when
the
wolves
bite

When the Wolves Bite

Copyright © 2024 by Madison Jo.

First Edition: November 2024

—and the rhythm of their heart keeps yours beating.

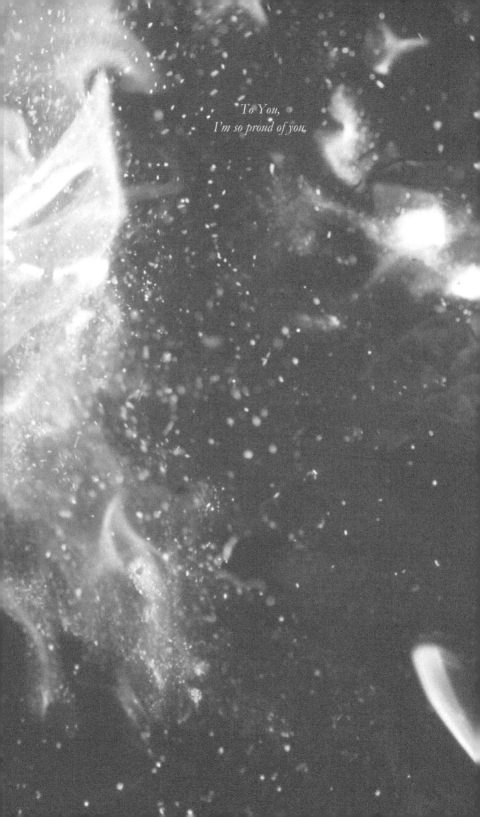

To You,
I'm so proud of you.

CONTENT WARNINGS

Animal abuse, Anxiety, Belting as punishment, Blood-play (third party), Coercion, Depression, Dogfighting, Drugs, Explicit rape, Explicit sexual situations, Explicit torture, Forced drug abuse, Graphic self-harm, Graphic violence, Pregnancy loss, PTSD, Subjugation

All events, situations, and stories have been fabricated from my grim imagination, insight passed along to me, and news media. It is intended for mature audiences and certain scenes may be unsettling.

Reader discretion advised.

There is audible dog abuse described in chapter 8 and a physical description of a dog losing a fight in chapter 15. They are both very brief.

Please reach out to me if you have any questions or concerns.

Your mental health matters.

madison.jo.author@gmail.com

@madison.jo.author

PLAYLIST

Rise up Dead Man (Instrumental) - Port Sulphur Band

Devil's Gonna Come - Raphael Lake & Royal Baggs

Prisoner - Raphael Lake, Aaron Levy & Daniel Ryan Murphy

Bones (feat. yuronono & Grimzlee - deer death

Numb - Sleep Theory

Chains - deer death & Nextime

Animal - Magnolia Park, Ethan Ross, PLVTINUM

Kintsugi - Like Moths to Flames

Chokehold Cherry Python - Ashnikko

Just Pretend - Bad Omens

Cursed - Ari Abdul

Eyes On Fire - Gold Souls

Blood on the Sheets - VIOLENT VIRA

My Body's a Zombie for You- Dead Man's Bones

Everything I Do Is For You - Amira Elfeky

SERPENTINE - Vana

Ascensionism - Sleep Token

The Offering - Sleep Token

Daddy - Ramsey

Howlin' for You - The Black Keys

Match Made In Hell - Dutch Melrose & benny mayne

Trust Me, Everything's Going To Be Fine - Nextime

Words can cut deep.
But a belt will always cut deeper.
Right?

CHAPTER ONE

TALA

Blinding bands of light spear through the cracks of my heavy eyes, and muffled masculine voices are coming from my right. There's a motion and hum that's twisting my nauseous stomach, flooding my mouth with warm saliva.

I go to sit up so that I don't choke on vomit, feeling a coarse texture binding my hands together.

Panic surges over my chest, overriding the haziness that's pervading my body. My vision clears lazily, but enough for me to see myself lying in the back of a moving SUV, thick rope cutting the circulation off my hands, and the two men sitting up front.

It all comes back.

Them storming through the gates, arguing with my dad—then shooting him in cold blood before tranquilizing the wolves.

Dread solidifies in my throat, amplifying the coiling of my stomach.

Do not fucking cry, Tala. Think and play your moves smartly.

"She'll be fed well. I don't want her to lose that ass of hers," Pyro snickers in the passenger seat.

"I'm sorry if this is overstepping, boss… But won't the other girls start picking fights with her if they see her getting special treatment?" the younger man in the driver seat asks.

"I don't want to be questioned, Shiloh. I find it greatly offensive. So, find yourself lucky I'm ridin' the high horse of gettin' my princess. Otherwise, you'd be the first meal to the wolves."

I need to jump out. I don't give a fuck about road rash.

My heart hammers, sending blood to my limbs to try and launch myself forward. The very second my waist tenses to pull my torso up, the SUV comes to a stop, blowing my dumb plan up in smoke.

It's not just me I have to save. I have to get the wolves too.

I don't know how the fuck I'm going to manage that.

"Well, look who's awake," Pyro says ardently, twisting his neck to smile at me. "Just in time, princess. You can walk… and I get to watch."

Shiloh hops out and promptly opens the back door by my feet. And all I can do is gape at the sick smile that's beaming at me from the front.

His hazel-brown eyes reflect the assault he's envisioning for me, trailing over my entire body.

"You're sick," I hiss, instantly biting my tongue.

His smile slowly falls into vexation, plaguing me with angst. "I already warned you, girl. You will respect me. Pull her out!" he shouts gruffly, swatting his hand through the air.

I finally flick my sight to the man grabbing my ankles. His tight face is clean shaven, dark eyes refusing to meet mine.

"I can do it myself," I bite out, and kick out of his grip, launching myself forward.

He throws his hands up in a surrender, backing away with his attention on the ground. My head starts violently spinning. I try blinking it away, inching myself out, but the spins catch up to me and I start falling forward out of the seat.

He swiftly moves in front of me, hands firmly gripping my shoulders and catching my weight. "You have to get it together," he murmurs. I barely hear him.

"Pull! Her! Out!" Pyro's rough voice booms over the SUV.

The air is cold yet doing nothing for the sweat prickling over my hot face. My heart is thundering against my ribs. It speeds up as his hands turn merciless, ripping me out of the seat.

My heavy head jerks back, sluggish feet staggering to the ground.

I cannot hold back the vomit anymore.

The hot iron floods my mouth and I throw my head forward, gagging as watery stomach bile travels up my throat and pours out in between our feet. It splashes all over his shoes, a sticky band falling from my lip and clinging to my bound hands.

I cough, trying my best to swallow the thick, acidic remnants down.

"I'm not letting you get me killed," he mutters, quickly dropping down and throwing a tight arm around my waist. He tosses me over his shoulder with a firm grip on the back of my thigh, and hastily begins carrying me off through the snow.

I didn't take in my surroundings when I sat up.

It's quiet, far away from everything else. I try pivoting my blood rushing head to look around. All I can see are the trees towering over us, the snow eerily dancing with the brisk wind, and the stone stairs he's trekking up.

I know what the frozen river smells like. My grandpa used to take me ice fishing. It's crisp and slightly fishy and wafting around like it's relatively close. I might be able to figure out which one it is.

After two flights of old stairs, the barks of dogs echo hauntingly through the trees, reverberating in my pulsing head.

"Whoever is on feedin' duty clearly didn't feed my fuckin' dogs today. Let me find out who it is... She won't make the same mistake twice," Pyro says darkly in front of us.

He's fucking enslaving them here.

My blood begins boiling and I almost slip up and hammer punch this asshole in the spine.

"Don't let the rage blind you. Every single movement needs to be methodically planned."

Jax's rich voice invades my mind like he's here with me.

It makes the whites of my eyes sting.

I close them. And stay quiet. And just let him carry me up the stupid fucking stairs until he steps up onto a landing that's freshly cleared.

My hands are throbbing, turning a dark shade of red from the tight rope that's flaying my skin. His shoulder is definitely bruising my stomach given the pain that's smarting dully across my navel.

A creaky door opens, and I gain the strength to pull my head up and look back.

The black front door has a covered entrance, four pillars holding up what I assume to be a balcony overhead. His steps are too fast for me to see anything other than the dark brick making up the large house swallowed by trees.

Shiloh carries me into the darkness, then sets me down on my feet. I eye the open door like it's a saving grace, and his foot swings back, kicking it closed. "Don't think about it," he murmurs, sliding his hand off my back. I glance up, noting the way he still won't look at me. A long scar runs from his dark hairline, all the way down to his clenched jaw. Seeing it—I want to reopen it and give him a matching one that slashes over his eyes.

Swallowing down the attitude that wants to spew out hateful words like lava, I turn around to the large, open living room.

Big, barred windows let in the light from the snow, reflecting off the brown leather couches. There are bookshelves tucked away, and board games stacked neatly on the octagon coffee table. A wide, black staircase sits to the left, winding up to the second story where a familiar looking woman is standing, overlooking the newcomer to Hell.

She's battered. I can see it from down here. She takes a good look, then quickly disappears down the dark hall illuminated by sconces.

"Welcome home, princess," Pyro smiles, hands stretched out to show off his goddamn prison.

My stomach knots, and I get nudged forward to start walking.

I don't want to. But I do. And I watch his smile stretch even wider, assaulting eyes eating up every movement of mine.

"Shiloh will show you to your room. I have some discipline to uphold, or I'd do it myself," he says wickedly, unbuckling his belt with a sly grin.

I might fucking throw up again.

My ears grow hot with the claws ripping open my chest. While he walks away towards the stairs, I stealthily box breathe. I don't want anyone to see any weakness of mine.

You just threw up everywhere. It's a little too late for that.

5

Shiloh steps out in front of me, faintly glancing over his shoulder. "Follow me. Don't do anything stupid or that belt will find you next," he warns quietly.

Following him, I crane my neck to the right to watch Pyro disappear down the hall, belt in hand and whistling a slow unnamed tune that has the hair on the back of my neck sticking straight up.

My hands are killing me. I try wiggling them for slack, taking the stairs right behind the asshole. I'm not saying shit to him though. Maybe if my hands fall off, they'll just throw me to the wolves since I won't be able to perform whatever duties they give out.

I hope the wolves are okay. And I really, really fucking hope my phone is still in my back pocket.

I look over each shoulder—getting disappointed over something that was stupid of me to hold out hope for.

I shake my head, wanting to jump over the railing and break my spine. But that would be giving up.

I can't give up yet. It's only just begun.

My heart lurches into my throat, sharp whipping and screams pouring out of the second door to the left. As much as I want to squeeze my eyes shut, I glance in at a blonde woman bent over a bare bed.

Her face is shoved down into the white sheets, sweatpants down at her ankles, and Pyro's whipping her with his belt. My heart begins racing aggressively, the heavy tempo pulsing my hot cheeks, and I look away, running straight into the asshole that for some reason stopped.

I rub my throbbing forehead with my numb hands, getting a brisk arm around the waist. I want to tell him to eat my shit. But the words disintegrate as he pushes me forward down the hall.

"Keep going," Shiloh orders.

I roll my eyes, passing more doors that are closed. "Right, because I was just going to stay and hangout," I mutter under my breath.

Reaching around me, he brutally cages my throat and shoves my back into the wall. My pulsing head thuds from the brute force, and he bends down, getting nose to nose with me. "Don't take my kindness for weakness, wolf princess. I will fuck those pretty eyes of yours blind. So, act fucking straight," he snarls.

I tighten my face, curling my lips in disgust. No words manage to come out before he yanks me into him by my neck. "The rest won't pass up the opportunity to put you in your place. Keep those comments sealed by those pouty lips of yours and walk your ass down the hall. Your room is around the corner," he whispers venomously.

"Is my princess already in trouble?" Floats down the hall.

My eyes widen, and his nostrils flare in tandem with the tic in his jaw. "I handled it." His voice carries, the panic in his eyes not leaving mine.

My chest is rising and falling with deep breaths that are only making me feel more lightheaded, and I begin trembling, unable to shun the volatile anxiety feasting on my nerve endings.

Brutus' heavy footsteps are menacing, rapidly getting closer to us. "Oh, but I don't think you did. Words can cut deep, Shiloh. But a belt will always cut deeper." He stops at our side, lanky height towering right over me. "I won't tolerate having weak men work for me. So, take her to her room and fuckin' handle it before I bash your head in!"

Shiloh's face screws up angrily, and in a swift exchange, his hand moves from my throat and into my hair. Pins and needles fire up on my scalp, and I wince, willing myself to suck it up and let him walk me like a goddamn dog.

The menacing footsteps don't retreat. They follow right behind us.

My palms grow sweaty, and my mouth runs dry as I heave for air. The tears nipping at my water lines are unstoppable, flooding over my hot cheeks. Showing them that I'm weak.

Going around the corner, Shiloh stops at the black door on the right and throws it open, forcibly shoving me inside.

I stumble, tripping over my platform boots, and my knees slam down into the floor, my bound arms catching the rest of my fall. I whine, not giving a shit if it makes me look pathetic. The sharp pain exploding in my numb arms feels like intense icy hot running through my veins.

I don't receive a single moment before he's brutally grabbing my waist and launching me onto the same bare bed I saw in the other room.

Adrenaline spikes my blood pressure. And I speedily flip over and send my foot flying through the air, kicking Shiloh straight across the face.

The barred window behind me is opaque, shedding enough light to see his head whip from the strike—but he stands still as stone, turning to look at me with darkened eyes and a busted lip.

"Ho-ly shit!" Pyro shouts excitedly from the door. "She's a brawler. That'll be useful for my plans." He walks in, a smile stretching on his face. "Teach her what happens when you act out of turn here. The belt won't cut deep enough now."

With Shiloh glaring at me from the end of the bed and Pyro stalking up to the side—I feel like a fawn circled by a pack of starving wolves.

It's not the Dark God making my heart race like prey.

And that's devastating.

The cracks shattering my heart force out the sob I've been trying so goddamn hard to hold back.

"Please stop. I'm sorry. I'm so sorry," I cry out.

Pyro groans, shaking his head with delight. "You're a pretty crier... I really like that. Shiloh, I might just take this discipline for myself. Unless you want to get payback for the split she put in your lip." He turns to Shiloh, waiting for his answer.

Using his thumb to wipe the blood from his lip, Shiloh peels his malicious glare from me. "All yours, boss," he utters, then shoots me a final look before leaving the room.

I cry harder, curling my knees up for a sense of safety.

Pyro walks over to the door, aiming his eyes at me while shutting it. "Was it back talk that got you in trouble with him?" he asks, a slight tilt in his head as he stalks back over to the end of the bed.

With tears streaming down my temples and soaking my hairline, I nod, unable to utter a word without blubbering.

"See? That just won't do, princess. I guess you'll be learnin' the hard way." He sets his belt down on the mattress and lunges for my ankles, yanking me down to the end of the bed.

"No!" I bellow, getting dragged right to him. My shirt rolls all the way up to underneath my arms, fully exposing my chest.

I'm ignorant and didn't put a bra on today.

He beams down at my boobs, and I try to smash my bound arms down to cover as much as I can. But he still saw them. And the glistening in his eyes tells me he liked it.

He smiles wickedly, running his hands up my legs. "I don't think I want to share you with anyone here. Is that selfish?" he asks rhetorically, then slides his scratchy ass hands over the skin on my waist.

I can't even try to fight this. I'll only make it worse, and I won't get far with my hands tied tightly together. I'm sure Shiloh would just drag me right back anyways. And who knows how many more are down there now.

"I'll-I'll behave. I promise," I choke out, my insides turning as his hands wedge under my arms, firmly palming my boobs. My body begins shaking with an uncontrollable sob, getting violated and pushed into the depths of hysteria.

He groans, squeezing them, potentially bruising them from how painful it is. "Your phone is buzzin'! You must be popular for bein' Anchorage's Wolf Princess. Let's see who's trying to get a hold of my property." He stands up, roughly pressing his jean-clad erection in between my legs.

Reaching into his back pocket, he pulls out my phone and starts snooping through my notifications.

He must be really dumb if he thinks Jax can't track it. He might even be on the way. I can't get my hopes up though. We're out in the middle of nowhere and Jax said that Brutus was living off the grid.

Clicking his tongue, he looks up at me with a sly, crooked smile. "I think your ex-boyfriend would like to see what you're up to. By the looks of it, I don't think he was ready for the breakup. So, be the princess I need you to be and say hi to the fuckin' camera."

"No," I shake my head, my numb lips quivering.

With one hand aiming my phone at me, the other rears back and cracks across my face, my head whipping to the side. "Next time it's the fuckin' belt!"

I cry out, holding the back of my hand to the heat radiating on my cheek. And the sob continues with no end in sight.

He barbarically rips open my leather pants, roughly jerking them down with one hand. "Please, not again," I cry out hoarsely, my entire body tensing up.

The door flies open, and my stiff body jolts, the sounds of Brutus' aggravated breath increasing the turmoil taking over me.

"Ryder's arm got ripped off," Shiloh rushes.

My eyes widen, knowing it must've been Valko. He's the only one that's ever given any inclination to snap.

"Please don't hurt the wolves," I plead.

Shoving my phone back into his pants, he snickers, "Gotta train them somehow, princess." He walks away, stopping at the threshold to look back at me. "Don't think we're done here. I'll be back," he warns arrogantly, then vanishes down the hall.

I crawl backwards up the bed, trying to roll my shirt back down and get my pants up my hips.

Shiloh stands in the door for a few beats. Just watching.

Grinding his teeth, he pulls a knife out from his pocket and storms over to the side of the bed. "Hold your arms out."

My tired, glazed over eyes want to roll. But I obey, straightening my elbows, and he grabs my left arm and starts sawing through the thick rope with his pocketknife.

"Are you gonna get in trouble?" I whisper

"What do you mean?" His brows knit, dark eyes briefly sweeping over my face. "After Pyro left, I ripped your bondage off to fuck the shit out of you without having anything in my way. You screamed and cried-" the rope snaps "-and you hated every second of it, eh? He knows I'm a biter, so you need to let me mark your back to make it believable. Or, my brain will be splattered on your bedroom floor, and he'll let everyone take turns inside your ass."

I hate both of my options here.

I just want to go home and feel Jax's heartbeat on the side of my head. The thought alone sends more tears to well in my eyes as I watch Shiloh close the door.

I throw the rope off me, the heaviness thudding to the floor, and rotate my skinned wrists to get the blood flowing. "Do I need to scream and cry in case he asks around?"

He shakes his head. "It's just you tucked away in the corner."

I don't trust this asshole. But I'd much rather let him do this, than get fucking gang raped.

I sit up dizzily, feeling the bed dip in behind me. It feels so wrong. My skin is crawling at the idea of another man touching me, and a loaded tear sheds down the hot handprint on my cheek.

"Take your shirt off," he orders gently.

Quietly crying to myself, I lift my shirt up and pull it off inside out until the long sleeves slip off my arms. I wad the black fabric up, shoving it to my tits before another man sees something not for them.

"I saw the tattoos on your hands. But I didn't think you'd have something so big." His fingertips draw over my tattoo, and my wet eyes tighten, bottom lip quivering. He trails them down my spine, brushing over to my side to rest his hand, the other one collecting my hair and pushing it over my shoulder. Not wasting anymore time, he bites down on the crook of my neck.

It's not the pain that makes me wince and cry.

It's just him.

He bites and leaves hickeys all along my right shoulder and down my shoulder blade. Each one being a knife to the heart and drawing out more tears.

He tilts my head, opening my neck up to him as he leans forward and pushes up Jax's collar. I sniffle, shoulders shaking with the sob trying to ease its way out, and his lips meet my neck, for some reason fucking kissing me, before sucking and drawing blood to the surface.

His invasive touch disappears from my body, the hard mattress rising back up behind me, and he quickly roughs up his hair while walking to the door. "Remember what I said and stick to it," he tells me over his shoulder.

Undoing his belt, he unzips his pants and throws the door open, storming out of it.

I quickly get up and run to the door, close it, and dart back to the sad bed. Getting my shirt right side out, I slip it back on, zip my pants up—and cry.

CHAPTER TWO

JAX

"See any you like?" Silas asks, gesturing to the wall of abused dogs locked in kennels.

Ready to whip my pistol out and shoot the fucker in between the eyes, my phone vibrates—and I get a violent twist in my stomach.

Ignoring his dumbass, I rip it out of my pocket, heart coming to an abrupt stop at the only message on my screen.

Tala: He's here.

My fingers fly over the screen to hit Call, and I hold it up to my ear while making hell for leather out of his fucked up shed and through his rank ass backyard. Without unlatching the gate, I thunder through it, breaking it straight off the hinges, the wood cracking and adding to the heavy melody pulsing in my head.

The call goes to voicemail.

I try again, ripping open my car door and throwing my ass into the seat. "Come the fuck on, baby," I growl through a frantic breath, firing the engine up.

Not a care to look, I shift into drive and punch the gas to pull out onto the road. I'm six fucking hours away, all the way in Fairbanks to take care of the fucker I should've taken care of several weeks ago.

Voicemail again.

I try her dad. Voicemail. I try her mom. Voicemail.

Drifting onto the highway, I switch into track mode to maintain a healthy speed that will eat the distance between us up.

I don't have my fucking laptop with me, or I'd quickly hack into the cameras at the sanctuary.

I call Leon, the dial tone only ringing once before he picks up.

"Hey, ma-"

"Hack into the cameras at *Howling Haven*. Now!"

"Shit, okay."

The clacking of his keys bleed into the thrumming in my temples. It feels like utter doom weighing down on my chest.

"This is so bad," he wavers edgily.

My heart drops. "What's fucking bad, Leon?"

"They're there, Jax. They have trailers with wire kennels, semi-automatics strapped to their chests, and… Tala is walking over to Brutus."

You've got to be fucking shitting me.

Even with my father getting shot directly in front of me—I've never felt so sick in my life. My blood is turning to lava under my skin, firing up in my tight, twitching face as I punch it to one-fifty. "Keep watching and run those fucking plates!" I snap.

Keeping him on the line, I drift around a bend and call Maverick. It rings a few times, drilling my vibrating mind with the annoying ass tone.

"What's up?" he asks quickly, knowing I don't call to chat.

"How fast can you get to *Howling Haven*?"

He's silent for a beat. "I'll head there now."

I hang up, switch back to Leon, and hit a patch of gravel that sounds like it's tearing the underside of my car up. "What do you see?" I wait a moment, no response. "Leon," I growl, black threatening my vision.

"A shot just came out of nowhere and hit her dad. None of them had their guns raised, Jax. And now she's thrashing and trying to break out of Brutus' grip while they swarm the place with darts."

The leather wheel groans in my tight grip, and I gnash my teeth together, splitting off into the oncoming lane to pass some dumbass in a van. I've already cut an hour's time off the distance. But it's not enough.

"Oh, mija," he cries under his breath.

"You can't do that, Leon. Speak the fuck up!"

"He just brutally slammed her face into the SUV. Her cries, man… I can't fucking do this."

"God-fuckin-damn it!" I hit the wheel, jerking back into the lane. "FaceTime me and look the hell away if you can't handle it!"

It's not fair to get irate with him. But Jesus fucking Christ, I'm beginning to not see straight. My mind is racing in tandem with my pounding heart, twisting my stomach into a pit.

The call switches to FaceTime, giving me an up-close shot of the most gut-wrenching sight that spreads heat down my dry throat.

His hand is maliciously fisting her hair and he's pressing into her. She cries, absolutely destroyed, and the scar that runs down my sternum for her sizzles like a hot knife.

Barely looking back to the road, I catch the sign telling me I have one hundred-forty miles left, then look right back to my cracking screen.

My nostrils flare, watching him pull a dart from his pocket and slam it down into her neck. His phone isn't picking up the audio, but the scream she lets out sends ravens flying from the trees—and I can't fucking blink.

The hot breaths jetting out of my nose are circulating a haze in my spinning mind. All I can do is gnash my teeth and watch her go limp in his grip, trying my best to to fly this distance, hoping and fucking praying that Maverick will grow some goddamn balls and start shooting.

I shouldn't have left today. If I would've killed the piece of shit the second I got word of him she wouldn't be getting shoved into the back of an SUV, being taken who knows where for who knows what.

There's a man who looks like a younger version of Damascus approaching Brutus as he ties her arms together in the back seat.

"Turn the volume up and see if you can hear what they're saying," I demand, words tight with distress.

The volume banner pops up, sliding all the way over. All I can hear is the wind whipping the cameras and distant, vicious snarling. My loud engine isn't helping shit. But I'm not slowing down.

God must be real and guiding my damn way. I haven't spared a glance to the highway and I'm still somehow on the damn thing.

"I-I can't hear what they're saying, man. The snow's smacking the mics. But with him looking similar to her dad, I did quick digging and that's her uncle, Enzo Huxley. He quite literally disappeared for an entire year and the bank foreclosed his house two months ago."

I hear him. I'm too frozen, drowning in my internal berating while being stuck on the unknown man hopping in the driver's seat.

17

I'll get to the wolves in a goddamn moment. Tala is top priority here and their shit isn't marked. I'm scanning the SUV up and down, just watching like a helpless piece of shit as he gets turned around and starts kicking snow back to peel out of there.

My brain is running in circles like a dog chasing its tail, vision panning and trying to give out. But that won't help shit.

I'm not letting them get away with this.

I will find her. And I will burn everything fucking down in the goddamn process.

Fifty miles, baby. Fifty miles.

Swiping out of the call, I pull up the app I've been using to track her phone. I didn't see him smash it or toss it to the side, so my heart is thundering with hope that I'll be able to track it.

"Is Maverick there?" I ask impatiently, tracking the icon of her phone down the mile long road out of the sanctuary.

"No, I'm looking over all of the feeds. All I can see is the wolves being carried off and thrown into the kennels. I'm so fucking sorry, man. I'm so sorry I can't do more."

He would've been there already.

"You're a bigger help than you think, Leon. But I don't have the time or capacity to coddle you right now. I'm not taking my eyes off of tracking her, so I need you to call Nadia and see if she answers."

"Si, jefe."

Passing another slow fuck in my way, I divert my attention back to her icon stopping on a crack that's splintered over my screen. "No! No, don't you fucking dare!"

I refresh it, hoping and praying it was just them coming to a stop. But the location doesn't update, and her icon disappears.

A growl thunders in my chest, closing out of the false sense of hope and pulling up my texts with her. I type the only thing I can without spiraling and send the text meant for my girl—and the sick fuck that's trying to take another piece of my heart.

Except, Tala is my heart. He's taking my life.

Me: I'm coming for you.

"Our souls are interwoven, Jax. You are etched into my veins and branded in my bones."

I hear her voice like it's here. Like she's sitting next to me. And it makes my eyes mist over.

I blink that shit away, man the fuck up, and swallow down the boulder forming in my throat.

All I can feel is the cataclysmic rage fueling my heart to keep it going. And I see the flames of everything I'm going to burn down.

Leon's caller ID pops up, and I answer, saying nothing.

"I tried calling her five times. No luck."

Well, isn't this just a big ol' fucking shit fest.

The rest of the drive I vibrate in a white-hot rage that boils my lungs, physically shaking from the wrath-filled adrenaline pump. My mind races with the sickening images of what she could already possibly be going through—what she will go through.

Brutus isn't a man to beat around a bush. And he sure as shit wouldn't allow his men to grace any sort of kindness.

They're all mentally fucking ill.

Probably dropped on their domes too much as kids. That's the only explanation for the twisted shit they do.

The snowy gravel thunks against the underside of my car, launching up and smacking the sides as I fly up to the open gates of *Howling Haven.*

19

MADISON JO

Seeing the life stripped from this place hollows my stomach and twists a knife into my chest. My wheels slide through the gravel, coming to an abrupt stop right where the terror unfolded.

Leaving my car on, I throw my door open to the eerie coos of birds from the trees.This place once was riddled with woofs and howls.

They're all gone. Every. Single. One of them.

Clenching my fists, I storm through the gates, passing over the crimson puddle where Damascus once laid. I'll look over the footage and see what happened to him. Right now, I'm hunting down anything that may have been dropped. Phone, keys, ID… a fucking arm.

It's lying in the snow over where the hammocks usually are. I kind of snicker while running over to it. Not that this is fucking funny. It's just pleasant seeing someone get what they deserve.

It's ripped off right at the shoulder, shredded meat hanging out of the tattered fabric and soaking the snow with crimson. I crouch down, inspecting the tattoo on the middle finger. It's a bone with the initials *IR* running vertically through the center.

I peel up the bloody and torn long sleeve, inspecting the gnarly gashes from wolf teeth latching on strong enough to rip it clean off. I flip it over, looking for more tattoos, huffing in disappointment when I don't see any.

IR is something to go off of.

Picking the cold arm up, I haul it around with me while scanning the ground and circling around the entire place.

It feels like a goddamn waste of time that I don't have. But even a shoe could give me a base idea on where they're living. Your tread gets worn down in certain ways, depending on what surfaces and terrain you're walking on.

20

I don't see shit though. Just the open chain link gates that used to have the wolves roaming at their liberty.

I stop, stiff as stone.

Damascus has mentioned having microchip trackers implanted in them. They're relatively fresh too. He got them done right after they tried buying the wolves.

Launching the arm into the trees like a Frisbee, I sprint back to the wooden gates and throw myself down into my seat. "Damascus, you fucking genius, man. I'd probably kiss you if I could," I mutter, feeling the high of hope rushing back in.

CHAPTER THREE
TALA

My cheeks are tight with dried tears. I don't know how much time has passed since Shiloh left. I've been curled up in a fetal position, slowly entering shock.

It's freezing in this room.

I honestly can't gauge if it's the temperature, or the nerves making me shiver uncontrollably.

The walls are an ugly cream color with nothing hung to fill the open space. The paint seems fresh though. No nicks or cracks.

Which is odd, considering the stone stairs and exterior of the house appear to be dated. But he's probably made enough money on pitting dogs and selling blow to revamp the place.

The door cracks open, bleeding in the dim light from the hallway.

I harden to stone, teeth chattering, gaping at the dark-haired woman walking in. It takes me a moment, but I recognize her.

It's Loxley Quinten.

She stiffly walks over to the side of my bed, the light completely drained from her blue eyes. "I'll show you the bathroom and help you get clothes," she says softly.

The heavy weight of my new reality, my new life, is crashing down on my chest. "Have you been here the whole time?" I whisper.

She barely nods, the movement getting lost in the shadows from the bars on the window. "We have to be kinda quick. I'm supposed to start dinner in an hour."

Right. Because what fucking world would I be in if a man wasn't expecting to be catered to?

With a million questions plaguing my broken mind, I uncurl from safety, slide across the bed, and haul my ass up.

Up close, I can see a jagged scar running across her snub nose. Her bottom lip is busted, just starting to scab over. There are bruises marring her protruding collar bones, a gnarly hickey on her neck, and she's very thin. She's always been petite. But she's starved. The tight, white long sleeve shirt showcases the evidence.

I follow her out of the bedroom and into the hall that belongs in a horror film. We go around the corner, and the men talking and laughing downstairs spreads heat up my tight chest.

She's immune to it, seemingly unbothered as she leads me right towards the den of dogs.

I, on the other hand, might just fucking piss my pants.

Looking over her shoulder at me, she murmurs, "Don't insert yourself and try to avoid eye contact unless you're spoken to. And definitely do not give sass."

23

I already learned my lesson there. I have at least twenty different sore spots running down my shoulder, reminding me that I could be raped at any given moment.

About to take the stairs, I briefly glance down to the living room at the six men sitting around with cigarettes and bantering like they're not scum of the Earth.

Keeping my steps in line with hers, I try to focus on which step creaks, and which doesn't, but the eyes penetrating me are like hot stones, rendering me incompetent.

One of the men starts barking, the irritating sound echoing off the high ceiling. I fight the visceral reaction powering up in my lungs, biting my tongue so I don't bark back.

I'm swallowing nothing, taking the last step. I want to look. I want to learn the faces that I'll slaughter. But I keep my sight set on Loxley and how she's methodically moving past the living room.

It's not confident, her shoulders are slightly dropped, she keeps her spine straight, steps quick but not rushed, and blatantly ignores the derogatory remarks coming from them.

There's an arched cased opening at the end of the tiny hall that extends from the living room. It leads to the kitchen, where Shiloh and another man are standing around the island.

I divert my eyes, stealthily crossing my fingers that it went unnoticed.

"Wolf girl," the other man calls out.

My skin ripples up, screaming at me to not turn around and to just keep going. But Loxley stops—so I stop. She looks back at me, eyes telling me to obey and see what the asshole wants.

She doesn't stay. She walks off and around the corner, disappearing down another hallway.

I turn around with a stoic mask, looking right at the man with dirty blonde hair and facial hair covering his long face. It's not covering the shit eating grin he's wearing.

Setting his beer bottle down, he beckons me with two fingers. "C'mere."

Every hair on my body stands up. I will myself to close the distance, each step spiking my heart rate, and stop on the opposite side of the island as the fucking freak.

He takes a drink, a sinister smile deepening his crow's feet. "I wanted you to come here." He points to his side. "So, crawl to me." He taps the island.

You have to be fucking kidding me.

The dark brown eyes boring into the side of my face are telling me to "not do anything stupid."

Clanking my teeth shut so that I don't snip, I flatten my palms to the island, haul my ass up until my knees meet the cold granite—and I crawl to him.

The demeaning act makes me want to cry. The knot is trying its hardest to work up the tears. But I suck it up, watch him adjust himself, and stop right in front of the pungent, yeasty smell emanating from him.

His pupils are blown out, leaving a sliver of shit green to wrap around his coked-out vision. He reaches out, running his dirty fingers through my hair. "You're a good girl, aren't you?"

My eye twitches, nasty words rushing to the tip of my tongue, but the eerie whistling coming from behind turns me to stone. He drops his hand, taking a single step back while fixing his eyes on Pyro walking in.

Who's getting a five-star view of my ass.

The whistling stops, his menacing steps getting closer. "Jeremy, Jeremy, Jeremy," Pyro chants disappointedly, walking around the island. "I thought I told you to leave my princess alone."

Jeremy gestures to my neck with his bottle. "Mine was all in good fun, boss. Shiloh marked her up."

I want to put it in reverse, slink down to the floor, and crawl away from the testosterone battle happening here.

"Shiloh got the approval. You didn't," Pyro says sharply. In a blink of an eye, he whips his gun out from his jeans and shoots Jeremy in between the eyes.

A head-splitting ring fires up in both my ears. I'd slap my hands to them if I wasn't stunned, visibly watching the life fade from Jeremy's eyes as he crashes dead weight into the floor.

Images of my dad getting shot flash through my head, and my burning eyes begin to sting. But I've cried myself empty today. And according to the oven... it's only five p.m.

It feels like it's been a week.

While raking over Jeremy's body and the broken bottle that's sitting in a puddle of beer, Pyro's boots stop in front of me.

He cups under my jaw, pulling my attention up to him, and starts wiping the warm splatters away with his thumb. Of course he's smiling. "You gonna say thank you?"

I could squash your head in between my thighs. How 'bout that as a thank you?

I haven't eaten all day. The nausea is coming back in a tide, brewing up nothing but stomach acid.

I swallow the burn down, along with my pride. "Thank you." Might as well be the acid on my tongue with how bad it tastes to say.

His eyes light up, and he tilts his head down to look at the mark Shiloh left on me. "I don't believe in double rounds of discipline unless provoked. And since you're bein' my good girl, I'll let you off the hook." He takes his scratchy hands off me, aiming his attention over to Shiloh who's still just fucking standing there. "Next time, don't mark her up so bad. I want my princess to look like a princess... She's goin' to be my money maker."

What the hell does that mean? And why does Shiloh get to touch me?

"Understood," Shiloh says reservedly.

Raising his relaxed knuckles to my face, I catch a glimpse of a tattoo on his middle finger. It's a bone with initials running down the middle. I can't see what they are though. He moves them too quickly, caressing the back of his fingers down my cheek.

"Help her down and take her to Loxley. It's about dinner time and I get angry when I'm hungry."

Him walking away is like the deep breath you take when coming back up to the surface of water. But his presence is replaced with Shiloh. Although he doesn't scare me as much—he's still a fucking freak.

He's pretty and could've gotten a career in modeling or acting. Instead, he chose something sick and inhumane.

"I can do it," I whisper, sliding my aching knees out from under me and sitting on my butt.

Holding his hands out for mine, he licks the puffy and bruised split in his lip. "I've been given an order, Tala. Just take my hands and hop down," he urges impassively.

Wow. The first time I've been called my name here.

Wanting to get the hell off this island, I rest my hands in his, spotting the same tattoo on his middle finger as he grips around my hands for support.

27

What is IR? …

I mentally run through numerous possibilities the entire walk through the kitchen, down the side hall, and into the laundry room.

Loxley is folding women's clothing, only in shades of white and black with some denim mixed in.

She neatly stacks a white shirt on top of the full laundry basket, sneaking a look out of the corner of her eye.

"Are those hers?" Shiloh asks, finally letting go of my hand.

Dude was walking me like I was a child that could get lost in the grocery store. I would have been cringing if my brain wasn't frying while trying to come up with what *IR* could mean. I settled on *Inhumane Reality* because it's fitting.

"Yes, sir," she answers submissively. "I'll take it to her room and get Brynn for dinner."

"No need." He grabs the basket from the center island, quickly whisking around with it. "I'll take it. You and Brynn need to get dinner going, eh? It's been a long day and he's getting hungry."

As he strides past me, Loxley and I share a slight look of confusion. She clears it from her face, turning around and silently closing the dryer.

"Princess."

I don't know why I was expecting him to leave me alone. I take it I won't really ever get a moment without a male being present.

And that sucks.

Knowing what's expected of me, I turn around, meeting the stern Roman features that are pinning me down from the hall.

I wish he'd go back to not looking at me.

It kind of made me feel superior. In a sense.

You'd think whoever does the shopping here has never seen a woman with curves before. The yoga pants are basically in my asshole and the tight long sleeve is smashing my tits, making them spill out of the V-neck.

Just what I need. Showing off every damn attribute while walking through a house full of feral dogs.

I wonder what Liam would say about my "tight ass shit." I can laugh about it now.

Well, not really. There's nothing fucking funny about this.

I still haven't met the other girls or learned any more names of the men. Shiloh took it upon himself to fill the dresser with "my clothes" and then walked me all the way back downstairs to the bathroom.

It's in the hall by the laundry room… Straight across from Pyro's bedroom.

The shower water is freezing, and we have to be supervised. I guess they don't trust us with the razors we're forced to use.

I rip the hair tie out of my hair, shaking out the loose bun I put up so that I didn't have icy water dripping down my back for several hours.

"I'm done," I say, looking at my tired reflection and the maroon mark on my neck.

Shiloh checks over his shoulder, catching my eyes in the mirror. "Be good. Pyro has already warned everyone that you are off limits. But a little attitude *will* make him change his mind."

My curiosity is overruling the need to play it smart. "So… why are you allowed to touch me?"

Saying that out loud is a smack to the face.

The only hands that should be touching me are large, calloused from killing assholes like this guy, and beautifully tattooed.

He turns all the way around, hands shoved in his denim pockets. "Because we've been paired."

Like fucking dogs?

I slowly blink, taking a moment to make sure I heard him correctly. When my eyes open, he's standing right behind me, ever so lightly grazing my ass and standing at least a foot taller.

"W-what does that mean?"

"That you belong to me." His fingers trail over the back of my neck, unclasping Jax's collar. It falls loose, and a sharp pain blooms on my heart.

"It stays on unless I take it off. Do you understand?"

I do, Jax. I do.

He stashes it in his pocket, relaxed eyes fixed on me. "The pairing is to keep things in check for Pyro. Every woman has a master, but they're still obligated to follow other men's orders and face their discipline. Cora, the blonde woman earlier, she was paired with Jeremy. That's why he got shot. He was already on thin ice for not keeping her in check."

Am I in a nightmare? Do I need to smack myself to wake up? Because this is entirely too fucked up to be real.

"Your situation is different. Pyro wants you for himself. You're the princess he's been going after for damn near two months. But… he's busy. He knows you need someone to keep you in line, eh?"

My stomach twists. This time, flooding my mouth with thick saliva I cannot choke down.

I skitter off to the left, slam open the toilet lid, and begin dry heaving through my raw throat, nothing coming out besides the spit streaming from my bottom lip.

My hair gets lifted out of the way, aside from a tendril falling over my eye and brushing over the bacteria infested toilet seat.

I groan in discomfort, also cringing over how many asses this toilet sees. I'm hovering above it with my hands gripping onto the germs, gagging from the swirling nausea.

A loud knock thunders on the door, the jolt of panic making me flinch.

"What?" Shiloh barks.

"She can suck your dick under the table! It's time to eat!"

Just when I thought my stomach was calming, it twists even tighter with a sharp pain in my shoulder.

My vision blurs-

CHAPTER FOUR

JAX

Her parents' front door is unlocked. I push it open, holding my phone up to my ear while Dr. Zion searches for Damascus' file.

He's old school and does all that shit by paper. It takes way too damn long, and I've told him several times to switch to digital. I'd even help him encrypt it just so it didn't take seven business days for him to sort through his files.

Maverick and Nadia still cannot be reached. So, Leon is going by her town house, and Viper is checking the club.

I'm trying to kill as many birds as possible with one stone right now. Even though I would rather be devoting all my time to Tala, I'm trying to figure out where the hell Evelyn is.

Scanning around the living room, I see nothing disarray and keep my steps light and quick into the kitchen, my wavering vision instantly darting down to the bare foot sticking out from the cabinets.

Fuck.

I run over, hearing the fucking papers rustling in my ear, and spot Evelyn sitting on the floor, back propped up against the cabinets and hands splayed around the knife sticking out of her stomach.

She's alive, but quickly bleeding out.

Crouching down next to her, I throw the call on speakerphone and toss my phone up onto the counter. "Evelyn, hey, look at me," I rush, reaching back for the towel draped over the sink and tucking it into my back pocket.

Her eyes lag trying to focus on me. "Enzo," she draws out hoarsely.

"We'll get to that, Ev. Right now, I need you to hang in there and keep pressure on that." I slide an arm under her knees, the other around her soaked back. "Dr. Z! I need a room open within five minutes!"

I pick her up, gritting my teeth over her cries of pain, and collect my phone from the counter before racing out of the house.

Her complexion is already fair like Tala's, but she's growing paler and sweating against the cold air that's biting at us as I haul her to the passenger seat.

My back seat would be better. It will take too much time cranking the damn seat forward, getting her in there, just to have to drag her back out through a crack. Instead of wasting time and putting her through even more pain, I squat down, get the seat laid back, and try my best to be gentle while setting her down. A groan of discomfort sticks in her throat, muffling behind her tight lips.

"I'm sorry," I utter. Whipping the towel out of my pocket, I move her bloody hands away from the knife, wrap the towel around it, and put her hands firmly back in place. "I don't know what was punctured, so I can't take the knife out. Hold that tight."

Three pints of blood and some stitches later, I get the call that Evelyn is doing just fine. I would've stayed by her side, but this is a goddamn shit show and I'm racing against time.

And time is unforgiving. There's no rewinding it.

Viper found Maverick with a busted head in the tunnels and Leon found Nadia bound, blindfolded, and gagged in her closet.

I needed to go home to switch to my truck and get my laptop and shit. So, I got into the club's cameras to see who the fuck waltzed in there, pistol whipped Maverick upside the head and shoved him down the metal stairs.

A little face recognition popped up Jeremy Fern. The nappy motherfucker didn't have plates on his truck. But his background is sickening enough to give me some leads.

I hacked into the street cams on Nadia's street. I didn't need third-party face recognition for her.

Kendra. Fucking. Balleger.

I've already dug into her. I know where she lives and that she's been left as primary guardian to her fourteen-year-old brother Samuel. That's why she works a double job as a server. Brutus doesn't pay her. She's working off a debt that her mom owes.

I'd like to have a little chat with her brother.

I have Leon in the passenger seat trying to get a ping on the wolves. If they're too far out, it won't pick up. And I fear that's why we're not getting shit on their location yet.

Hitting Call again, the ringing feels like flea-infested rodents running under my skin and gnawing on my heart.

"Hi, you've reached Tala. I'm sorry I didn't catch your call on time… I have better shit to do. You can leave a message if you want. I may or may not call back. Okay, byyee."

"Bitch, did you really make that your voi-"

Her fucking voice.

Locking my phone with an iron vice-grip, my lip begins twitching. So vigorously, it feeds into my eye and sends waves through the wash of red.

"I think they're too far, man. I'm running all their serial numbers, and the ping falls flat."

I snarl, cracking my vibrating phone.

I peel my eyes away from the snow that's wiping out the road, over to the black number that has a file attached to an empty message.

Already knowing what it is, my stomach sinks, veins getting loaded with ice, and I hesitantly tap on it.

Tala's cries instantly fill my truck.

A crater forms in my chest and my eyelids pin open, forcing me to watch her cry with her arms bound, covering her exposed breasts while someone records her lying on a white sheet.

"Be the princess I need you to be and say hi to the fuckin' camera."

"No," she sobs, shaking her head.

Brutus' hand flies down, cracking maliciously across her face. "Next time it's the fuckin' belt!" He snags the waistband of her leather pants, ruthlessly tearing them down.

My chest constricts, and she tenses up. "Please, not again," she cries brokenly.

A door opens and the video cuts off, snapping the thin cord that was holding me to-fuckin-gether.

Everything fades to black. All I can hear is barbaric roars and glass shattering. By the time I zone back in, my phone is in tiny pieces across my dash and embedded into my bloody palm.

"Jax... I know this is horrible and you have every right to lash out and start fucking shit up. But you have to hold it together. For Tala."

Heaving for air, I pull off onto the side of the road in front of Kendra's house, kicking myself in the ass for destroying my phone like that. "We could've tried tracking that," I say hoarsely.

"I can get it into your cloud and see if it synced."

Curling my fist, I scrape the glass out of my palm with my fingertips, glaring at the little duplex in a run-down neighborhood.

I won't kill a kid. But I will get payback and make her shit her fucking pants. Then, pluck every tooth out of her mouth and send my rats gnawing on her stomach until she fesses up.

The snow soaks through the sides of my sneakers, opening the back door for Sirohi. I grab his leash and tuck a knife into his tactical harness, watching him clomp down into the four inches of fluffy ice.

I have him with me to pick up scents.

I would've brought him to the sanctuary with me, but the wolves would've overpowered any of the musky shit left behind by the bastards.

I need to go back for that arm I launched into the trees. He might be able to pick something up off the tattered sleeve. But then again, the dude was in a tussle with a wolf and his arm has been sitting in snow.

My truck shuts off, and I stop halfway across the yard, turning back to Leon high stepping through the snow, holding his laptop up like an award trophy. "I need to keep moving to try and get this ping."

I nod, then continue to the wooden porch.

It's rotting, warping, and falling through at the corner. The white paint on the house is flaking off and the red door just pisses me off.

The rage twisting my arteries has me raising my foot, kicking the shoddy door down. Fuck being polite. This kid better tell me something good and not waste my time.

The door smacks the wall, knocking shit off onto the stained carpet. I take one step in—glaring at this kid being none the wiser to what the fuck is going on.

The back of the couch is facing me, and he's sitting there, playing video games with a headset strapped over his blonde hair, the shooting drowning out his hearing.

Over the loud huffs of Sirohi's nose getting to work, I hear an elderly woman's voice coming from the shared porch.

"All is well, ma'am. Just a little prank for his grades not being to Kendra's liking," Leon lies smoothly.

While he takes care of that, I stride in and round the couch, plopping my ass down next to Samuel. He jumps, blue eyes wide in horror, and swats his headset off. "Can I help you?" he asks, voice high pitched and cracking from his breakthrough to puberty.

"Yeah, man. You can. Thank you for asking." I throw my arm over the back of the couch. Right behind him. "Where's Kendra?"

He splays his hands around his controller, twisting half his face. "Um. Probably working a shift at *Aurora's*."

"Wrong. Try again."

My patience doesn't exist anymore. I won't get that back until I have Tala in my arms.

"I-I can call her."

I roughly pat his bony back, deadpanning at how easy he is to move. "That would be fucking great. Put her on speaker."

He slowly bends over to set his controller on the carpet, then stretches back to wrangle his phone from his sweatpants. "Are you gonna kill her?"

I clench my teeth, the tensed muscles pulling my ears back. "Why would you jump to that assumption if you weren't aware of what your sister is doing?"

Pulling her contact up, he says, "You're not the first man to bust in and ask for her. I know she has to do stuff because our mom fucked up. I just don't know what, or where she goes. She doesn't want me involved."

That hits close to home.

Except, I didn't have an older sibling to protect me.

If she would've taken Leon's advice by getting the fuck out of here and letting him create a new identity for her, I would have some respect for her. It is admirable that she took on the weight of caring for her brother, all while dealing with her mom's shit. But she had the chance to get out. And she chose not to.

She chose to continue fucking with what's mine.

Leon walks past the TV, holding his laptop in one hand and whizzing over the keys with the other.

The clacking, the dial tone from Samuel's phone, and Sirohi's huffs are lacing together, running alongside the explosive anger that's bubbling in my chest.

"Hey, Sammy-Sam. You doin' okay?"

I snap my head to him, tunneling my attention on anything in the background that could shed light on where she'd be.

He glances around, rolling his hand to come up with a lie. "Um, yeah. I was just wondering what you're up to. I noticed on the fridge that you're off today and I'm bored."

It's silent for a moment, the wind rustling against the speaker on her phone. "You know I can't tell you that."

He recoils, angrily tightening his face. "You can. You just choose not to, Kendra. I think I'm grown enough to handle whatever fucked up shit you're out doing."

My brows kind of raise in interest at this kid's fire. He wants to know. It's evident that it bothers him that she keeps him in the dark.

Leon skitters right in front of me, whisking his laptop around to show the coordinates he picked up on one of the wolves.

It's stationary though. Meaning—it was either plucked out or the wolf is dead.

Or…

In the middle of Kendra bickering at Samuel, I jump to my feet, eyeing both Samuel and Leon. "Truck. Now," I say loud enough to hear, quiet enough to not raise an alarm on Kendra's end.

Sirohi runs up to my side and I give him a pat on the rib, grabbing his leash and hauling ass out the door with Leon and the child on my heels.

Leon gets in the back with Sirohi so I can keep Samuel in my sight, and he connects his phone to the GPS on my dash.

The entire drive Samuel and Kendra bicker.

I don't know if it's his pent-up aggravation with her, or to keep her stalled long enough to see the twisted shit she does. Either way, he's doing a good job at getting her to yap her trap.

Daylight is burning out.

The curvy road the GPS is taking me on is packed with snow, crunching down with my tires like it hasn't seen any in several hours. We're in the middle of the fucking woods, rolling up to a little cabin that appears to be abandoned.

But the white car parked in the trees tells me someone is home.

I don't want to get too close and her take off out a back door or something. I'm not in the damn mood to chase her down.

I pull up into the tree line, whipping the wheel to dodge the big ass trees, and get myself turned around for a quick exit.

I cut the engine and step out, quietly closing my door. Keeping my eyes on the cabin, I spark a cigarette and grab the gas can from the bed of my truck.

"Ah, man," Leon sighs. "That video didn't sync in time. Looks like it got halfway before you smashed your shit to crumbs."

I figured.

Taking a drag that depletes a quarter of my cigarette, I stalk through the snow, gas sloshing in the can at my side, and do a double take at the lush, black tipped tail peeking out from the corner of the cabin.

I flag Leon down, pointing around the side for him to grab the wolf, and start dumping the gas around the perimeter of the worn-out logs.

I can hear her shouting in there. It's comical she still has no clue that I'm about to set this shit on fire.

I didn't expect Samuel to keep his lips sealed once he saw what I was doing. But the dude is leaning against the front of my truck—just watching—letting her yell at him.

Leon zips by, rushing along the gray wolf that's on a thick chain. By the pale-yellow eyes and crimson soaking his mouth and chest, I can almost guarantee it's Valko.

40

I bet it was him that finally snapped and ripped that dude's arm off. But why would Kendra have him?

Taking a final drag, I flick my cigarette down to the spilled gas. It takes a few beats. The snow is trying to play on the offense. But I don't play fair, I play to win. And I fucking smile while watching that shit catch up in a flame.

I circle around to the front door and station myself there, waiting for her to try and run out. There was no back door, and the only window was maybe six inches tall and eight wide.

This is her only escape.

There is no echo of an Angel anymore.

She'll run right into the hands of the Devil.

Once the flames catch onto the wood and start traveling up, the door flies open, and she frantically runs out. Her eyes pan up to my head at a tilt, steps coming to a skating stop and blowing up snow.

I contemplate giving her the option to walk her ass to the truck. You see, the Devil doesn't like that though.

I reach back into my waistband and grip around the handle of my handgun. She chants the pleas I don't accept, and I rack the slide to chamber a round, and shoot her in both thighs.

Her head falls back, a scream of agony tearing through her lungs, and she collapses down into the snow. Rolling from her stomach and onto her back, she grabs at her shot up thighs like it will help the shredding pain. "You don't understand!" she bellows.

Treading through the snow, I stop right above her screwed up face. "I do. I just don't give a fucking shit." I bend down and twist my hand into her shirt, ripping her up and dragging her right behind me.

She screams, clutching my hand and digging all her nails into my flesh. Her attempt to kick at the ground and break free is weak.

I easily drag her back to my truck.

I know she won't be able to run off, so I leave her ass lying on the ground while reaching into the bed of my truck. The yellow eyes focusing on me like lasers make me act quick and snatch up the rope.

Can't lose an arm. Tala likes them too much.

"What are you going to do to her?" His cracking voice filters through her insistent cries.

I grace him a single glance, bending over to bind her arms together. "Torture her until she coughs something up," I answer dryly.

Before you get your panties in a wad and pull the gender bullshit, she entered this game and now I'm making her play. I don't give a fuck about what you have in your pants. I will seek vengeance if you wrong me.

She helped rip my heart out of my chest.

And I will do the same.

Honey brown hair whips through the air, a crack following close behind and ringing off the cement walls.

It doesn't stop. It hasn't for at least four hours now.

I'll slice and dice a woman, but I won't raise my hand to her. Good thing feral Nadia has rage to let out.

The carnage that's designing my blood flow has black crowding my peripheral. I got way too close to sawing her legs off with metal wire.

She would've died before I had the chance to ask any questions.

So—Kendra is Nadia's punching bag.

Legitimately.

She's strung up by her wrists, toes barely touching the floor and offering her no support. I bet that pressure on her shot up legs feels like fucking hell.

Nadia shakes out her bruising hand, throwing her head back and hocking a loogie on Kendra's bloody nose. "Does cocaine cloud your morals too, or are you just fucking stupid?" Nadia bites out.

Kendra snarls, a mixture of spit and crimson seeping over her top lip, spreading through the cracks of her teeth.

"What's *IR*?" My voice booms with impatience.

Her head weighs heavy, hanging through the space of her overextended shoulders. She lazily lifts it back up with tears turning her eyes to glass. "*The Inner Realm*," she squeaks.

I stalk closer, daggers sharpening my eyes and knuckles cracking at my sides. "Let me fucking guess. Mayor Jenkins has something to do with it."

She nods, a yell tossing her head back as a right hook thuds into her rib.

For being a chihuahua, Nadia's got some strength to her.

"Why do you think he's gotten away with all of this? Why he has over thirteen properties all over Anchorage that are hidden in plain sight? Or, why it's impossible to get the fuck out?" Kendra strains out.

Hidden in plain sight.

This whole time he's been concealed by the mayor.

Nadia raises her fist, more than ready to strike again. I hold my hand up to put her on pause, not tearing my eyes away from the rat that's finally spilling shit. Out of my dark peripheral, I see her marred knuckles lower back down to her side.

"What does he get out of it? And why the fuck did you have a wolf?" I ask testily, lip twitching up a snarl.

"Money… Non-consensual sex… Shows. I don't fucking know. But he's the reason it all stays afloat. He's the reason there's no opt out. I had the wolf because the second he tore Ryder's arm off mayhem broke out and I knew I only had a few seconds to run off with it. If I wouldn't have, they would've boiled it alive."

The only sensation I have in my cement riddled body is my stomach knotting the fuck up.

Leon would've pointed her out if he saw her on the cameras. And when I went back to review the footage to torture myself and see what the hell happened to Damascus, it was all spliced.

"How'd you manage that?"

She sniffles, tears pouring out of her penitent eyes. "I tried," she wavers. "After my order, I sped there, parked my car in the woods and climbed the fence. I tried throwing little rocks to get her attention without being seen."

Nadia collapses to the ground, breaking out in a sob that rekindles the flames roaring in the hole where my heart should be.

"Keep going," I demand venomously.

She watches Nadia crying at her feet, her own streams dripping off her bruised chin. "Well, it didn't work. She didn't notice. So, I tucked myself away once I saw her walk off, heard the commotion, the shot, and her crying… That was the last wolf left. I think he got a faulty dart and just fucking snapped, ripped his arm right off. Two other men rushed over to carry Ryder off and stanch the wound, and the next thing I knew… I was picking up the dropped chain and sprinting off with a bloody wolf."

Hearing that she could've gotten away, that she could be by my side and looking for the wolves with me—makes this so much fucking worse.

I've been skating on the thin ice of a goddamn mental breakdown. I feel the cracks splintering under my feet, ready to give out and plunge me into the freezing water.

"How do you know how to hack and splice?"

"Books. I learned because I get watched on the street cams."

"And that cabin was yours?"

"Not legally. I needed a safe spot for Samuel and found it a few months ago. That's why I took the wolf there."

I run a rough hand down my face, cracking the vexation out of my neck both ways. "You do realize you could've told us, or Leon, from the very start, right? We would've helped you and your brother, my fucking girl would be here, and the wolves would be at home."

She cries, lowering her head back down.

Stepping around her, I grab my Sirohi sword off my workbench, shaking my head in disbelief while striking the rope. It snaps cleanly, sending her body crashing to the ground next to crying Nadia.

"Get the fuck up. You're my GPS," I mutter, tossing my sword back onto the workbench.

Kendra groans hysterically. "You shot my fucking legs!"

"That sucks. Figure it the fuck out and get up before I start dragging you by that rope."

Her tightened lips quiver, slowly inching up to her elbows and knees. Winces and cries ricochet off the epoxy floor, and she finally gets up, staggering to her feet.

CHAPTER FIVE

TALA

A high-pitched beep is resounding in my head. My heavy lids open, the bright light glaring across my unfocused eyes. My head is groggy, and cramps are aching dully through my uterus, all the way to my back.

I blink a few times, washing the blurriness away, and pan around the cabin-like room I'm in. I have a gown on and an IV in my hand that's on a steady drip.

Anxiety coasts over my chest and raises my heart rate. The beeping grows louder and faster, triggering the claws to dig in deeper.

What the fuck happened? Think, you dumb bitch.

The wooden door flies open with a panicked nurse running in. "You're awake!" She runs to my side, pressing buttons on the machine next to me.

The beeps finally stop, leaving me with white noise.

"How are you feeling?" she asks, resting her cold hand on my arm.

I lick my chapped lips, taking in a deep breath of dry air. "Uh," I say hoarsely, having to clear my throat. "Not amazing. I'm mostly confused though. What happened?"

She rubs my arm, offering a somber frown. "Honey, you were severely dehydrated and suffered a ruptured ectopic ovarian pregnancy."

The room begins spinning, darkness clouding around the border of my vision, and a boulder of distress sinks down into my aching stomach. "How... how far along was I?" I choke out.

"You were estimated to be about five weeks."

Jax told me I was, and I refused to believe him.

I just want him here with me. I want to see his devastatingly handsome face and smell his whiskey scent as his strong arms wrap around me, telling me we'll be okay in his rich voice.

I wipe the tears from my face, chest tightening in anguish. "How long have I been here?"

She grabs a cup of water from the bedside table, holding the straw up to my mouth. I curl my lips around it, taking a big drink that soothes my dry tongue and slides down like ice. "You had to have a laparotomy to remove the ruptured fallopian tube. It was hard on your body... You've been in and out of consciousness for three days."

"Three days," I echo in disbelief. "Has anyone been in here?"

Not that Jax would leave me if he found me, but it would simmer down the boiling anxiety hearing that he was here.

She faintly grins, walking over to the gloves on the wall. "He hasn't left. He's pacing up and down the hall right now."

I shoot up, face twisting with the violent ache running up my stomach. "Does he have a lot of tattoos?" I ask optimistically, voice twinging from pain.

She cocks her head, lips pursed and brows tight. "No, I don't think so." Snapping her gloves on, she lifts up my gown. "I need to check your staples, honey."

The optimism drifts from me like a snuffed flame.

I don't know why I got my hopes up.

I slam my cloudy head back into the bed, peering down at the horrific sight of staples running from my pubic bone, well past my navel.

I should be able to look away and into hunter eyes. Instead, I get to look up into the cold panel lighting.

The door creaks open, stealing my attention from the light I wish would take me away. Shiloh is striding in, black hair messy like he was running his hands through it.

I huff, not giving a shit about their weird discipline.

I quite literally look like Frankenstein and have a nurse poking and prodding the sensitive incision.

She quickly lays the gown back over me, sending a grin that reads, *all is well with the butcher of your stomach*, then walks out.

"Are you okay?" he asks, inviting himself to sit on the edge of my bed.

"No," I snip. "This is so fucked up, Shiloh! This entire thing is gut wrenching, and I shouldn't have a random kidnapper in my goddamn room after losing a fucking fallopian tube and getting stapled up like I'm the next Tim Burton Claymation!" I let out a deep breath, relishing how good it felt to pop my top on him.

He raises a brow, the faintest of a smirk tugging up the corner of his lips. "I bet that felt good."

I glare venomously at his amusement. "It did. Almost near as good as fucking your lip up with my boot."

He smiles, revealing his straight teeth and dimples. "You probably thought I was mad." I stare in shock, unable to say anything over his switch up. "I was really just thinking about putting my face in between your legs. Can't let the boss know that though."

He's a masochist. Great.

It's been four days since I woke up there. I was supposed to stay for observation for another twenty-four hours. But with the weird cabin just being a clinic under Pyro's payroll or some shit—I had to go back to the house. I was able to get the staples taken out this morning.

But I had to come right back.

I don't think it's fair of me to complain though. I have it better than the other women. I've been left alone to sulk in my room and tend to my bloody vagina.

Except Pyro stopping in to remind me that he's in control here and Shiloh shoving anti-inflammatories in my face. Loxley has come in a few times. Just to quietly chat for a few minutes.

But these walls are becoming my tomb.

I sing a little. And pretend like Jax is rocking out on his guitar at the end of my sad bed. Though, it doesn't help the corrosion rusting over my broken heart.

It makes it worse.

The only thing that's keeping me from falling down the rabbit hole of insanity is going through the few boxing movements Jax taught me.

Slowly, of course. My abdomen is still tender and healing. But it gets me up and going without having to run into an egotistical rapist.

The sun is shining through the barred window in my room. It'd be nice to see the trees. Even if the windows were clear, the snow would be mounding and collecting on them, wiping the outside in a blanket of white.

"I need to get up," I murmur to myself, then throw my legs over the side of the bed, wincing from the shooting pain in my stomach.

I manage to make it to the kitchen without running into someone.

Someone I haven't met yet.

His back is turned towards me and he's pouring coffee into a mug by the kitchen sink. His overgrown, black hair is flipped up around the bill of a backwards ball cap and the gray long sleeve he has on is, of course, clean without wrinkles.

I tread carefully by keeping my steps light and aim for the side hall. Once I get into the bathroom, I hit the light on and quietly close the door, cringing at the squeaky hinges.

I think I'm safe, but the door pushing back open, forcing me to step back, has me sucking in a sharp breath.

The panic eases over and I sigh in relief, taking in the blue eyes and scarred snub nose.

Loxley closes the door behind her, a secret dying to spill from her lips, and steps right into my bubble to press them to my ear. "I overheard a couple of the guys say we're all going to a fight and strip night this upcoming Friday." She pulls away, beaming at me.

I don't give a fuck about how appalling that sounds. I might be able to run off or bump into someone I know.

I'd fight *and* shake my ass for the chance to get the hell out of here.

"Wait," I whisper, then turn my head to get closer to her ear. "I know they're stupid, but they wouldn't let you guys leave since your faces have been in the paper."

"I thought the same. But then I heard them say masks."

I wrap my pinky around hers. "I promise to have your back. If there's an opportunity, you take it, Loxley. Even if that means leaving everyone else behind. Once I figure out what river we're by, I'll be able to start planning a way to get everyone out."

She pulls away, the light finally finding its way back to her ocean eyes. "And I have yours. Pinky promise." She bumps her shoulders up with a gleeful smile.

I smile back. It's nice seeing the hope return in her.

CHAPTER SIX

JAX

I took Jeremy's dog and burned his house down. He wasn't there, unfortunately. But a fuck ton of blow was. And with Kendra's crippled ass pointing me in the direction, I've raided and burned down four of Brutus' other properties.

Didn't find shit besides old couches and cots in little bedrooms.

Right now, I have a full fucking house of domes. Not a single one has raven silk and amber eyes. And that makes my ears ring at a high pitch frequency.

Maverick is concussed and spread eagle on the couch, Nadia and Evelyn are in spare bedrooms asleep, Kendra is pouting some-fuckin-where, Viper is hollering Russian over the phone, and Leon is clacking away next to me at the island.

Oh, shit.

Forgot to fucking mention the wolf I have in my backyard, Jeremy's Pit Bull over by the fireplace, and Samuel who's doing homework over at the dining table.

I'm going to lose my goddamn mind.

Distance from her in general makes my chest ache. Not knowing where she is and what she's going through is like drinking bleach.

It's eating my insides and killing me.

I'm trying to collect my thoughts and use logical thinking here. It would just be so much quicker to burn everything down to ash until I found her.

It's been three days. Three days of not being able to breathe. Three fucking days of her having to endure horrible goddamn shit because this motherfucker knows how to be a ghost.

"Geoffrey has his spies on the move," Viper says, dropping his phone down to the countertop.

I nod, pushing off the island. "We need to layer up. We have a lot of water ways to cover."

He looks around, unsure if he should say what's on the tip of his tongue. "What makes you think they'd be by water?"

He's being helpful. But the tsunami of vexation is making me intolerable to bullshit.

While I glower at him and make him uncomfortable, Leon's head oscillates back and forth in my peripheral. "B-because his name isn't attached to any water lines," Leon cuts in awkwardly. "He has to be pumping from a river. And with what Jax has told me about him, he wouldn't waste money on something he could catch for free… Fish."

Leon's looked through every single water line. He's gone through ID's, where they live, whether it's well or city.

All regular damn people.

The most incriminating thing he found was a shoplifter and someone that went too hard at the bar during the day.

I walk off, needing to get my drone off the charger and slap a beanie on. It's cold as fuck and I won't be able to find her if I die pathetically from hypothermia.

Passing Maverick on the couch, he shoots up, throwing his hand to his fucked-up head to clutch the migraine that's making him weak. "I'm going with," he grunts.

I slowly blink, realizing I'm picking up on Tala's mannerisms. It makes a goddamn boulder form low in my throat. "I don't have the time to babysit you." I pivot to my left and start hiking up the stairs two at a time, Sirohi clomping right by my side.

He misses her too.

"I'm not going to be a sitting duck!" Maverick shouts after me, a loud thud and groan following right behind.

Knowing he just fell off the couch, I don't turn around. I shake my head and keep going until I reach my office.

I push the door open, spotting the strawberry hair peeking out from the other side of my monitors. "The fuck do you think you're doing in here?" I ask abrasively, stalking in and rounding the desk to see why she's on my fucking computer.

I always lock it down. But I haven't cared about anything else other than finding Tala.

Her shoulders stiffen, eyes rounding with nerves, and she points, waving her shaky finger around. "Unless you have a map on hand, we'll easily get lost in the trees."

She's putting together maps for all the rivers, where they lead, what other beds of water they flow into. It's cool of her to think ahead but...

"Following water isn't a hard task," I grumble, and grab my drone to rip the charger out of the port.

"You're right, it's not. But with the snow and your full gas can... I figured I'd print these out to be safe and mark his other properties for you to burn down along the way. We'll end up coming across the other eight that I know about."

She's trying. And she did try. I just don't have anything in me that's willing to give a fuck about anything other than my missing girlfriend.

Trying isn't good enough right now. Doing is what will get results.

"Cool. Print them out and get out of my office."

"Yes, sir," she mumbles.

My stomach twists, and I glare at her. "Don't ever call me that again."

She clanks her teeth, audibly swallowing. "I'm sorry. It's a habit."

Jesus fucking Christ.

I need a cigarette before I start killing everyone.

Shaking the nozzle in the gas can, I pull it out and slam the handle back onto the rack. Something catches my eye at the pump to my left.

Not tearing my eyes away from Don Cromwell, the deputy mayor, I twist the cap back onto the gas can.

Pretty fucking ignorant of him to get his own gas with no one else around to watch him. The glacial air is keeping everyone at home. Including his security, I guess.

I pick the gas can up and reach over to set it in my truck bed—and paste on the fakest fucking smile I can manage. "Deputy Mayor," I say ardently, stepping around the pump and to his side.

He smiles, nose already turning red. "What can I do for you?"

I huff in amusement, swiftly dropping the fake shit from my face and balling my fist, striking him in the temple. His light goes out, his shoulders dropping limply and body tumbling into his truck.

I let him fall to the salted pavement, unclick the lock on the nozzle he was using, and set it back on the rack.

He's a well-rounded man. That's no problem though.

I grab under his arms and drag him around the pump, over to the rear door of my truck. It opens for me, a thin body scurrying away and peeking around with wide eyes. "What do I do if he wakes up?" Kendra squawks.

Having to activate my goddamn muscles for this gluttonous fuck, I shove him headfirst into the floorboard. "Punch him, kick him, stab him, I don't give a fucking shit," I grunt out, grabbing his knees and shoving his big ass all the way in.

His face grates along the floor, right towards Kendra's boots.

She winces and grabs her stitched up thighs while shooting her legs up, making room for the piece of shit.

I grab his ankles and throw his feet to his ass, then slam the door closed. While opening my driver's door, I glance to my right, glaring at the cashier staring through the window in shock.

I don't give a shit. This dude is useless, and everyone knows that. The police would probably give me a pat on the back if they actually cared enough to do their jobs.

Planting my ass in my seat, I close my door and instantly start the engine so Leon will stop chattering his teeth. "Dude, man the fuck up before I pull all your teeth out," I warn, shifting into drive and peeling the fuck out.

"I'm not built for Alaska, man. You know this. I'm meant for sand and salt water," he says breathlessly.

Kendra gasps. "Aw, I didn't know you were a mermaid."

My lip hasn't been able to settle the hell down. But hearing regular banter like Tala isn't fucking missing spikes the lightning in my face. "If you guys want to chat, that's fine. But fucking text each other. The only words out of your mouths should be regarding Tala. And if that's too fucking complicated get the hell out," I finish hostilely, the threat in my tone rumbling my chest.

My words hang in the air, the only sounds being the engine roaring and slushy shit smacking the mud flaps.

"Uh... how are you planning on getting information from him if we're walking the waters?" Leon asks cautiously.

"Make him fucking walk," I answer harshly.

CHAPTER SEVEN
TALA

"Fires are circulating the entire city. We have on account five in the city and eight, yes you heard me, eight on the outskirts," the blonde reporter on the TV says mechanically.

I pad down the last three steps, watching the slideshow of ash and embers out of the corner of my eye.

Pyro is sitting on the couch with his Cane Corso at his feet. As I step by, I cringe at his hand wound up in mushroom brown hair, him receiving a blowjob that was certainly not her decision.

That's Brynn. I did laundry with her yesterday. She's not much of a talker, but I can tell she has a fiery attitude that wants to slip out.

Much like me.

The physical restraint to not smack the shit out of him and tear her away—is painful. My hands are trembling with the urge as I stare down the hallway, wishing it would just teleport me to it so I don't have to pretend to be ignorant as I walk by this.

"Princess," he calls out, heavy breaths following.

I close my eyes and roll them, then strap on my sweet face, pivoting around to his smug smile.

Aside from the groping he did the first day I was here, I've gotten away with not being touched, or coerced to perform, or raped.

I don't think I'll get away with it much longer.

"Shilo's been doin' a peachy job with you. Let's see how peachy."

My heart plummets. And sweat begins percolating in my hairline.

A large hand rests on the small of my back, politely nudging me forward in passing. It's not Shiloh like I assumed. It's the man I saw in the kitchen the other day.

I learned that his name is Eli. He's paired with Sunny, whom I've only seen skitter down the hall and into her room.

Swallowing the rocks in my throat, I count the steps I was pushed into, only stopping when I reach Brynn.

Fifteen from the hallway to the couch. One dull creak at step seven.

His assaulting eyes look me up and down, still smiling like a smug pig. "That's a good girl," he drawls. "Now get on your knees, next to Brynn, and kiss her." He lifts her off his laughable cock, roughly yanking her over to make room.

Sitting my weight down onto my knees next to her, I smell his musk on her mouth. I can't let my lips curl like they're begging to. To power through it, I gradually exhale while leaning in, and I press my lips to her wet ones.

Expecting to be done, I start to pull away, but her hand slides up the back of my head and pushes me right back into her.

"Keep goin'," he orders, the sounds of him beating his dick right in my ear.

Her lips part against me, her tongue sliding through the seam and into my mouth, and sweaty, dirty skin smarts on my taste buds. I want to gag. It's not her fault though. And aside from the discipline, I wouldn't want to make her feel bad.

So, I suck it the fuck up and make out with her.

It's humiliating.

But I will admit that it's nice feeling a soft touch run up my thigh. It doesn't give me butterflies or weigh heavy in between my legs. It's just nice. She's tender and kisses well.

I'd probably enjoy myself if I wasn't longing for Satan, constantly feeling stitches run through my heart for him. Or, have a goddamn nut bag tugging his dick right next to my face.

"Look at my pretty girls," he marvels sickeningly. "Open wide for Daddy. Both of you."

A growl of vexation brews up my throat. I make it coast out as a breath, pulling away from her.

Her blood kissed lips are swollen, and she rolls the bottom one in between her teeth, looking at me like she wouldn't mind taking me to her room and exploring.

It's flattering. But having to turn and open my mouth for semen that has to be ash by now depletes the ego boost.

His leathery hand keeps stroking, aiming his tip towards us, and a loud groan belts out of his mouth, his lips curling into a satisfied smile while releasing his load.

I wince, tasting the horrible saltiness splatter on my tongue, the warm liquid spotting and roping over my face.

And once again, the whites of my eyes begin to burn.

He gets his dick out of my sight by tucking it back in and zipping up his jeans. Cupping under our chins, wafting his stinky musk around, he shoots us a wink and stands up. "Get some good sleep tonight," he says darkly, then steps around us and walks away with his dog.

We look at each other, both sharing looks riddled with anxious confusion. And his fucking cum.

If that's the worst I'll have to deal with while biding my time, I'll take it. It's not great. Obviously.

But clearly the sweetheart act works. And I'll keep strapping that mask on until I can methodically kill them all.

Reaching my fingers up to her hair, I brush it over her ear with my nails, leaning in until my own warm breath filters over my lips. "Your back is good. Is mine?" I ask, glancing around at the vacancy of men. She nods, running her hand over my hip. "Do you know what river we're close to?"

She tilts her head, grazing her lips over mine. "Knik," she murmurs against me, welding the words by smashing our lips together.

The stickiness will haunt me.

But I know where the Knik is.

I just have to start plotting and hope that my wilting brain allows me to retain a schematic plan to get us out.

The wolves are crying. I open my eyes to the cream wall that's highlighted with the cool light beaming in from the opaque window, the bars casting their own menacing shadows.

I haven't heard them a single time since coming here.

I don't sleep well, so their distant howls have me wide awake now, listening to the sound that used to mean home.

A lump lodges in my throat, tears glaze over my eyes—and I let them out silently. The drips roll over the bridge of my nose, splashing onto the white pillowcase, each one reminding me that I'm somewhere other than home.

I'm desperately trying to cling onto the flame before getting lost in the darkness. But the wick is rapidly burning down with the wax… and I don't have my extra candle by my side.

Using my sleeve to wipe my face, I roll over onto my back while drying my lashes, my other hand defeatedly slamming down to the mattress. I smack something hard, a sharp pain exploding through my wrist, and I snap my head to the left, meeting the dark eyes that are intently watching me.

I yelp in response, bolting upright and swiveling around in the sheets as if I saw a massive spider crawling in bed.

Nope. Just my kidnapper that's hanging out, arms tucked under his head and a whisper of a grin on his face.

"Can I help you?" I whisper-shout.

"I couldn't sleep," Shiloh says reservedly.

I squint, thinning my lips to pop them. "And you thought you'd find sleep in my bed?"

His eyes fall, landing on the boy short underwear I'm in. I claw at the sheets and jerk them over me, wanting to punch myself for thinking it was a good idea to sleep like this in a house full of rapists.

"No. But I knew I'd find you in it," he draws out, studying my face.

I blink with force, rubbing over the throb that's firing up on my scar, and ignore the way he's watching the action. "Okay… Why'd you want to find me?"

"Maybe I just wanted to talk."

"About what?"

"Come here," he lightly tips his chin, gesturing to his stomach.

Just when I thought he was doing so well at not coercing me.

He's a snake that's willing to strike at any moment. A bomb that has a faulty pin. He might let me get away with a little sass, but that doesn't mean I can disobey an order.

My skin itches from head to toe and it becomes impossible to swallow. But with each day, I get a little closer to an escape plan. So, I hesitantly peel the sheets from my hips, choke on fucking acid as I meander over on my knees, and straddle around his waist.

He wets his healed bottom lip, gazing at the sight of me on top of him. "How's your abdomen doing?"

My brows knit, thrown off guard by his sudden interest. "Fine," I drone. "I just get random dull aches along my scar."

He unfolds his arms to place his hands on my hips, skating them up my sides and sliding my shirt up with them.

I get rippling chills. Like, the chills you get when you're nauseous and you know you're about to throw up.

Analyzing my scar, he draws his fingertips over my rib, tracing down the straight line. I shiver, a twisted pit in my stomach and needles leaving evidence from his touch.

I can do nothing but watch him, and let him, and wither from the uncomfortable attack of fire and ice.

"You guys start training tomorrow," he whispers, moving his hands to rest on my thighs.

"For..."

He chews the inside of his cheek thoughtfully, unable to keep his eyes on my face. "Fighting. You already have bids on you."

My jaw falls slack, the sickly chills raising every hair on my body. "So, we're basically getting pitted like the dogs," I state the obvious. "Where are the wolves?"

Running his hands over my thighs, he wedges them under my ass, slightly lifting me up to set me down on his erection.

I bite the inside of my lip. So hard, iron bursts on the tip of my tongue. All so I don't snarl in repulsion and end up with the cotton-clad erection in my ass.

He sits up, tilting his chin down and getting eye to eye with me. "They're out back. And if I tell you this, you have to make sure you act completely shocked when Pyro discloses it to you girls. There can't be a sliver of already knowing on your pretty face."

This whole nightmare has shown me that I'm incredible at acting.

I nod in agreement. "I promise," I murmur, despising the proximity of our mouths.

"The wolves are getting pitted too. But it's not just a solo fight. You guys will be in the pit with them."

Panicked rage tightens my face. "Are you fucking insane?" I whisper-shout.

Dogs are one thing. Wolves are entirely different. We will be fucking slaughtered if they're back there beating the wolves the way they beat dogs to make them fighters.

64

Fingers crossed I can execute a plan before it boils down to that. I just don't know where the guys sleep.

And they're my biggest problem right now.

"It's not *my* doing, Tala," he says defensively, then pulls a leg out from under me and over the edge of the bed. "Get some sleep. I'll be dragging you out of bed at six." Lifting me off, he sets my ass back down on the bed, sparing one last glance before walking away and out the door.

Satan, I really need you to use your stalker skills.

CHAPTER EIGHT

TALA

I wasn't willing to get dragged out of bed. I put pants on and stayed up the rest of the night. I've just been sitting cross legged in bed, going over the creaks and moans the floors make, and watching the light gradually grow on the cream wall.

There's an unsticking noise my door makes once you start to push or pull it open. I hear it, watching the door slowly open to Shiloh carrying a stack of clothes, sneakers—and a bowl of oatmeal.

We either get granola bars or oatmeal for breakfast and lunch. He doesn't let the other girls have dinner. But to "maintain my ass," Pyro has whoever is on dinner duty make a tiny plate of salmon for me.

I don't eat it though.

Not only do I not have an appetite here, but that's also so fucking unfair.

I don't know why he's bringing breakfast to me. It's either slid under my door or set outside of it with a knock.

After kicking the door closed and throwing the sneakers down, he sets the clothes and the bowl on my dresser. "Come over here," he orders, pulling a water bottle out of his hoodie pocket and placing it next to the bowl.

No. I don't want to.

Internally frowning, I uncross my legs and crawl to the end of the bed, throwing my legs over to walk to the dresser.

"Good girl, keep that up today. Eat, drink. I'm getting you dressed."

I'm so fucking tired of, one, being called a good girl by these assholes, and two, being told what the hell to do.

I miss "*Attagirl*" out of Jax's full lips. I miss *him*.

Reality shoves me into the void of despair, and I go numb, as if I died in this room and became a ghost.

Maintaining my silence, I grab the bottom hem of my shirt, lift it up over my head and slip my arms out, letting it fall limp from my hands and to the floor.

I know he's eye fucking me.

I can see it out of my peripheral vision. But I don't feel it. And I don't know if that helps or makes it worse.

My mouth is really dry, and that water looks delicious. I grab it, making sure I can hear the cap crack open as I twist, and tilt it back to my parted lips for a gluttonous drink.

The dryness feels unquenchable.

I keep chugging, trying to pacify the desperation for hydration, only stopping when the empty bottle crackles.

He's holding up a black, spandex long sleeve shirt, staring at me like he's never seen someone thirsty before. "Are you staying hydrated?" he asks worriedly, stretching the shirt out and putting it over my head.

The tight fabric fits snug to my neck, shaping my hair to my head and leaving tendrils to obstruct my tired vision. "I do everything I can to avoid going down there. So, no. I'm not."

I do laundry every other day and help with dishes. Other than that, I only leave to change my panty liner.

I'm still spotting.

While lifting my arms and shoving them in the sleeves, he says, "Pyro will be pissed if you end up in the clinic again. He's already halted his plans for your healing. I need you to pull it together and take care of yourself."

Maybe I don't want to. Maybe the thought of not seeing Jax for another day is strong enough to push the knife into my heart.

All the guys carry one in their front pocket.

After forcing me to scarf down the oatmeal and dressing me in tight spandex, he pulls a collar out from his back pocket.

Not just a collar. A fucking shock collar.

My eyes round, tracking him as he slips behind me. The metal prongs float down my eyes, getting pressed into my bobbing throat.

He clips it, touching over Maiko's paw print before invading my space and stepping right in front of me. "It's just so you don't run off. We have to take the hills to get to your new gym."

I faintly shake my head, wanting to rip it off and gouge him in the eye with it, then turn it on the highest frequency and see if he likes it.

A small jolt runs across my throat, and I flinch, scrunching my face at the prick that just zapped me.

"Attitude check," he says haughtily, then smiles.

Fuck this shit.

I smile cunningly. "Where's the muzzle?"

I don't blink before he's slapping his hand to my mouth and walking me backwards into the wall. *Callously.*

My head thuds, stirring up the stars from exhaustion, and he presses his forehead to mine with eyes that are one tick away from exploding. "Right there, princess," he snarls. "Next time, it'll be my cock. So act fucking straight."

I believe him. He's a thread away from snapping.

Pain smarts on my ass cheek from his hand squeezing maliciously. Enough to make me wince, the sound vibrating the shock collar that's digging into my larynx.

Dropping his lids heavy, he slides his hand from my mouth, tugging my lips and cheek with force. He leans in, hot breath fanning my lips. "One little taste will set me over the edge… I'll do something stupid," he murmurs—as if he's talking to himself.

The scales are bobbing. His interest in me is crystal clear. I very well could get him wrapped around my finger and make him my fucking dog. But that thought mists over my eyes and churns the oatmeal in my stomach.

He parts his lips, moving them closer, and the sensation of them brushing mine produces a whine of terror.

A blood curdling scream comes from down the hall, loud enough to hear it through my closed door. My blood pressure spikes, spreading heat up my chest and nipping at my eyes.

He sighs, finally releasing my throbbing ass cheek and backing away. "We need to go before he gets mad," he says reservedly.

Grabbing my hand, he pulls me along to open the door, and straight into where the scream of horror came from.

I don't have to look to know what's happening in Rylie's room. The screams of agony, the fleshy slapping noises, and the bed creaking is enough to paint the picture.

My nose burns with the waves washing under my vision. It's so fucking painful not being able to do anything about this.

May your courage and bravery be strong enough, Tala. Become the weapon they're forcing you to be. The one your grandparents want you to be.

I get pulled along down the hall, down the stairs, through the kitchen, and to the back door that beckons me every time I go down the side hall.

Covering the spin lock with his body so I don't see, the whirring and clicks give way, and he opens the door to another door with six deadbolts running down it.

Each one with a different key.

He reaches a key up to the top one, and I do my best to not make it obvious I'm studying the keys in his hand.

It would probably take me too long to get the spin lock and all six deadbolts open.

But if they were all dead—it wouldn't matter.

While he finishes unlocking the door, I take note of the different shades of brass. There's not a stark contrast. But enough to tell me which one goes where.

I just need to get my hand in his pocket once I get an idea of the layout outside. This motherfucker blindfolded me and restrained my arms when he brought me to and from the clinic.

By the time the door is unlocked and open, Rylie's splotchy face and messed up ginger hair is behind me. I wish I could turn around and give her a hug, and shove Shiloh's knife in Jarvin's throat.

I follow Shiloh's steps out into the crisp, frigid air and the light that flash-bangs me. I haven't been outside in four days. I haven't had to feed the dogs yet. I kind of want that responsibility just so I can get fresh air.

Supervised, of fucking course.

That's why Cora got the belt. She wasn't able to get out of the locked-up door because Jeremy was too busy darting the wolves.

Yet she got disciplined for it.

It's not even the sun itself that's beaming into my eyes. The snow is so damn white and covering the ground with pops of green contrasting under the blankets on the trees.

Shiloh turns around, grabbing my hand and pulling me closer to him. "Stay in my steps. There are bear traps everywhere."

Oh. Good. That's just fucking great.

That makes my chances of escaping during winter slim to none. How the fuck am I going to see a bear trap that's been snowed on?

Another hand laces itself in mine.

I glance back at Riley and the green light on her shock collar and give her a somber grin. She offers one back, although the spark is gone from her glassy, blue eyes.

I whip my head back to Shiloh, closely following the steps he's making on the slim path that winds through the towering trees.

I didn't see Jarvis clutching onto her head. Unfortunately, I don't think it was a sudden and silent bear attack. I think he's locking the door like a piece of shit.

After a couple of minutes of stepping mindfully in his prints, we pass a little clearing to the right.

I quickly count how many wooden dog houses I see, lips barely moving with my internal dialogue.

I count twelve dog houses stationed in a U-shape and twelve thick, heavy chains that are anchored to the ground, giving them only enough grace to seek shelter from the weather.

They're all spaced out at least twelve to fifteen feet from one another, their bowls completely submerged in snow with no fresh water visible.

A long, black face with tan eyebrows peeks out of the second to the left. He looks identical to Sirohi. Except, his beady eyes don't hold a glimmer, and he has visible scars veining through his short fur.

My eyes start burning, the harsh breeze increasing the sting that's enticing tears. And the knot that's usually just in my throat—builds itself in my chest.

I'll save you, baby. Hang in there.

"The fuck you lookin' at mutt?" Jarvis asks cruelly.

My hand tenses in Shiloh's, my nails digging into his skin, and he looks over his shoulder with a warning glare already written on his face. Once he spots the tears begging to spill, his eyes soften, and he turns his head back to continue hauling me into the hills.

A chain rattles behind us, followed with the most gut twisting yelp—and I blanch.

My breathing picks up, inhaling the dry air with wide eyes. The latch around my hand gets tighter, and I get pulled into Shiloh's back, my arm wrapping around his waist. And I cry. I cry hearing the thuds and blows prompting screams from an innocent soul.

Riley wraps around the back of me—doing the same.

I have to stay strong for them. All of them.

The women, the dogs, and the wolves.

I don't know if that makes me a martyr. I really don't know how this will end for me. But I do know I will get them all out. The wolves will go home, the dogs will see the ranch, and the women will get their lives back.

They fucking deserve it. It should've never been stripped from them by sick bastards to begin with.

I will rain hellfire on this entire place.

Even if I go up in flames with it.

I dry my face on his back, shaking my hand to let him know I'm fine to use my own vision now.

He's hesitant, but he relaxes his grip.

I let Rylie take her time, hugging me and muffling her cry, and continue taking in the sights around me.

There's not much along the trail aside from a little clearing to the left. Poles are sticking out of the ground with balls attached to string, and treadmills are boarded up on the sides with tight leashes wrapped around the handles.

Forced "exercise."

From what Jax has told me, the poles are called spring poles. They make them jump up, latch around the ball, and hang to strengthen their jaws. The treadmills are explanatory. And the heavy chains they use increase muscle. Because the steroids and vitamins they inject them with aren't enough.

That was sarcasm by the way.

At the top of the hill, there's a metal building swallowed by towering trees. It's certainly newly built for his "plans" with us.

Shiloh leads us up to the white bay door, raising his free hand in a fist and knocking three times. Each one reverberates in my head, ringing an alarm under my skin.

I hold Riley's hand tighter, listening to the hum of the door opening. It slowly rolls up, first showing off the dirty boots, then the freshly clean denim, and finally the smug smile on Pyro's face.

His hands are out like they were when I first got to the house, as if we should be jumping up and down with excitement to see our form of forced exercise. "Well, don't you girls look pretty in my collars. Mmm!" He shakes his head with delight. "If I wasn't so excited to start makin' some money, I'd send the guys off and have some fun with you."

Thank fuck for greed.

Still smiling, he turns around for us to follow him inside.

The track lighting hanging from beams is menacing, casting its cold light down onto a boxing ring in the center. Punching bags hang in rows of two along the right wall, long ropes are hanging in the very back, and the regular shit like dumbbells and lifting machines are sporadically placed everywhere else.

It's just Rylie and I, though. I thought we'd all be here today. I was honestly hoping for a larger group of support.

Shiloh finally unhands me, stepping out in front of me and forcing me to a stop in an empty space by the rope. "Start stretching," he orders sternly.

I want to spit on his face.

Biting the sides of my tongue, I step back from him and stretch my right arm over my aching chest.

The last time I did any sort of training with stern orders—they were coming from Jax. I was happy to obey him. But I feel fucking sick letting Shiloh and everyone else have authority over me.

The entire time I stretch out Shiloh's eyes penetrate me, and Pyro's eyes assault me. The damn shock collar is irritating my skin. The prongs are digging into me and the itchy band feels like poison ivy is flaring up in a ring around my neck.

"Your warmup is over!" Pyro shouts from the center of the boxing ring. "Now, I get to see if you're worth a shit. Rylie on my right, Princess on my left. No gloves. Just brawl."

Our eyes connect from across the room. Her panic is real, mine is a show. I didn't know we'd be fighting today. But it doesn't surprise me that we're not getting offered legitimate training beforehand.

Shiloh slips around me, quickly gathering my hair up into a ponytail. Pulling it tight as hell. I almost wince from the snapping of some baby hairs, but the assaulting hazel eyes watching me leave no room to show weakness.

Shiloh pats my ass, and my eye instantly twitches something fierce. "Let the attitude out in the ring."

How about I do it right here and send a haymaker into your jaw?

Locking everything up in the box of my emotions, I stride forward, the shakes of adrenaline pumping through me, and climb up the little metal stairs on my side. Lifting the center rope up, I maneuver within them—and into the ring.

With both feet on the canvas, I don't see anything other than what's inside with me. Slenderman the assaulter and Rylie who's shaking like a lost dog caught in a storm.

Everything on the outside is depleted in black.

Eerie whistling circulates around us. My hair raises and my hands go numb, and with my sights set on Rylie's panic, I vaguely track Pyro waltzing around with his menacing tune.

"Three rounds. Three minutes each. Don't fuckin' piss me off and don't ask for a break. Whoever wins… gets to take a little field trip. Fight!"

Her eyes light up with the need to leave this place, and she screams like a banshee, tossing her hands up and going for my neck.

I sidestep out, using the tight canvas for fluid movement, and dodge her warned attempt. Bouncing on the balls of my feet with raised fists, I pendulum step a few feet away from the rabidness overtaking her.

She whisks around, seething with crazy eyes. "I deserve that!"

"You do!" I agree. "But I don't play fair. I play to win."

Call me fucked up all you want. But me leaving this place will give me a better understanding of where we are and raise the chances of me getting them out sooner.

She starts charging at me with a snarl, and with my right foot giving me more power, I strike my fist out, clocking her in the cheekbone.

Her head whips from the force, sending her in a tornado spiral down to the canvas in front of me.

I'll feel that in my hand and arm tomorrow. Right now, the adrenaline is numbing my body.

"Ho-ly shit! Time!"

A scream tears through her lungs, and she starts clawing at her neck, violently shaking as she flips onto her back.

Pyro stomps over to us, stopping right at her head and crouching down to her thrashing body. "I don't tolerate weakness! Get your fuckin' ass up and fight!" Twisting his hand in her shirt, he rips her up, throwing his free hand back and cracking his open palm across her face.

I start heaving for air, drying my lips and throat even more, and contain the words that could get me in trouble.

The next two rounds I try to go a easy on her. I let her get a hit to my ribs before roundhousing her clear across the ring and into the rope.

But my fucking stomach is killing me.

I'm almost certain I wasn't supposed to do anything vigorous for at least six weeks after getting opened up like a cadaver.

At least I get to leave tomorrow.

And then come right the hell back.

CHAPTER NINE

JAX

Tomorrow marks two fucking weeks.

One step forward, ten steps back. We're losing time. We're losing daylight. And I'm losing my fucking sanity.

I can't sleep.

I can't close my eyes without seeing her face. And it destroys me that the image is just a memory, not her standing in the flesh.

Don Cromwell died of a heart attack in the back of my truck. All he did was waste my fucking time and burden me with the disposal of a body I didn't even kill.

We've raided and burned down all the properties Kendra knew about. Same old couches. Same old cots.

I've tried using my drone to see where my eyes can't reach—and it's too fucking cold. The battery gets shot instantly.

Viper has some family from Russia that's trying to help sweep the trees, but with this goddamn weather everyone's needing breaks so that they don't lose fingers and toes.

"Jax… Hey, man." Sounds like an old record giving out. "Hey! … Hey!"

Loud ringing splits my ears, vision depleting to nothingness. All I see is her silhouette in a wash of white.

"I love you, Jax."

Her husky voice sounds so goddamn celestial echoing in my vacant mind. It rewinds, then restarts, conjuring up the horrific fucking reality that I'm not actually hearing it.

"Jax!" Cuts off the loop of her voice.

"What?" I snap, whipping my head to Leon who's trembling in a big ass coat.

With a shaky hand, he points to my chest. "You're fucking bleeding, man," he wavers.

I glance down at my hand curled into iron around my dog tag, crimson seeping up through the seams of my fingers and dripping onto the snow.

I relax my hand, wiping it off on my cold denim. "For all we fucking know, Tala has shed more blood than that."

"You can't think like that. It'll only darken the shadows."

Sirohi starts barking, snagging the hateful words off my tongue and spiking my blood pressure.

It's not vicious. He's picked up a scent.

He's stopped a few feet ahead of us, snow boots submerged in the snow and directing his alert straight ahead through the trees.

Holy fuckin' shit.

I jog up to his side and pat him on his coat. "Show me," I order desperately, snatching my gun from my waistband.

Clomping through the snow, we race along his side and weave through the trees I'm fucking sick of seeing. With each pounding stride, my heart races just a little faster. It sparks the hope that this may be a victory run towards Tala.

About a yard away, there's a cabin stationed on a cliff out of the tree line. The little bulb hanging over the front porch is on and there's a white sign hanging on the green door. I can't read that shit, but it appears to be a business of some sort.

He's still barking, still leading us straight towards it.

My heart is slamming against my chest and this goddamn air is so dry it's scorching my lungs.

We storm out of the tree line, running right up to the cabin, and I thunder up the wooden steps, glancing over the sign and read: Hemlock Walk-In.

It's a clinic.

I barely get the handle turned before pushing the door open and raising my gun at the brunette nurse sitting behind the front desk. "Tala! Where is she?" I shout gutturally.

Eyes wide, she vigorously shakes her head, following the movement of me getting closer. "I-I-I don't know who-"

I aim my sight at the log wall behind her head and pull the trigger. The pop makes her jump and shriek, her hands slapping over her ears as she hunkers down.

"Tell me before that hole is in your forehead!"

Leon zips around the desk, wrapping his hands around her chair and pushing her out of the way. Then he bends down and starts clacking away on the keyboard.

"I don't know!" she squawks, so high pitched it makes Sirohi stop sniffing and cock his head.

An older man in a lab coat holding a shotgun runs out of the hall, stopping at the side of the desk. He raises the barrel at me, shaking like a scared fucking dog. "Leave! I already warned the last one in here." He cocks the shotgun, attempting to use it as his stoic mask.

"Warned who?" I bark, still aiming at the trembling nurse.

"Whoever that idiot was that got his arm ripped off! I'm done with your kind!"

I lower my gun to my side, face vibrating with a rush of blood. "When I find the fucker, I'll drag him back here and let you do the honors. I'm looking for a woman that was taken by his group. She has long, raven hair and-"

"Amber eyes?" the nurse cuts in, whipping my attention to her. "I'm so sorry," she says softly, a tear spilling over her cheek.

The blood rush dissipates, turning my face gray. "Why are you sorry? What fucking happened to her?"

"I knew something was wrong when she asked if a different man had been here. Then, the man that brought her in barged into the room while I was checking her staples. I tried getting him to let her stay for observation so I could find... you... I guess. The man with tattoos."

"Staples for what?" I ask hoarsely, dread straining my larynx.

The old man sets the shotgun down on the desk, leaning against it with clasped hands. "She was brought in here unconscious with excessive vaginal bleeding."

Black brims my vision, sinking my concrete heart into my twisting stomach.

"I know what you're thinking, kid. I thought the same. But she suffered a ruptured ectopic ovarian pregnancy. I had to remove her left fallopian tube."

She was pregnant.

My baby girl was pregnant… with my baby. And she went through that without me there to hold her hand.

The ear-splitting ring comes back like bullets, muffling out the voices, my vision bugging around and turning everything to grain.

A distorted hand waves across my face. It lags and chops around, then the ringing dies off and I snap the fuck out of the desolation I was being sucked into. "What does ectopic mean and why did it rupture?"

I can only think of the worst right now. My chest is a giant knot that's trying to lodge itself in my throat.

"That little clump of cells wasn't growing in her uterus. That's where a baby has to be implanted in order for the mom and baby to survive. It was in her left fallopian tube and… just ruptured. It wasn't where it was supposed to be growing."

Mom and baby.

"So, she wasn't raped or beaten? It just happened?"

The nurse stands up, the chair rolling back and thudding into the wall. "I performed a sexual assault exam on her, solely because she had hemo… hickeys… along the side of her neck and down her shoulder with human bite marks. But she was not vaginally or anally raped. The only signs of abuse I noticed were light, raw rings around her wrists."

Jesus fucking Christ.

My heart is burning, propelling the flames and boiling my skin. Sweat is running down the back of my neck and I can guarantee my face is turning red with rage.

Leon waves me over, sorrow darkening his tired eyes. "You'll want to see this."

No, I fucking don't.

But it's my goddamn fault this is happening to her.

I swallow roughly and maneuver around the desk, having to roll the damn chair out of my way so I don't fucking launch it.

I immediately want to look away from the monitor.

She's unconscious, cradled in the fucker's arms that drove off with her. "What's his name?" I clip, tracking him as he quickly disappears down the hall.

"He wouldn't say. He demanded to be referred to as Sir," the nurse answers quietly.

Leon skips past injured hikers, pausing on the man carrying her out… Three fucking days later.

"She was here for three days. Three goddamn days and you didn't think to question her?" I volley between the supposed doctor who's cupping around his mouth and the nurse who's tensed up behind me.

"I tried," she mumbles. "She was in and out of consciousness the entire time. Once I saw her heart rate fly up, I raced in there and told him he had to stay in the hall in case it was too overwhelming for her. But I gave her too long to wake up. I was checking her staples and was about to ease in little questions… and he came in."

A deep, vexed breath jets out of my nose, and I roughly rub over my face. I miss her so much. This is sickening.

"Do you by chance know where One Arm went?" Leon asks. "I saw that he walked out alone. But you guys don't have a camera outside for me to see anymore."

I'm still fixed on her face, but I can see the doctor shake his head. "That guy was loony. He said something about returning to the trees."

Because that fucking helps narrow it down.

Glancing around the desk, I spot a notepad and cup full of pens. I pluck one out, click the end, and write down Leon's number since I destroyed my phone. "If you see any of them come back, call or text this number. I'll pay you for your time and pay for the damages on your wall." I toss the pen back in—and choke on the dread creeping up.

CHAPTER TEN

TALA

"Click." The sound that's supposed to taste like freedom, tastes like ash. It's not Jax clasping his well-thought-out collar on me. Instead, it's Shiloh snapping together a tracking dog collar and locking it on.

Four of us are lined up, wearing off the shoulder mini-dresses and strips of black lace covering our eyes. It's Brynn, Cora, Sunny—and me.

Bone chilling whistling draws closer. The slow tune echoes down the hall, filling the living room as Pyro stalks in, hands behind his back.

He stops a couple feet away from us, dropping the whistle and replacing it with a wide smile. "Wow!" he booms. Although I have lace obstructing my vision, I still see him assaulting us with his eyes. "Don't forget who you gussied up girls belong to tonight. And it's not the men standin' behind you… It's me. And you know how mad I get. Try somethin' fuckin' stupid and you'll end up wolf shit."

That's more appealing than being stuck in this house. At least I'd be able to see the moon.

"Tonight's field trip is for my winners to have a taste of fun. But it's also for you to take notes. I want you to study the forms of the men fightin' and implement them in the ring." He steps closer with shit eating smile and blown out pupils. "I'll let you in on my little secret… You'll be fightin' each other, but you'll also be fightin' off the wolves. Gotta get real strong for that, have a good form."

Panicked murmurs buzz down the line, and an unwelcome hand slides around my hip, squeezing in warning.

I don't need it though. Hearing it out of Pyro's mouth is much worse than when I heard it from Shiloh.

My lungs are trying to fill, but his twisted fucking mind doesn't allow any room to breathe.

Fuck the flies. Fuck the bees. I'm feeling the goddamn locusts skitter under my skin and swarm my body.

Brynn's shaky hand laces with mine, and I rub my thumb over hers, giving us both a sensation to cling to since we have coke eyes on us and can't breathe.

"Where's my thank you?" he asks sternly.

"Thank you," we hum mechanically.

It lights his face up, and he quickly targets Brynn and me. My cement lungs crumble to ash as he steps in front of us.

He bends down, leveling his mouth with both of our ears. "Don't think I don't notice your fondness for each other. That's fine. My pretty girls can play. But you both will be comin' to my room tonight," he says definitively, voice low with interest.

86

My stomach turns in on itself, trying to send up the two granola bars I've had today. I choke it down, watching his lanky ass stand back up and stride off.

Brynn's brown eyes are already on mine, etched with the need to run away. I'd nod in understanding if Shiloh wasn't boring into the side of my damn face.

Heels click down the hall, followed by menacing footsteps.

An older woman, maybe mid forties', with strawberry blonde hair is on a leash and holding a silver tray that appears to be empty. On the other end of the leash is Pyro and his stupid fucking smile.

He walks her in, stopping at Sunny's blonde curls that are on my right. This close up, I gape at the white lines and rolled up bill on the tray.

"Don't get greedy. Half a line each. The rest is for my boys that are doin' a peachy job at makin' sure I have obedient winners."

Brynn and I could probably prompt a damn earthquake with how vigorously our hands are shaking together. I've never done cocaine. Hell, I've barely smoked weed and even that was pushing it for me.

"I'm o-okay, sir. Thank you," Sunny says mousily.

His smile shapeshifts into a snarl, his eyes sharpening to daggers. "Now, girl!" he rages, face deepening with red and a curvy vein bulging out of his temple.

Fucking fuck. Fuck-fuck-fuck-fuck.

Sunny bends over the tray, grabbing the rolled-up bill with vibrating fingers. She levels it up to a line, then snorts up half the powder.

My heartbeat's dull, pulsing in an empty cave. I look down to my favorite boots, focusing on the faint scuffs on my toes from when Jax bent me over the seat of his bike.

I miss his touch, and the way he says my name, and the way he looks at me like he'd watch the world burn for me.

Chipped red polish and muddy boots step into my frame. I pan away from the memory, up to a freckled face that looks oddly familiar.

I can't linger though. My hair getting pulled away from my face reminds me that I don't have an option here.

Taking a discreet deep breath, I pick up the rolled-up bill that has residue from Sunny and pinpoint the half line. Brynn's still holding my hand, pushing oxygen into the bravery flame that's slowly snuffing itself out. The flame roars—and I snort the line before I can process anything.

The burn surging through my nasal pathway runs behind my eye. I drop the bill, and my brain begins fucking melting, skin tingling with euphoria. My vision enhances through the lace, catching the predatory wink Pyro shoots me before moving down to Brynn.

I give her the same encouragement squeeze, even though I feel like I should be running a goddamn track like a racehorse.

The sex crawling in my veins is a disgusting sensation to have in a house full of freaks. But I can't control it. It's only amplifying and demanding my body to move.

Good God, if I saw Jax right now, my one fallopian tube would have no problem teleporting babies to my uterus.

Images of him shirtless, water dripping from his messy hair and rolling down the black ink that designs his lean, behemoth body fills my numb mouth with saliva.

"I'm driving." Comes from behind me, ruining my brain porn.

It's for the best. I need to alter my hyperfocus on how to get out of here and swallow the drool trying to pour over my lip.

"He'll be watching the girl's movement like a hawk. He'll know, dude," Eli responds dryly.

Luke laughs, reaching out for Brynn to pull her into his lap. "And watching men fight will train them to fight wolves? That's fucking nuts."

Tuning out of their argument that's getting nowhere, I continue panning around the dancers.

The last of my high is gone and I feel like I've been smoked with a nasty hangover. There's a dull throb in my head and nausea is swirling behind my scar.

I'm so ready to go home. I haven't even been able to grieve my dad because of this shit.

"Wolf princess."

I slowly blink behind the lace, turning my attention to Shiloh who's manspreading in the leather lounge chair I'm leaning against.

He snakes his hand over my hip, patting his lap.

I want to fucking punch him. He'd probably jizz his jeans though. I already have to carry the weight of making Pyro come from simply kissing a woman.

I don't want to haul that around too.

He guides me around the chair, and I sit sideways across his lap, draping my legs over the leather arm so I don't have to feel his dick again.

With his face right in mine, he rests his hand over the leather covering my shins. "You're not going to his room tonight," he whispers, ire hidden in his tone.

"I don't think I have a choice, Shiloh."

His jaw tics, throat bobbing roughly. "You gotta stop saying my name. It sounds too good coming from your pouty lips."

Bile rises to the back of my tongue. I gulp the burn down, hoping he smells it on my breath and pushes me off into the floor.

He doesn't. He gets closer. "I'll do whatever it takes to make sure he doesn't touch you," he murmurs.

My face twists perplexingly. "Why?"

He runs his hand up my thigh, the other molding to the back of my head to push me closer, and I stiffen my neck, fighting the damn force he's using.

"As much shit as I talk, I know better. You don't belong to him. You don't belong to me. You have someone out there that's sick to his stomach that you're gone. All these women do. Now kiss me and don't make a scene, eh? We have eyes on us."

That's… not what I was expecting.

It's debilitating being away from Jax.

He's the other half of my soul. The man that constantly broke in just to love me.

The whites of my eyes burn, raising up the waves that distort my vision further before I close them. He presses his lips to mine, and a warm stream flows under the lace and down my cheek, dripping from my jaw and splashing cold on my chest.

His fingertips indent possessively around my thigh, and he languidly rolls his tongue through the seam of my lips, tilting his head to slide it over my dry tongue.

Letting him kiss me is poison. It's wilting my veins and burning a hole in the scattered pieces of my heart.

He means well. Even though he's volatile.

He pulls away, leaving a single inch between our mouths. "Fuck," he breathes, seemingly collecting himself. "I'm gonna kiss you again. This time, bite my lip and draw blood."

"Wha-"

"Trust me, Tala," he says my name on my lips, taking them like they belong to him.

His fingers move under the hem of my dress, prowling too high up and pissing me off.

I kiss him back, just to snap my teeth around his bottom lip. I bite. Hard. The skin breaks along my teeth, iron flooding over my tongue and fueling the hellish wrath that I've been keeping at a simmer.

He whimpers, quickly jumping into character and ripping away from me, brows furrowed tightly and blood steadily streaming down his chin. "You fuckin' bite me?" he shouts, capturing the attention of the rapists we're here with.

I'm trying to trust him. But you're not supposed to trust a mountain lion. You turn your back to it—and you're gone.

Panic of the unknown ruffles my skin. I wet my lips nervously, sweeping up more of the god-awful taste. When I say nothing, he ruthlessly grabs my waist and yanks me up with him.

An ache zips through my tender stomach, and I scuffle around trying to find footing, getting ripped away by my arm.

"Let me deal with this. Enjoy the fight," he grumbles.

"Ooh, wolf princess is in trouble," an asshole taunts me behind my back.

I'm too busy getting dragged past others enjoying the dancers to jot someone's name at the top of my shit list.

Once we're clear from their view and at the door, he loosens his bruising grip and grabs my hand.

The stride through the freezing parking lot is quiet. The only noise is muffled music pouring from the club and the busy road we're by.

We pace down the aisle he parked in, and a drawn black hood makes me double back, thinking it may be Jax.

My heart begins vibrating with a rush of hope, only to plummet into the pit of disappointment when it disappears.

Am I still high?

The SUVs headlights flick on, and he whips open the back door while releasing my hand.

I sigh, climbing in and maneuvering down the middle to sit on the bench seat in the very back. I know his rescues come at a price. A painful one. Mentally, physically, and emotionally.

He gets in, somehow contorting his body and slipping down the middle. He sits down next to me, then hooks under my knees to swivel my hips towards him and lays my legs over his thighs. "Pyro won't be interested in a body with fresh marks unless provoked."

Tired of feeling this scratchy lace over my eyes, I slide it off, nodding understandingly. "I get that… But I think his interest for me runs deeper than discipline." I cringe, not disguising the disgust curling my lips.

The light above us shuts off, washing us in the darkness that feels fitting. It doesn't hide his heavy lids and wandering eyes though.

"It does. I can change that and ruin the image he has of you."

"Why not just help me leave?" I snip, drawing blank over my word vomit. "I'm sorry."

"It's okay," he says softly, lowering his face down. "I've been trying to myself." He kisses my collarbone, then uses his tongue to siphon my fucking blood.

Working through the annoyance, I brush my hair out of my face and toss it all to my back. "Why haven't you been able to?"

He hooks his forefinger into the front of my dress, pulling it down until the top half of my boobs are out. I bite my tongue, watching him marvel at them. "I have a tracker embedded in my finger. We all do." He kisses my right boob, grazing his teeth over it before sucking.

My eye twitches, skin boiling from him marking it with temerity. But I'm trying to overfill the scale of knowing his story, so I don't start crying again. "Can you not cu-ow!" My brows pinch, peering down at his hollowed cheeks as he tries sucking me dry. "Can you not cut it out?"

The fatty skin pops from his lips, leaving me with the ache of broken capillaries and his blood smeared around the mark. He wipes it with his thumb, his free hand caressing up my legs. "I could. But the last guy who tried didn't get it halfway out before he was shot in the head. We're his soldiers. There's no turning back from a decision that some of us didn't even make."

A twinge of sympathy sparks up for them.

"How did you get mixed up in this mess?" I ask demurely.

He tugs my dress into place, slipping his arm around my back. "They made a pit stop in Alberta, Canada on their way to Anchorage. I was coming out of the gas station, felt a sharp pain in my neck... and lights out. I woke up the same way you did, but with another man bound in the seat next to me... Eli."

I frown, analyzing his shadowed face. I still don't know if I can trust him. But I need to know. "If I were to come up with a plan, would you and Eli be able to help?"

He chews his cheek, raising his hand to rub over his brows. "I don't know about Eli. But I'll do my best to help."

CHAPTER ELEVEN

JAX

Evelyn hasn't left the spare bedroom in two weeks. Nadia's been helping tend to her while the rest of us search for Tala. I've been trying to leave her alone to heal and process things the way she needs to. But I can't find shit on Enzo, and I know she'll have some answers.

"Hey, Ev," I say quietly, sitting down on the edge of the bed. Sirohi hops up, laying down next to her.

She lifts her hand to pet his head, looking up at me with a heartbroken stare. "Still nothing?"

The question is a knife to the heart.

I shake my head, trying to stay strong. "We came across a clinic she was taken to. The man that brought her there has been missing from Alberta, Canada since last September. Viper and Maverick are almost there to question his mother. But I need to ask you about Enzo."

She sits up, matted hair frizzing up on the back of her head. "I'll answer whatever... after you tell me why she was at the clinic," she rasps, despair straining her voice.

I've been having a hard time with processing that she lost our baby, and I wasn't fucking there for her. Trying to speak about it seems impossible. A knot is lodging in my throat, forcing me to clear it and blink before the burn hits.

"She uh... had an ectopic pregnancy rupture. The doctor had to remove her left fallopian tube. And the fucker just took her right back to wherever the hell they're staying."

A sob blubbers her lips, and she covers her mouth, tears welling in her eyes and dripping over the back of her hand.

"I know, Ev. Do you know where Enzo's been the past year, or why he disappeared in the first place?"

I hate to get the ball rolling so quickly. But time is ticking, and I'm done wasting it. I need her back.

She sniffles, wiping her splotchy face with her sleeve. "Damascus caught him mistreating Rose, one of the older wolves, and it sparked up a huge feud between them. He was told to never come back to the sanctuary and just... vanished. He stopped talking to their parents, stopped going to work, and wasn't paying his bills... I don't know where he went or where he's been. His ex-girlfriend might know. She was always really sweet to us and loved Tala."

Abusing the wolves, disappearing around the time Brutus showed up, and showing up the day they raided the place. It connects. But how the fuck did he get in with them?

"What's her name?" I ask, getting back on my feet.

She scratches Sirohi's side, throwing the covers off her legs. "Malia Gray. I'm going with you."

I'm not arguing with a woman on a mission.

The impatient Devil wants to kick the door down. But I raise my knuckles and knock fucking politely on the white door to Malia's apartment.

Three times. The normal amount.

Footsteps scuffle around, then the door opens to an espresso face. Her dark eyes widen, peering around the door. "Can I help you?" she asks cautiously.

I don't think she can see Evelyn behind me.

I step to the side, watching her face light up as she sees her. "Evelyn! Oh, my goodness, it's so nice to see you! Please, come in-come in!"

"I wish we were here on good news, Malia," Evelyn says somberly, wrapping her in a hug.

Malia draws back, brows pinched while stepping in with Evelyn. "What happened? Did Enzo start some more shit?"

I follow them inside, closing the door behind me, and stay standing while they sit down on a… cheetah print couch.

Tala would love that. One of her cheetah print blankets is at the house. It's debilitating to see it on my bed without her there.

Evelyn tries to speak, getting choked up on the storm of gloom.

"Tala's been taken," I speak up for her, startling Malia. "Enzo stabbed Evelyn and shot Damascus in the process of his buddies kidnapping her and stealing the wolves. We're trying to figure out if you'd know anything about who he fell in with prior to the fallout."

Malia gasps and grabs Evelyn's hand, distress dimming the light in her eyes. "Are you okay?"

Evelyn nods, roughly wiping her eyes. "Jax and Nadia have been taking care of me. We just really need to find Honey. It's been two weeks."

For being a hit man, I'm doing a horrible fucking job at finding the one person that matters to me. For fuck's sake... I've hunted people down in Russia. But I can't seem to find my goddamn girl in the city I've lived in for a year.

"Of course," Malia agrees softly. "He mentioned new online friends about two or three months before everything blew up. With the weird character change, I thought he was cheating on me. So, I went through his phone and didn't find anything. But when I got on his laptop, the dark web was already pulled up and he was looking at... um... women that were bruised and crying. He also had a tab open of horrible things happening to dogs." She shakes her head in disgust, recounting the images she had to see. "I didn't find any messages or anything. So, I followed him one day and he met up with Mayor Jenkins at Aurora's. I didn't get close enough to hear. And shortly after that, I broke up with him and moved into this apartment. I'm sorry I don't know more."

"Thank you, Malia," I say, heading for the door.

We need to pull up all the sketchy sites we can and see if anything's been posted.

"Can I get you some water or anything?" Malia asks.

I look over my shoulder, already having the door open. "No thank you, ma'am."

Evelyn stands up, flattening her hand to her stomach. "Thank you, Malia. I'll keep in touch," she strains out.

I don't want to be a dick and walk away from her in pain. So, I turn my ass around and hook my arm under hers.

She grins somberly, dark circles mapping under the permanent tired eyes she gave Tala. "We'll find her and figure out what happened to Damascus," she says softly with hope, walking out the door with me.

LEON

I'm used to these screens. But lately, I've been burning blue light into my eyeballs. I wipe them and get back to clacking on the keyboard that's begging for mercy. I may or may not have bugged Evelyn's phone to listen in on their conversation with that Malia chick.

Entering these sites isn't for the weak. And I am weak. I cannot stomach what Jax does.

"Aren't you afraid of viruses?" Kendra asks, tapping her nails on the counter next to me.

"Viruses are afraid of me," I chuckle.

"Okay, Mucinex," she retorts, analyzing the screen. "What do we do if we see Tala on here?"

My stomach twists at the thought. The images before me don't help. "Ah, well, I'll do my best to ping it, see where it was uploaded at and if there's a name. Either way, I'll take it down."

I don't want to see Mija on here. But if I do, that means she's alive.

Scrolling down the horrific images and videos of battered women for sale, I almost pass up two women in a boxing ring with shock collars on.

I stop, gaping intently at the extremely long, raven ponytail, and almost fall out of the stool from jumping out of my skin. "That's her!" I slam my finger into the mouse, clicking on the video.

The tips of my ears flame with nerves as I turn the volume up.

The fiery-haired chick on the left starts shrieking like a banshee, raising bony hands up towards Tala and running at her. Tala steps out, dodging her, and I smile, watching her bounce around like the fighter Jax was training her to be.

This is not the time to smile. I have no idea what the actual fuck is going on. Why would Brutus be having them fight each other?

"I deserve that!" the other chick shouts, face turning redder than a tomato.

The front door opens behind me, and I smack it on pause, swiveling around to the darkness that's haunting Jax's being. "You'll want to see this," I say urgently.

His scowl tightens to extreme lengths, turning even scarier as he storms across the house.

I swivel back around, getting chills up my spine from the Devil he's become. He's always scared the piss out of me. But it's like Jax isn't home. Only the carnage seeking shadows are.

He stops at my side, bending over to glower at the screen. "Are you fucking kidding me? He's fucking pitting them? Play it!"

I'm no stranger to his abrasiveness. I hit play, volleying between Tala and the crazy look in his eyes.

"You do!" Tala shouts back, fists raised. "But I don't play fair. I play to win."

The other woman charges her down with a snarl, but Tala's ready for it. At the right moment she strikes her fist out and knocks the chick in the cheek, sending her in a tornado spiral to the ground.

"Attagirl," Jax growls, slamming his fist down into the countertop.

I think I see cracks in the concrete...

The video cuts off, leaving, "*Bet On Princess and Watch Her LIVE,*" bannering over the dark box.

"You've got to be fucking shitting me!" Jax barks savagely, making Kendra jump like a Jack-in-the-Box.

I get to whizzing over the keys, typing in coding and attempting to route where the video came from.

All that comes up is Anchorage, Alaska. No name. No coordinates.

Jax's hands tighten ruthlessly on the edge of the countertop next to me, the concrete audibly cracking before a monstrous roar infiltrates the kitchen.

My eyes widen and Kendra falls out of the stool, a high-pitched yelp splitting my ear as her body thuds to the floor. I'm too scared to look away from the beast picking up a cup and throwing it at the fridge... So, hopefully she's all good.

The glass shatters, shards piercing through the air and clattering to the floor, and he stalks off, heaving for the air I know he feels guilty for breathing.

My eyeballs start stinging. And not from the blue light.

Because Jax finally learned how to give and receive love. And the gentle soul that kissed the Devil—is gone.

CHAPTER TWELVE

TALA

Gliding the charcoal point to finish the last tree, I lift up the mattress and shove my paper and pencil onto the wooden slats, setting it back down and silently booking it to the door.

Shiloh snuck me pencil and paper and got me on feeding duty for the wolves. It's all coming together. I just want all bases covered so there's no room for error.

The door unsticks as I pull it open, my one step over the threshold coming to a halt, terror sizzling under my skin.

His assaulting eyes target my bruised chest spilling out of the tight top, and he smiles, shoving his hands in his denim pockets. "I'm your partner today, princess. You get to show me how you handle the wolves… and I get a mighty fine view while doin' so."

Where the fuck are you, Shiloh?

My cheeks heat with panic. I can't let him see that, so I force a smile I know he'll eat up. "Well… shall we?"

"Mmm. We shall," he drawls, wrangling a hand out of his pocket to grab mine.

It's so fucking scratchy. And for what? From what I see and hear, he has everyone else doing dirty work for him.

He keeps his long strides in tune with the hustle I'm trying to have. The whole way through the hall and down the stairs, he wears his smug smile and intently watches the way my tits bounce with each step.

I'm getting a breast reduction after this shit. Or I'll chop them off and donate them. I don't want them anymore.

Entering the kitchen, a wave of relief calms the utter panic I had for Shiloh. He's leaning over the island, watching us pass by. My teeth marks are bruised into his skin, his bottom lip puffy and rosy with irritation.

I look away so Pyro doesn't grow suspicious and feel Shiloh's eyes penetrating my back as we turn left down the side hall.

"My boy must really enjoy your pussy," Pyro utters, spinning the lock on the first door. "That, or he's just really good at keepin' his eyes on you. I haven't made up my mind."

All this time, he still hasn't caught on to the way Shiloh helps the girls avoid getting raped and beaten.

I don't say anything. I can't without the possibility of leaking the venom poisoning me.

He opens the first door, quickly unlocking the six deadbolts. "You're supposed to be mine, ya know." He side-eyes me, a faint snarl beginning to form. "Yet, I haven't felt your little pussy around my cock. That'll change. No more gettin' out of it, princess. Even if Shiloh's in the middle of fuckin' you, I'll make him switch to a different hole. You were too damn expensive and cost me a lot of blow sales to not give me some action."

My head spins, guts twisting up a storm of nausea.

He's referring to losing the Guildons as losing business. Even though he makes plenty enough from dogfights and letting Jenkins and Cromwell pay for overnights with their girl of choice. I haven't seen it yet. But Loxley told me she's had to do it several times.

That's the sick shit they were doing in the castle.

Hopefully Jax has already killed them.

Instead of keeping straight on the trail towards the dogs and gym, he turns left down a narrower trail.

The wind's whispering through the trees and ravens are flapping their wings, fluttering snow around. It would be an enjoyable walk if I wasn't attached to a damn lunatic.

The silence between us is deafening. It's nice not having to hear his voice or the gut wrenching shit he says, but it feels like a walk to my demise.

After several minutes, my nose grows cold, and my toes go numb. The old barn about a yard or two away spikes my blood pressure, thawing out the ice overtaking my rather bare body.

He doesn't supply proper winter wear. We get long sleeves, yoga pants, leggings, denim, and sneakers.

No fucking coat.

Walking up to the open doors, my broken heart shatters. They're all on heavy chains with muzzles, spaced several feet from each other, and sitting on hay with no food or water.

I walk all the way in, choking on fucking rocks and blinking away the tsunami of tears. Void's gotten so big in just two weeks. Echo's miserable. Valko's gone. Ace and Spade are practically full grown.

Where… Where's…

"Where are the other eight?" I ask urgently, looking him dead in his malicious eyes.

He shrugs, releasing my hand to roam around. "They were too old and not worth my time."

It suddenly becomes impossible to hold my weight. I collapse to my knees, vision blurring into darkness. Through my dark peripheral, I see the contrast of Echo's white fur thrashing around, trying to break free. Her barks and the heavy chain clanking sound like a distorted record in my fucked-up head.

"Hey-hey!" a familiar masculine voice shouts gruffly. "Easy, girl."

I jerk my head to the left, to the voice, and blurrily see overgrown, black hair. "Dad?" I ask wearily, scurrying to my feet.

His heartbroken eyes turn to glass, taking in my appearance. "Hi, sweetheart."

The dam holding my tears back breaks, and streams run down my face as I stomp over hay, running to my dad. He stretches his arms out, wrapping me in the safety and comfort of home.

"I thought you died," I cry out.

"Enough!" Pyro shouts callously.

I don't listen. I hug Dad tighter, soaking his gray shirt with my tears.

A crack resounds in the barn, straight fire smarting on my ass cheek, and I scream in pain and tear away from my dad, unable to rub it over before another line of fire torches my other cheek.

"Stop! Stop hurting her!" Dad yells protectively over my cries, stirring up the wolves.

Pyro claws at the back of my head, grabbing a tight fistful. "Bad girls get punished, Damascus!" He rips me back, shoving me by my head to the center of the barn.

I flail, smoking my hands and knees on the concrete floor, and the immediate riptide of pain institutes a bellow of agony. Another crack, this time on my back and with what feels like the metal fucking buckle.

Every muscle tenses up, my body turning to stone as a scream shreds my lungs and throat. Stiffly, I try crawling away—but another—another—and another.

I'm not sure if anything's coming out of my mouth. The pain is throwing my body into shock. Everything warps and a mind drilling ring bleeds into the vicious growls and barks.

I collapse onto the cold concrete, getting my hips jerked up and pants ripped down to my thighs.

I can't fight.

And I can't hear the wolves anymore.

I'm shivering from the cold, but the blood soaking my shirt is keeping me a little warm. Almost as if my body is trying to hug itself, offer some comfort while I endure another barbaric man taking something he wants.

He forces himself inside me, the flaming ouroboros not being enough to snap me out of shock.

My throat's bleeding from my screams. I just can't hear it. I can only taste the iron on my dry tongue. I'm moving with each shredding pain that's surely splitting me open. Yet I can't fight it. Even if I wasn't whipped with a belt prior—I'd have to just let him.

I manage to close my wet eyes, hoping this is a nightmare I can wake up from.

I'm so sorry, Jax. I'm so fucking sorry. I'm sorry I froze up and didn't fight the way you trained me.

The trauma my body is enduring is unbearable. I'm numb but feel everything. It's a clash of fire and ice, battling each other to see who can take me out first.

I'd say fire. My back is bleeding so heavily it's seeping out of my shirt and rolling up the back of my neck. My vagina feels like a volcano, brewing up the molten lava that's radiating through my veins.

"You're so tight," he groans, breaking through the constant ringing in my ears.

I feel him pull out, but the agony persists.

So, I just lie here. Unable to move. Again.

I'm not sure how long it takes someone to pull my pants up. Then right after, they hook an arm under my chest, peeling me up from the floor and holding me in a cradle.

Everything hurts. There's no way to pinpoint a precise feeling when my entire body is lit up with excruciating torment. It's pulsing my vision, but I'm able to make out Eli's black facial hair and backwards ball cap. I think he's taking me back to prison.

I'd prefer to get thrown over the hills though.

"I'm so sorry," he mumbles.

Unable to speak, I weakly raise my hand to his chest, lazily patting to acknowledge him.

Every step he takes through the snow is like thousands of hot pokers stabbing into my muscles. And every breath is disconnected and unfulfilled because I cannot fill my lungs without the back of my ribs breaking.

That's what it feels like anyway.

He stops outside the back door, raising his arm and rattling my brain with a thundering knock. I faintly hear the deadbolts unlocking. The clicks weave into the pulsing ring that won't go away.

In a desperate attempt to shut the noise out, I turn my head and shove my face into his hoodie. The pressure on my forehead is somewhat relieving but doesn't do shit for my fucked-up body or the insistent drilling that's driving me insane.

"What fucking happened to her?" Shiloh rushes.

"Let's get her in the bathroom and I'll tell you."

The hair-raising coldness of the house runs over my aching skin, practically taunting me that I had to come back inside of it.

The creaky bathroom door closes, and I lift my head up, blurrily watching Shiloh rip open the clear shower curtain and turn on the water.

"I didn't see what happened to her back, but I know he raped her," Eli grumbles, maneuvering me into a burly arm to take my sneakers off.

Shiloh's face tightens, nostrils flaring as he closes the few steps between us. "I'm so sorry, Tala. I told you…" He stops, glancing around the walls that could possibly tell on him.

"It's not either of your guys' fault," I murmur.

Shiloh brushes his fingers through my hair, probably picking hay out of it. "I knew something was up when he told me he was taking you to the wolves. He knew… He knew you would get excited over your dad," he whispers, then grabs under my arms as Eli sets me down on my feet.

I wince, face twisting in pain from the weight shift. Shiloh's helping support me, but my bones are weak. I clutch onto his arms, getting my pants gently eased down by Eli. "You knew my dad was here?" I rasp.

He nods, not saying anything.

110

I can't be upset that he didn't tell me. Every action of mine can cost him his life.

I look down at my bare legs, noting the crimson streaming down my inner thighs. Makes sense. My vagina's in shreds.

While Eli lifts my shirt up, a sharp breath runs through my teeth, the tight fabric peeling painfully from the damage. "Oh… my God," Eli draws out distraughtly.

I don't want to look.

I raise my arms, Shiloh's hands moving to my bare, aching ribs, and force away the tears in the darkness of my shirt.

My matted hair gets pulled through, and Eli catches it before it can fall and cling to my back.

I should be concerned about being fully nude in front of them. But the plaguing agony makes me not give a fucking shit.

Shiloh walks backwards, guiding my way to the shower. He steps over the tub, right into the running water and helping my wobbly steps in. The freezing water needles into my back, washing my blood down my legs and swirling it around the drain.

I shouldn't bitch about it. This tub is stained from how much blood it sees. I'm not sure bleach would even get it out.

Eli keeps my hair gathered and drapes it over Shiloh's shoulder, walking away to unlock the hutch above the toilet. He pulls out a washcloth, then returns to the shower to start dabbing at my back.

I squeeze my eyes, the uncontrollable sting drawing out a whine. I'm not sure how many times he ended up hitting me. I lost the ability to count after four.

Shiloh cranes his neck down, getting level with my ear. "Eli and I will handle the wolves and dogs. But with us outside, that means you'll have to handle everyone inside… Including Pyro."

I think Jax burned their houses down.

They've been sleeping in the living room or in their mistress' room. Which could be helpful if I can get the girls on board with stabbing some heads.

"Thank you, guys," I rasp, letting my heavy head thud to the sopping hoodie covering Shiloh's chest.

Now, I have to wait a few days in order to move stealthily. There's no way I'll be able to go down the stairs without falling down them and waking everybody up.

CHAPTER THIRTEEN

JAX

The bell chimes as I enter *Wyvern's Ink*, and Paxton's glazed over eyes meet mine. It takes him a whole goddamn moment, but he eventually recognizes me and offers a dimpled smile.

"What's up, Jax? Finally getting that dagger on your face?"

"No." I hold Leon's phone out, showing him a picture of the *IR* tattoo on that dude's finger. "Does this look familiar?"

He stretches his eyebrows up, inspecting the tattoo. "That looks like Diego's work. He's in the back prepping for his next appointment. I'll take you to his station."

"Thanks, man," I grumble, fighting off the volatile urge to start ripping everything to shreds.

I follow him to the back, passing rooms that are buzzing with machines and playing rock music. It's petty to get pissed off over people going about their lives, enjoying their days and making it to tattoo appointments. But the reason I breathe is getting pitted like a fucking dog.

And I still cannot find her.

Mayor Jenkins is MIA. We finally cracked his security cameras, and he hasn't been home since I killed the Guildons.

I considered burning his humble abode down. But I really like the idea of sitting and waiting for him in the dark.

"Diego!" Paxton hollers raspily over the music. "Hey, man, my buddy here is wondering if you'd know anything about this tattoo."

Diego whirls around with petroleum jelly on the end of a wooden stick, and he peeks over his glasses. I walk into his room, already holding the picture up for him.

He looks at it, instantly tossing his head back on a laugh, and starts sticking ink cups down to his tray. "Those guys were fucking crazy. It does *not* surprise me they have hits on them," he titters.

"What makes you say that?" I ask.

"Oh, man," he shakes his head, still chuckling. "You know what subdermal implants are?"

"Sure."

"Those fucking freaks brought in small, disc-like trackers to be implanted under the fat of their middle fingers. They all lined up like they were going to recess or some shit."

I'm not surprised. I'd like to know more about the trackers though.

"And you implanted them?"

"Hell yeah, I did," he laughs, looking back at me. "I'm not a man to pass up big bills. Plus, I doubled it by having to ink their fingers." He tips his head, gesturing to his phone by the sink. "I got a picture of those discs. I snuck one to send to our group chat with the other local artists."

Taking the hint, I stalk over to his phone and grab it, then walk my ass back over to him for his Face ID. It scans and opens up, and he uses his knuckle to click around until he gets to it.

"That shit right there. That's crazy, dog."

I flip his phone around, narrowing my eyes at the pea-sized, flat disc. I've never seen a tracker like that.

"You cool with me taking a picture of this?" I ask, pulling up Leon's camera anyway.

"I don't give a shit. As long as I don't get caught up in the crossfire. I got kids and a wife at home."

I snap the picture, then set his phone back down on the sink. "If something happens, ask Paxton for Leon's number."

I turn for the door, almost barreling over Paxton.

"I don't know who Leon is. I don't think I have his number," Paxton says sedately.

"You sure?" I ask, slipping past him.

He glances around the ceiling, racking his fried brain.

I pat his scrawny shoulder, furrowing my brows over how easy he is to move. "I programmed it into your phone. Thank you. Both of you." I spare a glance at Diego's slack jaw and stride out.

Let's fucking hope Leon's big mind can figure out how to track these.

"These are in their fingers?" Leon asks disgustedly.

He drops his phone on the island, side-eying the picture with curled lips as he starts clacking on his keyboard.

"Mm-hmm." I run my hand through my hair, brutally rubbing over my scalp to try and relieve some of the pressure.

My body was adjusted to minimal sleep for the longest time. But once I started sharing a bed with Tala, the feeling of being home let me get some rest. I got greedy—and now my body is trying to give out on me for not sleeping. But how the fuck am I supposed to?

"No task is too big for Tech Boy," he says self-assuredly. "Give me a few and I'll see what I can dig up."

I nod and push off the island, watching the front door open.

Viper and Maverick have been in Canada trying to get information from Shiloh Cyr's mother. The last I heard she wouldn't open the door for them.

They walk across the house, stopping to gather around the island. "So?" I ask impatiently.

"She threw a frying pan at me," Viper pouts.

I glower at him, but Maverick beats me to it. "You'll live, Viper," he snarls, fixing him with a hard stare before flicking his attention to me. "She said he stopped by a gas station after work one day and never came home. Which was in the news. But what wasn't, was the feed of him getting a dart to the neck. And then another man, Eli King, got darted right after him. They kidnapped them."

"Did you see them or their vehicles?"

Maverick pulls his phone out, tapping away on his screen. "No vehicles, but men in masks. I recorded it for you."

I watch it over, shaking my head in disbelief that this happened in broad daylight with other people around, not doing shit. Some old fuck walks right past Shiloh as he collapses to the ground, then two men in masks grab him and run out of frame—and not a single soul steps in. The same for Eli.

116

"Why are you even here?" Nadia yells from the living room, capturing all of our attention.

"Unlike you, I'm actually useful," Kendra snips.

I can't tolerate their drama. Tala is so fucking serene compared to the yapping chihuahuas that are constantly picking fights with each other. I know it's probably rough on Nadia to see Kendra, but she's been helping Leon while I've been scouting with Sirohi.

Nadia laughs—psychotically. Pretending to turn around and walk away, she whirls around and backhands Kendra across the face.

Viper chuckles, Maverick storms to the rescue, and I deadpan. Now, Sirohi thinks there's a threat and is anxiously pacing around with perked up ears.

Even with Maverick picking Nadia up like a child, she's still kicking at Kendra who's clinging on to her, both screaming nonsense at each other.

"Tala will fucking kill you! You batshit bitch!" Nadia screams, getting a mighty fine kick to Kendra's chest and knocking her on her ass.

"Jax, please stop them, man. I can't concentrate with MMA going on," Leon sighs.

"Hey!" I shout, voice booming across the house. "Knock it the fuck off or get the hell out!" I toss Maverick's phone down, glaring at the awkward pause they're in while taking my ass to the back door for a goddamn cigarette.

I slam the sliding door behind me, looking at the pale-yellow eyes that have been hanging out in my backyard. Evelyn's smoking a cigarette in one of the chairs I just recently put out by the hot tub.

Tala never said anything, but I could tell she was not fond of my minimalism. So, I started filling more space to make her feel more at home. And now—she's not here.

She's not home.

Just looking at the hot tub makes my nose burn with the water washing over my eyes.

It's where she kissed me after I shared the story that no one else knows. Leon knows bits and pieces. But Tala's the only one I've been vulnerable with.

I take a seat in the chair next to Evelyn, reaching in my pocket for my pack. I huff the knot out of my throat, watching the vapor carry my breath in a cloud, and spark up some cancer.

Cancer is nothing when your body is plagued with the crippling despair of longing for the other half of your soul.

"How far along was she?" Ev asks, disassociating on the snow.

I couldn't bring myself to ask the doctor. But her avoiding sex before the gala made me do the math of when the last day of her period was. I knew then she was ovulating. I even watched her pop Plan B with strawberry ice cream when we got home.

She kept throwing up and blaming stress and blaming the pill for her late period. I told her I thought she was pregnant. But I guess it doesn't matter. The baby wasn't growing right and tried killing her.

And I wasn't fucking there for her.

"Around five weeks," I mumble.

Using her thumb, she wipes her glossy eyes, ash falling in her hair. "My baby girl," she squeaks.

The sliding door flings open, Viper leaping outside with a grave expression. "Irina's drone caught something by the Knik River," he says quickly, Russian accent jumbling his words.

I hear him though. And I lunge out of the chair to storm inside behind him.

118

Dear God, you better be a-fuckin-live, baby.

My heart is thundering. Yet it only feels like an echo pulsing in my veins, beating the dull melody Tala loves to tap out onto my chest.

Viper stops by the TV, hitting play on his phone to get the drone footage going.

I don't give a fuck if I'm in someone's way. I'm standing right in front of it, analyzing the frozen river, snow covered trees, and the flock of damn ravens randomly taking off in the distance. "Turn the volume up," I demand tonelessly.

The volume turns all the way up, giving light to the most heart shattering battle cries pouring from deep in the trees and resounding through the still air. I already fucking know it's Tala. But the wolves crying in a symphony with her sets that in stone.

The entire world flips upside down, causing me to stagger back with a sharp pain spearing through my heart. "Get those coordinates from Irina and tell her to send that drone in." My ears whoosh as I turn to face Maverick. "How fast can you load a gun?"

CHAPTER FOURTEEN

TALA

Loxley managed to round up the other four and get them into my room. In a different world, this would be cute. It looks like we're having a sleepover, all piled on my shitty bed. It's dark outside, so we only have the moon and snow casting through the prison window.

"I'll make this quick," I say quietly to the eager eyes beaming at me. "Tomorrow night, we're leaving."

Brynn throws her arms around me, the pain sending up a grunt that gets trapped in my throat. "Sorry, baby, I got excited," she whispers, relaxing her arms.

"What do we need to do?" Rylie asks.

I wave at Brynn, letting her know she's fine, and pay even attention to everyone around me. "Whoever has someone in their room, it's your job to sneak their knife and quietly, I mean so fucking quietly, stab them in the head," I say directly.

"What about the rest?" Sunny whisper-shouts.

I sigh, taking on a battle that doesn't give grace to any fuck ups. "I'll handle the rest."

I'm not mentioning Shiloh or Eli yet. Cora's chewing on her nub nails and anxiously looking around.

It's making me nervous that she may be a rat.

She notices me analyzing her and sweeps her blonde hair from her face. "I don't know if I can do it, Tala. That's so scary," she says timidly.

Loxley leans over to her, gently rubbing her knee. "You can, Cora. You'll get to see your boyfriend, your parents, and your cat again."

"I don't know if that's enough to make me brave," Cora whines silently.

Brynn slaps her hands in the middle of the bed, languidly leaning over to Cora, and she tilts her head, softly pressing her lips to hers.

I think Brynn is longing for tender touch. I get it. They've been here for a year, suffering worse shit than what I went through yesterday.

Cora whines, and Brynn draws back a bit. "Did that feel good?" she asks. Cora nods, cheeks flushing pink. "Yeah, baby. Think about how good you'll feel all the time leaving this place."

"What if we get in trouble?" Cora asks, glancing around in panic as Brynn sits back.

"Who are we going to get in trouble with?" I question. "They'll all be dead."

"The police. Mayor Jenkins," Cora rushes.

"Oh, my fucking God, Cora. I was the first one brought here and I'll be damned if I let you ruin this. I'm ready to go the fuck home," Riley whisper-shouts aggressively.

I kind of feel bad for not letting her win the "field trip." But if I wouldn't have gone, I'm not sure I would've ever gotten to talk to Shiloh like that.

I'd be planning his death too.

"So… are we taking their vehicles?" Sunny asks. "I never got my license and don't know how to drive."

I shake my head, gaining wide eyes from everyone. "In order for us to stay together, we have to walk. We're taking the dogs and wolves too and I don't know where they put the trailers they hauled the wolves in on. You know that river at the end of the drive?"

Everyone shakes their heads, the rush of what we're plotting sparkling in their eyes.

"Oh. Well, if we cut across that and troop through the weather for a few hours, we'll reach my family's sanctuary. Their house is on the property too, so we'll have somewhere to sleep until light breaks. If my dad's still alive, he'll help us get there."

I get nods in agreement, and curly, blonde hair crawling over my bed. "Can I sleep in here tonight?" Sunny asks, laying her head in my lap.

Sunny was seventeen when she was kidnapped. She had to spend her eighteenth birthday here, instead of cruising around town with friends.

I coil my finger around a curl laying across her temple. "I don't mind. My best friend Nadia has conditioned me to enjoy sharing my bed."

Nadia's been breaking into my room for as long as I can remember. Even when I was living with my parents, I'd wake up to her crawling into my bed at the ass crack of dawn.

The memory makes me grin to myself.

But the aches of missing everyone overrule the drop of happiness.

My door unsticks. I don't know how long I dozed off for. I foggily look around the curled-up bodies on my bed, spotting long, blonde hair drifting through the cracked door.

What are you up to? …

I pry Brynn's arm off me, holding back the groan of agony as I slide off the edge of the bed. Stiffly straightening my spine, I quietly rush over to the door. It's open enough for me to slip through. I guess my bland diet is making me lose my ass. My waist looks great, but Jax will be pissed.

I jolt, the air getting stripped right from my lungs as I spot a shadowy figure lying on the ground next to my door. I bend down to look closer, finally taking a breath over the clean-shaven, Roman features.

I think he's been sleeping there every night.

I quietly walk away and turn the corner, catching the top of Cora's head going down the stairs.

If she was snitching on us, she'd be going into her room where Kevin is. Unless she's telling Pyro…

Adrenaline coasts through my blood, numbing the pain in my muscles and lightening my quick steps. I keep my eyes on her while taking the stairs, avoiding the third and seventh step that creak like a bitch, and faintly snarl as she turns right through the kitchen.

Bitch, you better just be taking a piss.

I side-eye the four men taking up the couches and the four lying on the floor. They're all passed out, mouths wide open—and so fucking vulnerable right now.

I spot the asshole that got his arm ripped off. But I'm hunting down a possible rat and can't go over and stomp his face in.

I nimbly walk through the kitchen and down the side hall, briefly peeking in through the tiny crack of Pyro's door.

Ew.

He's naked and star fishing on his bed with that older woman I saw the other day. His Cane Corso is at the foot of his bed, asleep on the floor. And that's exactly what I was worried about with configuring the plan.

I don't want to have to tranquilize him.

But if he's in my way—I will.

The bathroom light is seeping under the door, a faint rustling sound coming from within.

She could be changing her tampon or something. I just don't trust her. Not after seeing how fidgety she was earlier.

Grabbing the handle, I lift and twist, avoiding the awful creak it makes while opening. I silently close it behind me, staring in shock at the blade she has in her hand.

Eli must've accidentally left the hutch unlocked yesterday. She's somehow taken apart a razor for a single blade.

"Cora," I drone, deftly moving towards her.

"I can't do it," she squeaks. "I'm not brave like you guys." She storms over to the tub, keeping her back towards me.

"You are brave. This is a terrifying situation and we're all facing our own battles with it. I can slip by your room and help you. But please, please put it down," I whisper, stalking up behind her.

"If I can't do it myself, I don't deserve to get out," she mumbles.

A drip audibly splashes on the edge of the tub, and my eyes zip down to the spreading crimson, my hands unwillingly darting out to her waist. "Cora," I whisper-shout.

"What?" she shrieks, whisking around with the blade raised up.

Even through the aches and pains, I can isolate the line of embers surging over my throat. Warmth begins bubbling and trickling from it, and panic widens her blue eyes as she realizes what the fuck just happened.

My heart begins thundering and tingles bloom in my hot face. I calmly reach up, wrapping a hand around my wet throat, and pray to the Dark God it's just a scratch.

"I'm so sorry, I'm so sorry," she chants edgily, tears welling in her frantic eyes.

"I need you to calm the fuck down so I don't freak out," I whisper harshly through gritted teeth.

She nods jaggedly, dropping the blade at our feet and clawing at her roots in distress. "Should I go get someone? What do I do?"

The cracks of my fingers are filling with the sticky warmth. I keep pressure on my throat, reaching over with my free hand to rummage through the open hutch.

"Find some peroxide or rubbing alcohol and clean your arm. I'll handle… this."

"Tala, you're bleeding really bad," she cries.

Must be why it's running down my chest and my lips are going numb.

I grab the box of gauze hidden in the back, then reluctantly step over to the mirror above the sink.

The door creaks open, and if I weren't in the middle of pacifying my racing heart, I'd probably pass out from high blood pressure.

Shiloh's dark eyes connect with mine in the mirror, and I bite the bullet, panning down to the massacre on my chest.

He closes the door, flashing to my side to start unpacking gauze. "What the fuck happened?" he asks roughly, yet silently.

"I'm sorry, Shiloh, I didn't mean to. I wasn't thinking straight and-"

"Cora, breathe," I interrupt, removing my hand from my throat.

It's maybe three to four inches long, deep enough to bleed like a motherfucker, but not deep enough to need stitches.

I shall survive—this time.

"Will you pick up the pieces of the razor before someone sees?" I ask Shiloh. "I can clean this up."

He shoves gauze to my throat, holding it firmly with anger burning in his eyes. "It doesn't matter if they see it or not, Tala. They're gonna see your neck, her arm, and the fucking bloodbath in here, eh?" He glares at Cora, darkness bordering his hard stare. "What the fuck were you thinking?" he asks sharply.

She squats down, blood dripping from her slashed arm and onto the floor as she picks up the blade. "That I'm weak," she chokes out, temptation laced in her wavering voice.

"Cora, look at me," I demand calmly.

Looking at me with wet lashes, she holds the blade in between two fingers, contemplating something irrational.

"I need you. The other girls need you."

She frowns, flattening her brows. "You need me?"

"We do," I nod. "Please pick your mess up and put it in the trash and smack a bandage on that."

"Yes, ma'am. I'm so sorry," she mumbles, quickly snatching up the pieces of razor.

Well, I didn't think the de-escalation would end with a knot forming in my sliced throat.

No one has ever called me ma'am—until Jax.

While Cora picks up and tends to the slash in her arm, Shiloh and I finish wiping up the drying blood from my chest. The slice is already coagulating. But it'll leave a scar.

"Will you do me a favor really quick?" I ask Shiloh, smearing ointment over the sizzling line.

"Anything," he insists, tossing the bloody gauze in the trash.

I lift my shirt up from my back, wincing from the dull aches in my ribs. "Will you lift me up so I can see my back?"

The mirror is a small square and I can't see higher than the middle of my chest. But I'm ready to see what that motherfucker did to me.

"Of course," he agrees. Stopping in front of me, he crouches down, hooking his arms around my thighs and lifting me up.

Holding my boobs in place so they don't fall out, I check over my shoulder—and my jaw drops.

Not only do I have over ten buckle shaped bruises and scabs marring my back, but this asshole also sliced through Jax's last name.

The rage begins boiling my blood.

CHAPTER FIFTEEN

TALA

Ire has fused my battered body, negating the sensation of pain. I focus on how fucking mad I am and the fifty ways I'd torture these assholes just to hear them echo the screams they've derived from the women and dogs.

It moves my body for me, and I send right hooks and rear handed punches into the punching bag like it's Pyro's face I'm beating in.

"Ho-ly shit!" Pyro slows down in passing, gaping at my neck with a smile. "I didn't know you were into playin' with knives, Shiloh."

Does he take his hearing aids out at night or something? Cora was shrieking right across from his bedroom, and he never woke up. It's good he doesn't know what happened. But this old fucker should be in assisted living if he's that easy to sneak up on.

That's probably the only reason he lets his dog sleep in his room. He's usually locked up on a chain in between two trees by the back door.

I don't know how Shiloh responded. I've been striking the bag, diving headfirst into the sea of red that's clouding my vision.

It appears we're all doing the same.

Loxley, Brynn, Sunny, Riley, and Cora are in here too, all tearing into the bags as if we've been personally victimized by them.

"Alright, pretty girls! I'm not a total asshole. I won't send you straight in with the wolves. So-" Pyro claps annoyingly "-you get a starter with the dogs. Bring 'em in!"

Two dogs get walked in on heavy chains, and I catch the panicking eyes that are darting around, looking at me for answers.

I faintly nod, signaling we have to do this and endure the torture for a few more hours.

"Everyone will be in here to watch, so I'm gonna slip away and find your dad. I need you to put on a show and keep them entertained until I can get back." Shiloh whispers, roughly tying my hair up. "If you get knocked down, you have to get back up. If he doesn't see me shocking you, he'll catch on that I'm not here."

Right, the shock collar that's pulling on my scab.

Luckily the slice is closer to my collar bones and isn't being rubbed. But the itchy fabric is tight and stretching my skin. It just might bust back open by the end of this.

"Princess and Brynn!" Pyro calls out. "You're so fond of each other... Let's see how well you fight each other." He smiles, stretching his hands out to either side of the ring.

Skimming over one another, we walk off in separate directions, taking the stairs up into the ring. I slip through the ropes, adrenaline spiking from the chanting I can't see.

A man emerges from the shadows behind Brynn, walking up the despondent Doberman Pinscher I saw the other day.

I don't have to turn around. I feel the violating presence behind me and hear the heavy chain.

This is so fucking crazy. Absolutely batshit.

"You know the drill. Three minutes. Three rounds... Just don't get bit," he finishes with a snicker. "These dogs got strong jaws and can rip the muscle right from your bones. That'll be a quick way to piss me off."

Oh, whatever shall we do if you get in your feelings over the consequences of your own actions? Idiot.

He steps to the front, kicking back against the ropes for his show. "Well. Fight!"

A bell dings, the chain slipping off the dog behind Brynn, and the fight-or-flight rushing through my body throws me into orthodox stance.

Not only do I have to pay attention to her movements, I have to keep a goddamn eye I don't have on two dogs that are already stalking each other down.

Her left fist flies towards my face, and I dip back, just barely missing a crack to the jaw. With her body still in motion, I take the opportunity to send a right hook into her rib. She grunts in pain, getting winded from the collision, and quickly spins around, kicking her right leg out.

Her foot hooks behind my knees and brutally forces me straight onto my back, my head ricocheting off the tight canvas. The throbbing aches sift through the adrenal rush, and I swear I just landed on a goddamn wooden board.

I groan, willing away the stiff pain and stars flickering in my vision, and lunge back to my feet.

The growling and yelping almost distract me as I pendulum step around her, watching the gears turn to plot her next move.

"Pay attention to their footwork. It will tell you their next move."

I'm fucking trying, Jax.

She lunges with her left foot, telling me to dodge the punch getting thrown towards my chest. I bounce on the balls of my feet to swiftly cut left, throwing her off and making her stumble forward.

I hold my weight in my waist to swivel into a haymaker, and my knuckles hit the back of her ribs, making her scream and fly onto her stomach.

"Time! Get the fuck up!" Pyro booms.

The dogs are tornadoing around Brynn, crimson dripping from their coats and smattering the white canvas.

She cries out, trying to get up with shaky hands. It gets the Pit Bull's attention, and he tears away from the Doberman, lunging for her face.

Panic widens my eyes and shoots another burst of adrenaline through my veins. And I don't know why I do what I do, but I pounce towards the dog, hooking my arm around his neck and throwing my weight over him, landing roughly on my side.

I tighten my eyes, pulling my arm back to keep his thrashing, wet body in a chokehold until she can get up.

Dear God, why did you make me a fucking martyr?

"Well, look at this, boys!" Pyro shouts through the chanting.

I open my eyes, unable to tell if the blood on my chest is his or the slice on my throat busting open. The dog is jerking my entire body around, snapping his jaws back at me.

I didn't think this through. I don't know how to get up without him getting a hold of me and these fucking assholes aren't doing anything about it.

I wince, and speedily let him go while crawling backwards to get some space. He instantly turns around and charges, a vicious growl rumbling in his snapping mouth.

Fuck-fuck-fuck!

He pushes off his paws to lunge, and the moment he catches air, a long, black coat side tackles him. They tornado together and roll on the ground, a loud yelp ringing in my ears.

I stumble to my feet, and blanch, helplessly watching the light drain from the Pit Bull's eyes. He stays lying on his side, the snarl fading from his motionless mouth.

"Kill-er! Kill-er!" the crowd chants.

I almost think they're saying, "Kill her," until it dawns on me that the dog that just saved my ass has the same nickname Maverick gave me in high school.

"Look at that!" Pyro shouts ardently, stepping into my line of sight. "It looks like we have ourselves two winners! Can't beat that show! Good God almighty, you're gonna make me big money, princess." He hooks his rapist hands around my shoulders, swiveling my shocked body around and forcing me to hold a fist up.

The crowd is whistling and chanting, yet I can't see anyone.

I really hope Shiloh is back by now.

He lets my fist down, then ushers me off towards the stairs. I have to step over the poor baby that just lost its life for doing what it was trained to do.

Out of everything I've seen and heard here—this is the worst. Coldness is creeping over my skin, pushing me back into the dark void that's hard to get out of.

He lifts the rope for me, smacking my ass as I step through. I grit my teeth; contemplating using the rope to swing over and latch my thighs around his head until it pops like a pumpkin.

"Go on and get cleaned up, girl. You've paid your time today and we got laundry pilin' up."

Shiloh rushes up the stairs, snatching my hand to help me down. He nods, telling me we're in the clear.

I'm going to make Pyro wish for death.

The shiny point glistens in the moonlight. I twirl it around, withering in nerves and excitement.

After we got back to the house, I cleaned myself up, had the perfect opportunity to get the girls' laundry done and laid out for them, and snuck a dart gun into my room.

You shouldn't leave something lying out if you don't want it to end up in unwanted hands.

I eye my sneakers, undecided if I should get them on so I can leave quicker or keep them off so that my steps are quiet.

I set Shiloh's spare Damascus knife on the bed I won't miss and slip my socks on, so my skin won't stick to the floor.

Don't fucking slip down the stairs.

My door unsticks, and I slap my hand over the knife in case it's someone coming in for a midnight fucking rape.

133

Riley's red hair and blood smattered face creep through the crack she made, and she slithers in, wet pocketknife in hand. "I'm so ready," she whispers eerily, eyes bugging out with adrenaline.

I knew I wouldn't have an issue with her fulfilling her end. I didn't think she'd do it so fast though.

I nod, grabbing the knife and standing up a few feet away from her. "Will you swing by Cora's room and help her? I don't think she can do it," I whisper, barely moving my mouth to keep my words noiseless.

She eagerly nods, instantly turning around to slither back out.

Squatting down, I reach under the bed and grab the dart pistol. It only has one dart loaded in it. I couldn't find any more with the minimal time I had. So, here's to fucking hoping I'm a good shot.

My hands are starting to shake.

With the knife in my right hand and the gun in my left, I take a deep, calming breath while slipping through the door, and slowly exhale through my lips during the walk down the hallway. The menacing sconces are lit, casting the dim light of their demise. It's so silent you could hear a pin drop. Which is good. However, very intimidating.

One fuck up could wake the whole house.

While approaching the stairs, I peer over the curved railing. The same eight men are down there. Four on the couches, four on the floor, all sleeping like they deserve rest.

I grip the handrail with three fingers, slowly going down the stairs in my socks. Almost stepping down on the third step, I quickly catch myself and hold on for dear life as I stretch my foot over it, continuing my silent commute to fuck these guys' heads up.

Making it down noiselessly, trepidation begins vibrating my body. Every second is valuable though, so I get my shit together and walk on the pads of my feet over to the back of the closest couch.

Glancing around the still bodies, the rhythm of my fast heart starts spreading over my chest. I grip the handle of the knife with a vice-grip, reach over, and hover the blade above the first man's temple.

And drive it down.

I clench my teeth, hating the pressure and squelch, but quickly withdraw it and move down to the second man.

He stirs a little, rolling onto his back.

I hold my breath, ready to squat down like lightning if his eyes open. Only his mouth does, letting out a snore that pisses me off enough to angle my blade to the top of his head and ram it in.

I cringe. That was a lot more pressure. The break of his skull vibrated the handle.

I keep it flowing gracefully silent, taking out the last two on the couch and squatting down to the assholes on the floor. Seven have faced the fatality of my loaned blade.

I'd be striding on a high if the last asshole wasn't scratching his face.

I halt in a half squat, glaring at him as his lashes flutter.

Think, bitch. Fucking think.

The only thing I can think of at the moment is *Possession of a Weapon*. Why am I thinking of a song?

No fucking clue. But it works.

I quietly place the dart gun on the floor, bending the blade up behind my arm. His eyes open as I languidly crawl over to him, putting on my best fuck-me eyes.

"What do you thi-oh. Oh, hell yeah." His dumbass brain melts as I straddle him. "I've been thinking about your pussy since I watched you walk down those stairs," he whispers.

I bend over him, hiding the blade on the side of his head. "Yeah? Consensually or forcibly?"

He smirks, grabbing my ass. "If I asked you to fuck, would you have said yes?"

I roll my eyes in annoyance, then jam the knife into the side of his head. "Stupid, stupid man," I murmur to myself, watching the light go out in his eyes.

I stand up over him, admiring the massacre in the living room of Hell. I smile like a crazy bitch, and bend at my hips to undo his belt, pulling it from the loops of his jeans.

Draping it around the back of my neck, I snatch the dart gun off the floor and feel eyes on me from the staircase. I glance up, meeting the smiles and slack jaws of the women that are about to taste their freedom.

We're in the home stretch. I just don't know what I'm going to do about the woman in his bed. I have no clue how she'll react. I've only seen her out of his room that one time when she was serving blow on a tray.

I point to my feet with the dripping blade, hinting that I need shoes to whoever will understand. Loxley nods and quickly disappears, leaving the rest to quietly take the stairs.

Swapping the knife and dart gun around, I tread past the cased opening of the kitchen, using the tiny window above the sink as my light to head towards the side hall.

Just as always, his door is slightly ajar, and he's butt naked next to that woman. Aiming my sights for his dog, every muscle turns to stone.

Cropped, slate gray ears are right in front of the door, looking at me through the crack with light amber eyes.

CHAPTER SIXTEEN

JAX

Those trackers were one of a kind. Leon couldn't find shit on them and Irina's drone went down before she could move it into the trees. She didn't think it'd go up in the first place because of how fucking cold it is, so she wasn't paying attention to where she was flying it.

All we know is that Tala is by the Knik River.

Viper's family had to get back to Russia. So, it's been Nadia, Leon, Viper, Maverick, Kendra, and me trying to cover as much ground as possible. We've been scouting through the woods for two days, only stopping when people whine about their feet hurting.

I know this shit is taxing.

And I know some are starting to give up hope. But I can feel Tala.

I know I'm getting closer, and I don't want to fucking stop until I find her.

My body's getting tired though.

It's well after midnight now, dark with only the moon and stars slipping through the trees and reflecting off the snow. The only sounds are chattering teeth and small talk happening around me.

"I'll start a fire right here," Viper mumbles behind me.

"That sounds great. I think my asshole's freezing over," Nadia says with a sigh, looking at me as if she needs approval.

I side-eye her and keep walking. I'm not giving a grown woman permission to sit the fuck down. I don't care if she does.

I'm not. I can smell the fishiness of the river and for some bizarre reason it's calling me like the siren herself, telling me to get closer.

"Jax, you should really sit down for a minute, man," Leon says cautiously.

"I'll sit when I find her," I grumble, barely mustering the energy for speech.

I keep walking, getting a twinge of hope as I notice the tree line about a yard away.

Come on, baby. I need a fucking sign that you're here.

My legs are screaming at me to sit my ass down, but I keep pushing, hearing the steps crunch through the snow at my sides.

"I know you miss her, Jax," Kendra croons, digging under my damn skin. "But you can't find her if you don't take care of yourself."

My lip twitches, ready to whip around and tell her how I really fucking feel about her damn presence. But I snap my teeth shut and preserve the tears I know I would cause.

She fed into this. She played her part.

And I can't stand to look at her.

"You know, Kendra," slips through the tight cracks of my teeth. "She lost our fucking baby during this. She's most likely been raped and beaten by the men you fell in with. Remember that the next time you lay your head down." I glare at her, wanting her to shrink back and feel like shit.

She looks away, frowning and curling her arms around herself.

I stop at the tree line to take in my surroundings, and a loud pop resounds through the night air, coming from the other side of the river where it looks like a hidden driveway is tucked into the trees.

Heat spreads up my icy cold chest and my entire face tightens.

"Was that a shot?" Leon chatters.

I don't answer. I dig my heels into the packed snow and make hell for leather towards the frozen river.

The snow is a dense layer on top of the ice, crunching under my soaked sneakers and filtering up with each heavy glide. I'm huffing straight fucking ice into my burning lungs, powering through the lock up trying to overtake my stiff muscles.

"Wait, Jax! No!" Kendra shrieks behind me.

Jesus fucking Christ.

I drift, snow and slush blowing up under my jeans and biting into my cold skin, and I come to a stop. Taking a big ass deep breath, I swivel around, huffing out pure smoke. "What?" I bark, absolutely at my goddamn limit.

From halfway across the river, I can see her eyes blown out to saucers, hands tucked into her hair in distress. "You can't walk on that! It won't support-"

I don't hear anything else other than the cracking under my feet.

I look down at the splinters that are forming like lighting, each one cracking abrasively and echoing my demise.

"Fuck."

In a split second, the ice gives out, breaking off in a whole chunk underneath me.

The freezing water hits my feet first, then my entire body plummets in the deep water of my despair.

That ice that was holding me together—finally broke.

And the darkness feels like the closest I'll get to home.

CHAPTER SEVENTEEN
TALA

"Hey, buddy," I whisper softly.

He cocks his head, pinning me down with intense eyes.

Making no sudden movements, I gently nudge the door open a hair more. His little nub tail is wiggling, so I make an ignorant decision by reaching my hand down.

He sniffs it, and I ease the door open some more, smoothing over his soft head with my bloody knuckles. He strides past me, most likely making a break for freedom.

I can't take my eyes off Pyro. I just cross my fingers and hope one of the girls distracts him.

Slipping through the door, I raise the dart gun up at him and walk around his bed.

Night, night.

I aim the sight at his neck—and pull the trigger. A pink, fluffy dart shoots out, embedding itself into his leathery, old man skin.

His eyes flash open, and I toss the gun and knife to the ground, instantly grabbing his arm and using all my strength to drag the old fuck out of bed.

"Are you fuckin' stup-" He eats his words, his body thudding violently onto the hardwood. He grunts, stretching an arm over his stomach to sit up. "Boys," he groans lazily.

The dart's already affecting him. I look back at the scared woman, tipping my head to the door, and she scrambles out of bed, crying as she awkwardly runs out of the room.

Sliding the belt from my neck, I look down at him, laughing at how pathetic he is. "Words can cut deep. But a belt will always cut deeper. Right?" I taunt, then smash my foot to his forehead and kick him back down, the reverberation from his head rumbling the floor.

"You won't get away with shit," he grunts drowsily.

I hold onto the tail end of the belt, smiling cunningly. "I already have."

While he's still with us, I throw my arm back and crack the metal buckle over his stomach. He lets out a garbled, guttural cry of agony. And I do it again—and again—and again.

The horseshoe shaped welts begin leaking crimson through the hair on his stomach. I'd keep going, but he's losing consciousness.

Speedily dropping the belt, I whisk around for the knife and crouch over his head. "Jax will have so much fun with you," I smile, carving "J.S." into his forehead.

He passes out in the middle of my work. Which, I find kind of fucking rude. But *I'm on the high horse of gettin' the fuck out of here.* Or whatever stupid shit he said.

I shove the knife into the waistband of my leggings and put his hands together in a prayer. Then, I bind those scratchy fuckers together with the belt I beat him with.

Hooking my fingers into the knotted-up belt, I use my glutes and thighs to drag his heavy body through the door. The pain is starting to ease its way back into my body.

Ignoring the aches, I keep pulling him, grunting and breathing heavily the entire way to the front door.

"Oh, my God… You really did it," Sunny says.

I straighten my spine, dropping his limp arms to his chest. "*We* did it. Yes," I say breathlessly, and thank Loxley as she hands me my shoes.

I look around the beautiful faces that already have the glimmer coming back to their eyes, noticing the woman shaking like she's next for the belt. "What's your name?" I ask her, sliding my sneakers on. "You look really familiar."

"Uh-I-I'm Valerie. You might know my daughter, Kendra," she wavers.

Holy shit. The waitress I thought was flirting with me but was actually trying to kidnap me.

"What a small world," I cheer sarcastically, snatching Pyro by the belt and opening the door.

Pyro's dog is by Riley's side. If he for some reason takes off, I'll find him. I'm just eager to watch this asshole slide down the stairs on his back.

I drag him behind me until I get to the stone stairs. Then, I skitter around to his feet and squat down, grunting as I shove him headfirst down the stairs.

"Wee," Cora and Brynn hum, watching his naked body take a bumpy ride down.

That'll hurt when he wakes up.

Every step down feels like a beam of warm sun. The smiles are radiant, they're laughing and chatting with each other, and it almost feels too good to be true.

It kind of feels wrong to be so excited to leave.

I didn't pay as much time as they did. I didn't endure horrible shit the way they did. In retrospect, I had it so fucking easy compared to the foul treatment they suffered.

The guilt starts gnawing on my aching bones as I shove him down the second flight.

I should've stepped in when I witnessed shit happening to them. I was so caught up in saving my own ass and playing the sweetheart role.

Would it have done anything if I spoke up or started decking people? No. But at least I'd be able to walk away not feeling like a coward.

Once we get down the second flight, the floodlights surrounding the round driveway shed a beacon on my dad holding onto the wolves and Eli and Shiloh holding onto the dogs.

The gleeful cheers and scampers make me smile, and I push through the pain to run up to my dad.

The cold air bites into the tears spilling down my cheeks. But it's a sting of freedom.

I leap up and throw my arms around him, his arms tightly wrapping around my waist, and he cries into the crook of my neck, amplifying my own emotions.

"I'm so sorry, sweetheart. I'm so sorry. That son of a bitch knocked me out with a pitchfork."

I rip away, grabbing his face to look it over. "Oh my God, Dad," I panic, spotting the gnarly knot and bruise on the side of his forehead.

"Are you okay?" he asks, a quiver in his lip and streams pouring down to his full beard.

I've never seen my dad with facial hair. Mom always props herself up on the bathroom counter to shave his face for him.

"I'm okay," I insist softly. "Let's get out of here."

I peek behind him, frowning as I remember what happened to the wolves that have been around since I was a teenager.

"I didn't kill them, kiddo."

My brows pinch, looking at him perplexingly.

"I told him I killed them and tossed their bodies down the hills... I sent them on home. I promise they'll be there."

A weight I didn't know I was holding on my shoulders instantly gets lifted off. I sigh in relief and make my way around him to love on their fury heads as our voyage begins.

I get stuck on Echo for a moment, petting her while we follow behind my dad. "You tried saving me, girl. That means more to me than you'll ever comprehend." I bend down and place an awkward kiss on her head, trying not to fall in the rocks.

I move down to Void, more worried about the rocks building in my throat. "You've suffered horrible shit twice now. And I am so sorry, Void." I kiss his head too, watching the drips splash from my eyes and onto his black fur.

"Hey, Dad?"

"Yeah, kiddo."

"What happened to Valko?"

He looks over his shoulder, the moonlight washing over the contemplation deepening his crow's feet. "He wasn't with them, sweetheart. I think he escaped or hid. I'm not sure. But we'll find him. I just gotta shake his treats around and he'll come runnin' home."

I pat my cheeks dry with my sleeve, catching myself smiling over what a freak Valko is. I think out of all my memories with him, him biting at the four-wheeler and amusing Jax is my favorite.

Oh, my God. Jax. I finally get to see him.

To shun the images trying to spark desire in an unsavory moment, I love on Ace and Spade, then meander back to Killer who's walking alongside Shiloh.

"Thank you," I say, volleying between both the man and dog.

"You gave me the courage to be brave, Tala. So, thank you," Shiloh says adoringly.

I pat his arm, and the whisper of a grin that wanted to form dissolves, the realization of my party foul sinking my chest with panic. "Oh, shit! I forgot him back there."

He laughs, throwing his head forward and tightening his eyes. "Eli grabbed him," he titters, attempting to wipe the dimpled smile from his face.

I wipe my forehead in relief. I was about to be so pissed if I had to turn around for his naked ass.

He grabs my wrist, and I instantly enter defense mode, fixing him with a hard stare and tensing my arm up. "Open your hand," he urges.

Hesitantly, I uncurl my fist, holding my palm up. He drops something cold in it, winking as he pulls his hand away.

I look over the thin chain and crimson charm, heart swelling that he saved it for me. "You kept it," I state, faintly pouting my bottom lip.

"It wasn't mine to take off. But I knew Pyro would catch on to what it was and do something to hurt you both."

"Thank you, Shiloh," I croon, clasping it back on. It'd feel better having Jax do it. But I don't have pockets, and I'd punch myself if I lost it after getting it back. "Why didn't you look at me at first?"

He chews the inside of his cheek, casting me a small glance. "I knew I'd either end up getting killed or wrapped around your finger." He gestures around, pointing out that we're in the middle of escaping.

My lips purse and I nod, ready to leave it at that and soak in the silence that doesn't riddle me with the plaguing thoughts of anxiety.

We've been walking for what feels like forever.

I finally see the end of the driveway, and suck in a deep breath of the crisp air that burns my lungs.

You're no longer breathing in stiff, toxic masculinity.

A loud pop comes from behind me, resounding through the still air. I jump out of my skin, whirling around with wide eyes. All the girls are freaked out too, looking back at Eli who's holding a pistol in one hand and dragging Pyro in the other, guiding the leashed dogs on his belt loop.

"Sorry. He started talking so I shot him in the dick," Eli grumbles.

I tighten my numb lips, shunning a smile over his act of retribution, and whisk back around, carrying on my way.

"Wait, Jax! No!" a feminine voice shrieks in the distance.

Heat spreads up my chest, the increasing beat of my heart traveling up my throat. Before I can protest the impulse in my body, I'm pounding into the gravel and sprinting past Dad and the wolves.

"What?" Jax barks, vexation roughening his voice and echoing through the trees.

My hands begin shaking, and I push, I push my body past its limits and keep running through the burn. The blood whooshing in my ears overpowers the shouting, so I have no fucking clue what is being said as I run out of the tree line.

Like a moth to a flame, my eyes instantly attach themselves to Jax standing on the frozen river.

A loud crack echoes over the ice, and in a snap of a finger he falls through.

My eyes round, cloudy puffs of air jetting out furiously in front of my face. "Dad! Unclip Void and Echo!" I shout desperately, sprinting over the flat patch of snow.

I blurrily see two others on the other side, my vision is shaking with an influx of adrenaline and dopamine.

Sprinting onto the river, Void and Echo both appear at my sides, the ice crunching under my feet and blowing loose snow up onto my ankles.

I don't know why Jax hasn't come up yet.

"Mija!"

I hear Leon, and it forms a knot in my throat while drifting and sliding down to my hip. I stop myself at the hole Jax fell through, and I don't think, I just take a deep breath and dive in.

I've been enduring freezing cold showers. Little did I know it would prepare me to dive into the frozen river.

After a fucking behemoth.

I swim down, holding my eyes open to look through the murky water. Just a few feet below me, his black hair is swaying around.

Why aren't you swimming?

I scoop and kick myself down, grabbing him by his hoodie and furrowing my brows at him.

He opens his sharp, hunter eyes, looking at me as if I'm a figment of his imagination.

Although my rapid heartbeat is swelling tenfold over seeing him—I'm pissed off. I snarl at his perfect face, yanking him with me as I swim back up to the fucking hole he just fell from.

Halfway up, I feel his large hands slide over my hips.

Even under freezing water—his touch is electrifying—zapping my veins awake and making me feel alive again.

The second my head gets above water, I gasp for air, jerking his face closer to mine. "What the fuck is wrong with you, Jax?" I shout, raking down to his full beard.

He shakes his long hair from his eyes, pulling my body tight to his and analyzing my face. "Are you really here, or did I die?" he questions.

Ignoring the way his rich voice gives me butterflies, I shove him towards Echo, watching her latch around his hoodie to pull his big ass out.

It's not my first damn ice hole to crawl out of.

I meticulously splay my hands over the ice and swoop my leg over. I don't make it far before Void bites the back of my shirt and pulls me out.

I get up, shaking from nerves, adrenaline, and the frigid air whipping into my soaking wet body. And I hunt Jax's sexy ass down.

What the fuck was that shit?

He stands up next to the bitch that tried drugging me. I'll ask him about that later. Right now, I'm fighting the urge to smack him in the face. "Why weren't you swimming?" I holler angrily, closing the space that seems so far away.

Apparently not learning his lesson, he runs back out onto the ice, charging straight at me.

I'd shake my head if he wasn't such a sight.

He skates to a stop in front of me, grabbing under my arms and hauling me up into him.

The skin on my back stretches and pulls at the scabs. I'm not protesting the love I've been missing though.

I don't dare.

I wrap around his lean body, smelling his dark spices—and staring at him. His jaw tics, and he holds me tight while sprinting back across.

The ice cracks under each inhumanly fast stride. I hold on just a little bit tighter, resting my head against his neck and watching everyone else ease their way over the river with Dad guiding the way.

"Tala!" Nadia shrieks behind me.

Jax steps onto land, and I look over my shoulder to misty, hazel eyes. I grin somberly at her angelic face, and my eyes begin burning while panning over the relief softening the exhausted faces of Maverick, Viper, and Leon.

And for some Kendra.

The hand sliding down my back gets my attention, and I turn back to the obsidian that's glassing over. "I can't believe I'm looking at you right now, little wolf."

I lazily rub the tip of my cold nose against his, squeezing my legs around him. "I got you a present," I whisper.

He tilts his head, moving closer to my lips. "Hmm, I just want you, baby."

Oh, how I've missed his voice.

"Mom?" Kendra shouts.

I shy away from the Dark God, lips trembling from the glacial bite overtaking my body. His hunter eyes are zeroed in on me, but the happy faces skating over the river and the prancy paws making a freedom walk are my top priority right now. "I hope you have space on the ranch. Otherwise, we'll have fourt… thirteen dogs now."

That's a tough pill to swallow.

If I would've ovaried up last night, the Pit Bull that lost his life would be coming with us.

He spins around, keeping me in his sight while taking in everyone else. He wants to smile. The sharpened daggers are preventing it.

I cup under his jaw, not used to feeling longer facial hair, and turn his face to me. "Don't. We can talk about it another time. Right now, focus on the naked old man that's leaving a blood trail over the river."

"Yes, ma'am," he grins.

"Jax!" Dad shouts excitedly.

I spin my damn spine again, smiling at the pure joy Dad has from seeing Jax.

Dad steps onto land, guiding Ace and Spade on their rope, and stretches his arms out to sandwich me in between him and Jax.

"Damn, Damascus. You took a bullet and you're still standing?" Jax enlivens him.

He pats Jax's back, smiling brightly. "Not the first time I've been shot, son. Remind me to show you my scars."

Chatter fills the air with Kendra reuniting with her mom, Nads tending to the girls and guiding them through the trees, and Maverick and Viper helping with the dogs.

Leon approaches with damp cheeks, stretching an arm out to wrap around my back. "If no one else is going to ask you, mija. I will... Did someone try slicing open your throat?"

"Leon," Jax warns.

"What?" Leon cries, wiping the streams pouring out.

My cheeks begin hurting from the violent smile tugging on my tired face. "No," I laugh. "It was an accident."

Jax's thick brows furrow, and he starts carrying me through the trees. "How the fuck is that an accident?"

I stretch up and to the side, wrangling the knife from my waistband. "That's another story for another time. We're both soaked and I think my nipples are going to fall off."

He smiles sharply, the moon kissing his dangerous teeth. "God, I fucking missed you."

I tightly wrap my arms around his neck, holding the blade that just killed eight men behind his head.

I want to kiss him until my blue lips turn purple.

But once again. I might be poisonous.

CHAPTER EIGHTEEN

JAX

I can't take my eyes off her.

I have the man that I've had a vendetta against for fifteen years strapped to my torture chair in the shop and two men that participated in kidnapping her somewhere in my fucking house. Yet I don't care.

I'll get to them.

I flip the faucet up, turning the shower on the hottest setting. She's kicking her shoes off while petting Sirohi, and although my heart is pumping hot with completion—it breaks seeing how much weight she's lost in two weeks.

Stepping back over to her, I rip my damp hoodie off and toss it to the floor. She eyes me as I start undoing my belt. But it's not the same look of interest I caught her doing often.

She's wary.

"What happened?" I ask, slowly easing my belt off.

Sighing like she doesn't want to tell me, she turns around, peeling her wet shirt up and slipping it off her arms. As she pulls her hair over her shoulder, revealing the black and blue belt buckle imprints marring her back, my stomach twists up into my chest, lodging a knot in my throat that burns my eyes.

I fall to my knees, getting eye level with the fucking torture she was put through, and pry down the waistband of her leggings.

Not only are there scabs lining the countless bruises, but there's also a straight line through my last name in between her dimples of Venus. I gently wrap my hands around her hips, pressing my lips to each mark holding pain.

I've been fighting the annoying fucking water in my eyes.

I can't fight it anymore. Not with the sight before me.

The warm liquid races down my cheeks, and I kiss her back, smoothing my thumbs in comforting strokes over her hips. "I'm so sorry, Tala." I kiss another bruise. "I should've started burning all the trees down."

I thought about it. A lot. And I should've.

She spins around in my hands, narrowing her golden eyes at me. "I would've been so mad if you killed innocent animals just to find me." She raises her hand, wiping my cheeks with her fingers.

I can't help but lock in on the hickeys on her breast and neck. They're faded into a light reddish-brown color. So, they're not new.

But they're there.

She runs her fingers through my hair, gliding her sharp nails over my scalp, drawing up chills. "I know how hard it is to see. No matter what I say… it's sickening. But I do want you to know, Shiloh used hickeys as a way for the women to get out of discipline."

The visual of him sucking all over her makes my lip twitch.

Before she can see it, I rub down my face, standing up to unbutton my jeans. "I'll let him see his mom one time. You know, to say goodbye. But he and Eli won't see Christmas."

She peels her leggings off, glaring at me. "If that's the case, then I'm killing Kendra. You know, your new friend you got all cozy with while I was being ordered around, beaten, jizzed on, and raped."

Black clouds swarm the periphery of my vision, the air becoming too damn stiff to breathe. I swallow nothing, watching her stomp towards the shower and turn her back to me under the water.

As if the wrath is moving for me, I stalk out of the bathroom, making it all the way downstairs before running into Nadia.

She widens her eyes at me, bracing her hands on the back of the couch like she's in trouble. "She's in my shower. Keep an eye on her for a minute," I grumble, barely acknowledging the living room full of domes.

I thunder over to the front door, rip it open, and huff the cold air into my collapsing lungs as I walk my ass over to the shop on the side of the house.

I don't want her thinking I give a shit about Kendra's existence. I'll pacify that in a bit. I have pent up aggression to let out and a dickless, piece of shit, rapist waiting with my initials carved into his forehead.

She's so fucking hot for that. I still can't believe she stabbed eight domes and pulled the fucker out of bed, then shoved his ass down two flights of stairs.

Damascus is returning with my truck as I smash the pin into the keypad for the bay door.

He and Evelyn took the wolves home, and Leon somehow loaded up the dogs in his SUV to take to the ranch. Once everything settles down, we'll organize an adoption event and get them into homes.

The bay door whirs itself open, flicking on the automatic light to the shop. "Can I get a strike at him?" Damascus asks.

"Yes, sir." I dip down under the door and stride in.

He eagerly walks behind me through the shop and down the hall to the metal door. I throw it open, vengeance tunneling my vision in on…

The empty motherfucking chair.

"You. Have got. To be fucking shitting me!" I kick a bucket, launching it across the room and knocking a line of drills off a shelf.

I inspect the chair and floor like a madman, spotting a few drops of blood on the epoxy floor and a smear where his tattered dick was resting on the seat.

"Oh, that son of a bitch," Damascus mutters, following me out of the room.

I bolt back to the house, flying through the door I left open, and search around the living room until I spot Kendra. "Where the fuck is your mom?" I ask abrasively.

She shakes her head, staring at me with bug eyes. "I-I don't know. She said she was going to the bathroom."

"When? An hour ago?"

Her cheeks grow red, and she peers around at the nervous eyes that are glancing back and forth.

"Fucking find her!" I snap, beyond sick of this girl being around. She's nothing but a problem.

"What's going on?" my favorite voice asks behind me.

"Someone let what's his nuts out, sweetheart."

Kendra squints, recoiling her head. "She wouldn't do that."

Warm vanilla looms around me, calming my racing mind. Her long hair is wet and dripping down a black shirt she took from my closet. And her face. God, her fucking face.

Her divine features are really here. Right next to me.

"She very well could have Stockholm Syndrome, Kendra," Tala says tiredly.

Kendra's brows raise. "What did you say about my mom?"

"Did I stutter?" Tala clips.

Fuck. I was so sick of hearing Nadia and Kendra bicker. But Tala holds a power that's quick and cuts down to the bone.

"I don't know you, baby," Brynn chimes. "But I watched her kill eight men in the dark with one knife."

I press my knuckles to my lips, stifling a groan. I was trying to not get hard in a shitty fucking moment. But apparently my siren girlfriend is now an assassin.

"Why are you still sitting there?" Tala asks, cocking her head. "You heard him. Go. Find. Her."

Oh, fuck.

Targeting Eli and Shiloh in the armchairs by the fireplace, I say, "Watch the girls." They nod, and I grab Tala's hand, swiveling around to Viper and Maverick at the island. "Lock the house down once she leaves."

I look long enough for agreement, then make my way up the stairs. Once we get in the hall, she wiggles her hand from mine. "What are you doing, Jax?"

I lift a brow, stopping at my office. "We're looking at the cameras." I push open the door and stalk over to my desk chair.

Following me in, she stops on the other side of my desk, arms folded under her chest. "I'm sorry. I'm just not ready for... Yeah."

I know what she means. And I know why.

And the fucker responsible is out on the loose.

"I know, baby," I say as softly as possible, pulling up the cameras on the outside of my house.

She maneuvers around my desk and throws an arm around my neck, sliding into my lap.

My body temperature rises, tingles spreading from my chest to my knees. Her vanilla is penetrating my mind, and I want to run my hand up her thigh, feel her soft skin and kiss her pouty lips. But I don't want her to feel like I'm pressuring her.

While I rewind the footage to the past two hours we've been back at the house, she tucks her arm in between us and rests her wet head on my bare shoulder.

I found home in her. I knew when I first saw her that our designs connected. Me feeling her pulse that night, the rhythm of her heart on my fingertips... That's when I really knew that she is the embodiment of my comfort.

A hum drifts from her lips. And although I'm watching Kendra's mom open the side door to my shop, I smile over how pretty every noise is out of her mouth.

I only looked for confirmation. I also wanted to make sure Kendra's sneaky ass wasn't out there helping her.

I fast forward until I see her propping his limping body up, helping him escape towards the woods.

He doesn't have anywhere to go besides back to that house. Maybe the mayor's house. Either way, I'll get him once Tala has some rest in her.

I switch back to the live feed of all twenty cameras and a knock comes from my office door. I look over the edge of my monitors, meeting

Damascus' eyes in the doorway. "Hey, son. Will you let Sweetheart know all the wolves are home? Evelyn's here to pick my old ass up so I can get back to them."

"Yes, sir. I gave you Leon's number, right?"

"You did indeed. I'll give you a holler if anything happens. And thank you. For everything. You're a good man, Jax. We're lucky to call you family." He tips his head, quickly making his departure.

A good man would've been able to find his lost loved ones within twenty-four hours. And I didn't even find them. *She* found me. *She* saved me. And *she* is the one that got them out of there.

You know, she sat on her parents' couch and felt inadequate about finding the missing women to fill her grandparents' shoes. Yet she constructed a whole goddamn plan and killed people to bring them home.

I look down at her—and my heart skips a beat. Her long, dark lashes are fanning her cheeks and there's a small gap in between her plump lips, and she's curled up in my lap, finally getting some sleep.

Sirohi's beady eyes are fixed on her from the side of my chair. I'm not sure he'll ever look away from her now. I know I don't want to.

I got so distracted by the hickeys earlier, I didn't even look at her stomach. Gently, I hook a finger into the bottom hem of her shirt, lifting the baggy fabric up until I see her slim stomach.

I clench my jaw, staring at the purple line running from the bottom of her ribs, through her navel, and to the hem of her underwear.

Contrition bites into my skin, and I ease her shirt back down, wrapping my arms around her. "I love you, little wolf. I'm so sorry I wasn't there," I murmur.

She jumps, pushing her hands into my chest and staring at me with panicked, bloodshot eyes.

"I'm here," I whisper, coasting my palm over her hip.

She sighs relievedly, her shoulders relaxing. "I'm sorry," she mumbles, dropping her head back down.

I brush the wet hair from her incredible face, tucking it behind her ear. "Don't be sorry, baby girl. I'm here for you. I'll help you get through this."

I know all too well the panic of realizing you fell asleep in an unsafe environment. It ingrains into you.

But she's safe. And she's finally in my arms again.

CHAPTER NINETEEN

TALA

I think I'm going into shock. A lot has happened in two weeks. Almost too much to digest without nausea paralyzing me.

Staring at the pancakes, eggs, and bacon before me, silverware clanks against the plates lining the long dining table.

You'd think I'd be scarfing it down the way Brynn and Cora are. Their lips are glistening with syrup and grease.

I'm just processing everything.

Riley and Sunny both ate while making calls to home, said their thanks, and returned to their families.

Eli was a little glum to see Sunny go. Apparently, they formed a nice friendship, and he'd sneak her his portion of dinner. But Sunny's young, she was ready to burn the horror movie and pop in a musical. Riley was just ready to get the fuck out of here.

Rightfully so.

Loxley passes Nadia her phone back, melancholic tears rolling down her pale cheeks as she takes her seat in between Shiloh and Cora.

Scalding embers are melting the side of my face. I look out of the corner of my eye, getting the semi-blurry image of Jax facing me in his chair—just watching me.

I grab the iced coffee he made me, tilting the glass to my lips and attempting to wash my nerves down with the rich bitterness. The buzzing chatter morphs into gibberish, leaving me with the rhythm of my heart thumping in my ears, the beat gradually increasing.

The aroma of jasmine spreads warmly through the heavy smell of breakfast, caramel arms tenderly wrapping around the back of me, honey brown hair draping down my chest.

"I love you. Please eat," Nadia whispers in the crook of my neck.

I set my glass down, wiping the precipitation on my hand off on my leggings, and mellowly rub her arms. "I love you. I will, I promise. I want to make sure the girls get enough."

She leans forward, craning her neck to get face to face with me. Happiness is trying to deplete the sorrow, but it still weighs heavy in her hazel eyes. "You know Jax will make more if they want more. Eat."

"Angel," Maverick warns from the seat next to me. She moves her head back, both of us looking at the exhaustion darkening his face. "I know you mean well, but I don't think barking orders at her is something she needs right now."

"Oh, shit," she mutters under her breath and looks back at me. "I'm so sorry, babe. I'm just worried about you. You never pass up pancakes and you sure as hell don't refuse chocolate chips."

Not only did I get accustomed to the bland diet of oats, but my stomach is still a mess from getting opened up.

I don't know how to tell them about that. Maybe I should just text Paxton and get my entire stomach tattooed so I can avoid a difficult conversation.

Not knowing what to say, I nod understandingly, peeling away from the worry veiling their faces.

A large hand runs up my thigh, wafting the intoxicating dark spices that formulate his tattooed skin. "Is it your stomach, baby?" Jax asks, leaning in too close with knowing eyes.

I glance around dazedly, landing on the tiny scar on his lip. "No," I draw out.

He hikes a brow, and Nadia releases her arms to crouch down next to me, clearly awaiting the truth. I volley her and Maverick, swiveling my head to the demon that's gotten closer.

The attention is too much right now. It's lighting a torch and holding it to the bees buzzing under my skin.

I abruptly scoot back, the chair dully scraping the hardwood and snapping even more eyes to me, and I step over Nadia's tiny body. I know I can't run away from it forever. But it's the last thing I want to discuss at the moment.

Pointy ears follow my side to the backdoor. I gently pet over his soft head and snatch Jax's cigarettes off the island in passing.

I don't know why. I'm sure it'll be ripped from my mouth before I can spark a flame.

"Do you want a friend, Sirohi?" I ask, sliding the door open.

His beady eyes are glued to me, stepping out into the frigid air of freedom. I don't close the door. The tingles vibrating my back tell me my shadow is on my heels.

It slides, faintly thudding behind me as I walk barefoot through the snow, over to the new furniture Jax got. He stalks past me, raising my blood pressure simply from granting me the sight of him, and he sits down in one of the chairs.

He pats his lap, devouring my movement. "Talk to me," he urges lovingly, reaching a hand out and placing it on my lower back.

My cheeks pulse in tandem with my heartbeat, sitting sideways down on his lap. I throw an arm around him, curling my legs up and spotting the silver chain he still wears.

Flipping his pack open, I hold it up for him to take one. "I'd rather talk about why the hell you got cozy with Kendra."

He takes one, fetching out his Zippo with his long fingers, and faintly grins. Apparently amused with my bitterness.

"There was nothing *cozy* about it, baby girl. I shot her in both legs, dragged her ass through the snow, and hung her up as a punching bag for Nadia."

My eyes thin to hateful slits, watching his full lips form to the filter. The metal clinks, a flame burning the end, a cherry blazing as he inhales. "You tied her up?" I question irritably.

Turning his face closer to mine, he exhales the notes of tobacco, the smoke looming around the gap in between us. "Hmm, don't get jealous, little wolf. I promise it wasn't enjoyable for anyone besides Nadia. I have two reasons for not killing her. And I think I know you well enough to know that you'll agree with me."

I reach up, prying the cigarette from him. "Go ahead. Make it good." I tuck the paper in between my lips, lightly inhaling the herby warmth and inspecting the desire sharpening his hungry eyes.

"Mmm, yes, ma'am," he drawls. "One, she tried getting your attention to help get you the fuck out of there. The cameras were spliced, so there's no video evidence of it, but her saving Valko was evidence enough of her being there and playing on the defense after fulfilling her fucked up order. Two, she has a kid brother. If her life was taken, he'd end up in the system because his loony ass mom wouldn't be able to take care of him. I can't just let that shit happen, baby. And I'm not taking in a fifteen-year-old."

My vision waves with the buzz running through my blood, and butterflies flap obnoxiously in my empty stomach. He's so compassionate, yet he's the scariest person I've ever met.

I almost pass the cigarette back, awkwardly freezing and pulling it away from his tattooed fingers. "I didn't know she had a brother… What was her fucked up order?"

Eyes ensnared to mine, he wedges the cigarette in between two fingers, prying it from my light grip and taking a drag.

I sigh. I don't want to give him something, even though I know he doesn't care. He'd take a pill or get a shot with me.

"She struck Nadia upside the head with one of Nadia's trophies from cheerleading. It knocked her out. And then she tied her up, shoved socks in her mouth, blinded her with a scarf, and locked her in a closet," he says directly, thin smoke sifting through his teeth.

I slowly blink, attempting to calm the raging waters of wrath. It's rising and crashing into me—and I honestly can't look at him right now.

Setting his pack down on his chest, I spare him a hateful glance, my right eye beginning to twitch, and I slip off his lap. My blood is boiling, reaching the point of combustion. I don't even feel the snow melting under my feet while walking away.

I rip open the sliding door for Sirohi, stepping inside after him and trying to gain distance.

"Tala, she was just extra eyes looking for you," Satan says defeatedly behind me.

I make eye contact with Maverick who's loading the dishwasher, getting a small head shake from him.

He has seen me blow up. It's not often that I reach the point of volatility that makes my hands shake and vision fade.

But it's how I got my nickname.

I'm unable to suppress the fury that's rupturing out like lava. I whip around, face screwed up in rage and force the behemoth to stop in his tracks. "That's so fucking disrespectful!" I snap.

He slightly draws his head back, eyes widening at my outburst.

"That's not only a slap to my face, but Nadia's too! You might as well pull your stupid fucking knife out and slam it into my heart! … You already broke it," I finish despondently.

Taking a step back, I turn around and absorb the speechlessness coming from both the living room and dining room.

How dare he?

Sparing her life is understandable.

Her brother doesn't deserve to face the consequences of her actions. But to let her hang around, constantly taunt Nadia with the face that hurt her… I just can't believe him. I want to go home.

To *my* home.

With the goal of yanking shoes on and getting the fuck out of here, I speed up the stairs, only making it to the fourth one before Jax is grabbing my waist. "Tala, running-"

Against my will, I twist around, cracking my open palm against stone that doesn't move. "Don't fucking touch me," I hiss, pointing my sharp nail in the face that's rapidly growing dark.

Fuming, I turn around and sprint up the stairs.

Embers are popping under the skin on my palm. I rub it on my thigh, racing down the hall and battling the rain that pours after a cataclysm.

"Fucking asshole," I mutter, clenching my teeth and turning into his sad bedroom.

I hate that I just laid a hand on him. It's making my chest tight and forcing out the waterworks.

I wipe my eyes and rush over to his bed, ripping off my blanket and storming over to his closet. I smack the light on, whiz around like a fly until I have socks and sneakers on, then snatch my keys from the top of his dresser.

Hauling ass out of his room, I glance around, still not understanding the bleakness he finds comfort in. It's only pissing me off further, and I run down the hall with a twitch in my eye.

He's still at the bottom of the stairs, one hand latched tightly in his roots, jaw ticking beneath his facial hair.

I instantly look away, wadding my blanket up so I don't trip over it, and run down the stairs.

"Please talk to me," he pleads hoarsely.

Saying nothing, I avoid him and wave bye to all the eyes stitched to me. "Call or text Nads when you guys get home safely. I'll reach out once I get a new phone," I tell the girls while scratching Sirohi's head, then walk to the door.

Jax strides by, able to eat up the distance with a few steps, and stops in front of me. "No, I just got you back. I'm not fuckin' losing you again, Tala."

"Can't lose what's not yours," I counter quickly, stepping closer to the twitch in his lip. "You promised. You promised me you wouldn't break my heart."

Affliction weighs his eyelids heavy, and he reaches out to touch me.

The door opening behind him interrupts the touch I was going to accept. I tilt my head, peering around the behemoth, and the strawberry blonde hair—makes me laugh.

Not because it's funny. Because it's ironic she just waltzes into his home. She was clearly given the pin to the keypad to get in.

I locked it up after Sunny and no one has left since.

I shake my head, and shove past the asshole, walking around the bitch who's eyeing him. She still has tan marks marring her face from Nadia getting payback.

Yet she holds temerity. As if she has a right to be here.

Storming out the door, my heart sinks into a pit, echoing the broken rhythm up into my temples. The air whipping my skin seems warmer than the coldness beginning to plague my body.

Hello, darkness. I see we're meeting again this year.

CHAPTER TWENTY

JAX

"You promised. You promised me you wouldn't break my heart," she says dolefully, amber eyes scanning my face—but missing the twinkle that normally shines when she looks at me.

I didn't mean to, little wolf. I didn't have any energy to exert into keeping a rat out. I just wanted to get you home.

My chest is ramrod stiff, closing off my throat and paralyzing my tongue. I reach out, just wanting to fucking touch her, hold her close and never let go.

My fingers almost reach her hair, ready to brush those silky locks of raven behind her decorated ear. She doesn't move away or swat my hand like I thought she would.

I just barely get the silky texture on my fingertips before the door opens behind me.

I huff, and drop my hand, checking over my shoulder to the worst sight I could ever fucking take in.

It's honestly mortifying.

Several stitches run through my heart and my stomach twists. The crazy laugh coming from Tala only paralyzes me further, rippling my skin and running my hands cold.

Breaking Tala's heart—has broken mine.

I've never felt this before. I feel like a useless sack of fucking shit, just standing here, watching the love of my life run out the door. Meanwhile Kendra's dumbass has the audacity to act clueless.

"Get the fuck out of my house!" I bark volcanically.

My vision begins pulsing, blackness crowding around the way she basically leaps out of her skin. "I-I tried calling Leon. I was able to get into some deer cams. I saw them stumbling their way back towards the Knik."

I hear her fucking stutter, I'm more focused on Tala flying down the driveway.

I know she's going home. But I don't want there to be a second of her missing from my sight.

"Just leave, Kendra," Nadia snips, appearing at my frozen side. "You are nothing but a fucking plague that keeps coming back where it's not wanted."

I don't have time for this shit.

I look around until I spot Maverick watching the shit show from the kitchen. "Can you keep an eye on the place and make sure the girls get back to their families safely?"

"Absolutely," he nods. "But it may be smarter to send Nadia or myself after her."

I furrow my brows, almost not letting him finish.

"Once you lose her trust, man... it's gone. If she says you broke her heart... it's shattered. We-" he gestures to the domes that have been looking for her "-know it wasn't ill intent on your part. We heard you talking to Kendra like shit. But Tala doesn't know that. And I'm honestly not sure if any words will change that now."

I can't live without her. And there's no way in fucking hell I'm sending another man to console her.

I broke those pieces. I'm the one that will pick them up, stitch them back in place, and kiss over the wounds until the scars fade. Even then, I'll caress her flesh and soul until she begs me to stop.

I won't though. I won't ever stop.

I palm the chihuahua's heads, prying apart the bitch fest happening. "If I have to tell you to get the fuck out of my house one more motherfucking time, it won't be words floating through that dense mind of yours. It'll be a bullet," I grumble, then give Kendra the damn nudge she apparently needs.

She quietly stumbles backwards through the open door, eyes misting over as she finally walks the hell away and stomps down the concrete steps.

"Maybe it's not Stockholm Syndrome that her mom has," Viper quips from the living room.

I scoff. "Make sure she doesn't come back. If she does, by all means shoot her. Let's go, Nadia." I head out the door with Sirohi by my side.

"Okay, but if she starts throwing knives at you... I'm out of there."

"You think she will?" I ask with a sliver of hope.

She races up to my side, out of breath to keep up with me. "Well, the last time I saw her blow up like that was freshman year. Granted, it wasn't kitchen knives she was throwing. But my girl's leveled up now. I would not be surprised to open a drawer and see a machete in it."

"What happened freshman year?"

"You know Tala," she croons. "She's an empath. She didn't even know Mav yet and she stormed across the cafeteria because she saw his black eyes."

She stops for a moment, the anticipation gnawing on me while I open the rear door for Sirohi and get into my truck. Her little ass crawls up into the passenger seat like a purse pooch as I start it up.

"She stomped her sexy boots up onto his table, threw her food off her tray, and snapped it right over her knee, demanding to know who did that to him... I was watching in shock from our table, but I guess Mav was all like, *"Woah*, easy, *killer."* And that's how she got her nickname."

"You were ready to go to war for me and didn't even know my name."

It makes sense now. All of it.

Of course he'd be protective over her. He was being abused at home and her big ass heart and infectious compassion probably felt like the most loving hug.

You'd think more people would be unsettled with a kid showing up to school with bruises. In reality, no one gives a shit unless it directly affects themselves.

Sure, they can see that shit and *want* to speak up. But then they think of the paperwork that consists of. The paperwork that leads to an in-home visit. And once the suit claims you're in a loving home and passes you off and tosses the fucking paperwork—you get hit again.

The system is a joke.

The drive to Tala's house is relatively silent. It's given me time to sit with the heavy, foreign feelings of... Despair?

I'm not sure. But it feels like toxins are taking over my bloodstream and turning my lungs to ash.

I'd rather take a million pretty palms to the face as a form of her touch, than to feel her try and cut the cord tying us together.

She tried breaking up with me. I don't accept that.

Nadia rips her spare key out of the door, shoving it open and stepping to the side. "Remember, Jax, the darkness consumes her. She might not even speak or look at you. I didn't see her pretty eyes for three weeks when Ruby and Blade passed away... Just be gentle with her..."

I nod and eagerly squeeze by.

Maple syrup and vanilla... Oh, how I've missed you.

I'd grin at the zebra print runner if this wasn't a walk to her crippling depression. It's knotting my stomach knowing I'm the root cause of it.

My heart begins beating maliciously, stalking down the hall, and seeing her door closed.

It's never closed.

I swallow roughly, then push down on the handle to open her door.

The hinges faintly squeak—and she just lies there, swallowed in fur, her raven silk draping across the animal print pillows.

Kicking my shoes off, I walk over to her bed, lifting up the blankets until I figure out how many she's under, then slide in behind her.

Somehow—she's cold to the touch.

I wrap my arm around her waist, molding my body to hers and lacing her fingers with mine so she can see that it's me. Her sharp nails stay sticking up though. She doesn't squeeze like she normally does.

"You want to know a secret, little wolf?" I ask quietly and kiss the back of her shoulder.

Nadia freezes by the end of the bed, an awkward frown tugging her lips as she backpedals out of the room.

I don't really mind if she hears it or not. But I wait until I hear her chunky sneakers thud down the hall to continue.

"Up until my father died, my life was the dojo. If I wasn't in school, I would be there training with him. After he died, I only saw dog abuse, drugs, and my own blood. I graduated from my online courses when I was eighteen and used the trust fund my father set up for me to go to college. I only went to learn how to hack and code because I knew that was my best shot at hunting down Brutus. I knew his slimy ass would slip up and post a stream at some point. Therefore, my entire life has been consumed by work or wrath, both being disciplining and unaccepting of outside distractions... Until you."

Saying nothing, her little fingers slowly bend down to sit flush with the top of my hand, and I feel her heart rate pick up against my wrist.

"On September first, you gave me a purpose. I've never felt my heart beat against my sternum until I saw you... I've never even been with a woman before you... You've been my first everything, Tala. You are quite literally the object of all my desires... and the comfort of home."

Twisting her neck, she looks back at me with bloodshot, golden eyes, her wet lashes sticking together. "There's no way," she mumbles.

I laugh lightheartedly, grinning and propping myself up to see her better. "I'm no liar, baby."

Looking at me with adoration, the beautiful twinkle returning in her eyes, she rotates around and lays on her back—still holding my hand. "Is that why you didn't just ask me for my number, or ask me out on a date?"

Blinking, I glance around, realizing I never even took that into consideration. She laughs quietly, the gentle rasp drawing my attention right back to the face that still doesn't seem like it's here.

"I think maybe I had gotten so accustomed to hunting and... well, stalking... that I didn't know how else to get my hands on you. I just knew I needed you."

Her eyes roam my face intently, and she squeezes my hand tighter, running her thumb over my pinky. Sirohi starts whining, begging to get up here with us, and her focus on me breaks.

"Yes," she says, patting the surplus of blankets.

His big ass jumps up, instantly leaping over me and to her side, laying down next to her.

All I can do is take in the beautiful sight of her being home, wrapped up in fur, lying under me and throwing an arm around the dog that would kill for her.

I lower my hand, gently swiping my fingertips through the notch of her collarbone. Goosebumps rise on her creamy skin, and her eyes of Venus find mine.

"I'm so sorry, little wolf. I didn't mean to hurt you, and I didn't mean to freeze up when you needed reassurance. Kendra knows how to hack and splice, so Leon kind of took her under his wing to show her more shit. But if her death is what will bring you peace, then I'll pull her death card and let you do the honors."

"Jax," she purrs, running her hand up my arm. Making my fucking stomach flip. "I'm mad enough to curb stomp her face until there's nothing left but bone matter and chunks of hair... I shall move on. As long as she does."

CHAPTER TWENTY-ONE

TALA

I slept all day. The only reason I woke up is because Nadia slithered into my bed and hugged me a little too hard.

Hugs shouldn't be painful.

During the winter, night breaks through daylight a lot quicker. We get a few hours of beaming sun, then the moon eats it away and washes the sky in shades of orange and pink before raining down its blue-hued glow through the darkness.

The sherbet lighting is diffusing through my bedroom window, casting a euphoric halo around honey brown and mushroom brown hair at the end of my bed.

Cora and Loxley both went home to their families yesterday. They've been sending photos and texts to Nadia's phone.

Brynn hasn't called anyone though.

"Thank you, Jenny," Nadia says sweetly, and hangs up, tossing her phone into the pile of fur. "You both have appointments tomorrow."

"Thanks, Nads," I say, watching Brynn pull her into a hug. I lean over my crossed legs, peeking around the doorframe to make sure our babysitter isn't eavesdropping, then shuffle my hips to get closer to them. "Brynn, do you know if Py-Brutus used condoms, or if he'd pull out?" I ask quietly.

Nadia's eyes well with water, but Brynn's unphased. That was her life. "He'd mostly use condoms. You know him, that would be even more discipline if we ended up pregnant... Why, baby?"

I vaguely shake my head. "I was just wondering."

Wouldn't want a lunatic's seed clogging up my one fallopian tube.

I still need to talk to Jax about that. He's downstairs with Sirohi, cooking something that's making my mouth water.

Uncrossing my legs and crawling over my bed, I say, "You guys can hang out here if you want. I'm gonna go talk to Satan."

Brynn's sweet laugh sounds like heaven, the halo around her adding an extra celestial touch. "Why do you call him Satan?"

An obnoxious smile forms on my face, and I glance over my shoulder to her amusement with his nickname.

"Because he's a big, sexy hit man that stalked her," Nadia titters.

That reminds me.

I turn on my heel, quickly walking around the end of my bed while eyeing the dog tag still hanging from my moon lamp. I grab it and slip it on. For the first time.

I'm not sure why I don't wear it. I just liked the way the moon would reflect off it when I couldn't sleep at night. I guess I kept it in the same spot because in a way... it was like looking at him. Beautifully sharp in the moonlight.

Walking out of my bedroom, I pass Leon who's clacking away on his laptop, holding it in one hand and breezing over the keys with the other. "Hey, mija," he greets softly, pushing off the wall and following alongside me.

"What are you doing?" I ask curiously.

He offers a smile, wearing dark circles I've never seen him wear. "Right now, I'm hunting down Ashton Prior, the man that manufactured those trackers we pulled out of Shiloh and Eli."

I cringe, shifting my focus on the stairs so I don't snap my neck. "You guys pulled them out?"

"Si, querida. Jax did, and then had Dr. Z stitch 'em up." He stops on the last step, tired eyes trailing over me. "It's good to see you home. I'm really sorry to ask again… but I can't sleep not knowing if someone tried slicing open your throat."

The Dark God appears in the cased opening, sexually leaning against the wall, waiting for the story that's not exciting.

"No. Like I said, it was an accident. There was a hutch above the toilet that was kept locked so we couldn't get into it. Well, it was left open, and Cora took apart a razor for a single blade. I got too close and startled her, and she whisked around and got me. The end."

Leon curls his hand over his mouth, the disappointment reaching his eyes, and Jax slowly blinks. It makes me want to jump up and down.

He's picking up on my silent attitude.

In order to not call him out and possibly never see it again, I walk past him, inhaling a big breath of crab and Cajun seasoning as I get closer to the kitchen.

Butterflies flutter in my stomach and shock veils my face, taking in the organized mess of this man making my top comfort food.

179

His hands glide around my waist, stopping my steps and pulling me into stone. "I still need to take you to Savannah, little wolf. You'd really enjoy the soul food down south."

I take a steady breath, skin tingling from his touch. "Can I talk to you about something?"

The kitchen blurs as he spins me around by my waist, the butterflies increasing tenfold. "Always," he insists.

I need to sit down for this. Blowing my cheeks up with nervous air, I slip from his hands and hop up onto the island.

Still nowhere near his height.

I let the air out, trilling my lips as it slips through. "Your baby tried killing me. I know you know. But I don't know how you know."

Easing himself in between my legs, his hands encase my hips, tenderly rubbing his thumbs across my lower stomach.

"Sirohi led us to the clinic you were taken to. I don't know how he picked your scent up a week later, nor do I know how the fuck Shiloh got you there before you bled out." He shakes his head, self-contempt hardening his eyes. "There were so many times you needed me over the span of two weeks… and I wasn't there. I'm so sorry. I'm here now, baby girl. There's no way you're getting rid of me." His gaze wanders down to the dog tag, and a small grin forms on the lips I cannot stop staring at. "You're finally wearing it."

I nod, zoning in on his mouth. "You had Sirohi out in the cold?"

He wets his lips, flashing a tease of his teeth. "He had shoes and a coat on."

I missed the sight of him dressing his dog?

I groan and fall forward, crashing my forehead into his chest. He lightly rubs up my back, most likely feeling the fucking scabs through my shirt. "Lay back," he demands lovingly.

Panic runs under my skin, and I snap my spine straight, looking at him as if he just smacked me across the face. "Jax," I draw out.

"I'm not going to hurt you. Lay back."

Blood thumps against my cheeks, pounding the erratic beat my heart is running at. But I obey. And lay back on the cold countertop.

"Attagirl," he growls, trailing his hands up my sides, my shirt up inching up with the gentle glide.

I tighten my lips, containing a whine over how much I missed hearing that. It slips out through my nose, watching his devastating face lower to my stomach. He peels my sweatpants down and presses his soft lips to the bottom of my scar. Right on my pelvis.

"Jax," I breathe needily, combing my fingers through his long hair.

His lips smack with every longing kiss, his silky tongue erasing the pain, and he takes his time capturing the demons I didn't know I was still housing.

He doesn't stop. He keeps going, pressing desperate kisses up to the dagger on my sternum and sinking his body into the thrum lighting up in between my thighs.

You're disgusting. You were just raped five days ago and you're getting wet.

Reality kicks in and I tense up, shoving his face away from me. Ignoring the conflict in his eyes and his blood kissed lips, I swing my leg from around him and scramble off the island.

I don't make it far. I rarely ever do.

His hand slides across my chest, arm wrapping around my shoulders and spinning me right back into him. Quickly locking me in with his other arm, he holds me tight—like he's afraid I'll vanish again. "I won't ever do something you're not comfortable with. Just let me love you, Tala. Let me kill the monsters that are attacking you."

Breathing in his intoxicating scent, I wrap around his waist, turning my head to rest against his heartbeat. "Thank you for lighting a candle for me," I whisper.

A hand travels up the back of my head, latching in my hair just enough to pull my attention up at his worried face. "What?"

I laugh lazily, resting my chin on stone. "It's a metaphor, babe. Not only did you light a candle, you held my hand and guided me out of the darkness… No one's been able to before… But your voice alone called me back home."

He drops his shoulders in relief, molding his hand to my head and tucking me back into safety. "I'd let the world burn if that meant bringing you home."

CHAPTER TWENTY-TWO

JAX

Long, dark lashes flutter over pools of amber. So close, I can see the one black spot that sits under her right pupil. It adds to her own personal constellation of sporadic freckles on her fair face.

She rolls her lips, intently watching as she guides the trimmer down my cheek. Her little hand is gently wrapped around my throat, using her forefinger and thumb to tilt my head in the direction she needs.

I look into the mirror, studying the way her silky hair flows down her back and bends with the curvature of her hips. But the face of a siren calls me right back to it.

She turns the trimmer off, blowing cold air on my cheek and brushing the loose hairs down. "So handsome," she smiles, getting stuck on my lips.

I wet them, and her thumb glides right through the fresh saliva. "We should probably go," she murmurs, slowly inching closer.

She makes me so fucking lightheaded.

My hands wander up her thighs, the simple contact sizzling my nerve endings. "Do you actually want to? Or are you just distracting yourself from what you really want?"

Her sharp nails slide along my jaw and under my ear, right into my hair. "Both."

"You can have your cake and eat it too."

She shakes her head, nose almost skimming mine. "It could be poisonous," she whispers glumly.

I move in more, feeling her breath coast over my scruff. "Then we'll take the antidote together."

"I can't do that to you, Jax. You know that." She slips away, pulling her leg in and jumping down to the floor.

I don't want her to feel pressured. But I also don't want her to think it's a deal breaker and feel bad about something that's out of her control.

I'd never think any less of her. I never have.

"Remember, keep your finger off the trigger unless your site is lined up on your target."

"I know how to shoot a gun, Jax. Who do you think used to help my dad bring all the meat in for the wolves?"

I smile at her, eyeing the way tendrils of raven flow around her face as she treks up the driveway she escaped from two days ago.

Eli and Shiloh are in front, domes vulnerable and easy to take out.

I'll push my goddamn pride to the side and admit they're good dudes that got caught up in horrible shit. They did what they could to survive and found roundabouts through the fuckery that was instilled.

I still want to carve Shiloh's tongue out for marking my girl like that. He had no reason to go that low on her chest.

You're just pissing yourself off when you should be vigilant.

I look away from the back of his head, taking in the cluster fuck of trees encasing the stone stairs and the circle drive full of trucks.

"Fuck," she curses under her breath. "His SUV is gone."

I scan around the blanket of white, gripping around the handle of my pistol and pulling it from my waistband.

"What? A bunch of oafs live here?" Viper quips behind us.

"Oafs indeed," Eli grumbles quietly.

Hiking up the snow dusted stone, I almost laugh at the image of Tala pushing his old, naked ass down them. But the vile images of what horrors this house contains eats away any humor.

Her fingers hook into my waistband, gripping on for comfort.

"You got this, little wolf. You have eyes all around you."

Trepidation radiates off her the rest of the way up the two flights of stairs. We come up to a landing around the entrance of a dark brick, bizarrely shaped house.

It screams sinister.

The eerie wind blows the unnerving feeling around, smacking me in the face with the reality of this is where Tala was fucking taken. This is where she was most definitely battling anxiety while being transported into the haunting darkness.

Shiloh creeps the door open, Eli checking overhead, and Viper and I scanning around the goddamn trees.

They swallow the place. Even with a drone you wouldn't get a single shot of anything besides maybe the circle drive.

The gut twisting stench of rot wafts out as he pushes the door wide open, and Tala spins around, covering a gag with the sleeve of her shirt.

Unfortunately, I'm accustomed to the foul smell. But it's still fucking sickening.

"Viper can stand out here with you," I say quietly, standing in the doorway.

"I'm fine." She waves her sharp nails through the air, then pulls her sleeve over her hand, pinning it over her mouth and following me in.

I internally laugh, scanning over the eight bloated bodies lying around the living room. They all have knife wounds to their domes.

Slayed during their slumber.

Using her free hand, she laces it with mine, eyes watering from the rancid odor fuming up to the high beam ceiling, and she tips her head towards the stairs.

I can only assume what that hallway contains.

Firmly holding her hand, gun at my side, I sidestep up the stairs, noticing the way she intentionally misses two of them. And it boils my fucking blood that she had to stoop to stealth out of fear of what would happen to her if she were seen.

Eight doors line the straight stretch, four on either side. I open each one, scanning around the empty bedrooms aside from three bodies, the last one being absolutely mutilated.

"Riley. She was excited to go," Tala whispers.

I nod, moving along to the left turn.

How do I already know this is where they kept her?

Any scrape of moisture depletes from my mouth, and she turns the handle, squinting up at the unsticking noise that comes from the top of the door as she pushes it open.

She rushes in, lifting up the mattress that only has two white sheets and a hard looking pillow.

The mattress she was on in the video that was sent to me.

My lip twitches, black spreading around my vision and sweat beading up through my pores.

I am so fucking sorry.

I rub over my mouth, glancing around the bare walls I know drove her fucking nuts. She whips out a piece of paper, then speeds over to get behind the door, picking up the boots I memorized the sound of.

"Did you bring your gas cans?" she asks softly, exiting the room.

"Mm-hmm. They're in the truck." I step in line with her, focusing on any sounds.

But it's dead silent. Even her steps.

Getting back downstairs, we pass Eli, Shiloh, and Viper standing on guard around the living room and stride through the kitchen.

Taking the side hall, I huff at the spin lock on the back door. Ire explodes within me, running rampant under my skin and spiking my body temperature.

I have to force myself to breathe through it, otherwise it'll get the best of me, and I might start beating the drywall in.

She points to a lone door on the left while peeking through the open bathroom.

I grab the handle, slowly cracking it open with my gun raised and ready.

There's no mistaking the blue bug eyes that are staring at the door. With no hesitation, I shove it open and point my gun at the bitch that took off with Brutus.

She screams, crawling backwards up the bed, and I move in, ready to shoot her in the strawberry hair I'm so fucking sick of seeing. "Get your ass up," I demand sharply.

In the blink of an eye, Tala is mounting the bed and sending a roundhouse right to her temple, knocking her the hell out. "Took too long," Tala mutters, snatching her limp head up by her hair.

Am I... Am I getting fucking hard right now?

I watch in shock and unholy desire as she tosses her dead weight into the floor, sending her face first.

She doesn't need a weapon. She *is* a weapon.

I put my back to the door, keeping an eye on all entry points, the other on the way she's flipping her body over. She looks around, doubling taking my waist.

I know what she wants.

Using one hand, I pry my belt buckle open, slipping it through the loops and observing her wariness flash into lust. "Attagirl," I growl, tossing it over to her.

She catches it, the leather cracking as she whips it down, and starts binding Valerie's hands together. In a prayer.

I'm sweating bullets from how hot she makes my blood run.

"It's so gross how they came back here and were living with those bodies," she rasps, dragging Valerie over to me. "Do you want the bitch, or my boots?"

I kind of want to see her departure method for sending unconscious bodies down the stairs.

I hook my free hand into the belt, feeling her fingers slide over mine with the switch off. "Baby, I'm having a hard time thinking about anything other than you saddling my face and riding my tongue right now. I need you to stop being my sexy, little samurai for just a moment so I can think straight."

A light laugh slips through her nose, a foxy grin curling her pouty lips up, and she bends over to pick up the paper and her fuck-me boots from the floor.

I bite my lip, distracting myself from dropping Valerie and reaching out to smooth a hand down her curves. Iron bursts over the tip of my tongue, and I tear my eyes away before I end up adding another unsolicited touch to the walls that have seen it all.

She straightens her spine, snapping a look of panic back to me. "Did you guys get the trackers out of the dogs?"

I glance at her paper, and a stitch runs through my heart as I take in the map she drew of what I'm assuming the back is. She even drew doghouses and chains. "Yes, ma'am."

I'll tell her about Dr. Zion going by the ranch and how the dogs are all living their best lives once we're not in a place where possible ears could be.

Dragging Valerie to the putrid living room, I guess the stench zaps her little brain awake. She shrieks and starts thrashing around—doing nothing to break free of my hold.

"Let me go!"

"No. You've made the wrong enemy, Valerie," I grumble, hauling her out the front door. She blubbers, glassy eyes darting around everyone. "Don't look at anyone besides the raven-haired vixen behind me. *She's* the one you should be shitting your pants over."

I won't be a total dick and shred her back open.

She's a little silly upstairs and thinks they're in love.

So, I curl my arm up and let her bare feet stumble backwards down the stairs.

Tala's teeth chomp behind me and Valerie screams bloody murder, eyes wide the fuck open like a slasher is after her.

My lips tighten, harboring the laugh that's tingling my chest. The debilitating self-loathing has it dissipating as fast as it came, and I huff to myself, tuning out Valerie's thrashes and cries while walking her backwards.

Viper, Eli, and Shiloh stay back with the nut job while Tala and I coat the house in gasoline. She has me follow in her steps to the barn of horrors, the gym where she was pitted like a dog, making our last stop at the doghouses.

She rips the chains out of the ground, coiling them in her hands while I pour the remaining gas over the tiny houses that provided little to no shelter against the glacial weather.

I let her do the honor of striking the last matches.

She smiles, watching each orange flame sway, flicking them to all twelve dog houses.

"Will you take me to the ranch?" she asks, not looking away from the second doghouse on the left.

"Whatever you want, baby. I'm there. Is there someone you're wanting to bring home?"

Not tearing away from the flames rolling through the white canvas, she nods.

CHAPTER TWENTY-THREE

TALA

Eagerly hopping out of the truck, I scan around the ranch in utter awe. The cabin itself is stunning with warm logs designing the exterior and a large porch that has a breathtaking view of the mountains in the distance. The acreage is open, sporadic trees filling space and providing shade for the dogs in the summer.

I was really concerned about the possibility of Brutus weaseling in here and getting ahold of the dogs. But the massive wooden fence surrounding the property and influx of visible cameras depleted the high waters of paranoia. The password to get into the gates took Jax a solid two minutes to enter. Even if someone did know it, they'd be caught on camera and shot in the head before getting halfway through typing it.

The snow crunches under my furry boots, ambling past Leon thundering down the front porch steps with a big smile.

The ranch is so much more than I expected. I knew Jax would have the dogs set up right. But he created a haven for them.

There are dogs filing in and out of the barn that's emitting a cozy glow, tails wagging at warp speed as paws drift through the snow, kicking it up into the gentle breeze.

"Ah? You dig it, mija?" Leon asks ardently, running up to the side that's not occupied by my silent shadow.

Jax is just watching me. Obsessively observing every micro-expression of mine.

"It's perfect, guys." I look over both of them, knowing both of their hearts get poured into this. "Why go through the adoption process if they're happy here?" I ask curiously.

Walking closer to the fur zooming around, Jax says, "To give them a family. Here, yeah, they have each other and Leon, but they don't have their own humans. They don't have someone to be attached to, to go on walks with or play fetch with. We've only had one dog get returned out of his own unhappiness with the move. The rest are happier and getting fat as hell. We get sent updates and go by their homes just to ensure the dogs are actually being taken care of."

I somehow fall harder for him every single day.

The buzzing under my skin is pleasant, activated by the love that continues to grow for Jax Scythe.

"Who was returned?" I ask, petting a scarred, boxy head in passing.

Using a long, tattooed finger, he puts at the two Dobermans chasing each other. "Gemini, he's the stockier one. I was actually going to see if you'd get along with him a while back."

"Ah, I remember that. I was excited to see her and you showed up without raven hair."

Gemini's playing with Killer.

I stop a few feet away from the heart-warming sight, chest swelling tenfold as Sirohi zooms up to them. Watching three sets of pointy ears run around, I slide my earmuffs down the back of my neck, wanting to hear the sound of peace better. "Why didn't you bring me?"

"Because he threatened to kill you," Leon rushes, a hint of a grudge edged in his tone.

A laugh ruptures out of me, and I turn to the scowl aimed at Leon. "This is where you were wanting to bring me?" His obsidian eyes slide over to me, instantly softening with a nod. "We need to go back to the storage unit at some point. I'm honestly not sure if that bike will work with how long it's been sitting there," I ramble, fixing my attention back on the dogs.

"We'll get it started, and I'll teach you how to ride," Jax drawls lasciviously.

Desire warms my cheeks, a lewd comment rushing to the tip of my tongue. I swallow it down, peeking at the flustered face next to me.

Swatting my hair over my shoulder, I focus on the reason for coming. "They're playing with Killer." I point lazily. "He saved my face from snapping jaws."

"Hmm," Jax growls, containing a blow up that's sizzling his skin. "What do you mean by that?"

"Ah," Leon chimes anxiously. "I know I should've shown you the second I saw it. But with her being home… I just wanted to take it down and let everyone move on."

"What. The fuck. Did you see, Leon?"

I'm not surprised it was recorded. But I really don't want Jax seeing that. So, I'm crossing my fingers that Leon wiped it away completely.

"Tala and Brynn fighting with dogs in the ring," Leon says with bated breath, curling his lips down in a cringe.

An aggravated breath thunders from Jax, kind of startling me and making me side-eye him.

"You better have a backup of it," he warns, then laces his fingers with mine and whistles at the dogs. Their ears perk up, beady eyes darting to the apparent dog whisperer. "Come on, boys. Let's go home… We have a monster to catch," he finishes with a muttered breath.

With Brutus being on the loose, it's safer for everyone to stay together at Jax's house. Therefore, I brought all my pillows and blankets, some more clothes—and even some rugs.

Jax doesn't mind in the slightest. I actually think he likes it. Viper seems to as well. He's rolling around on the fur rug in the living room with Gemini.

Jax is in the studio room with Eli, probing Valerie for answers on where the hell Brutus could've gone, and Leon's sitting at the island, still trying to track that Ashton guy.

Apparently, he's not even in Anchorage. Or Alaska for that matter. Which is why he's jumping through hoops trying to find him.

Shiloh… I haven't spoken a word to. He's usually wandering around outside or peering out windows. Maverick is manspreading on the other couch, keeping tabs on *Club Sin*.

Sirohi and Killer are laying their sweet faces on my crossed legs on the couch, and Nadia is filling the wine glasses Brynn's dragging out of the kitchen cabinet.

They'd probably have dust on them if Jax wasn't a clean freak. I'm still appalled over taking his virginity. I know he doesn't lie, but no one moves their hips like that without experience.

Must be the training that's consumed his life.

"Tala!" Nadia shouts from the kitchen, mid pour. "Get your sexy bikini on and get in the hot tub with us!"

I shouldn't. But that sounds really nice.

Feeling like shit about it, I gently move the sleeping heads from my lap and haul my ass up from the couch.

Maverick sighs, locking his phone and jumping to his feet. "Stay your ass there, Viper," he grumbles irritably, aiming daggers at Viper attempting to get up.

"I don't think we need a babysitter, Mav. The hot tub is right outside," I say placidly, walking out in front of him.

"You were surrounded by wolves and still managed to get kidnapped, Tala," he counters.

I purse my lips in fairness and take the stairs, each one giving way to the rich voice that gives me butterflies.

While passing the studio room, I glance in and almost choke on the influx of saliva flooding my tongue. He's sitting backwards in a chair, muscular arms resting savagely on the back of it, and gracing Valerie who's strung up by her wrists with the sexiest scowl.

Bitch, you better run and take your birth control.

I quickly walk away from the wet dream and rush into his room. My blood panel results came back and I'm somehow clean, so I can't use that as an excuse—once again.

Grabbing my black bikini out of the dresser, I slip it on, staring at my scar while tying the strings around my neck.

I need to text Paxton.

It's not that I want to run from the memory. I'd just prefer to hide the constant reminder of my fallopian tube exploding and my kidnapper taking me to the doctor.

Six beady eyes pin me down from the bottom of the stairs. I smile, going down the steps and waving to the triplets. "You guys are so cute," I coo, rubbing all three heads as I reach the bottom. "I need to grow a third arm to love on you guys." Looking back up and walking with my Hellhounds, my smile drifts and lets in the self-consciousness.

Leon, Maverick, Viper, and Shiloh are all staring at me, not disguising their curiosity of my ugly scar. "Look while you can. It'll be covered soon," I say dryly, walking right through the cluster of men.

"I think you should keep it," Viper chimes. "It's pretty cool. Looks like you took down a bear."

"Viper," Maverick warns from the sliding door, gun in hand.

I've never seen him hold a deadly weapon before. I know that's ironic, all things considered. But Mav refrains from violence.

He steps to the side as I approach, and I turn around, loving on the sweet faces while stepping out backwards. "Stay here. It's cold."

Guilt runs up my chest while closing the glass door, but the drunken hollering coming from the hot tub puts me in mom mode.

The freezing air nips at my skin, and I hurry over to the hot tub, practically jumping in while flipping my hair onto the concrete so it doesn't get wet.

"Your poison, my queen," Nadia says theatrically, stretching a full glass of wine over the bubbles.

Gaping at it, I take it from her hand, steadily bringing it closer to my face. "I will drown if I drink all of this."

Brynn laughs, cheeks flushed from the wine. "Baby, I had to stop after two sips. I haven't had alcohol in a year and I'm already entering space."

"Whatever you don't want, I will guzzle down like your own personal slut," Nadia smiles, tossing back the rest of her glass.

"I'm sure you have a lot of people in your phone that have that as your contact's name," Maverick retorts passive aggressively, and sits down in the chair next to the hot tub.

Nadia's eyes thin at him. "If my presence makes you so goddamn miserable, Maverick, there's the door," she bites out.

"I'm not out here for you, angel," he counters bitterly.

I take a big ass drink and swallow it down, setting my glass down heavily behind me. "You guys need to fuck, or kiss, or something. I'm so fucking tired of the bickering. It's been nine years."

Nadia smiles cunningly, and I thin my lips, knowing what's circulating in her pretty head. She stands up abruptly, water sloshing and rolling off her toned, caramel body, and suavely exits the hot tub.

"What are you doing, angel?" Maverick asks edgily, gazing at the way she's swaying over to him in her pink bikini.

Brynn plugs her nose and disappears under the water, bubbles of her laughter exploding at the surface.

The wine's already making my face warm. I have to cover my mouth with my hand to conceal my amusement, watching Nadia straddle Maverick's lap.

He's caught in her trance, chocolate eyes not straying from the angelic face getting closer to his. "You're getting me wet," he states languidly, and sets his gun down on the side table, gliding his hands around her hips.

Brynn comes back up, wet hair molded to her head and a bright smile showing her teeth. "I haven't seen something consensual without the influence of drugs in so long. I don't know wha-"

A loud shot pierces through the night air, a cavity appearing in the middle of Brynn's forehead and stopping her motor skills.

My eyes widen in horror and complete fucking shock, unable to move as she goes under—lifeless.

With a high pitch ringing in my ears, the dogs barking against the glass is muffled. I can't tear away from the crimson swirling through the blue water, turning the comforting bubbles into a macabre nightmare.

A hand latches in my hair, painfully gripping at my roots and forcing me out of the water. "That's annoying. That was meant for you," a feminine voice says impassively through my cries of agony.

"Let her go, Kendra," Maverick warns, standing in front of Nadia and pointing his gun—hopefully behind me—as I scuffle to my feet.

Her hand tightens, snapping little hairs and lighting my scalp up with pinpricks. "She's trying to take what I claimed!" she shrieks, shoving the cold barrel to my temple. "Your blanket is really comfortable by the way. Too bad I claimed that too, otherwise I'd bury you with it," she spits into my ear.

Hysteria and volatility run through my veins like electric fire. I speedily step my right foot out, hooking my left one behind her calves and kicking her legs out from underneath her.

The sliding door shatters, the fractured glass flying through the air and clattering as my head gets ripped back by my hair.

"You crazy fucking bitch," I growl, coming down right on top of her and locking my legs around her hips.

A winded groan comes out of her screwed up face, and the crimson dripping through the corner of my eye makes me see red. Metaphorically.

And literally.

The rage constricts my hand around her neck, completely cutting off her oxygen as I grip around the barrel of her gun and yank it from her grasp.

Another shot pierces my ears. This time, a hot vibration rattles my palm. I don't know where the bullet went, I'm in pursuit of rearing the handle through the air. And with all my might, I strike it across her reddening face.

Warmth trickles down the side of my abdomen, tearing my attention away from her unconscious head whipping from the blow.

Oh. Well, that fucking sucks.

Blood drips off the tip of my nose, focusing on the leaking bullet hole that's now starting to burst into a stinging pain across my stomach and back.

Distorted shouting intertwines with the insistent echoes of the dogs barking, and large hands grab under my arms, hastily lifting my body through the air.

Black splotches begin depleting my blurring vision, the pain turning volcanic as I'm thrown into a cradle—faintly seeing the fear that's widening the hunter eyes I fell in love with. "Stay with me, baby." His deep voice thunders into the wall blocking my hearing off.

The pain evolves into pinpricks along my entire torso and the side of my head, my lips becoming unbearably numb. "Did you know she has feelings for you?" I mumble, sinking into his arms.

"Not a fucking clue, little wolf. Keep your Venus eyes on me and keep talking," he says gravely. "Somebody get some fucking towels over here!"

"I'm here, I'm here." Leon's blurry face emerges through the shadows swelling around my pupils.

Even on the precipice of death—I find myself wandering back to Jax. I say a sappy goodbye in my head—just in case. "I love you," I whisper, a warm stream rolling down my cold cheek.

"Don't do that. Please don't fucking do that," he wavers. "I need you, Tala. If you die, I'm coming right with you."

I can't fight the exhaustion eating my body.

Running my fingers over his erratic heartbeat... I succumb to fate, letting my lashes close over the water welling in my eyes.

The fireweed sways in the warm breeze, the western hemlock rattling its sound of comfort from above. I close the cream pages in my lap, looking over at the black fur and amber eyes next to me. "Maiko?" I ask quietly, shock freezing my face.

His head turns, golden eyes meeting mine. A gust of wind carries my hair and thaws out my frozen muscles, and I chuck my book into the grass, lunging and wrapping my arms around him. "I've missed you so much, boy."

I don't feel sadness or grief.

It's warm and happy, and vibrant with colors that don't exist.

CHAPTER TWENTY-FOUR

JAX

My heart stops, watching the most magical fucking eyes close on me, tears slipping through her dark lashes and streaking through the crimson that keeps spreading. "No-no-no. Come on, baby, let me see those eyes," I plead hoarsely, ripping a towel from the pile on the island.

Her raven locks are in the way, so I can't tell what the fuck happened to the side of her head. But it's bleeding heavily down her face and neck.

I apply pressure, doom sinking my stomach as she progressively grows paler. "Someone make sure that fucking cunt gets hung up next to her crazy ass mom!" I shout over my shoulder.

"On it," Eli grumbles, dragging Kendra past the island by her hair.

Snapping my attention back to Tala, I frantically roam her lifeless face, chest solidifying with the boulder working its way up my throat. Leon's firmly holding a black towel to the gunshot wound on her abdomen—and it's getting soaked, her blood spreading on his hand and rolling off her side. Dripping. And forming a puddle underneath us.

The oxygen has been stripped from me. I'm heaving for the air that refuses to fill my lungs, in turn making my head spin like I'm defying gravity and feeling Earth's rotation.

The front door flies open, Dr. Zion rushing in like the savior he is. "What the hell happened?" His voice carries vexation across the house.

"It's my fault," Nadia cries. "I was distracting Maverick and-"

"Playing victim isn't going to save her!" Leon snaps.

I can't pay much attention to anything other than my lifeline growing colder in my arms. The rosiness that makes up her lips is rapidly depleting.

"Set her down. Let me see her," Dr. Z rushes, throwing fucking puppy pads on the island.

I don't want to let her go.

I don't want her to slip away without me holding her.

Stepping over the puddle of her blood, my chest draws taut as I lay her limp body on the island. "I need you here with me," I choke out, and press my lips to her icy forehead.

Dr. Z snaps his gloves on and throws open his carrying case of instruments. "How fresh is that laparotomy?" he asks quickly, shoving packing gauze to the bleeding cavity.

"Three weeks," I answer, grabbing her little hand.

"Leon, run out to my truck and speed back with the heart monitor... She's trying to drift away from us."

Dread constricts my throat, heart falling into a cold abyss of desolation. "Tala! Come on, baby!" I shout gruffly through gritted teeth and lower my forehead to her chest.

I can't feel her heartbeat.

It always thumps beautifully against her sternum. Yet the rhythm of comfort is only a mere tap inside the woman I found home in.

"Hey, Damascus," Nadia sniffles. "I think you might want to wake Evelyn up and-"

"No," Maverick cuts her off. "Give me that, angel. This could be a fucking ploy... I'm sorry about that, Damascus. Everything's fine, just stay extra vigilant and don't let Evelyn out of your sight."

Still holding pressure on her head, I lift my face over hers, and the whites of my eyes get attacked with stinging tears. I swallow through the knot—and let them out. "You know what I think, baby girl? I think you were given Venus eyes so anyone who looked into them could feel love. Even the strongest, most ruthless beast would fall to his knees before you."

A tiny hand rubs my shoulder, and Nadia stands at my side, face blotchy and top lip quivering alongside her heartbroken tears. She runs her hands through Tala's hair, pulling it out from under her and draping raven silk over the edge of the island.

I hate it. It looks like my girl is on an embalming table.

Six beady eyes and pointy ears are whimpering and whining by her head, watching the girl *they too* fell in love with get hooked up to a heart monitor.

"Jax, what's her blood type?" Dr. Z asks.

"O negative. Same as mine."

"Great. We're tapping from the source."

I'd rip my heart out and give it to her if that meant hers would continue beating.

My tears become loaded, muffling the guttural roar that's knocking on my tight chest. Sniffling like a big baby, I close my eyes and lightly press my lips to the pout I haven't felt in three weeks. "I love you, little wolf."

CHAPTER TWENTY-FIVE

TALA

I sit up with fireworks popping on my lips—and tears that are not mine dripping on my cheeks. The sherbet colors swirl together, engulfing my body with serenity—and taking my lost loved one away again.

The stars flickering in the distance beckon me. I'm somehow standing up in the peachy light, feet moving against my will towards the dark blues and vibrant whites.

An ear-splitting beep resounds in my head, my straining eyes lazily cracking open to a light casting a silhouette above my face.

I blink roughly, clearing the fog altering my vision, and my heart begins to burn over the sight of a dangerous man tightly closing his eyes as tears drip from them, his spilled love splashing on my cheeks.

His sharp eyes open, obsidian pools swimming in irritated blood vessels. "There you are," he breathes deeply, a crack splintering through his words.

Jax's arm is strung over me, an IV running from his vein to mine, and Dr. Zion is fishing around in my new wound. Must be pulling my intestines out from the god-awful weight that's twisting and turning my stomach.

Before I can watch more of the gory movie, the Dark God claims my vision. "You're so fucking strong, Tala. Keep fighting and listen to my voice."

Weakly lifting my heavy arm, I trace his defined lips with my finger. "I saw Maiko."

His warm breath jets over the top of my hand, and he blinks roughly, dropping another tear on me.

I cup his face, using my thumb to dry his cheeks. "Did you break the sliding door?" I ask mutely.

He nods. "I didn't want to waste time sliding it open."

I clear a rattle from my throat, amplifying the rasp in my exhausted voice. "So... you just ran through it?"

"Yes, ma'am," he murmurs, gazing deep into my eyes.

He's not human.

I faintly shake my head, amused with the behemoth who can power through glass and walk away without a scratch. Then flashes of Brynn pollute my mind, wiping the half-ass smile from my face. "Did you guys get her out of the water?"

"Shiloh did. He's outside trying to reach her family to proceed with whatever her wishes may be, and Eli and Viper have the circus in check upstairs. Just focus on you right now, little wolf."

"Are Nadia and Maverick okay?"

"We're here, killer."

I tilt my head back to his voice, seeing him, Nads, and Leon.

"I'm so sorry, Tala," Nadia wavers, honey hair stuck to the tears on her cheeks.

"Don't burden yourself with that, Nads," I rasp, then zip my head down to the piercing sting and horrible pressure. "Ow," I whine through gritted teeth.

"Got it!" Dr. Zion holds up a bullet wedged in between metal forceps. "I'll clean it off and let you keep it, Tala. A souvenir for surviving your first shot."

"Okay," I half cry, half laugh.

He sets it down in a metal bowl, reaching over and holding up a curved needle. "I pulled your old man's bullet out in the eighties. I'm sure he still has it lying around somewhere."

I have to look away or I might pass out.

Good thing I have a beautiful distraction hovering right above my face, his dog tag resting in between my collar bones. "I'll take the pain away, baby," Jax says languidly.

My face tightens, sucking in a sharp breath as the needle pierces my skin and slides through. "Mm-hmm," I hum.

His lips part, turning the sizzling pain into frantic butterflies, and he lowers himself down with the perfect tilt, capturing my lips tenderly.

I fervently run my hand to the back of his head, coiling my fingers in his hair and escaping into the dose of ecstasy his kiss gives me.

He lightly groans and pulls back, just to tilt his head the other way and brand the shape of his lips with mine again.

Kissing him lights my body up like a solar flare, shocking my tired soul awake and mending the wounds that haunt me. The coldness that was once lying still over my skin—breaks out into flames.

I'm convinced the narcotic Jax gave me is sending me to Heaven. Honestly, I could be drooling on myself, and I'd have no clue.

I'm light as a feather and stiff as a board.

Slothfully blinking, I track the Dark God sitting down on the end of the bed with an acoustic guitar I've only ever seen on the wall in his bat cave.

He turns to face me, the remorse hardening his eyes not matching his lighthearted grin. Before he can say what's on his tongue, I shake my head, wanting to stop him before he kills himself with guilt.

"You couldn't have known, babe. No one did. And don't let what happened be the compass for future decisions. Your heart was in the right place, and you tried giving her the benefit of the doubt. But you cannot help someone that doesn't want help. She was mentally unwell and facing demons that weren't hers," I say languidly, each word feeling like cotton.

He stares at me quietly for a moment, a light softness easing into his obsidian. Holding his guitar up with one hand, he scoots closer to me and lays down on his back, bringing his guitar over his torso.

"I just don't enjoy the feeling of letting someone off the hook, only for it to bite me in the ass, little wolf." He turns to me, twisting his lips contemplatively. "I thought I was going to lose you, all because I was concerned about some kid ending up in a home like the one I was in. I really didn't give a fuck if she tried to help you. But I knew you'd care."

Wrangling my damn ghost arm out from the blankets, I rake my nails through his hair—just admiring him. "I'm not sure there's anything I can say to help how you're feeling about it. But that's just the thing, Jax… You're feeling. And you're allowing yourself to."

He raises a brow, a faint grin tugging his lips up. He doesn't say whatever cocky remark is brewing in his beautiful head. He adjusts his guitar and begins strumming a familiar tune.

Tears nip at my eyes, a lump forming in my dry throat, and I continue playing with his hair.

Soaking in the sound of *Keep the Wolves Away*.

I don't expect him to start singing. The velvety rich voice stuns me, my eyes locking on his full lips—as if my mind doesn't believe that the Big Bad Wolf is serenading me.

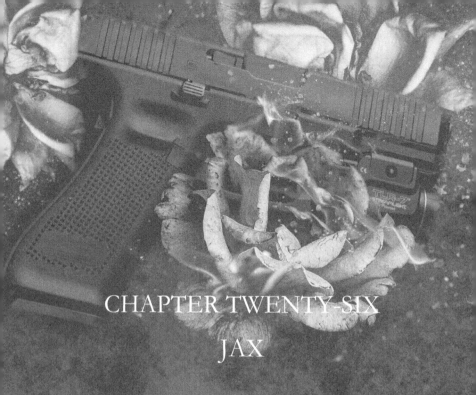

CHAPTER TWENTY-SIX

JAX

I've done a lot of shit. Delivering a sheet covered body to the family of the deceased has never been one.

First for fucking everything. Unfortunately.

The white door opens as I carry Brynn up the front porch, anguish weaseling under my flesh and solidifying my chest.

The short woman with glasses slaps her hand to her mouth, a heartbreaking wail piercing through the air.

I'm not sure why Brynn opted out on getting in touch with her family. She said she needed time. But I think it was more than that. And the bald man appearing behind her crying mother—may just be the reason with how sinister his blue eyes are.

"I'm terribly sorry, ma'am," I say heavily, stopping a few feet from the door.

The embers poking through my hoodie and searing my back make me pin down Mr. Clean who's not focused on his dead daughter, rather my fucking girl who's supposed to be sitting in the truck.

Tala strides by me, lips tight to hold her pain in. Because, you know, she was just fucking shot last night. She wraps loving arms around Mrs. Morgan, and I check back in with the freak who's looking at her like he'd cut off a lock of her hair to sniff it while jerking off.

"I should've made her call. I just didn't want her to feel forced after what she had been through. I'm so sorry, Mrs. Morgan," Tala says wistfully.

"Did she... did she at least have a few good days?" Mrs. Morgan chokes out.

"The best," Tala insists softly. "She was smiling, laughing, enjoying good food and company... Her killer isn't getting away with it. Neither is the man responsible."

While studying Baldy, I catch his sly eye roll.

It pisses me the fuck off. No one rolls their eyes at Tala.

"There a problem?" I defend.

He curls his lips in a wry grin, a wobbly shrug lifting his shoulders. "No problem," he says confidently, his twitching fingers saying otherwise.

I'm not leaving Brynn's body here with him. I don't have a good feeling about it.

"The cremation has already been arranged," I lie smoothly, wanting to chew my tongue off. "Mrs. Morgan, I'd like for you to stay in contact with Tala and let her know your vision for Brynn's funeral. We'll take care of it for you. Once her ashes are ready, I'll personally hand deliver them to you."

"Oh, I couldn't accept-"

"No!" he snaps, ire sharpening his eerie eyes. "Set her down on the couch and be on your way. I think you heathens have done enough."

Heathens? Shit. Haven't heard that since I was like ten. This dude needs to pick up a thesaurus.

"Tala, get in the truck," I demand, not ripping away from the mask slipping from his face. "You're more than welcome to lift the sheet and say your goodbyes. But Brynn's body will not be entering this house."

I note the plethora of crosses hanging along the walls. It makes a good ol' jolly fucking chuckle brew in my chest.

He tries being slick while reaching over, arm getting lost behind the wall, and he whips out a sawed-off shotgun.

But you see… My girl's quick.

The metal clanks deliciously as she whips her matte black handgun out, steadily aiming right at his head.

My brow raises. "Bet you didn't see that coming."

Mrs. Morgan might piss her pajama pants. She's silent, frozen with fear and stuck on the gun strewn across her face.

A vexed growl slips through his bared teeth. "Get the fuck out of here! Both of you!" Like the child he is, he slams the door in our faces, Tala's raven hair blowing back from the velocity.

She lowers her gun, amber eyes darting to me. Her lips tighten, and knowing a laugh is about to bubble smokily out of her—makes me fucking laugh.

With both of us laughing our asses off, we go down the stairs and walk through the snowy yard. "Ow," she titters choppily, bracing a hand to her stomach while opening the backdoor.

Reality smokes me like a freight train, dissipating my amusement. "Get in your seat, little wolf."

Like the good girl she is, she obeys while I place Brynn back on top of the bags of ice in the back seat. I know her wishes are to be turned to ash, but it wouldn't sit right with me to let her rapidly rot while we get our shit together.

Hauling my ass up into my seat, guilt gnaws on my brain, peeking at her stitched-up wound as she checks on it.

I should've just killed Kendra from the start. The Devil was more than eager to and had the metal wire wrapped around one of her legs.

I guess I just have a soft spot for Samuel.

I did some digging last night while Tala slept in my lap. Turns out, they have a loving aunt and uncle in Fairbanks who are already on their way to get him.

I reach over, ever so gently lifting the top section of her hair up. The bullet that hit Brynn lightly grazed the side of her head. It's small, but if it would've been an inch over, she would've fucking died.

Tala's not even upset about the proximity it was to her brain. She's pissed as hell over the "hair it broke off." She has so goddamn much you can't tell she's hiding a shot that was meant for her head.

"I'm okay," she insists, then lays her seat back to relax. "Where are we taking her?"

I pause, knowing she's going to hate what I'm about to say. "The only place we can take her where we won't be probed with questions is Dr. Zion's," I rumble, and she slowly blinks at me. "I know, baby. It's not ideal. But we need Jenkins to come out of hiding. Wherever the fuck he went." I start my truck up, grabbing Tala's new phone from the cup holder and passing it to her. "Nadia's blowing your shit up."

"Stalker," she mutters, shooting me a coy grin.

I stare at her infatuatedly, obsessing over how perfect her design is. "I don't want to miss a breath of yours, Tala. Every flutter of your long lashes, I want to see. Every word that smokes out of your pouty lips, I want to hear. Fuck, I just want to stare at you, baby. I want you in my lap right now... Just so I know that you are really here. With me... To know that you're home."

Her bottom lip lightly curls between her teeth, and she reaches over, rubbing my thigh in comforting strokes. "I love you, Jax. I'm here."

"I love you, little wolf."

Gary Morgan. What an awful name. Looks like he and his buddies were convicted back in the eighties for attempted manslaughter.

They drugged a group of girls, raped them, beat them with bats, and told them to run for their lives through the woods. With a goddamn miracle, the girls made hell for leather and stumbled upon an old cabin to hide out in.

They're alive to this day. And the monsters are walking the streets, working nine to fives, breeding, and getting the white picket fence they don't deserve.

I want to take that luxury from them.

Peeling my eyes away from the blue light fucking my corneas, I look at the goddess who's sitting up in fur, leaning back against animal print pillows while arranging Brynn's funeral on her laptop.

Her long hair's up in a clip and flowing like a waterfall down her back, and she's wearing the silkiest pajamas that show off her creamy skin.

We're going to have to get a bigger bed. Sharing it with three Dobermans doesn't give me shit for room and Sirohi is always wedged in between us. I barely get to feel my girl.

"Don't stack your plate with more than you can eat, Jax." She peeks at me, then returns to her screen.

I close my laptop, bringing my hand over to her and lightly rubbing over the bruises on her upper back. "You know I'm a man with an appetite," I say hungrily.

Drawing in a long breath, her throat bobs with a nervous swallow. "I was thinking maybe I should stay here tomorrow," she suggests, and I tilt my head, brows furrowing tightly. "I don't like leaving the dogs here with the nut jobs hanging up a few rooms down. I know they're constantly being watched, but it takes one slip up and Shiloh seems to be absent-minded lately."

Irritation sizzles my veins. I slide my hand up the back of her neck, using my fingers to push her jaw, getting her eyes on me. "You know him well enough to read that?"

She wrinkles her nose. "No, Jax, I actually don't know shit about him other than him being a ticking time bomb. It's the energy he's giving off. It lingers like a bad smelling incense after he leaves the room. If you want to play the immature game, let's fucking play. Why the actual fuck was Kendra in your bedroom to know what my blanket felt like?"

"Little wolf, I wasn't always around. I wasn't just kickin' back here and hoping you'd show up. Most of my days were spent covering as much ground as I could with Sirohi. Leon was her damn babysitter, but she's clearly a sneaky fuckin' snake."

She closes her laptop and slides it across the fur blanket. "Dad's always told me that snakes are good to have around. But when they start spreading their venom… you shoot them." She gets off the bed, attempting to muffle a wince.

I stack my laptop on top of hers, get off my side, and walk my ass to the door to open it. Gun in hand, she sways her sexy ass right past me, and I follow her down the hall and into the studio room.

With how magnetic she is, all eyes fall on her as she walks in. Viper lingers a little longer than I'd like, but Eli returns his focus to the two dumbasses hanging like heavy bags.

Without warning, Tala raises her gun at Valerie, prompting muffled yelling to filter through the bandanas shoved in their mouths. "Although you didn't grant me the same courtesy, I'll let you say final words to your mom." She reaches her free hand over, ripping out the bandana from Kendra's mouth.

"Jax wouldn't have kept me around if he didn't like what he saw," Kendra sneers, the dried blood on her dome leaking watery with her sweat.

Repulsion tightens my face. I have half a mind to throw my bali through her forehead. But the dead meat belongs to Tala.

"Tsk, tsk," Tala clicks shamefully. "You wasted your goodbye."

Kendra's eyes bug out, and the trigger gets pulled, a pop echoing around the room as a bullet bites through Valerie's forehead.

Good fuckin' God. This is the woman that wears my blood. The siren I lay with at night. The damn masterpiece I get to marry.

"I'm going to fucking kill you!" Kendra spits. Legitimately. Swinging around like a rotisserie chicken from her wrists.

"Didn't you already try?" Tala tilts her head, raven silk flowing with the movement around her shoulder.

Thundering steps bolt into the room, Nadia and Maverick both sliding across the floor in their socks, still wearing their slumber on their faces.

"Holy shit," Nadia says breathlessly, tired eyes widening at the sight of Tala freshly killing someone.

Tala barely pays any mind to them. She's pinning Kendra's red face down with golden, bedroom eyes that are pervaded with murder.

Goddamn. I kind of want her to look at me like that.

It's making my dick tingle.

"You knew all along where Brutus lived, didn't you?" Tala asks. "That's why you yelled at Jax. You knew the river was safe to walk over as long as you didn't linger on it. You knew he'd fall through if he stopped. You didn't want him to get too close without being able to warn Brutus, Pyro, whatever the fuck you call him."

I think my girl exceeds my analytical thinking.

"You're just now piecing the puzzle together?" Kendra snickers. "Your uncle said you were dumb but-"

"The fuck did you just say?" I bark protectively, the mirrors carrying the boom of my rage.

Kendra jumps like a little bitch, and Tala's hand raises to me, eyes still ensnared to Kendra. "I guess so. Usually when there's shit on my shoe, I don't think too much of it, I just wash it off... But you stink," Tala hums.

Honey brown hair flashes out of the room, a throaty laugh exploding in the hallway.

I'd probably find amusement in it too if I wasn't so pissed off. It boils my blood that people think they can talk to her like that.

Tala aims her barrel at Kendra's stomach, firing off a shot that makes Kendra's head fall back in between her shoulders on a crybaby scream that splits my ears.

"Where are Brutus and Enzo?" Tala snaps.

"I don't know!" Kendra wails toward the ceiling. "I know Mayor Jenkins has a hideaway in Maui. He's been there ever since the Guildon's house was set on fire," she strains out.

"Oh, baby, you hear that?" I ask, her sultry eyes sliding over to me. "Looks like we're going to Hawaii." I flash her a sharp smile.

"Can I go?" Viper asks, another shot resounding in the room.

Tearing away from the bullet hole in Kendra's forehead, I look over to Eli and Viper, and Shiloh who apparently snuck in the room. "I need you guys to watch the ranch, take care of the dogs and keep your heads on swivels. I'll triple your pay and make sure you guys are set up for a couple of days. But when I call or text, I expect an answer."

They nod in agreement with no odd mannerisms being displayed to make me wary.

"Don't fuck up," I warn

CHAPTER TWENTY-SEVEN
TALA

Beelzebub's flies are swarming my chest and lungs. I should be thrilled while packing for Hawaii. But Jax took Shiloh with him to go kill Gary and his friends, and who knows when they'll be back.

A cold, wet mark blooms on my thigh. I look down at Sirohi, running my nails over his head. "How do you cope with the anxiety of not knowing if you'll see him walk back through that door?"

His beady eyes just stare at me, a light whine traveling up his throat.

"Yeah," I breathe pensively. "That's about where I'm at too, boy."

Killer and Gemini are sitting outside the closet, backs turned to me and watching the bedroom door intently.

I give Sirohi another scratch and hit the light off as I walk through the gap of my guard dogs.

With Cerberus on my heels, I collect my phone from the end of the bed, frowning over the notifications only being from my mom.

She and Dad are doing really well by the way. The wolves are happy and safe, and for some reason she felt the need to let me know that their "alone time" has been "eventful."

I didn't need to know that.

I still haven't told them about almost dying on puppy pads. I have a lot of truth to spill. I just don't really want to. At least not right now.

The boys follow me through the hall, down the stairs, and into the kitchen. Leon's in his designated spot at the island. He's still tracking Ashton and thinks he might be in Canada now. He's also running feeds in Maui to see if he can decipher where the hell the mayor's hideaway is before we leave tomorrow.

"Mija, will you convince Jax to let us have some fun in Maui?" he asks persuasively, shooting me puppy eyes.

Leon is ecstatic to go. I think it's really sweet that Jax already had him included in the plans when it formed in his mind.

I laugh, opening the fridge for the vase of water. "Leon, I just have to look at Jax and he says "yes, ma'am." I attempt his subtle accent, amusing Leon with it.

Snatching a cup from the cabinet, I spin around and start filling my glass across from Leon at the island. "Can I ask you something?" I question wearily, and quickly shove the vase back in the fridge, cringing at the package of chicken feet.

"Si, querida. Anything."

I take a drink, trying to form my words correctly. "Are you upset that I killed Kendra?"

His brows knit, and he stretches back in his stool. "Not at all. You reap what you sow, mija. I really did believe she was in need of escaping that life. I offered to give her and Samuel new names of their choosing and help get them set up somewhere away from here. I could've gotten her an incredible job and she chose to ghost me… I thought she was in danger. Turns out, she just knows how to splice and move undetected. She played with us."

"Why didn't you answer her call the other day?"

Yeah, I heard her stutter as I was flying out the door, thinking Jax might've possibly taken interest or some shit in her. It just didn't make sense as to why she was around. That is until he actually spoke to me about it and didn't freeze up like he was guilty.

"Ah… I kinda saw it coming. Not her trying to kill you, otherwise I would've said something. But I caught her snooping around your guys' room and had a feeling that tiny crush wasn't reciprocated… I still have no idea how she got weird about Jax. He treated her like shit."

I'm happy Jax wasn't cordial to her. But I'm also sad that Leon developed feelings for someone just for her to turn out to be batshit.

Stepping around Gemini, I round the island glumly, stretching my arms out. He smiles, welcoming the soft hug I wrap around his shoulders. "I'm sorry, Leon. You're destined for a special kind of love. The universe knows that," I say quietly, then pull away.

"Thank you, mija," he croons. "You always smell good. What is that?"

I laugh, walking back to the fridge to start dinner for the humans and dogs. "My secret weapon," I hum, glancing at my phone on the counter.

Still nothing from Jax.

"Ah, okay. I see how it is," Leon teases.

I make the dogs their bowls of brain, liver, feet, pumpkin puree, egg, and some more nasty shit. After scrubbing the hell out of my hands and giving them fresh water, I start making steak, steamed broccoli, and baked potatoes for the army that lives here now.

Making small talk with Leon as the food cooks, Nadia busts through the front door, a huge smile stretched on her angelic face, and both arms full of bags. "I got us slutty stuff!" She kicks the door closed behind her, only reminding me that it's dark and Jax still isn't home.

The bags smacking each other as she scrambles to the kitchen distracts me from having a mental breakdown. Sirohi booping my leg does too.

I need to get him a service dog harness and take him everywhere. Sometimes I'll be on the verge of tears trying to decide what ice cream to get. Even though I always end up with strawberry.

"Where's Mav?" I ask, watching her throw the bags down by the fridge.

She flutters her fingers towards the door. "He was on the phone and took too long to get out of the car."

I nod, and swivel around to flip the ten steaks I'm cooking all at once.

"What do you do for work, Nadia?" Leon asks.

"Eh, just some interior design stuff. It's mostly online. Look at this!"

I look away from my stress, over to the asymmetrical, mesh wrap dress she's holding up with a smile.

"I got it for you because your curves would look bangin' in it! Your one fallopian tube better be primed and ready this time."

Leon's hand smacks to his mouth. But I find it hilarious and laugh, turning the stovetop off. "Thanks, Nads. I'll have a word with it tonight."

"Anything for you, my queen. I'll set your bags on your bed for now. I want a slutty fashion show later."

I think I smile. I'm beginning to get in my head over how long Jax has been gone. Him giving me his direct blood flow has made me clingier.

While making everyone's plates, Eli comes in through the new sliding door, holding fresh wood in his arms. "Hey, Eli," I greet him sweetly, getting a small head tip in return. "Dinner's done. I'll set your guys' plates at the table."

He tosses the wood in the fireplace, practically sprinting back to the kitchen. My eyes widen at his speed, holding his and Viper's plates in my hands.

"That's not necessary, Tala," he rumbles, taking both plates from me. "Thank you for feeding us. I'll never decline a meal. But I'd prefer to take the steps to grab my plate."

"Okay," I say, offering a lighthearted grin.

I know it's because the girls were expected to make the meals, set the table, and clean up after the feral dogs.

He gives me a polite nod and walks off to the dining room. Viper appears from somewhere. I'm not sure I want to know what he was doing. I passed by the hall bathroom last night to get water, and I accidentally saw him jerking off in the dark.

Why did he have the door open? No fucking clue. Why he was in the bathroom and not his bedroom? That's an even better question.

"Thank you!" Viper shouts aggressively, hauling ass to the dining table. I just smile some more, passing Leon his plate.

"Thank you, mija."

"You are so welcome," I say mechanically, overwhelmed by everyone's gratitude over a simple meal.

I tap my nails on the island, robotically handing Nadia and Maverick their plates—just staring at the door.

"He's okay, killer. I promise." Maverick flashes his pretty smile, grabbing a ginger ale from the fridge.

Not saying anything, I stab a piece of steak, gingerly swirling it in the puddle of sauce.

"Mija, come sit by me. I'll show you where we're going to be staying."

I trill my lips, sliding my plate across the island. I have three shadows that follow me over to the other side, sitting on their haunches around me as I sit on the stool next to Leon.

My breath is instantly stolen.

The resort itself is gorgeous, and the little beach house that we'll be staying in is right next to the water, secluded by palm trees and vibrant flowers.

"Leon, did you choose the most extravagant place in hopes that Jax will extend our stay for pleasure, rather than business?"

He curls his lips to his teeth, flicking his eyes to me and back to the screen. "Ah, I hope there's some pleasure in Maui," he says lewdly.

I hope for his sake there is. I personally cannot fathom the idea of taking Satan's monster cock for at least a few months.

Speak of the Devil.

Fiery tingles spark across my back, dark spices floating warmly around my face.

A tattooed hand slides over my chest, caressing up my neck and caging snugly underneath my jaw. My stomach flips, and he tilts my head back to the sharp features of a god.

"Miss me, little wolf?" he drawls, voice deliciously deep.

I nod, not willing to use my strained larynx. I catch the clear plastic on the side of his neck and whip out of his grip, swiveling around to inspect it.

He smiles sharply, satisfied with my interest. "The wolves ate well today. We didn't even cut their bodies up. They were ready to rip apart limbs."

I stand up on the footrest, gaining some inches so I can see clearer.

"It was... something," Shiloh says tonelessly behind me.

My jaw is on the floor, marveling at the cherry red lips tattooed over black ink. It drops even further as he casually pulls a dark bouquet of dead flowers from behind his back.

Stunned, I stare at his face, catching even more fucking plastic. I comb his hair back, tilting my head to see the small dagger with raven wings as the handle tattooed close to his ear.

"What the fuck, Jax? I would've gone with you," I whine.

"It was a surprise, baby. Where do you want your flowers?"

I plop down on the stool, getting way too close to the metal teeth containing something I'm not ready for—but want. "You can set them down next to me. I'll find a home for them. Thank you." I swivel back around, tightening my eyes and lips so I don't moan in the middle of the fucking kitchen.

"Thank you for dinner, Tala," Shiloh says placidly.

I forgot he was there.

I relax my face, flashing him a smile as he walks off to the dining room.

The demon sits next to me, reaching over for the bite I stabbed but didn't consume. "Show me those pretty jaws," he demands, bringing the fork to my mouth.

My chest burns with nerves, and I open my mouth, watching his lids grow heavier as I curl my lips to the metal. Garlic butter and the blend of sweet and salty bloom over my tongue, capturing the slice of meat and pulling my mouth from the fork.

He groans in contentment, biting his bottom lip and piercing another piece. Bringing it to his own mouth, he salaciously bites it off, intentionally flashing his canines.

You... are so fucked.

CHAPTER TWENTY-EIGHT

JAX

Squealing and chunky sneakers skittering across the salted pavement has me deadpanning at the suitcase I'm pulling out of my trunk.

"Angel, it's four in the morning," Maverick sighs.

"I'll jump around with you, Nadia," Leon chimes.

I rip the suitcase out, turning around to the sight of two grown adults jumping up and down in the light spearing out of the private jet's door. Maverick locks eyes with me, exasperatedly shaking his head.

"Not everyone is dead inside, babe," Tala rasps while closing the trunk. She winces, and then pretends like her abdomen didn't just electrocute her.

I follow behind her and Sirohi, doing nothing to stop my hungry eyes falling down her body.

I even tilt my fucking head, in utter shock with the way her bodysuit flaunts her hourglass curves.

Stopping halfway up the boarding stairs, she looks back at me, fully catching me in the middle of eye fucking her. She zips away nervously, fleeing the scene and up the remaining steps with Sirohi.

My chest constricts with a small laugh, and I pass our suitcase off to the pilot. "Appreciate it, Flynn," I say politely, and walk my ass up the stairs.

Met him back when I did the hits in Russia. He's quiet, but he's a cool dude. He doesn't ask questions. He just picks you up and drops you off. I'm able to bring my barrels and blades without him poking around through my shit.

The warm glow is raining down on my vixen, her furry boots draped over the armrest of the seat in the very back. I walk past Sirohi who's staring at her from the floor, and I run my hand over her knee. "You know where your seat is."

She scans down my body, burning my skin with her eyes of fire and caressing my bones.

I need her on top of me as soon as possible.

I wedge my hand under her bent knees, bending over and wrapping my other arm around her back. "Easy," she breathes, lips separating as she roams my face.

"I'll be gentle, baby… take it slow," I whisper, easing her up with me.

She rubs up my chest, targeting her lips tattooed on my neck. "What if it hurts?" she murmurs.

I sit down, keeping her in my arms. "I won't let it."

Discreetly inching her face closer, she slightly tilts her head, zeroing in on my mouth. The anticipation of her making the first move weighs heavily in between our faces, and my heart skips a beat.

She's about to ice the cake, press her coconut gloss to my lips—and fucking Leon leaps into the seat in front of us.

None the wiser to the tension he just interrupted, he whips his laptop out and cracks open an energy drink. "Alright, man, where you hidin'?"

Glowering at him, a little hand curls under my jaw, pulling my attention to Venus eyes and a glossy pout. "Why the raven wings on your dagger?"

Lifting her up a little, I adjust my hips underneath her, and smile at the nerves widening her eyes as she feels me. It falls though, and I briefly take in Maverick and Nadia bickering before returning to the grim subject.

"Viper's cousin had a drone flying by the Knik. She wasn't able to keep it up long enough to get coordinates, but the ravens taking off from the trees stabbed a blade into my chest. I knew it was you. I knew you were hurt, or being hurt. So, to remind myself of the blade that no longer bites my heart, I got it tattooed where I'd have to see it every day. Wounds heal and scars fade, little wolf. But I never want to forget my fuck up. I don't want to get so caught up in loving you and being happy you're back in my arms... I neglect the truth."

Venus' functioning water cycle gets restored. She blinks her tears away. Only allowing a singular drop to roll down her largest freckle that's remarkably shaped like a heart. "It's not your fault, Jax. He *legally* purchased us. It would've happened regardless and who knows, maybe if you would've been there... you wouldn't be here. The universe has a funny way of putting us exactly where we need to be."

"Guys," Leon cries, sniffling obnoxiously. "I'm sorry to interrupt something so beautiful. But we have a black-tie Christmas dinner to shop for and a plan to come up with."

"Tonight?" I ask.

He nods, wiping the snot from his face. "It's invite only, so we'll be crashing it. But you won't believe where it's being hosted."

I stare at him, not in the mood to chase a dog.

"The resort we're staying at. The event is under his name and everything. I guess our boy's been livin' it up in Maui with... Anyone? Anyone want to guess?"

"Enzo," Tala states.

"Ding-ding-ding! Tala's our win-" His face drops in horror, realizing he might've possibly picked the scab off a healing wound. "I'm so sorry, mija. That was insensitive."

She furrows her brows. "I'm not made of glass, Leon."

I can't help myself.

I lower my lips to her raven covered ear, smelling her coconut shampoo. "I'll treat your pussy like it's made of glass. Not just any glass, baby. Fragile, stained glass that can shatter from one wrong touch," I whisper languidly.

She shudders, and methodically moves her legs to straddle my lap. I rest my head back, cock stiffening from her weight and the sight of my girl getting hungry. "Be a good boy and I'll put a bow on it and give it to you for Christmas," she says foxily, running her nails up the sides of my head.

"Hmm, yes, ma'am."

She arches her back, bringing her chest closer to me, wafting the intoxicating scent that makes my head foggy. Then, she rolls her pussy over my dick, letting out the faintest moan that she knows will drive me crazy.

"Should I go sit somewhere else?" Leon asks.

Rubbing my hands up her thighs, I firmly grab her hips, the juiciness overflowing through the cracks of my fingers. "That might be best," I answer, not looking away from the snakes turning me into stone.

"You're fine to stay there, Leon," she says smokily, then slides off my lap. "Is the bathroom back here?" she asks, pointing a sharp nail towards the little hall.

I nod, watching a fine piece of art scurry away.

CHAPTER TWENTY-NINE

TALA

"You're so fucking stupid," I murmur to myself, throwing my back against the bathroom door.

My vagina always wants to take charge, even though she was just violated a week ago. Hell, I have a pretty fresh gunshot wound and am still seeing flashes of Brynn dying in front of me.

I'm a whore.

Taking a few steps over to the little sink, I turn the faucet on the coldest setting and hold my hands under the water until they turn red.

You can wash your hands, but you can't wash the black from your soul.

Maybe I should admit myself to purgatory. I've taken the Devil's hand and his monster cock. Therefore, I've fallen in his unholy steps of abomination.

I smack the water off with a numb hand, and rip paper towels down to dry my stinging skin off. I toss them in the trash, give myself a light smack to the face in the mirror, and let out my held breath while leaving the bathroom.

Walking past Sirohi, I glance at Jax looking sexy while typing on his laptop and sit down in the seat across from Nadia. I need to check on Killer and Gemini. They're at the ranch because we weren't sure how well they'd do with traveling. Gemini loves Viper and Killer is acclimated to the tender hands Shiloh and Eli have always given him.

I have to go claim my phone from Jax though…

Meeting Nadia's concerned eyes, I roll my top lip over my septum ring, fidgeting so I don't let my vagina mount the Dark Stallion. "Do you have Viper's number?" I ask. She slowly nods, darting her eyes over to Maverick as if she'll get in trouble. "Will you ask him how my babies are doing?"

"Did you forget your phone?" she questions, one brow hiking up.

Jax's eyes are burning through my clothes.

"It's not in my possession at the moment," I say dryly, refusing to meet the obsidian pools that always get their way.

Her French tips clack against her screen, then she quickly goes back to the website she was browsing. "I'll let you know what he says. What do you think about this?" She turns her screen to me, showing me a halter neck, satin dress. "Do you think my tits would look good in it?"

I hum in thought. "Smash your hands to them, let me see." Without a question, she drops her phone to her thighs, smashing her hands to her boobs and pushing her cleavage up through her V-neck. "Looks great. How are you gonna get it in time for dinner?"

She shrugs, grabbing her phone from her lap. "It's the site Jax sent me. He's ordering all our stuff."

"Alright, folks. You see those seat belts? Buckle them up. We're taking off," the pilot says robotically over the intercom.

Nadia's face scrunches, a laugh slipping through her shocked expression, and her jaw drops. "Oh, my God! We're popping your air travel cherry!"

"Mm-hmm." I frantically buckle my ass in, searching around for a bag in case I start vomiting everywhere.

Of course, Jax is beckoning me as we're about to fucking take off into the sky.

I shake my head, and his eyes sharpen dangerously thin. Growling in annoyance, I unclick my seat belt and scamper over to him.

The moment I reach him, horrifying whirring comes from outside of the jet. I whine, neglecting the burst of pain while launching myself into his lap, and I squeeze around him, hiding my face in his warm neck.

Strong arms encage me, and his rich laugh begins shaking his chest. "I got you, little wolf." His deep voice numbs my panicking mind.

After the bumpy take off makes me bounce on his weapon, we get the clear to roam around—but I stay clinging to my lifeline.

I'm using fear as my excuse to be molded against him, inhaling the whiskey that gives me butterflies.

"Do you want to see the dress I picked out for you, or do you want to be surprised again?"

I lift my head from his shoulder, lingering over his lips as I swivel my head back to his laptop. "I can pick my own clothes out, you know?"

Just as before, I am baffled to see a stunning dress I would pick out myself. Though, I'm more appalled by the price tag.

Whipping back to him, my eyes narrow assertively. "You are not paying that much for lace, Jax."

He shoots a criminal smile. "I already did."

"People will be able to see my bruises and scars," I say dismally.

He rubs up my back, the chills forcing me to sit taller. "Don't worry about that, Tala. You're a goddamn warrior. You came out of battle with marks signifying you survived." His other hand grazes my chest, gently lifting my dog tag up. "Do you know why I chose a dog tag of all things?"

I shake my head, getting lost in obsidian.

"Because you're never alone, baby girl. I'm always fighting for you."

The blue waves are rolling gently, the water swelling over the sand. There's a tropical and salty scent blowing within the warm air. It almost smells identical to the lotion I lather on every day.

Sirohi finishes going pee on the nearest tree to the porch, and excitedly returns to me to walk inside, his nub tail wiggling away.

There's only two bedrooms, so Nadia and Maverick are already arguing over who gets the bed.

I bet they end up in it together. I almost got to witness them cave and kiss. And here we are, in a magical place that welcomes showing off your skin. They're going to rip each other apart.

And I might get ripped to my ass.

Starving hunter eyes are tracking my movement like a predator. He's on the phone with Viper, and I guarantee pornographic images are playing in his mind.

I need to take these damn furry boots off. I thought they'd be the most comfortable for the flight. But they're too damn hot for Hawaii.

Slipping past the hungry wolf, I head towards our room in the very back, and Leon comes out of the bathroom shirtless and in swimming trunks.

The shock freezing my brain almost reaches my face. I knew he had tattoos on his arms, but I didn't expect him to be covered in ink. I'm not sure what all the design entails. I snap my eyes away before my curiosity can get fabricated.

"I'm going to get your requested daiquiri, mija. I'll scope the place out a bit so we can strengthen our plan."

"Thank you!" I dart into the bohemian room, and Sirohi chases after me, thinking we're playing and zooming out in front of me.

Pain smarts on my stomach and I skid to a stop, bracing my hand to the stitches poking through my body suit. Everything needs to come off before I start having a panic attack. It's hot and the Alaskan outfit I have on is not letting a breeze in.

The sliding door in our room leads out to a circular clearing of palm trees with hammocks and a fire pit to enjoy. They said the trail winds through the other houses, ending off with a massive waterfall.

I close the linen curtains, dimming the flash-bang of green that seems to be everywhere, and hastily rip my boots off. Walking past the large mirror, I start peeling my body suit down. Though, my exposed skin doesn't breathe. Instead, it tingles.

Hunter eyes are watching me from the door I accidentally left open. He has seen me undress and shower several times since I've been back. But for some reason—I'm shy as hell right now.

I gulp, and freeze up, unsure about what to do as he walks closer, grabbing the back of his collar and seductively slipping his shirt off.

His ink is so dark and prominent. It's impossible to not stare in awe at the beast before me.

He tosses his shirt to the floor, tilting his head with an intense gaze. "You can touch me, baby."

The temperature spikes, burning my cheeks and drying my throat. His cocky smile pisses me off, and I rip my body suit down until my boobs bounce out. "What time is dinner?" I ask, shimmying the tight fabric from my arms.

Raising his fist to his mouth, he bites his knuckle, eyes eating the flesh from my bones. He roughly drags his teeth over his skin, finishing with a groan that makes me throb. "Five. You have four hours to get ready."

I gasp, and frantically hook my thumbs into my body suit to teeter it off. "Jax, do you realize how long it takes me to do the waves you like?"

A glimmer lights his eyes up, and he lifts a brow.

"Too long, dude. Too long."

His amusement disappears, his resting scowl slowly hardening. "Did you just call me Dude?"

With my body suit still clinging to my ass, I dart around the behemoth, running for the bathroom with my tits out.

It was stupid of me to think I'd get far.

His hand secures my throat, obstructing my windpipe as he pulls me back into his trap. "Jax," I whine, horrified of someone peeking back here and seeing my fucking nipples.

Pulling me flush against him, his other hand draws up my side, and he tilts my head back. "Let me wash that word from your pretty mouth," he grumbles.

As if I'm his puppet and he's my string puller, my lips part and my jaw opens. While he collects his preferred amount of saliva, my nipples tighten into painful peaks from the goosebumps his feathery touch is prompting up my stomach.

Angling his head, a clear bead slips through the small part in his lips. It streams down, breaking halfway and splashing cold on my tongue.

The sweet bead of his DNA starts running back to my throat. Before I can swallow it, his tongue flattens over his bottom lip, and he bends over me, sliding his tongue against mine.

I whimper, latching my fingers underneath his belt and driving my ass into him. His scruffy beard is rubbing my nose and upper lip, his tongue leisurely swiping up to the back of my bottom teeth.

The radioactive thrum pulsing in between my thighs is infuriating. I crash them together, pants of my desperation jetting from my nose.

His lips stretch into a smile above me, and he sucks my bottom lip into his mouth, biting and scraping his teeth along it.

Just enough to leave a tingle as evidence.

"Such a good girl for me," he drawls quietly.

And lets me free of his trap.

CHAPTER THIRTY

JAX

I'm stuck on black lace conformed to the body of a goddess and raven waves that bend harmonically alongside a structured, heart-shaped face.

From below her breasts and down to her thighs, the lace appears to be sheer with creamy silk lining the inside. The dress hugs her hourglass phenomenally, flowing elegantly around her thin heels.

A dress fit for my dark siren.

She stops on the top step, raising a brow at me. I might fucking choke on the influx of saliva that's flooding my mouth.

I get down on one knee on the bottom step, and a wicked smile creeps up my face at the panic widening her smoky eyes. "Do you honestly believe I'd propose to you in a cliché way?" I ask, pulling her lace garter and black balisong out of my pocket.

She exhales, shoulders dropping in relief. "No, but seeing you drop to one knee after staring at me for ten minutes made me question it."

I eye her dress, tipping my chin for her to lift it up. "You won't see it coming, little wolf." Watching her leg come out from the lace, I glide my hand around her smooth calf, lifting her pretty heel up. "Do you remember how to roll out your knife?"

Hanging the garter loosely, I fit it over her heel, using both hands to slowly slide it up her leg.

"Mm-hmm." She rolls her cherry lips. "I still remember all the tricks you taught me. Too bad I didn't have it shoved up my ass when I was kidnapped. I could've gotten out a lot sooner," she finishes with a laugh.

Working the lace up to her thigh, I look up with barbed eyes. I'm not amused with it, but if humor helps her cope—I'll keep my trap shut. She shrugs, her fiery attitude rushing to the tip of her tongue, and I hook my hand under her knee, turning her leg out.

"Jax," she hisses, latching onto the handrail for support.

Keeping my eyes stitched to hers, I lean in and press my lips to her inner thigh. "That's my name, baby." I kiss her soft skin again, this time over the faintest scar from a flame. "It's actually Kintsugi Otake. But I renamed myself before going to college."

She recoils, her waves bouncing around the rosiness in her flushed cheeks. "Were you ever going to tell me-oh, Jax, wait. No, stop." She falls apart, wanting to accept my hand traveling towards her lace thong.

But she's not ready.

I respect her, and stash the black metal in her garter, then stand my ass up. I lick my lips, tasting the sweetness she's made up of and watching her frenziedly smooth her dress back down. "I just did." I smile at her narrowed eyes.

"Your dad named you, didn't he?"

"Yes, ma'am."

"Why didn't you want to keep it?"

I swipe my tongue over my teeth in thought. But I've never been dishonest, and I won't start now. "Because it haunted me. I covered the scars and got rid of the name that once meant resilience but ended up only making me sick." I stick my hand out to her. "Come on, baby girl. We have domes to stab."

Gazing at me, she places her hand in mine and walks down the steps. As her heel meets the other on the last step, I gently yank her arm and spin her ethereal ass around. She yelps and stumbles back, and I throw my arm out to catch her.

"Maybe if you were romantic like that and didn't bitch so much, you'd get laid," Nadia bites out.

I don't have to look to know it's Maverick on the receiving end.

I'm glued to the siren in my arms. God, her fucking eyes. They're draining the golden glow from the sunset, popping in contrast to the cherry red on her lips, and smoked out in a sultry, foxy look.

I unlatch my hand from hers, dipping down to hook under her legs. She laughs, placing her little, tattooed hand on my chest as I stand up and carry her off.

"Maverick!" Nadia squeals behind us.

"You won't be able to find an old man to mooch off of if you have sand caked in your pink toenails," he mutters.

"It's fine, guys," Leon chimes glumly. "I'll hold Sirohi."

I shake my head, taking the trail to the resort. "Don't pick my fucking dog up," I grumble.

Tala peeks around my shoulder, tensing her cheeks to avoid a laugh. I snap my head back, catching him in the act of putting Sirohi back down.

"What? He loves it."

Must be why he's prancing back to Tala and me.

I say nothing. I just glare at him, then continue carrying my goddamn queen through the sand.

I don't care about watching where I'm going. I can't take my eyes off her. I'm curious to know what she'd want for our wedding, what dress she'd pick out, if she'd put her siren waves in her hair or if she'd pin it up.

I groan in delight, shaking my head at her extraterrestrial beauty, and she side-eyes me, raking her pools of gold down my face. "Sorry, baby, you're just so goddamn captivating," I say vehemently.

She deadpans at me. Still hypnotic as fuck to look at. "I won't be captivating anymore if you trip, and I tumble through the sand. Jesus, Jax. Are you even watching where you're walking?"

Warmth spreads over my chest, emitting a laugh that makes her lean back over my arm, pretending to pass out. "I'm not going to trip." I lift the drama queen back up, bringing her in closer to my chest. "You need to sit up, so you don't bust your stitches."

She wrinkles her nose at me, and before she can get feisty, the celestial music filtering from the resort gets her attention.

We pass the pool full of kids doing cannonballs and playing chicken, their squeals and laughter overpowering the music. I catch Tala watching them with a wistful grin, and pangs of guilt zap my heart.

I lower my face, kissing her forehead and rubbing the side of her thigh. She snaps her eyes away from the kids, focusing on the suits and dresses wandering around in the courtyard.

"I have a feeling they're not here. We're probably just wasting our time," she rasps, shunning the emotions I know she'll never speak about.

Walking through the archway made from palm trees, I scan around the faces that are well known for their big donations at the gala. "Even if we did come all this way and leave without them, it's not wasted time, Tala. That's not possible when you're around."

She gazes at me, eyes absorbing the golden hour and twinkling with adoration. Her cherry pout purses deliciously, and she kisses the damn air before turning her attention back to the black tables.

I'm not convinced I can go the rest of the evening without tasting what's on her tongue.

She pats my chest, wanting to be set down. I don't want to let go of her. I quite like having her in my arms. But I stop, keeping her steady as she slips away from me.

A woman with a tablet approaches us with an anxious smile. "Good afternoon," she says modestly, paying even attention to all of us. "I'd like to inform you all that Mayor Jenkins will not be joining us. Dinner is still scheduled as programmed. So please, connect with others and enjoy the champagne."

Her eyes dart down to Sirohi by Tala's heels, and she looks away without saying anything about him.

Tala peers up at me, eyes shouting, *I told you so.*

"Wasn't this event organized by the man himself?" Maverick asks reservedly, shoving his hands into his pockets.

She nods curtly. "Yes, sir. It was. But it seems as though he had important matters to tend to."

Her demeanor tells me she's aggravated about it. So, I'm wondering if she knows what he's actually up to. Because if it really was important his absence would be understandable.

"It's no problem, ma'am. We appreciate you informing us," I say placidly. Even though I'd like to light a cigarette and flick it towards the wall of fucking palm trees surrounding us.

241

It's not her fault though. Maybe if we kill her with kindness, she'll spill something.

Tipping her chin down, she turns on her heels and begins walking away. "One second," Tala says softly, then quickly catches up to her with Sirohi by her side.

"Tala!" I call out.

Not even turning to look at me, she extends her arm back and flips me off.

"I'll go with her," Nadia sighs, and heads their direction.

I don't like her waltzing off without me. But the last thing I want is for her to feel chained down.

Here's to fucking hoping she actually remembers how to swiftly roll her blade open.

I watch her siren ass disappear inside, growing more frustrated by the damn second.

"Now what?" Leon asks, appearing at my side.

I huff, tearing my eyes away from the open door. "Walk around, pretend to be interested in conversation, see what we can figure out," I say irritably.

Leon smiles, adjusting his tie and scanning around. "Leave the chicks to me, man. I'll work my Latino charm."

I shake my head, watching the dude stroll off towards a group of dresses sipping on flutes.

Twenty minutes go by of us entertaining yapping traps, bullshitting our way through conversations that lead nowhere.

And Tala still isn't back.

I excuse myself from Maverick and some old fuck's conversation about the financial opportunity behind film and walk my ass across the courtyard.

Getting inside the resort, my attention gravitates to the siren brushing a raven wave from her eye, holding a flute of champagne up to her cherry lips. She's still chatting up with the woman from earlier and Nadia's swaying the attention of Ben Roland.

The man that bought every single piece of art that was displayed at last year's gala.

I stand by the door, shoving my hands in my pockets—watching the siren use her enchanting charm. She appears to be getting somewhere, given the relaxed state the woman is in now.

You get to sleep next to that enthralling creature every night.

She whips her hair from her face, turning to pin her insatiable eyes on me. And my fucking knees turn to paper-mache.

I tilt my head, pulling a hand from my pocket and beckoning her with two fingers.

She eye fucks me, then gently places a hand on the woman's arm, saying her goodbyes before walking my way with Sirohi.

"Goddamn," I murmur to myself, shamelessly gawking at her wild ass body.

Maverick stops next to me. And I don't have to look to know he's shooting daggers at Ben. He's a relatively calm guy. But Nadia knows how to get under his skin and make him emit a murderous rage.

He never says anything though.

The numbing scent of seductive vanilla immerses me, her pretty hand snaking up my chest and hooking around the back of my neck. Knowing what she wants, I bend down into her haze, stifling an aggravated growl as her lips skim my ear.

"He bet a million on a horse and lost it all. Apparently, he can't even pay for this event. That's why she's wound tight. She's his secretary and has to deal with the assholes hounding her because of his fuck up. Now, pretend like I just whispered sweet nothings to you." She draws back, eyelids heavy and champagne dancing on her tongue.

"Hmm. I don't have to pretend when your voice sends Hell through my veins," I grumble, and rest my hand on the small of her back, pulling her closer into me.

She flashes a white smile, and spins around. Rubbing her ass right against my dick.

And that wouldn't be enough to fucking torment me.

She presses into me, snatching my hand and placing it on her waist.

I meet Maverick's eyes, attempting to not lose my shit and bend her over the bathroom sink. "You have any gambling contacts here?" I ask quietly.

He nods. "I'll give him a call."

CHAPTER THIRTY-ONE
TALA

All three of the guys are pissed off, manspreading on the couch in the living room and going over the next move.

I'm not letting a sweet trip to Hawaii turn sour. Neither is Nadia.

We've been in Jax and I's room, giggling from the champagne and stripping down to our skimpy bikinis. The number of photos and videos we've taken is throwing me back to high school days. Except, we're in Hawaii. We're not stumbling around my parents' house after they've gone to bed.

Nadia gasps, excited eyes landing on me. "Satan's piss," she whisper-shouts gleefully.

Satan's piss is our go to "messy drink." It's vodka and pineapple juice and entirely too dangerous.

Hence why I randomly started objectifying Maverick at *Harvest & Horrors* before Satan appeared out of thin air.

"Okay-okay," I giggle, and flee for the door with her and Sirohi on my heels.

I silently open the door, smacking a sober face on while walking down the little hall. I was going to play it calm and not draw attention to the two rays of sunshine beaming through the tornadic storm, but Nadia's feral ass zooms past me. Laughing.

Maverick huffs, shaking his head in disappointment, and Leon's face lights up.

I'm being hunted by obsidian.

His dress shirt is unbuttoned, exposing the dog tag glistening against his black ink. He rests his head over the back of the couch, stalking my movement as I pass by their manly conversation.

I rip my eyes away, furrowing my brows at the sight of Nadia already having the drinks poured in the kitchen. "Who wants one?" she shouts over her shoulder.

"Jax doesn't drink vodka," I tell her, stopping at her side and propping my arms up on the counter.

"He'd probably drink it from your mouth," she mumbles, smirking while sliding a glass to me.

Great. Now that image is in my mind and making my pussy clench.

I snap my spine straight, raising the glass to my lips for a desperate drink. I know Nads makes her drinks way too strong and I'll most likely black out from this, but the edge needs to be taken off before I drown myself in the ocean.

"Are you going to make it for me, Nadia?" Leon asks salaciously, walking up behind us.

The ethanol is already warming my blood and burning my cheeks. I smile in amusement over my glass, volleying between the eye contact they're sharing.

"If you get on your knees and let me pour it in your mouth," she tests him.

Eyes ensnared to hers, he loosens his tie and smoothly slides it off. I start guzzling my drink, unable to look away from him getting on his knees for her, a flirty smile appearing on his face, his fingers slowly unbuttoning his shirt.

What the hell? What happened to awkward Leon?

I slurp up the last drop of sweet and acidic butane, vision waving and skin crawling with adventure. I have to do something other than watch Nadia pour her drink down his throat.

Not knowing what to do or where to go, I awkwardly start opening the cabinets, searching for a fucking snack or something.

I'm sweating. My skin is melting. And I can barely see anything anymore. Good thing I already wiped my makeup off. Jax would wake up to a damn raccoon that survived Freddy Krueger.

Ending up with the pre-sliced fruit from the fridge, I whisk around to shirtless Leon who is seemingly getting hit as hard as I am. I pop the lid off, stabbing a piece of pineapple with my nail and munching down on it while Leon rips his pants off.

A laugh explodes out of my lungs, and he turns his thin eyes to me, a laugh of his own coming out. "Don't hurt my feelings, mija. I'll cry… Can I have a bite of that?"

I stab a piece of dragon fruit, then pass the tub off to the man standing in his briefs and socks.

Nadia's ogling his dick imprint, jaw slack, and not giving a shit. "Wow," she marvels, getting a bashful grin from him. "I didn't think it would be that big."

I frown, and bite around the dragon fruit on my nail, ripping it off and stumbling away. I chew it up and swallow it, getting lured towards the Dark God in the living room. I have no clue what I interrupted, but I continue plopping down on the rug and lay back.

The ground's moving underneath me and the ceiling's rolling like a wave.

"Damn, killer. I haven't seen you this drunk since high school."

The world spins, panning over to the sly smile on Maverick's face. "I've had a pretty fucked up month, man."

His smile disappears, realization twisting his lips.

I sit up, bracing my hands to the floor so I don't collapse backwards. "I was forced to do cocaine," I admit.

His chocolate eyes blow out, and Jax sits up, elbows propped on his knees and gorgeous hands laced in between his legs like a stern dad. "Excuse me?"

Maybe Daddy does suit you…

I nod, and wobbly stand up. "Don't ever let me do blow when you're around. My other fallopian tube would probably rupture," I titter.

He stands up, stalking over to me with darkness afflicting his eyes. "The fuck does that mean?" he asks callously.

I'm too drunk for this.

Nadia and Leon are sprinting out the front door, likely aiming for the magical water. And I'm getting pinned down with a twitching lip. All because I have no filter when I drink.

I back up, being followed by Satan. "It means my mind was playing porn of you shirtless. I had to alter my hyperfocus on escaping, so I didn't get soaked in the middle of a living room with rapists," I clip, and walk away from the pissed off beast.

I'm not letting his abrasiveness ruin my night. I open the front door, peeking out to make sure Nadia and Leon aren't in the middle of something. They're being cute as hell in the water, laughing and splashing each other.

I step out, close the door behind me, and walk across the porch.

The moon's casting a vibrant glow over the sand and reflecting off the dark water. I know we need to get back and handle unfinished business in the morning, but Maui almost brings me the same peace that death did.

I wish we could stay longer.

"Mija! Get in here!"

A smile rips at my numb face, and I jog through the sand and into the warm water until it reaches my hips. He crashes through the water, wading over to me with a playful grin.

"I've got vodka in me this time. I won't feel the pain until tomorrow when I wake up with a hangover."

I don't have time to react. He speedily crouches down and hooks an arm under my legs, the other behind my back, and I squeal, getting lifted out of the water and spun around. My vision blurs further, and I latch around his neck, giggling—forgetting about the nightmare for just a moment.

"Look, I'm a mermaid!" Nadia hollers drunkenly.

Leon stops Tilt-A-Whirl, letting me hazily watch Nadia swan dive into the water. "Hold your breath," he rushes.

"Uh-oh." I gasp for air and plug my nose, surprisingly getting lifted pretty high for how big my ass is compared to him.

My stomach swirls, flying through the air and plunging into the deeper water.

Suddenly—all noise ceases to exist. I'm swallowed in the darkness. Except, crippling desolation isn't coiling around me like a python, constricting my lungs and killing me.

It's peaceful.

A massive, distorted splash invades my quiet. I spin myself around, scooping my arms out and kicking my feet until sand grazes my toes, and I stand up, letting out my deep breath as I rise through the surface.

Nadia is still flipping around and diving. I might just be missing him because my eyes are lagging right now, but I don't see Leon.

A goddamn geyser erupts behind me, and I lazily look over my shoulder. "Oh, my God," I whisper to myself, gawking at the tattooed behemoth hunting me down a few feet away.

"What the fuck, baby?" he shouts brusquely.

I lift my hands out of the water, turning my palms up. "What'd I do?" I question, fixating on his hair raining down on his muscles.

"You don't play in deep water when you're drunk." Hips rolling like the waves, he comes around my side and stops in front of me. "About gave me a fuckin' heart attack," he grumbles under his breath, then picks me up by under my arms like a wet dog.

I lock my arms behind his neck, my legs encircling his slutty waist. "Is Leon alive?"

"He's fine," he growls, caging me in his arms and carrying me back to the house.

Splashing to my left gets my attention, tearing me away from the droplets rolling down Jax's sultry scowl. Maverick's shirtless, walking out to where Nadia is still playing mermaids all by herself. The black ink wrapping the left side of his back and connecting to a sleeve I wasn't aware of has me squinting my stupid eyes. I think it's a phoenix with flames.

I don't know.

I'm drunk as fuck and didn't even know Maverick had any tattoos.

"I'm sorry for rough housing with you, mija," Leon says grimly from the front porch.

I bow my head back to see him, feeling bad as I take in his pouty expression. "I was having a good time. Maybe we can convince Satan to get us dinner to sober us up and go back out into the water."

He smiles, before he can say anything, Jax hauls me past him and into the house.

It's fun hanging like this. I relax my arms and drop them with my weight, giggling as I dangle in his strong grasp and see Sirohi's upside down face. It doesn't last for more than a second. One of his hands cups the back of my head, pulling me up to him. "You're going to bust your stitches," he says tonelessly.

I roll my eyes at Mr. Party Pooper, gasping at the immediate pop that zips lightning across my ass cheek. "Don't roll your eyes at me or I'll give you a reason to roll them."

"Sir, yes, sir," I purr, flattening my body to his.

My guard is down, allowing the carnal fire to rush through my veins and move my body for me.

His jaw tics, walking us into the bedroom lit up with lanterns and fairy lights. Maintaining his stern silence, he tosses me onto the bed.

I land on my ass first, then flop onto my back. My heart hammers, eyeing the predator standing in the gap of the white canopy hung above the bed.

Hooking my thumbs into my bikini bottoms, I slide them down and toss my wet bottoms to him, biting the smile back as he speedily catches them. Keeping my knees bent, I widen my legs and flatten my feet to the bed. "You can look. Don't touch."

I want him to touch me. But he won't since I'm drunk. So, I'd rather set a boundary, that way I don't overthink and take it personal when he rejects me.

He bends over, sliding his hands up the bed and firmly gripping the sheets at my hips. Marveling at my pussy.

Not caring about the music filtering through the open door, I untie my top and yank it off. "How bad do you want it?" I ask huskily, using his own words against him.

His heavy eyes scan up my waist, over my boobs, and land on my numb face. "Are you teasing me, little wolf?"

I smile cunningly and toss my top to the floor. His eyes darken, reading me like an open book and seeing what's coming next. I cup under his jaw, pulling his eyes down to my other hand slithering towards my clit. The simple touch of my finger rubbing over my pulsing nerves has a whiny moan escaping my lips. He groans against my palm, and I slowly, so fucking slowly, dip a finger inside.

"God fucking damn it, Tala," he growls through gritted teeth, brutally gripping the sheets.

I moan to make it worse for him and slide my wet finger out. "Look at me," I demand.

His sharp eyes flick up, his nostrils flaring.

I smear my juices over his lips, licking my own at the sight of my arousal highlighting the fullness of his mouth. "Taste it," I whisper.

He draws his bottom lip in between his teeth, leisurely sucking my taste off. An aggravated breath thunders in his chest, and he stands up, finally letting the damn sheets breath, and beckons me with two fingers.

The vodka disappears from my bloodstream. In place of it, the scared, little rabbit nerves swarm in.

I sit up, doing nothing besides manually breathing and gaping at him.

"Relax, Tala. You need to shower so the salt doesn't dry your hair out," he says impassively.

My wide eyes fall with my ignorant heart. I know it's not me. But my brain's telling me that it is.

I scoot off the bed, pushing the dick out of my way.

What if he really did have feelings for Kendra? What if he's been lying and he was just sitting at home, letting her sit in his lap while they swapped fucking spit?

I smack myself in the forehead. "Stupid fucking bitch," I mutter, moseying my naked ass down the hall and locking eyes with Leon in the living room.

His jaw drops, and he scurries away before the murderer can see it. I'm too pissed to get enjoyment from his reaction. Otherwise, I'd laugh, possibly feel flattered.

I close the bathroom door behind me, lock it, and let the burn invade my eyes. "Why would he want you? You're disgusting," I snip under my breath, cringing at my reflection.

I walk away from my self-deprecation and over to the shower. As I turn the nozzle, the rain falls from the shower head—and from my eyes.

I take my time lathering my hair and conditioning it, washing my body, and letting my insecurity drain out without anyone seeing.

Must've been leaking straight vodka from my face. The last of my buzz is gone. I'm left with the grogginess and a horrible taste on my tongue.

I'm not convinced it's just the alcohol though.

After brushing my teeth and drying off, I tap the light switch and walk out to Nadia and Leon dancing in the living room.

Jax isn't even waiting for me, or in our room for that matter. You can't expect anyone to help pick up the pieces. You have to do it yourself if you want to avoid disappointment.

Good thing I had gotten used to it.

I pull on a pair of leggings and a cropped tank top, then do something I never thought would feel right to do.

The metal clasp widens, and I lower the chain from my neck, trilling my lips as I set his collar down on the vanity next to our suitcase.

Honestly, he never started making me feel insecure—until he made those comments about my mom. I had the plaguing questions when I saw the red rope. But he immediately eased my mind once he saw my face.

He never said anything about Thanksgiving. Nor has he said anything about the way he viewed Kendra. Maybe it's too expecting of me to assume he would.

I crawl under the covers, reach over for the little remote on the nightstand, and hit the button that blankets me in what I know best.

The darkness that constricts and claims my life as its own.

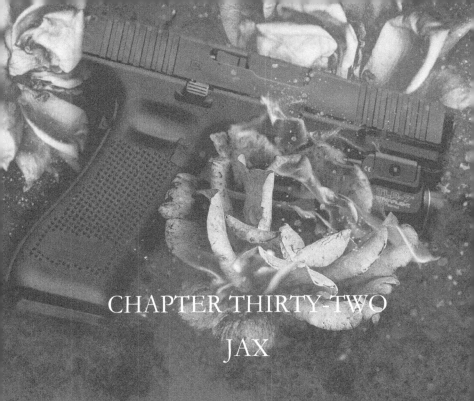

CHAPTER THIRTY-TWO

JAX

Sucking the sweetest form of intoxication from my bottom lip, a wild craving I've been suppressing sparks in my veins.

I can't take advantage of her. I don't care if she fucking begs. I will not do something that might make her resent me in the morning when alcohol isn't overruling her thought process.

Letting a bit of my aggravation slip, I stand my ass up, almost letting the Devil take control and dive me right into her pussy.

I beckon her to sit up, observing the way her sultry eyes widen, the fear racing her heart as she does.

That right there.

That's why I'm not giving her what she's subtly hinting at.

"Relax, Tala. You need to shower so the salt doesn't dry your hair out."

I start to reach out, wanting to carry my ethereal creature to a nice shower and wash her silky hair for her. But she looks at me as if she's repulsed, then scoots off the bed and shoves me. Her little ass can't move me. So, I move me for her.

And once again—watch my girl fly out the door.

Nude this time.

I glower down the hall, ire turning my aggravation into a flaming fury across my chest as Leon's fucking jaw drops.

The bathroom door shuts and the lock clicks, and I whip my belt off to rip my soaked dress pants down before I end up killing him. He's already on my shit list for touching Tala and throwing her out into the goddamn ocean. And now he just saw her pretty tits and sexy landing strip.

I throw on dry briefs, a pair of black shorts, and socks and sneakers, then crack my neck while walking down the hall—so I don't crack Leon's.

Pulling my Zippo and a cigarette from my pack, I tuck the poison in between my lips, stopping in my tracks over this dude bouncing around like a little girl with Nadia.

He's beyond fucked up. Jesus. That's embarrassing.

I shake my head, heading towards the front door with Sirohi. Maverick's on the porch, smoking a cigarette I've never seen him raise to his mouth. I close the door after Sirohi, eagerly flipping my Zippo open and burning a cherry into my stick of cancer.

I've never been to Hawaii. It's gorgeous. Yet it looks bleak in comparison to the beauty Tala holds.

I think she may have ruined sightseeing for me.

Without her, there would be no stars, no planets, no galaxies—no life. *She* is dark matter. And I get to wake up to that incredible sight every day.

"I'm gonna walk up there and get some food," I tell Maverick, ashing my cigarette off the steps.

"I'll walk with you," he sighs, pushing off the railing.

I'm not getting in the middle of his and Nadia's shit. But I'm nosy as fuck and curious. "Why not just tell her?" I ask, walking over to the trail.

Keeping his steps in line with mine, he ruffles Sirohi's head, attempting to put a mask on. "Tell who what?"

I side-eye him, filling my lungs with tobacco.

His lips thin, and he shrugs with a defeated head shake. "It wouldn't matter. Nadia sees men as objects, as toys for her to use when she's bored."

The lights from the resort beam into my fucking eyes, and the music they're playing for the night swimmers makes me want to stab myself in the ears.

I shake it off, aiming my sights on the shack about a yard away in the sand. "Man, I'm not one to say shit about relationships, but I think you need to drop the good boy act and be who you fucking are. Maybe that's what she's waiting for."

He nods, evidently agreeing with me.

"Nice ink by the way. I didn't know you had any."

He checks it out, a humble smile lifting his pouting face. "No one did. Until an hour ago."

I'm not doing tricks for a bone. If he wants to tell me more, he's more than welcome to.

I let the conversation fall off, regretting my choice of bringing Sirohi as a group of little Yorkies start cooing and squealing.

I huff in annoyance, seeing blonde hair whipping around in my peripheral. "Awh! Doggy! Can I pet him?"

"No," I answer coldly, and keep walking to get my girl some food.

"Jackass," she snips.

Maverick chuckles, trying to wipe the amusement from his face. "Is Tala the only woman you've ever liked? I've had women in my office before and you acted as if they didn't exist."

"Mm-hmm."

"Why's that? Just too busy?"

"Honestly, dude. I had it in my head that all women were pieces of shit. I didn't have any interest in getting to know anyone. I had my goal of finding Brutus and taking down as many rings as I could, and I kept it at that. That was until I hacked your shit and broke into your office. Then I became extra busy."

He twists his face, unsure if he wants to question me, or laugh over the memory. He's never been one to pry. And I think that's why we've gotten along pretty well.

He lets out a little laugh, scanning the menu as we approach the shack. "Tala would get a kick out of that. She always told me I was stupid for not taking extra precautions to protect my money. Then, she disappeared for almost eight months," he finishes under his breath. "You know he used to beat her, right?"

"Mm-hmm." Sweat begins rolling down my back, and no matter how hard I fucking try—I cannot fill my lungs. I look over the filter in between my fingers and shove it in my pocket. "I obviously overheard you guys on Thanksgiving, so I know you tried to intervene, but Damascus didn't?"

"He did," he nods. "She was quite literally getting smacked into loving him. She didn't want to listen to anyone. She couldn't. He had her so brainwashed, she stopped going to the sanctuary, stopped speaking to Nads and me… I still to this day don't know what happened. She never did tell us."

It's not my place to say anything. If she wanted them to know, she'd tell them.

We order way too much food that's going to get thrown up everywhere, then head back to the house. The silence between us isn't awkward. It's nice not being expected to hold conversation.

We walk in, not at all surprised to see Nadia dancing and bopping around. But Leon and Tala are both missing from the living room.

I set the food down in the kitchen and stalk down the hall. The bathroom door is closed, the light shining through the crack at the bottom. I turn the handle and push it open, upper lip curling in disgust with Leon white knuckling the toilet seat and vomiting.

I close the door back, sighing as I get closer to the bedroom door that's shut without light emitting from it.

Walking into her darkness, I let Sirohi follow me in before closing the door back. I know the thin blanket isn't doing shit to keep her warm.

Kicking my shoes off, I lift the shitty blanket up and slide in behind her. I fit my body to hers and prop my head against my knuckles to look over her. My brows furrow, and I lean in even closer, getting a stitch in my heart as I see the only thing on her throat being her scar.

I swivel my goddamn head around, spotting the silver chain on the vanity.

What. The. Fuck?

Swallowing down my aggravation, I reach over and tuck her hair behind her ear. Her celestial earrings twinkle enchantingly with the moonlight spearing in. It steals my breath for a beat.

"Please don't touch me, Jax," she hisses silently.

Might as well slap me in the face again with how rough that feels. I roll onto my back—even though it hurts separating from her. "What's wrong, little wolf?" I wait for what feels like an eternity. No response. "Talk to me about it."

Like a goddamn ninja, she rips the blanket off and whisks around, mounting me and tacking the sharp tip of her black blade to my throat.

Thrill explodes under my skin, pumping my dick painfully stiff. I don't touch the succubus. I tuck my hands under my head, enjoying the wild show.

"Did you fuck Kendra?" she asks cuttingly, adrenaline blowing her pupils out.

My face tightens. "You better be fuckin' playin' with me right now, Tala."

"I'm not." Placing her free hand by my head, she moves closer, a wet, raven curtain falling over the side of her body, shadowing half of her face.

"If you think I would ever be capable of doing something like that to you, just go ahead and push your blade in. I don't want to breathe if I'm not making you feel loved."

"Answer the fucking question, Jax," she bites out.

"No," I clip sharply, in goddamn disbelief she'd question that. "Aside from cutting her up for the wolves, the only time I touched her body was when I palmed the top of her head like a fucking basketball and pushed her out the door."

The blade scratches up my throat, scraping through the facial hair under my chin. "I don't enjoy the parasites polluting my brain with obsessive thoughts, Jax," she says smokily, a little crazy in her one visible eye.

I untuck my hands from behind my head, gradually caressing up her unhinging thighs. "What did I do, baby?"

She slides the blade over my lips, her other hand possessing my throat, making the sizzling desire unbearable. "I didn't have them bothering me until you made those comments about my mom. So now, they jump at the chance to eat at me."

I sigh in realization, and she rolls her hips back, flattening her stomach to me.

"I don't want to be with you if this is going to be a problem… Even if that means I have to kill you to get you to leave me alone." She rotates the blade, covering my lips with the smooth side—and fucking kisses it.

I've been letting her own her power. But the rush of blood flow setting my skin on fire is running alongside the frustration with what she just said.

I cup under her ass, speedily flipping us over and throwing my hands out to either side of her head. "You won't ever fucking escape me, Tala. You've already granted me permission to haunt you." I widen my legs, rolling my hips to fit snugly in between her open thighs.

Her lids fall heavier, and she starts slowly dragging the sharp point down my abdomen, her other claws scratching over my shoulder.

"I'm sorry, baby girl. That was fucked up of me to say about your mom. Speaking out of anger has never done me any favors. I should've taken my ass for a walk to cool off."

Rolling her knife around underneath me, she closes the blade and sets it on the bed. "It's not right of me to hold a grudge. Not only did I do it back, I got mad and screamed at you. I let my anger take control and I hit you. I'm really sorry, Jax."

"Hmm," I growl, lowering myself down to her. "I liked it. I wasn't happy that you were upset. But it made my dick hard seeing the fire erupt inside you. You got a mean smack on you, baby. You almost had my head spinning."

"Don't honey over me smacking you," she says pensively, and forms both of her hands to the back of my head, brushing her pouty lips against mine.

"I'll automatically honey over everything that you do because I'll never see anything wrong with it," I whisper onto her.

The door flies open, and I growl in utter vexation, barely turning my head to look at Maverick storming in and flipping the bright ass light on.

"Sorry not sorry," he rushes, still holding his phone to his ear. "Our boys are hitting an illegal gambling room right now."

I spring up and slide across the bed. "Get your shoes on, little wolf. You're coming with."

"What about Sirohi?" she questions, scurrying off the bed after me.

"We'll take him with us."

"They're going to let us?"

I stare at her pretty ass face for a moment. "Who's going to tell me no?"

She slowly blinks, and then hits play on her frantic race to throw socks and sneakers on.

I slip my sneakers on and bolt past her, grabbing the collar that wasn't supposed to come off of her. She bends over to fix her shit, and I stop right behind her, letting her get a feel of my hard cock through the thin layers separating us.

She snaps straight, and with me being ready, I quickly center the charm to her throat and clasp it back on. "Don't ever take that off again," I grumble, then give her a pat on the ass.

I almost forget that we need to make hell for leather out of here. The simplest pat causes massive waves that roll and crash through her leggings.

Satan give me the fucking strength.

CHAPTER THIRTY-THREE

TALA

My lungs are still burning from running all the way from the house to the front of the resort. I haven't been able to fully breathe because I've been sitting on top of Jax's monster cock.

I'm convinced he's permanently hard. There's no reason I should be able to make out the entire shape from simply sitting on his lap.

Refusing to meet his eyes, I watch the palm trees blur by until we roll to a stop outside of a souvenir gift shop.

"Thanks, man," Jax says, passing a wad of cash to the driver.

I pull the handle, stopping as obsidian burns through my skull. His hand slides over mine and he opens the door, and I quickly shuffle to get out, slightly rolling my fucking ankle and almost face planting on the pavement.

I steady myself and skitter off to the side, not letting Jax see my twisted face and the pain induced tears forming in my eyes from my stitches snagging on my leggings.

I stealthily jab my thumb down into my waistband, prying the fabric away and smiling at the tactical harness Sirohi is wearing.

It's like some John Wick shit.

Jax grabs my hand, tightly lacing his fingers with mine. "Do not wander off."

With Sirohi walking in between us and Maverick taking place on my right side, we walk towards the side of the shop. "Right, because I was just gonna go for a little field trip and mosey around."

"Tala," Jax warns.

I seal my lips, still getting over the fact that he managed to make me so upset the ethanol in my blood evaporated. But he's so beautiful—it hurts.

Seeing snow collect in his lashes and blow around his black hair will forever hold a special place in my heart. There's just something about seeing a black short sleeve hugging his lean body and showboating his tattoos while walking around Maui.

I feel like a hungry animal driven by instinct.

He comes to an abrupt stop, looking down with hunter eyes and an arched brow. "I love that you're eye fucking me right now, baby girl. But we're about to walk into a den of snakes and you're making my dick hard."

I look at it, clenching my teeth and sealing my tongue to the roof of my mouth to block my laugh off.

Those thin shorts are doing nothing to hide it.

Maverick shoves his hands in his pockets, short sleeve shirt displaying the feathers and flames designing his left arm.

"This guy's name is Wayne. He's laid back but won't tolerate any attention being drawn. Gambling is illegal here and that's how he makes a shit ton of money. He won't let anyone jeopardize that. So, we have to be quick, stealthy, and figure out how the fuck were going to walk two grown men back to the house without anyone seeing. We also have to take into account the two guards in there with Jenkins."

I flash Jax a cunning grin. He reads my thoughts instantly, licking over his teeth and sucking his canine.

Pulling my tank top down, I shimmy my tits to get them in place and look up through my lashes at the behemoth. "It's my first time. Can you show me how to do it?" I ask coyly.

His lip twitches. "Are you trying to make them jizz their jeans?"

"Killer, I don't approve of you using your attributes to sway men's attention. But I think we might need to use it tonight to keep our brains hole-free."

I gesture my thumb to Mav. "See? My tits were meant for more than just your hands and mouth."

Jax's eyes darken, and he doesn't blink.

"Please let me help." I pucker my bottom lip.

A heavy breath rumbles from him, and he lightly shakes his head, telling me I won. "Pay attention to what you're doing and what's going on around you. We're in Maui, Tala. So, unless you really want to see me burn the fucking world down in order to find you, you need to stay vigilant. Worst case scenario, use that scrapper smack of yours and yell "pervert" or some shit."

"Yes, sir," I smile.

He growls, and lightly chomps his teeth at me.

Hey, vagina. It's me. Again. Stop fucking pulsing.

Pulling me along with him, he knocks three times on the black metal door. Within a few seconds, it opens to a burly man who scans over them before landing on me.

I smile, slightly tilting my head, and he nods, moving the hell out of the way.

"Thank you," I say sweetly, and get guided in by pissed off Satan.

I know he hates it. His blood is probably reaching the point of combustion.

"Let Wayne know we'll be quick," Maverick says quietly behind me.

I follow Jax and Sirohi down the dark stairs, growing more nervous with each one. Mayor Jenkins is aware that I was literally fucking bought. He's the one that helped arrange it. And I haven't seen my uncle in over a year, aside from faintly seeing him as I was tranquilized.

Get it together and breathe. Four seconds in, four seconds out. You cannot fuck this up.

Dim, warm lighting, chatter, and loud games bleed into the bottom of the stairwell. I've never been in a casino before. But this is exactly what I see in movies.

"They're in the private room in the very back and the guards are standing outside of it," Maverick relays.

Jax nods, grasp on my hand turning lethal as he walks past people playing slot machines. His other hand reaches into his pocket, pulling out a whole fucking roll of cash. "I'll watch until you get them to the slots. But Maverick and I both have to deal with the dumbasses. Keep Sirohi with you and use this to play your game." He stops in the middle of the walkway, unzipping my leg bag and shoving the cash into it.

"How are you going to get them out of here?" I ask, for some reason getting butterflies as he zips it back.

How did I know his hand would stray from its objective?

He trails over my hip and up my side, possessively yanking me into him. I swallow thickly, peering up at the conflicted eyes of Hell. "Don't worry about that, little wolf. When you see Sirohi's ears perk up, ditch the fuckers and meet us back in the stairwell."

I nod, thoughts of ripping his shirt off and climbing him like a tree circulating in my mind.

He caresses up my exposed cleavage and runs gentle fingers through the notch of my collarbone.

I don't have a damn bra on, and my nipples are little fucking rats.

I need to get the hell away from him before my crying vagina seeps through my leggings.

I wrangle my hand from his, shoot his sexy ass a wink, and walk away with a smile. Sirohi is sticking close to my side, easing over the trepidation of having to jiggle my tits and play sweetheart for two men.

It's warranting a lot of attention though.

Passing obnoxious shouting coming from the rows of oval tables, I set my sights on the two men posted outside of a red door in the back corner. "Mask on, Sirohi."

I roll my glossed lips, make sure the girls are still spilling out, and veil my face with sugar while heading in their direction.

The blonde man on the left spots me. Greedily eye fucking me, he nudges the brunette man next to him. They share unintelligible words— and I keep my good girl face strapped on.

Jax probably has a death grip on his knife, watching from the shadows with a twitching lip.

It makes me smile as I take the last few steps to the horn-dogs about to blow their loads over some cleavage. They watch my tits bounce as I come to a stop, the blonde man blushing aggressively and fixing his eyes on my face. "Hi," I purr, pretending to drink him up.

He smiles, stashing his hands in his pockets. "Hey, sugar. What are you looking for?"

Gag me.

I give the other man a little attention. Just enough to take in him staring at my boobs like he's never seen a woman before. "It's my first time. I was wondering if you guys could show me how to do it."

"We're working, baby girl," the brunette says, just now tearing away from my tits.

"Oh, come on, Barry. He won't know."

"Oh, come on, Cooper. Yes. Yes, he will."

I pop my lips, not letting my grin fall. "I promise I'm a fast learner. I just need-" I oscillate a finger over them "-teaching hands to guide mine."

Cooper's jaw drops and Barry's cheeks finally blush.

"Why do you have your dog here?" Barry questions.

I pet Sirohi who's guarding me from in between my legs. "Anxiety. He's a professional working dog."

"I'll go with her," Cooper says ardently, taking a step closer. "Wouldn't want something so sweet to panic."

Barry's brows knit. "You stay here. I'll go."

Oh, my God. Shoot me.

"No, dude-"

"I want you both," I interrupt. I'm growing too impatient, and it will start slipping if both these assholes don't fall into my fucking trap right now.

Barry wipes his mouth in contemplation, eyes roaming my body. "Okay," he agrees. "We have to get back here though, baby girl. We'll show you a few slots, but then you're on your own."

"Yay!" I bounce on my heels, smiling even harder at the dogs chasing a ball. "I'll be a good girl and not waste your time."

Cooper tilts his head back, stomach tensing as if he's harboring a groan.

I don't really want to look at them anymore, so I turn around with Sirohi and begin rolling my hips with every step.

I can feel their eyes boring into my ass. But it's a show I must entertain them with.

"Why are you here alone?" Cooper asks loudly over the music and chatter.

I glance back at them with a forced grin. "Just a lone wolf I guess."

"No friends?" Barry questions, looking a little too predatorial for my liking.

What an odd question. What if I really didn't have friends? Maybe I should start crying to make him feel bad.

I don't. I squint my eyes playfully as he saunters up to my side. "Why? You want to be my friend?"

He cracks a smile. "Sure. We can call it that."

Cooper rushes to the other side of Sirohi, staring daggers at Barry. "Don't you have a wife back home?"

I look away from the imbeciles arguing, and my veins get zapped with electricity, locking on hunter eyes.

No. He's not in the shadows. He's right where I left him. And making it too obvious he's thinking about all the ways he could slaughter these guys.

I smile at him, getting sickening fucking butterflies from the subtle, and I mean subtle, grin he gives me. I flutter my fingers, walking through the dark spices that encircle him.

Maverick curls his lips to hide a smile, and Jax's head turns to track my movement.

I'm not sure why it's igniting excitement over my chest to be walking past him with other men. Maybe because only we know I'll be going home with him.

He's my dirty little secret. Just for right now.

"Uh," Cooper drones, looking over his shoulder at Jax. "Maybe we should sit with you until you leave."

Yeah, asshole. That's my plan.

I walk them around the corner, pretending to be interested in the slots. I'd say we're out of Jax's sight, but he can see straight over the machines. "Which ones do you guys like to play?"

"Baby girl, we play poker and roulette. None of this sissy shit."

I'm going to bite a hole in his face if he calls me that one more time.

I straddle around the farthest stool, sitting down in front of Wheel of Fortune. The neon purple light is kind of intimidating. It's basically a fucking beacon, shining a bright light on the dumbass who doesn't know what she's doing.

Cooper points to the money slot. "You'll stick your cash in here."

I twist my waist, unzipping the leg bag on my thigh and pulling out the absurd wad of cash Jax shoved into it. Sirohi is sitting in between my legs, keeping even attention on me and the strange men.

"Holy shit. What do you do for work?" Barry asks.

I take out a solo Benjamin Franklin and shove the rest back in, making sure to zip it back in case this guy has sticky fingers. "What do you think?" I croon, sliding the bill into the machine.

Guilt weighs on my chest.

I know he gave it to me to use it for this, but I honestly hate not working for my own money. I was going to bartend at *Club Sin* while working on my autobiography. But Liam told me it would "ruin his image at the bank."

He just liked keeping me isolated.

Barry crouches down next to me, assaulting me with eyes that look too similar to the murky blue that veiled the evil in Liam. "You want the truth?" he asks. I shrug coyly, slightly nodding. "I think you sell your body. Porn, dancing, stripping, either of them. Hell, I'd pay for it."

This man has a wife at home. Possibly kids.

I blatantly look at his wedding band, and he crosses his hand over it to conceal it. I slide back up to his conniving eyes, keeping the sass on the back of my tongue. "There you go. There's your answer." I bump my brows, then fix my attention on Cooper touching a button that starts rolling the screen.

"It's just a game of luck," Cooper says reservedly, tipping his hand and gesturing to the screen. I nod, watching it stop on three sevens. "And apparently you, my friend, are lucky."

A natural laugh comes out lightly. "You know angel numbers?" I ask, not giving a shit about the game still spinning.

He smiles bashfully, startling me by lifting his shirt. I dart my eyes away. But I end up looking over to the three ones running vertically down his rib.

"I got it for achievement and new opportunities." He lets his shirt fall back down, tucking it behind his belt. "Not even a week later, I got a job that changed not only mine, but my mom's life."

That's kind of sweet of him to take care of her.

I'm not here to be his friend though.

I paste a smile on, getting yelled at by the machine to spin again. I wrinkle my nose at it and press the needy button.

"Did you really just try using your one tattoo and your mommy to get this girl's attention?" Barry asks, jealousy evident in his tone.

I slowly blink, hiding the way I'm rolling my eyes so far back I can see my tired brain crying.

I'm not sure how long I sit there, tuning out the way they bicker like Nadia and Maverick. Long enough for my money to run out and a receipt to print.

I rip it off and hold it up to my face.

My eyes round, and the muscles in my jaw turn to pudding.

How. The fuck. Did I just win ten thousand dollars?

I quite literally sat there and looked pretty.

They don't notice me wandering off with Sirohi and my receipt. Astonishment is racing my heart and kissing my cheeks as I scan around, spotting the cashier's window close to the game I was just "playing."

The woman smiles sweetly, folding her arms on the counter and leaning closer. "What'd you get?"

I scratch my eyebrow and slide the receipt her way. "Does that happen often?" I ask perplexingly.

She weighs her head, still wearing her smile. "More often than you'd think. We're steady here all day, every day." She clicks around on her screen, humming to herself. "You're getting cashed out seven thousand even. Taxes still exist when it's illegal," she finishes with a lighthearted laugh.

She could've told me I was walking away with two hundred and I'd still be happy.

The exchange is quick. I just shove the money in my bag, pay my thanks, and glance back at them still yelling at each other.

Sirohi's ears are perking up, head tilting both ways at an incredible angle. "Let's go surprise Daddy," I whisper giddily, and walk around the slot machines.

A hand latches around my arm, yanking me back and spinning me around. "Did you get what you wanted from us and just walk away?" Barry asks, rage screwing his face up. "That's what all you fucking sluts do. Play games with men for your own benefit."

I don't tolerate being talked to like that. Anymore.

Sirohi starts growling, and I sharpen my eyes to swords. "Did you want me to break up your bitch fest so I could lift my leg and show you how I'm bleeding through my pants?"

His lips curl in disgust and he drops my arm. Because apparently the curse placed on women's bodies is repulsive.

Maybe he should consider the possibility that the room will be rainbow if he steps out of the closet.

He flinches at Sirohi, prompting him to quickly step closer and chomp his snarling teeth. "Get your fucking mutt on a leash before he hurts a kid."

Volatility flash-bangs in my chest and ripples my vision. I can't make a goddamn scene, otherwise I'd punch him in the nose. "Right. Because there are children here manhandling me. Fuck off."

His face twitches, and Cooper grabs his shoulders, pulling him away. "You're gonna get your dick ripped off, Barry."

I roll my eyes and run the hell away. Jax is probably already worried and there are concerned eyes sticking to me.

Ignoring my snagging stitches, I sprint with Sirohi past the slot machines and cut right into the stairwell. Almost running smack into Jax's big ass, my shoes squeak in agony from my abrupt halt.

"Are you okay?" Jax rushes, sharply analyzing me and hauling Enzo's unconscious body up the stairs by handcuffs.

Maverick is dragging Mayor Jenkins' unconscious body. And I am beyond baffled. I have to take a moment and file up the stairs behind them in silence.

"Tala," Jax growls sternly.

I slurp my drool up and pry my eyes away from his muscles bulging out of his shirt. "I'm more than okay." I follow them out the door, unzipping my bag and pulling out his paper bound winnings. "I won you this," I smile.

Maverick looks over his shoulder, both of their jaws growing slack. Jax sets his back in place, shaking his head. "You are mind blowing, little wolf. That's yours."

I'm not keeping it.

"Mm-hmm. Where did you get handcuffs?"

He smirks devilishly. "I've had them."

"In your ass?"

His sharp canines flash out, a laugh rumbling low in his chest. "My fucking pocket, baby."

A van is sitting where we were dropped off, the back door slid open and the trunk popped, seemingly ready for our escape.

Maverick grunts, hauling Mayor Jenkins up and dragging him into the trunk. "How much did you put in, killer?" he asks breathlessly.

"A hundred," I reply.

Jax throws Enzo in like a rag doll, turning to me with furrowed brows. "And how much is in your hand?"

I grab his large hand, twisting his palm up and placing the stack in it. "Seven thousand." I skitter away before he can force me to take it back and leap up into the van.

"Hi," I breathe speedily, smiling at the tired, tan face watching me crawl towards the back bench seat.

"Hello," he says modestly, and cranes his neck to check out Sirohi plopping down by my legs.

I lose interest in the stranger, becoming infatuated with the way Jax has to bend to get inside.

CHAPTER THIRTY-FOUR

JAX

"Where did he go?" I snap, glaring at the bloody faces that thought they were getting away with this shit.

Enzo sends a wad of crimson flying from his mouth. It splats next to my sneaker, smattering the white rubber.

I've already been a little testy. We've been back in Alaska with these fuckers for five hours now. They'd rather get beat, than spill something. So, the disrespect that just got sent my way makes me see red.

Cracking my bloody knuckles at my sides, I strike Enzo's nose, the bone snapping in tandem with his head ricocheting off the dining chair.

I can't stop. The pent-up aggression is pumping my muscles and using his face as an outlet.

I'm supposed to be saving him for Damascus and Evelyn.

I send one last powerhouse to his jaw, finally getting a scream of agony from him.

I turn to Wily Jenkins, the man that will no longer be the mayor in approximately five minutes.

His disoriented eyes lag around, the teeth already stripped from his mouth. Tala's somehow turning his and Liam's teeth into earrings in the living room right now.

"How many more of you are there?" I ask.

He grunts, a stream of blood rolling over his withered bottom lip.

"Wow. That was really fucking insightful," I say dryly. "You're wasting the oxygen my girl needs." I grab my balisong from the table, flipping it around a little, getting enjoyment from the panicked, garbled yelling coming from his nasty mouth.

A siren appears at my side, holding up two earrings with wisdom teeth dangling from them. The excited smile on her face coasts over my body like a cool breeze on a hot day.

I grab Jenkins' crimson matted hair, still looking at her over my shoulder. "I like those, baby. You want his ribs to make knives with?" I hammer my knife into his head, hardly hearing the thick squelch over Enzo's blubbering.

"You guys are fucking crazy!" Enzo shouts.

Ignoring him, she places the earrings in her hand and pets Killer's scarred head. "You know how to do that?" she asks interestedly.

I dislodge my blade from his dome, a spurt of crimson following my knife out and speckling my face. "Yes, ma'am."

She notes the warm liquid settling into my skin, and desire fires up in her amber eyes. I continue wiping my bali off, sharing heated eye contact with her—and getting overloaded with need.

It's prickling my skin.

"Si-Silas White," Enzo stammers.

Now this dude wants to speak up as I'm noting Tala's chest rising and falling quicker, like the desire is getting to her too.

Her throat bobs and she whips around, speed walking away with her three boys.

I hate to see you go, little wolf. But damn, I love to watch you walk away.

Tearing my eyes from her ass, I fix my scowl on the dude that just interrupted me. "What about Silas White?"

He rests his head to the back of the chair, one eye twitching and rapidly blinking from the blood seeping into it. "Middleman. He got us in contact."

I figured. And hearing it's true is a punch to the gut.

"Is that where Brutus is?" I ask, tone sharp with annoyance. He shrugs slothfully, then begins hacking up a damn lung. I don't blink. I just stare at him until he gets himself together. "How did Ashton Prior get involved?"

Viper, Shiloh, and Eli are heading to Canada to grab the dude. We'll see if it's just Viper returning with him.

He chokes down the iron filling his mouth, black and blue swirling around his tan complexion underneath the blood raining from his hairline. "He set Jenkins' security system up. His contact info got passed along to Pyro and he paid him to build trackers. He liked him, kept paying him to keep tabs on the guys and upload the videos sent to him."

"Hmm. What videos?"

I'm not dense. I know. I just want to hear him say it.

A sinister smirk lifts his face. "Dogs fighting and getting beat, women getting beat... my brother's whore fucking daughter getting beaten with a belt and put in her place. I don't know why-"

I black out, only hearing thuds and blows that warrant grunts and wheezes. The hostility transiting through my body is numbing my blows. I truly have no clue how long I've been knocking his teeth down his throat. I only tune back into reality once I hear Damascus' voice.

Heaving for air, I take a few steps back, watching a tan, balled up knuckle strike the side of Enzo's head. "I apologize, sir. He pissed me off," I grumble, peeling my pulsing vision from Enzo's unrecognizable face.

Damascus steps over to my side, giving me a firm pat on the back. "No worries, son. Evelyn and I just want to tie the score and then toss him to Rose."

I nod. "Who was in the barn with you guys?"

He squints thoughtfully. "It was just Sweetheart. My old ass got knocked out, so I'm not positive if someone else popped in. It was already dark when Eli woke me up. He was the one patrolling me."

My lip twitches, jumping straight into what I hate doing.

Assuming.

"I'll be upstairs, Damascus. Holler if you need anything."

He nods, contrition tightening his face. He's not at fault, but I have a rather difficult task to deal with and can't be bothered to pacify him.

My chest tightens with angst, passing by Evelyn combing through Tala's hair in the living room. Tala's golden eyes land on me, and she tips her head, asking what's wrong.

I can't hold eye contact with her without breaking the fuck down.

I clench my teeth, looking away from her and hauling my ass up the stairs. I don't notice Sirohi following me until I get halfway down the hall.

I pet his head while stepping into my office. "Go get Mama," I mutter.

A jolt runs through my heart, watching him turn around and walk back towards the stairs. I feel bad.

But Tala needs his comfort more than I do.

I close the door, swallowing roughly as I lock it, and stalk over to my desk. I remember the sketchy, dark site the video of her fighting Rylie was posted on. I sit down, type my shit in, and pull it up.

The large monitors give me room to cover all bases and have as many tabs as I need open. It also ensures that I can't escape the barbaric acts that are happening every second of every day.

I can't get lost in the sea of horrific images.

With each scroll, my stomach twists a hair more. It keeps ringing itself out, riddling my nervous system with torment.

My heart stops, combusting into flames of wrath as I spot Tala on all fours on loose hay and the muzzled wolves on goddamn chains in the background.

The fire spreads, constricting my throat and percolating sweat across my forehead. I briefly look away, then grow the balls and click on it.

Her battle cries pour from the speakers, piercing my igneous heart and shattering it to dust.

I rub over my mouth, eyes stinging something fierce, and firmly hold my face in place, watching Brutus whip her back with the metal fucking buckle of his belt.

CHAPTER THIRTY-FIVE

TALA

Mom wipes her wet cheeks, reaching over to tuck my hair behind my ear. "I'm so sorry you had to go through that alone, honey."

I finally talked to her about our baby trying to kill me.

I know I should be more engaged in the conversation and assure her that I'm okay. But Jax went upstairs with Sirohi, wearing a tormented face and barely sparing me a glance. And Sirohi came back down without him.

I lean over and hug her, tenderly squeezing into the coffee that spreads warmly from her fuzzy coat. "It's long forgotten, Mom," I assure, and pull away.

Her tearful eyes roam aimlessly around my face. I rub her arm, standing up from the couch and maneuvering around the boys.

"Alright, Ev!" Dad hollers from the dining room. "Get your pretty booty in here!"

"Honey."

I stop, and spin around on my heel.

"Will you ever try again?" she asks somberly.

I purse my lips glumly, letting a bubble out that vibrates them. "Well, I didn't try the first time… But no, I won't. That was pretty traumatic. Besides, you have three grandbabies already." I gesture to the dogs, a small laugh breezing out.

"Okay," she murmurs, and pats her legs while standing up.

"Mom," I croon, tilting my head with pinched brows. "Jax and I have been together for two months. It's way too early to even consider changing my mind."

Mom loves kids. She wanted me to have siblings, but after her first miscarriage they stopped trying. So, in a way, she understands the trauma that inflicts.

She smiles and walks past me, drawing over my shoulder blades with her fingertips. "So there's a chance," she hums.

I shake my head, proceeding on to the stairs. I've been tuning out the sounds of torture since we got back this morning. Yet I'm still stunned to pass by my dad punching his own brother in his messed-up face.

Sirohi, Killer, and Gemini follow me up the stairs and down the hall. I look into his office, frowning at his chair spun at an angle. He's anal about it and always pushes it in straight. I meander past the spare bedrooms Nadia and Leon are still sleeping in, reaching Jax's bedroom at the end of the hall.

My heartbeat bombs into my throat, and I grab the handle, opening the door to whatever is spiking my adrenaline.

My eyes widen, and chills roll goosebumps over my hot skin. He's standing shirtless in the middle of the room, belt in hand—waiting for me.

"W-what are you doing, Jax?" I waver, closing the door behind me.

Maybe it wasn't a good idea to close the dogs out.

I don't think he'd hurt me… But I'm not sure Jax is home right now. Darkness is haunting his eyes, stripping the life from his face.

"Come here," he orders darkly.

My heart might fall out of my ass.

I slowly approach the beast, eyes stinging and welling with tears from my refusal to blink.

"Attagirl," he whispers. Gently grabbing my hand, he turns my palm up and places the leather into it. "Thirteen times."

"Thirteen times what?"

He cups under my chin, tilting my head up to him. "That's how many times you're going to strike my back with the belt in your hand," he says definitively.

I shake my head, eyes wide in fear. "No, I'm not hurting you."

"Don't think of it that way." He lowers his hand, walking over to the end of the bed and dropping to his knees. "Your pain is mine, little wolf. So, share it with me. Make me feel what you did," he says hoarsely, and folds his arms on the bed, lengthening the oni mask on his back.

"No!" I snap in disbelief.

"Now. Tala."

My face scrunches, heart palpitating and pulsing in my ears. I pace over to him, getting on my knees and chucking the belt onto the bed. Grabbing his perfect fucking face, I twist his head, looking him dead in his black eyes. "I will never hurt you like that. I love that you don't want me to feel alone with the torture I endured. But you've suffered from your own, Jax. We're partners. We can release our pain to each other in ways that feel good."

"I need to know, baby. I need to know what you felt when I wasn't there to protect you," he whispers, affliction hardening his scowl.

I think I have a way. One that doesn't involve buckle shaped bruises hiding under his ink.

"Do you trust me?" I ask.

Without relaxing his brows, he hikes one up. "More than anyone, Tala."

I grin, standing up and guiding his eyes to stay on mine. "I want to take our time." I lick my free thumb, wiping off the smattered crimson from his face. "Let's go downstairs, crack open some energy drinks, and take care of the assholes ruining your floor... I'll try to be done with you by the time the guys get back from Canada."

The darkness shadowing his eyes slowly retreats, a faint shimmer of excitement lighting his obsidian up.

While Jax and my dad take care of the bodies, my mom and I break out the cleaning supplies. The cat litter in the closet is a bit perplexing. But I throw that shit on the puddles soaking into the wood. It absorbs the moisture really well. All I have to do is wipe it up, stash the slimy paper towels in a trash bag, and get on my knees to scrub the remnants up with soapy water and bleach.

By the time we're done, Nadia's bedhead is wandering around in the kitchen, groans of her hangover echoing into the dining room.

We left the second we got the dumbasses back to the house. Nads and Leon have been sleeping since we got home and Maverick's at *Club Sin* handling "some business."

While washing my hands and scrubbing under my nails in the kitchen, Nadia plops down at the island with a bowl of cereal. "How are you murdering people right now?" she mumbles.

I check over my shoulder, noting the time on the oven. "It's been twenty-four hours since alcohol invaded my blood stream."

She stares at me, caramel face washed out with nausea. "I almost fucked Leon," she confesses, and shoves a spoonful of cinnamon Cheerios in her mouth.

I'm not shocked. I'm more taken aback that they didn't after he got down on his knees and stripped for her.

The cereal crunches in her mouth, filling the silence of me not knowing what to say. She hastily works her jaws, swallowing with thin lips. "He started crying about how pretty you are."

I clench my teeth, holding in a laugh and watching her throw the back of her hand to forehead. "Oh, mija. What I would do to get in between those cheeks," she says theatrically.

"Nadia," I hiss, getting her lazy focus on me. "Are you trying to get him killed?"

Shoving another spoonful of cereal in her mouth, she says, "If Jax didn't kill him for launching you to the sharks, I don't think he'll kill him for fantasizing about putting it in your butt."

It takes me a second to decipher her cereal congested words. Horror-struck, I stare at her munching down without a care in the world and pop my lips. "Did he say that? Verbatim?"

She shakes her head. "No, I'm making it up. The sappy boy was crying about you though. It was revolting."

Mom whizzes into the kitchen, tossing her hair up in a clip. "Alright, honey, we're out of here. We're gonna get that meat to the wolves before it tastes even more bitter."

Is it fucked up that we're feeding human meat to the wolves that kids take field trips to go see?

Maybe. No one needs to know that though.

285

I hug Mom, unable to pull away without bunny kisses tickling my nose. "You know once word gets out about the Cheechako no longer being mayor, Dad's phone is going to blow up with people asking him to run for the election, right?"

She smiles. "Dad's too humble for that." Walking away, she wraps behind Nadia and kisses her temple, then walks towards the front door.

The front door Satan is walking through. Blood splattered up on his face and both hands drenched in the sticky liquid.

I might start howling like a fucking wolf.

He stops by the stairs, tipping his head towards them and beckoning me with crimson soaked fingers.

My cheeks burn with need, and I swallow roughly. "Uh, I'll be back, Nads."

Taking a bite of cereal, she spins around in her stool, taking in the sight of bloody Satan waiting for me. "Oh, my God." She spins back around, eyebrows raised over wide eyes. "Will it be the first time since you've been home?" she asks curiously.

I narrow my eyes at her and keep walking towards Jax. My blood pressure rises with each step, locking on the hellish hunger that's cruising down my body. I step up in front of him and deftly roll my hips up the stairs, already hitting play on: How pissed can I make him?

Oh, yeah.

I'm going to piss him off, make him lose the control he constantly seems to have. It's the only way I can think of that will make him feel the way that I did—without hurting him.

My ass is on fire as I walk down the hall. His eyes are searing through my leggings, tingling my flesh with chaotic embers.

I stop in front of the studio, flashing a cunning grin at his confused scowl as I open the door. The ropes from Valerie and Kendra are still hanging from the hooks in the ceiling.

I turn around and walk backwards toward them. "Lock the door and get undressed. Now," I order.

He hikes a brow, but drops it and quickly locks the door, watching me strip my shirt off. Doing as he was told, he gets undressed without letting his eyes stray from me, stepping closer with each removed piece of clothing.

Stepping out of my leggings, I turn my back to him, hooking my thumbs into my thong and teasing them down. I know he's staring at my wet pussy as I double over before him.

An aggravated breath rumbles from him, and I stand straight with my cheetah print thong in hand, turning to face him. His jaw tics, and my eyes zip down to the monster cock I haven't seen in almost a month.

It's somehow even more horrifying now. Yet it makes my mouth water, and my thighs grow slick.

I tear away from the pussy drenching sight, peering up at the amusement barely showing his teeth. "You miss it, baby?" he asks languidly, and steps close enough for it to graze my lower stomach.

Yes.

"No. Get on your knees, Jax," I demand bitterly.

I don't know if I can do it. My chest is already tightening from being abrasive towards him.

His nostrils flare, eyes sharpening to slits, and his cock smacks my inner thigh as he lowers himself to his knees—sitting as tall as I stand. "What's your goal here, Tala?" he asks gruffly.

I look up, volleying between the ropes. "String you up, strip you of your control, and piss you off." I smile at his glare. "Show me your magical tongue."

His eyes slide down to the thong in my hand. And the asshole smiles. Then, looks me dead in the eyes, opening his mouth for me.

Facing the crotch lining towards him, I grab the back of his head and slide the wet trail over his tongue. He grabs my hips and groans, the heat of his desire blowing over my fingers and swirling my stomach. "You miss it, daddy?" I ask, wanting to punch myself in the forehead.

But he likes it for some reason.

He yanks me into him, obsidian darkening with the rapture of his starvation. I shove my thong into his mouth so that I don't kiss him, and grab his blood-stained hands, forcing them off me. "I didn't say you could touch me," I utter, and stick his large hands up in the air.

His lip twitches with a thunderous growl, letting me know I'm finally provoking him.

Grabbing the rope to my left and knotting it around his wrist, I say, "A few nights before we escaped, we had to fight each other to win a field trip to a fight and strip night. I won. And before we left, we were forced to do cocaine. I'm assuming it was in hopes of altering our perception so we wouldn't run or take in our surroundings. But I did. That's how I knew we were by the Knik." Ignoring his death glare, I pull the knot tight and move on to the other one. "While we were there, Shiloh kissed me to conceal what we were talking about."

He spits my thong out, the fabric launching over my shoulder and smacking the floor. "Are you fucking kidding me, Tala?" he asks abrasively, searing into my face with the rage roaring in his eyes.

I know I didn't do anything wrong. But my heart drops thinking I did. It's not like I enjoyed it.

Shiloh saved me in diabolical ways that saved him too.

I pull the knot extra tight, backing away as he stands up. "I was supposed to return to Brutus' room when we got back. Brynn and I both were. He wanted to do disgusting stuff with us because in his vile mind, forcing us to make out for his pleasure meant he could force us to fuck him at the same time. And Shiloh was in the middle of telling me he wouldn't let that happen when eyes started falling on us. So, he did what he had to do to save both of our asses. Mine literally. If I would've fucked up, Jax, I would've been gang-raped in my ass."

Grabbing the weight under one side of the rope, I grunt, hauling it up and clipping it to the existing hook. He's staring out the window, jaw ticking and arm getting stretched up as I drop the weight down.

I manage to do the other side in silence.

I step back, the beat of my heart thumping in my ears, anxiety buzzing under my chest.

He looks at me coldly. "Did you like it?"

Out of everything I just said… that's what he's hung up on.

I slowly blink, taking a deep breath to calm the volatile storm that's creeping in. "No. It felt like poison in my veins, and I cried." I walk around to the back of him, giving him a firm crack on his tattooed ass.

His back muscle tense up, a grunt getting trapped in his throat, and he snaps his eyes over his shoulder at me. "I'm not trying to pass over what you went through. But I am having a really hard fucking time with the fact that's he's been staying under our roof, and you are *just now* telling me."

"I think that should be the least of your worries considering Brutus is still running around," I clip, and reach my arms up, tacking my nails to his shoulders and dragging them down his back.

His head falls back, goosebumps rippling his inked flesh, and a husky moan smokes out of his mouth. I grin, dragging my nails down his lower back, then slide them around his hips and up his abs.

"I'm aware he's on the loose, Tala," he breathes.

I press my lips to a line of circular scars on his back, skating my nails back down to his hips. "What happened here?" I ask, and kiss over them again, sliding a palm over the shaven, coarse hairs on his hilt.

He groans, yanking on the ropes and tensing his back muscles up. "A spiked club. I tried running out of the pit... Never tried again."

I flatten my tongue and lick up them, wrapping my hand around his thick shaft.

"Baby girl, you know I can get out of these, right? You start pumping my shit and I swear to fucking God, I'll rip them out of the ceiling."

"No, you won't... You want to know why?" I slowly stroke up, prompting a moan from him that makes my pussy tingle. "Because I didn't tell you that you could. You're not in control, Jax... I am." I stroke him, rubbing up his side and stopping on the long, jagged line that runs over his ribs.

His breathing grows heavier, lifting his chest higher and making it fall deeper. "Wooden break stick," he says through clenched teeth.

Leaning over, I kiss along the scar and release his inhumane cock. He growls in annoyance, and I capture the violence with a form of gentle love all the way around his rib.

I step in between his parted feet, gazing up at the irritation setting his jaw back and sharpening his hunter eyes. "Do you want to touch me?" I ask.

He licks over his teeth, sucking on his canine and flashing it at me. "I want to do more than touch you, Tala. I want to taste every inch of your body, hear your husky moans and whines in my ear, and, fuck, I want to watch your pretty eyes roll back as I feel your tight pussy stretch around my cock."

The thrum in between my thighs spills its neediness through the seal containing my hungry vagina. I can't admit that I want that too. Not yet. I'm getting him right where I want him. "And how does it feel knowing you can't do any of it?" I ask, and lower myself to my knees, gliding my hands down the soft hair on his thighs.

Without warning, I grab his shaft and open my mouth, sliding my lips and tongue around his outrageous size. I look up through my lashes, watching the groan fall past his parted lips, his muscular arms drawing taut as they rip at the rope holding his hands hostage. "Fuck, baby, it's boiling my goddamn blood," he bites out, brows pinched tight. "It feels like a fire is spreading rapidly under my skin and cremating me from the inside out."

My eyes water, taking as much as I can down my throat. I hollow my cheeks, using my tongue for extra stimulation as I bob my head.

The sweet taste of his musk makes me want to keep going. So do his moans.

But he's enjoying himself too much.

I gradually work my mouth to his rosy tip, letting it pop free, and I stand up underneath the heavy breaths jetting out of his flaring nostrils. "Squat down a little bit," I demand.

His already vexed face tightens perplexingly, defiance rippling his lip. He doesn't defy me He heeds my command, creating enough of a flat surface for me to brace my foot on.

I hop up, grabbing both ropes for support. And this fucking asshole instantly catches a nipple in his mouth, swirling his tongue around it and instituting pleasure to flower over my boob.

"Jax, no," I moan. Contradicting myself.

He smiles, nipping at it with his teeth before letting it go. He tilts his head to look at me, clearly satisfied with the minimal contact he just got. "Sorry, baby, I couldn't help myself."

I shake my head, climbing up the behemoth and steadying my weight on one leg, swinging the other over his shoulder.

"Oh, fuck. Okay," he breathes, staring at my pussy.

Adjusting my hands farther up on the rope, I throw myself forward and lift my weight, getting my other leg on his free shoulder.

I laugh, scooting my pussy right into his awaiting tongue. Practically smothering him. My giggle burns into a slutty moan, feeling the silkiness of his wet tongue languidly swipe up my soaked entrance and over my touch deprived clit. "Oh, my God," I whine, head already fucking spinning in the clouds.

He groans in contentment and stands straight, giving me several incredible views of Satan chowing down in the mirrors.

Hunter eyes gazing up at me with unholy passion, he draws me into his magical mouth, and my head falls back on a raspy moan that bounces off the ceiling.

When I did cocaine, I didn't realize I was already hooked on a violent substance that blasts through my veins in a demanding fury. The high Jax gives me is transcendental, taking me to nirvana. Except, soul-absorbing desire is all that I feel in my body as I'm sent to a wavelength that only exists around him.

I almost forget about the whole point of bringing him in here. I don't want to lose the orgasm that's building in between my hips. But I'm supposed to be stripping him of everything he wants.

Breathing heavily, I rock my hips back and break out of his suction. He tries diving back in, glistening tongue out and enticing me to just give in and forget about playing with him. Instead of breaking, I engage the muscles in my arms and lift my weight, speedily bringing my legs back in from his tight shoulders.

I keep fucking forgetting about my stitches.

They stretch as I dangle down in front of pissed off Satan, warranting my face to draw taut in pain, a wince rattling my throat.

"Are you okay?" he asks worriedly, brows furrowed over roaming eyes.

"Mm-hmm," I nod, and circle my legs around his trim waist.

I'm face to face with killer eyes and dangerous lips. Dried crimson is smattered up his beige skin, clinging to his dark facial hair and thick eyebrows.

I'm weak. And needy. And a goddamn fool for this man.

Releasing my grip on the ropes, I squeeze my thighs around him and fervently latch my hands into the hair on the back of his head, crashing my lips to his.

Our jaws stretch open in desperate tandem, his tongue sweeping over mine and dispensing my sweet musk onto my taste buds. I whimper, grinding against his abs and panting into his parted mouth before tilting my head and skating my tongue through another dose.

Our lips smack as I tear away, and I scramble to detach from him. Dropping down to the floor, I avoid the ire thundering in his chest and walk away from him.

"Tala!" he barks barbarically, the mirrors and windows carrying his frustration.

I'd grin over breaking him if it didn't feel like the plague was infesting my euphoric high.

My inner thighs are soaked, rubbing my arousement around with every step towards the door. I course through his scattered clothes, body locking up from the inhumane growl resounding through the room.

Eyes wide, I pivot, jaw dropping from the sight of a beast engaging his strong arms and back, ripping the hooks out of the studs in the ceiling.

Oh. My. Fucking. God.

I knew he'd be capable of doing it. I didn't think he would, though.

He turns to me, shredding the knotted rope from his wrists. In a weak attempt at fleeing from the Big Bad Wolf hunting me, I back pedal into the door with a racing heart.

Not because I'm scared of him.

Because I'm finally living out a fantasy.

He's instilling a rush of adrenaline that's convincing my brain that it's run or die.

And that's thrilling. With him.

"Run, little wolf, run," he growls, stalking closer.

CHAPTER THIRTY-SIX

TALA

Hysteria coils down my spine, weaving into the electrifying pump of desire. And I run. To him.

He smiles wickedly, licking over his teeth and snapping them shut. "Attagirl," he snarls enthusiastically, words sifting through clenched teeth.

Like a hungry animal, I lunge for him, wrapping around his neck and waist, and he palms both my ass cheeks, roughly taking my lips within his. The high spreads through my body, lighting it up in a warm vibration.

I rip away from my drug, running a hand down his dog tag. "No, this isn't how this was supposed to go. The rage didn't make me a horny fucking monster. It made me murderous," I say breathlessly.

He teases his lips over mine, a faint smile showing his sharp teeth. "Baby, I am murderous… Your pussy is at the top of my hit list."

I'm unable to say anything. He steals my mouth and ravenously swirls his tongue inside. All rational thinking ceases to exist in my light head. I'm fading into my favorite black, consumed with the sensation of him against me, taking slow, deep turns tasting everything we can within each other.

At this point, my pieces are bonded together with gold. They have been, really. But now?

Everything that happened just feels like a nightmare that scarred my bones. I'll always carry that with me. And that's not necessarily a bad thing. We can't grow without rain. And sometimes that rain consists of a cataclysm that fucks everything up. But we build it back and move on stronger than we were before.

"Kintsugi," I whisper against him, and fervently fuse our lips back together, cracking my eyes open to his smile that has his teeth colliding into mine.

The shower hisses, giving way to the rainfall that patters onto the stone tile. I wasn't aware that we left the studio. I'm almost certain Jax is capable of floating through walls.

He's too… soundless. It's horrifying, yet peaceful.

The hot water cascades over us, streaming down our faces and filling the seams of our battling lips. It mutes the sweetness of his tongue, but it doesn't hinder how intoxicating he is.

A silky texture runs up my thigh and over my ass, wafting up the scent of coconut. I pry away from his swollen lips, looking down at the red tinted soap rinsing from my skin and swirling around the drain underneath his tattooed feet.

Panic flash-bangs in my chest.

Most of my time in that house I had to watch my own blood stream down my legs and cloud the water collecting in the stained tub. I bled heavily for a few days after my fallopian tube ruptured. And right as it started lightening up—Brutus took what he wanted.

Not only does the red water resurface trauma I'm actively getting over, but it also floods my mind with the images of Brynn taking the shot meant for me.

"I'm here, little wolf," Jax says warmly, pulling my attention to the rivers flowing down his structured face.

His voice alone subsides the hurricane of barbaric images. But his eyes. They caress my flesh open and exterminate the parasites, blanketing me in seventh heaven.

He sets me down on my feet, backing me up into the cold glass. "Don't think. Just feel, baby," he urges, the sound soft and longing, and he gets down on his knees.

The sight of a wet savage spreading my legs and looking up through his lashes has me tongue tied. All I can do is nod in agreement, lifting a leg and bracing my foot to the glass wall next to us.

He runs two fingers through my slit, spreading them around my throbbing bud while easing a finger inside my horrified vagina.

I latch into his hair, tensing up and whining from the pops of pleasure. He leans in, swiping his silky tongue up my isolated clit and tapping my inner walls. The immediate pressure stretches my jaw open for a raspy moan, my brows knitting tightly over my hooded eyes.

My muscles relax, and he retracts his finger, just to slip it back in with a second one.

He's still watching me, drawing me into his mouth and curling his fingers into the pressure that's expanding. "Fuck," I breathe, slamming my head into the glass.

Watching his jaws work languidly, I relax my hands in his hair, combing through his wet roots. His fingers around my clit massage vertically, adding

297

extra stimulation that makes it impossible to hold the sounds of my pleasure.

He's lustrating me. Purifying my cursed, violated vessel.

Chants of his name and husky cries circulate around the glass, echoing the ballad of my release from the rusty chains anchoring me to the pit of haunting memories.

Red hot pleasure shoots up my spine, spreading the heat of carnal flames through my entire abdomen. I let go of his hair, slapping my palms into an unforgettable prayer—and pray to the Dark God who's lighting my soul on fire. "Oh, my fucking God, Jax" I moan, hips and stomach twitching.

It's cathartic. Celestial even.

My bud pops from his mouth and he smiles, withdrawing his fingers. "Atta-fuckin-girl, baby," he drawls. "I'm proud of you for remembering who you pray to." He raises his glistening, inked fingers to his lips, salaciously opening his mouth and cleaning them off.

Breathing heavily, I drop my foot and find myself wanting to become one with the water swirling down the drain. "Wait, what's your name again?" I tease.

He narrows his eyes and stands up. His terrifying cock rubs up my thumping pussy, instilling nerves to rattle my damn Jello bones. "Hmm," he growls dangerously, brushing the wet hair from my face. "Do you need another visible lesson? 'Cause from what I remember, baby, you were whining it while coming all over my cock."

My cheeks burn from the memory. I'll blame it on the steam penetrating my skin, just so he doesn't have the satisfaction of knowing I'd do it again because it was hot. "And from what I remember, that was the first time you ever felt pussy. Unless you lied to me, of course."

Grabbing under my arms, he picks me up, and I eagerly cage the wet behemoth, getting large hands on my hips. The tip of his cock rubbing my entrance makes reality set in and my eyes round in panic.

He remains neutral, exuding a calmness that's somehow ravenous. "I'd never intentionally lie to you, Tala. So, yeah, the first pussy I felt just happened to belong to a siren. And fuck, she sings so pretty when I'm riding her waves," he finishes with a rumbling whisper, pushing my back against the cold glass.

Speaking of waves. Jesus Christ. There's no chance he doesn't feel me spilling down his abdomen.

Getting out of my head about it, I reach a hand in between us and spread myself open for him. He looks down, breezing back up to my face with a twinkle of excitement. "You have to be careful, Jax," I croon, and drop my hips a bit lower.

"I told you I'd treat your pussy like stained glass, baby girl. Tell me you want it and it's yours." He rocks his hips back, centering himself to my entrance.

Paranoia of it hurting is eating at my mind. But I must admit that I miss having my eyes knocked around in my skull.

I take a deep breath, falling into his obsidian. "I wouldn't be spreading myself wide open for you if I didn't want it."

He raises a brow, slowly rolling his hips forward. "Is that attitude I hear?" My jaw grows slack, stinging from the stretch that's moving my fingers. "In case you've forgotten, Tala. I fill you the fuck up and correct that shit."

I clank my teeth shut, whining behind them and clawing into his shoulder. I haven't forgotten about his monster cock making a seamless fit inside me. It's just been so long, and each centimeter feels like too much.

He presses his forehead to mine, letting out a husky moan that coasts warmly over my lips and makes my pussy tingle. "You say the word and we'll stop. Don't force yourself to enjoy it," he says breathlessly, voice hoarse with need.

"I don't want to stop." I rock forward, sliding down another inch. My misted forehead rubs across his, my throat stretching open for a slutty whine directed over his head.

I think his dick is touching my fucking brain.

Once again, my inner walls are beginning to accept his shape, molding around him and soothing the discomfort into pleasure.

He kisses my throat, pushing in until his hilt wedges my fingers in between us. The smoky moan that ruptures out of me seems so foreign.

It's not. He's inflicted carnal sounds out of my lungs too many times to count. Something's different though.

It's as if our souls have officially merged into one, the way the universe planned. And connecting like this is the only way we'll physically feel it ourselves.

It's the same sensation as a steep drop on a roller coaster. Except, our flames are catastrophic, rolling around and dancing within each other.

It's dynamite.

I was worried that when it blew up, I'd be left broken-hearted. Little did I know, we were supposed to blow up to transcend. Together.

He groans against my neck, sucking the sensitive skin into his warm mouth, and starts languid thrusts that make me feel. Every. Single. Inch.

Sliding my hand up his moving abdomen and over his chest, I latch into the hair on the back of his head, belting out the raspy moans and heavy breaths he's drawing out of me.

His tongue sweeps up the mist on my throat, lapping over my chin and plunging inside my mouth. I mewl, rocking my hips into his momentum as our tongues fervently swirl around each other.

He tears away, moaning onto my pulsing lips and slapping a hand to the glass. Precipitation is drizzling down his face that's taut with carnality, his hunter eyes heavy with lust. "Are you doin' okay?" he rasps out.

My cheeks are already blood kissed from the humidity. So, his gentleness just tosses more fuel on the fire, spiking my body temperature and percolating sweat on the back of my neck. "Yes, sir," I breathe.

He smiles lazily, husky pants falling between his parted teeth. "God, you look so fucking divine taking my cock. And you take it so well, baby. You want it a little deeper? A little faster?"

His Poseidon powered hips are sending waves crashing throughout my entire body. I feel weightless, yet heavy with the pressure that's beginning to contract my abdomen. "You're already fucking my skull, Jax. But I-"

He rocks in deeper. Harder. Hitting something that makes my eyes roll back and a loud moan to echo off the glass.

My nails dig into his shoulder and the back of his head, and a fire wrapped hurricane shreds my body, leaving me withering, whining, and geysering on his cock.

Everything washes out to black. My soul leaves my fucking body, getting sent somewhere that's lit up in my own displays of Aurora.

Re-entering my sizzling skin, I vaguely hear chants of his name and staccato moans escaping my hoarse throat. It's hard to focus on anything when you're being lustrated and are overdosing on desire.

But I hear him.

His moans are rich and velvety with infatuation, edged with his gruffness. And *right* in my ear.

I don't get the chance to come down from the soul-binding orgasm. The sounds of his pleasure and the way he rolls his slutty hips into me is creating a vortex that's hollowing my stomach.

His hand coasts up my sweaty spine, fingers wrapping around the hair on the back of my head, and he rips me away from the glass wall. Moving his face into mine, he captures my lips, backing us up underneath the water—still fucking me senseless.

The water rains down on us, slipping through the seams of our connected bodies. My ass was already smacking off his thighs. Now, the sounds are vulgar.

"God fuckin' damn it, baby, I can't hang on any longer," he breathes aggressively against my panting mouth.

My head's spinning and I've officially reached the point of puddling into him. I really don't want to end up losing my other fallopian tube because my body doesn't know how to carry babies. But I'm lost at sea and don't care at the moment. "Come for me," I whisper.

He groans, quickly dropping to his knees and placing my back on the cold floor. As if he could read my mind, he braces a hand by my head, using his other to pull out and pump his cock in between my legs. "Fuck, Tala. I love you," he breathes heavily, tightening his eyes as his cum ropes out onto my stomach.

I retract my claws, caressing down his savage face and twirling a finger around his dog tag. "I love you."

He opens his eyes, letting his cock bob free of his hand. The water is washing away his cum. But he smooths his hand up through it, rubbing it up to my throat and taking my neck into his possession.

"*Divine and all mine,*" he growls with a faint smile, and lowers himself down, kissing me longingly.

He stands my limp body up and we wash each other, taking our time and sensually gliding our hands around the curvatures of our vessels.

I've never received aftercare—until Jax.

We dry off and put comfortable clothes on. And he cuddles me. And kisses me. And makes bullshit small talk like he didn't just consume my soul.

I lay my head on his chest, tapping out the strong rhythm of my comfort. He rubs down my back, hooking his other hand under my knee and bringing my leg over him. "I need to ask you something, little wolf," he grumbles, guilt tightening his words.

My face scrunches, and I slide my cheek over his chest to look up at him. "Okay," I draw out.

The returning torment in his eyes makes me sit up. I note the large wet mark on his shirt from my hair and shift my weight over to straddle his waist.

"Who else was in the barn with you besides your father?" he asks tepidly, gliding his hands up my hips.

I frown, hating having to reflect on it. But he's asking for a reason. "Uh, I don't really know who watched... But Eli's the one that picked me up and carried me back."

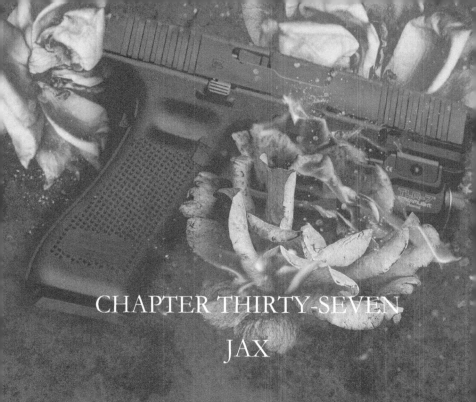

CHAPTER THIRTY-SEVEN

JAX

The bright headlights coming up the driveway fuck my barbed eyes for a second. But I'm too irate to even blink.

Viper's SUV rolls to a stop in front of me, and I zero in on Shiloh getting out of the passenger side before sliding my vision over to Eli dragging Ashton out of the back seat.

I know Tala's watching from Nadia's room.

I can feel her fiery eyes searing through my hoodie.

"Where do you want him, boss?" Viper asks, cautiously approaching with a simple expression.

I faintly tip my head towards the shop. "In the chair. I need to speak with Shiloh and Eli."

Shiloh stops off to the side, bringing his hands together in front of his stiff body. My knuckles crack inside my hoodie pocket, staring at him until his throat bobs nervously. Eli passes the unconscious dweeb off to Viper, and he soldiers up, stopping on the opposite side of Shiloh.

I've never seen Eli get nervous. Dude barely even speaks. So, he remains neutral, maintaining moderate eye contact with me.

"Who recorded Tala getting beaten and raped?" I ask Eli directly.

Penitence thins his eyes, and he lets out a deep breath that clears his face, scratching the long facial hair on his chin. "Jarvin. I didn't know Tala would be there. He made it clear that she wasn't allowed to know about her dad or see the wolves. I was doing my usual check in and I... I got there too late."

My lip twitches, blood boiling my fucking heart. "How is it that I heard her from a drone that was roughly two miles away, but neither of you heard her screams?" I ask abrasively, looking over them both.

I'm aware they were in a shitty position where they lacked power to do anything. But the barn was isolated from everything else. Someone could've done something.

Shiloh chews the inside of his cheek. "He had all the walls ripped open and re-insulated so the hikers on the other side of the river wouldn't hear anything. Eli was starting coffee because he always snuck a mug to Damascus. And I... I was standing in the kitchen like a piece of shit. I was supposed to be monitoring her feeding the wolves. And I just fucking let him switch everything up."

I'm sure Brutus was smug as hell, knowing exactly what he was doing and how she'd respond to seeing her father.

A vexed breath rumbles my chest, and I just barely acknowledge Leon awkwardly walking around Eli, stopping behind me. "And then what?" I lock eyes with Eli. "You said you got there too late. How so?"

"I passed by him and Jarvin on my way up. He was smiling and fixing his belt while Jarvin had the phone held up for him. I waited until the trees blocked our view of each other and then ran to the barn to see what he did…"

"Mm-hmm. Keep going."

He cracks. Finally swallowing roughly and glancing around. "She was… crying on the ground with her pants down. Damascus was knocked out in the corner. I pulled her pants up, picked her up, and carried her back to the house."

I glower at him. Waiting for him to continue.

"She couldn't stand up. She could hardly move. But her shirt was soaked with blood, so Shiloh held onto her while I cleaned her back."

I'm not naive. I know they stripped her down and got her in the shower. And I'm trying my best not to rip their fucking eyes out with my bare fingers. But I can't be mad at them for helping her.

I *can* be mad at Shiloh for kissing her though.

Oh, I can be fucking livid. And I am.

I glance up at the sexiest silhouette watching me from the top floor, rubbing over my mouth in thought. "Thank you, Eli. You can go do whatever the fuck it is that you were going to do."

He nods curtly, then walks off towards the shop.

Setting my rage thinned eyes on Shiloh, I tighten my fist and strike him in the cheekbone before he can blink.

His head whips, and his body smacks the pavement, a groan of agony puffing out of his lungs.

"Ah, shit," Leon mumbles behind me.

My jaw locks, the plaguing images of Shiloh taking something that didn't belong to him scorching my chest.

"I was willing to move past the marks because I believe you really were trying to help her. But kissing her is a different story. She views that shit as special. It's intimate for her. And you just fucking took that shit," I finish with a snarl.

He pushes himself up, staggering to his feet and rubbing his face. "I know, man. I'm not fucking proud of it," he says grimly.

I can't stand to look at him any longer. I'm too volatile and might rip his damn spine out.

I turn my ass around and head inside the shop. Now, I have to deal with the bastard that was posting the horrific videos.

Viper's leaning against the tailgate of my truck, scratching the side of his fade and shooting me shocked eyes as I pass by. "Thanks for going and getting the fucking punk," I grumble, then aim my sights on the little hallway.

Walking in through the metal door, I stalk past Eli who's kicked back against the wall, staring at Ashton's dizzy face.

I stop in front of Ashton, his eyes blowing out in horror as they land on me. "Ashton Prior. You are a sick piece of shit," I say tonelessly, and send a powerhouse punch straight to his honker that can probably smell a mile away.

His eyes squeeze shut, head slamming back into the chair. Crimson instantly sprays down his pathetic excuse for a mustache, filling the seams of his twisted lips.

The scream that claws out of him makes my brows furrow, and I strike his nose again, this time snapping the bones.

Blood splatters onto my knuckles and gushes down his face, seeping through his gray crewneck.

His eyes roll around, grunts of distress filtering between his red teeth. "It was just money," he strains out. "My insulin is expensive."

"Then you should've gotten a job," I counter. "You could've found a well-paying career in tech that didn't involve you posting barbaric torture for the whole fucking world to see. How'd you even get in contact with Jenkins? I'm aware you set his security system up. But why would he seek out someone in Canada?"

"M-mutual connection," he grunts.

My brow raises. "Silas White?"

He nods jaggedly, tears veining down his tense face.

"Is Brutus Tuffin with him?" I ask impatiently.

He spits a wad of blood into his lap, shaking his dense head and crying like a fucking baby. "Who?" he wavers.

"Pyro!" I snap.

He flinches. "I-I think so. You can trace his last text to me." He lazily lifts his hip, pointing out the phone in his pocket.

"I'll take that," Leon chimes gleefully, digging into Ashton's pocket and fetching his phone out.

The rusty door opens, leaving only a screen storm door in between Silas's short ass and myself.

His eyes widen, nervously scratching over the sweat stain on the front of his shirt. "The dogs are gone now. And you fucked up my backyard."

"Sorry about that, man. I had something important come up. Now, instead of lying about the dogs I can hear and smell, why don't you just open this door and invite your guests in," I suggest firmly, tone laced with threat.

"Guests?" he questions, a dumbass look on his face.

"Hm, the pretty, little thing hiding behind me. Careful though… She bites."

His brows jump up, craning his neck to see the anxious vixen that's clawing into my back with her sharp nails. She steps to the side, and his eyes light up from being graced by the presence of a divine specimen.

"Sorry," she says sweetly. "I'm just really excited to see your dogs. I had to put myself in timeout for a moment."

He smirks, scanning her head to toe. "I wouldn't want to make you wait any longer, sweets. I'll slip my shoes on and show you around back. You'll have to excuse my destroyed gate." He glances at my twitching lip, wiping the smile right off his face. "It's okay. I'm not mad about it."

"Actually," she chimes, grabbing the handle of the door. "I was wondering if you could show me your trophy wall."

Fuckin' hell, little wolf.

Can't help but fantasize about all the positions I could get her into inside my truck. I reach out, rubbing over the top of her ass while doofus here smiles at her, showing off his decaying, chipped front tooth.

"Come on in, sweets," he says sleazily.

I wrap my hand around hers on the handle, glaring at him while opening the door. His greedy eyes don't stray from her as we walk in. Probably about to jizz his crusty, flannel pants over Heaven and Hell being in his house.

It smells like cat piss and dog shit.

Cigarette butts are spilling off the coffee table, littering the floor alongside the trash and sketchy stains. I can see his kitchen sink from the front door. Dirty dishes are piled up in it and scattered over the roach infested countertop.

Probably some fucking rats too. Jesus.

"You have company often?" I ask, scanning around while he guides the way down a claustrophobic hall.

I analyze the way he's lifting his shirt, grabbing what I assume to be a gun shoved in his sleep pants.

Adrenaline pops in my veins and I wrap my arm around Tala's shoulders, shoving her in between the wall and myself, all while ripping my gun out of the waistband of my jeans.

He spins around, raising a puny pistol at me. Apparently not expecting my barrel to already be pointed at his greasy dome with the way his sly grin dissolves.

"Where's Brutus?" I ask, finger on the trigger and sight lined up in between his brows.

He squints his eyes as if he has the upper hand. "Probably several blocks over by now. Even for an old man, he's got some juice to him."

Viper. Eli, and Shiloh are surrounding the house. There's not a chance he slipped past them unless the fucker is a sorcerer and opened a damn portal.

"Thanks." I pull the trigger, a noisy pop echoing through the hallway.

Wasn't just mine though.

The cavity in between his shocked eyes leaks crimson, his body thudding heavily to the piss-filled carpet.

"Are you okay?" I ask Tala, inspecting her panicking face.

Her pupils are dilated, diminishing the golden amber as she stares at my shoulder. "Babe… you got shot."

Must be why I feel a pinch in my shoulder.

"I'm fine. Are *you* fine?" I move the hair from her neck, caging my hand around the back of it to pull her closer.

"Mm-hmm," she hums, not blinking. She reaches up, scraping her sharp nails along my flesh as she hooks her fingers into my crew neck, prying it open to look at my shoulder.

That was too fucking close. She could've been shot. Again.

"I'm fine, baby." I wipe a stray tear falling over her cheek. "We need to get those dogs loaded up and pop some Ibuprofen."

She flattens her brows, gazing at me with concern. "I don't think Ibuprofen will do much for a gunshot wound."

I slide my gun back into my waistband, a laugh coming out over how fucking cute she is. "Not for the gunshot, baby. For our thumping domes."

I offer her my hand, tightly lacing her fingers with mine to get the fuck out of here.

We walk through the heinous living room, and I whip the front door open. She gasps lightly, and I point to Brutus thrashing around in Eli's grip, a bandana gagging his smug mouth. "And that's why we'll have headaches, little wolf."

She laughs out of relief, raising our joined hands to her mouth and pressing her glossy lips to the back of my hand. "I'll saddle up on your lap and play doctor with you later. If you're lucky, I'll sing to you like you sang to me."

I halt, staring at her silently.

I've seen her singing to herself before. But I never let the Devil control my finger to turn the volume up to actually hear it.

Fuck. I know it's sweet and husky.

"Do you know how to play guitar too?" I ask her, stomping my ass through the snow, not looking away from my little mystery.

She grins, amber eyes absorbing the reflective wash of white. "Mm-hmm. I used to play with Dad and Grandpa. So, I'm probably a little rusty now. Good thing I know a demon with magical hands."

Desire rolls under my skin like dice, and I harbor the groan brewing in my chest.

The dogs are at the ranch. That makes thirty-two of them now. All running around, doing whatever their heart desires.

Brutus and Ashton are both chained and bolted up in the shop. I'll let them starve for a few days, then fuck them up.

I might let my rats eat them.

Now, I have creamy skin, Venus eyes, and raven silk up close. Her maddening thighs and curvy hips are straddling my lap at the dining table.

I coast my hands over her curves, taking my mind off the way she's digging in my flaming shoulder with forceps.

She gasps sarcastically, focused on fishing around for the bullet. "Mr. Scythe, is it appropriate for a patient to caress their doctor?"

My cock lengthens underneath her, only my sweatpants and her thin leggings creating a barrier in between us. She wets her lips, cheeks flushing rosily, and glances at me before returning to her work. "A wise woman once told me, *It's so much more fun when you break some rules.*"

I feel her clamp around the metal lodged in my meat, and I clench my teeth, getting her pussy to roll over my cock in return. "Such a good boy," she whispers, easing out the bullet. She reaches over and lets the bloody metal clank down into the metal pan.

I grab her hips, the juiciness overfilling my hands, and yank her pretty ass closer to me. She drops the forceps on the ground, desperately entwining her fingers in my hair. "Little wolf, I'm two seconds away from tearing your pants in half and letting everyone watch as you come all over my cock."

A whiny breath drifts from her parted lips, skating over my own like it belongs to be trapped in my mouth. "You need to get stitched up," she counters.

"Boooo! Let him bleed and ride that stallion!" Nadia shouts, watching from the other side of the table.

For once—I agree with the feral chihuahua.

"Are you kids done playing around so I can do what I came here for?" Dr. Zion asks exasperatedly, holding a needle and thread up with gloved hands.

Her forehead presses into mine, and she shakes her head with an embarrassed grin. "You're trouble, Jax Scythe. Whatever your middle name is." She lifts off, throwing her leg over me and leaving me with the ghost of her body on top of mine.

"I don't have a middle name, baby. I opted out of normalcy."

While she hops up on the table in front of me, relaxing back on her hands, Dr. Z begins cleaning my shoulder and tearing a needle through my flesh.

She smiles, the dim light raining over how euphoric she is. "Can I give you a middle name?" she questions.

"Hmm. And what would that be?"

She weighs her head, amber eyes breezing over the ceiling in a theatrical thought. "Jax. Reaper. Scythe," she finishes with a dramatic whisper.

CHAPTER THIRTY-EIGHT

TALA

I'm going to do something stupid. But in my defense, Jax constantly surprises me with meaningful gifts, and he spoiled the fuck out of me for the late Christmas we celebrated.

Dark red peonies fill the house that's now cluttered with animal print, fur, ornate mirrors and frames, and bundles of dead flowers.

I didn't want him to change the house for me.

I love Jax for who he is and would do anything for him. Tolerating the bleakness that made the walls cold, and the rooms feel like voids wasn't a concern of mine anymore.

When I'm with him, I'm home.

I don't need the eclectic chaos to keep me sane when I have obsidian eyes to fall into and strong hands that caress me.

I don't dare tell him that though.

He was so happy to show me and obsessively analyzed my reaction to everything.

Not only did the sex demon redo the house. He cleared out a spare room and turned it into a home office. The monitor is massive. I told him I didn't need that much space to work from, but he insisted it would "give me room to have my files open while writing."

All I did for him was dress up in red lingerie and put waves in my hair. That's pathetic.

He's currently delivering Brynn's ashes to her mom while Eli and Viper watch Brutus and Ashton in the shop. Which gives me an opening to sneak out.

I just have to get past Shiloh and hope that the dogs don't freak the fuck out and rat on me. I fed them before fleeing upstairs to throw my Chucks on. So, fingers crossed they're still chowing down.

Leaving my phone on my nightstand, I grab my keys and walk out of the bedroom. Nadia's on the phone with her newest client, talking with her hand and pacing around the room she's been staying in.

Which is all pink now.

I stride past her and quickly walk down the hall, taking the stairs as quietly as I can in sneakers. The boys are still eating, wagging their nub tails in the kitchen. It makes me grin and take in the cute image as I walk towards the door.

Right as I think I'm in the clear, I run straight into a damn wall. Pain jolts down my chest, and I whip my head straight, widely staring into black fabric.

I pan up to stern Roman features with a bruised cheekbone, attempting to swallow down the bees that are beginning to buzz up my throat.

Son of a bitch.

"What are you doing?" Shiloh asks reservedly.

Flashes of him sucking on my skin and brutally slamming me up against walls play behind my panicking eyes. I remind myself that we're no longer in that house and pop my numb lips. "Just grabbing my spare lip gloss from my car."

His eyes narrow, raking over my face. "Okay. But I'm supposed to make sure you and Nadia stay in the house. So, hustle back in, eh?"

I snarl at him, eyebrows pinched tight at his audacity.

"Please, Tala."

I gasp sarcastically. "Well, since you asked *so* nicely. Dick." I push past him and rush out the front door, closing it behind me and jogging through the snow to my SUV.

Knowing he's watching my active escape makes me laugh, throwing myself into my seat and slamming my door closed. I don't waste time starting the engine and shifting into drive.

Did I just get him killed? Possibly.

But Jax will really like his surprise.

Ignoring Shiloh sprinting out the front door, I turn the radio up and speed down the driveway, flying through the slush covering the back road that leads into town.

The city roads are mostly clear, yet not many people are out due to the snowstorm coming in tonight. Supposedly people were panicking yesterday and buying out all the stores to make sure they're stocked up for the apparent apocalypse.

Brynn's funeral was scheduled for tomorrow. But with the incoming snow, her mom called it off and said she'd prefer to wait until Spring when everything is colorful.

I'm just glad she's getting her ashes today.

The wooden gates are already open for me as I roll up to *Howling Haven*. I pull up in front of my smiling Dad who has Echo and Void on either side of him, and shut my SUV off, jumping out with a giddy smile.

He hits the button to close the gates, and I reach down to love on the awaiting furry heads. "Jax has no idea. So, if he calls, pretend I'm not here."

He cringes, tipping his head towards the ICU cabin. "I don't like that, sweetheart." I fall in line with his steps, briefly waving at Valko's crazy ass watching me from behind a tree. "But I suppose I'll lie for the sake of romance," he croons.

I grab his arm and lean into him, crunching down the frosty rocks with my sneakers. "Thank you for not casting judgment on our macabre love."

"What's there to judge, kiddo? Mom and I think it's really special."

"Is she in the cabin?" I ask, looking up at his blushed cheeks.

He nods. "She and Paxton already have it all set up for you."

I knew I wouldn't be able to go to *Wyvern's Ink* without Satan showing up there. I also wanted to kill three birds with one stone so this wouldn't take too long and make him crack his molars.

I sigh, realizing he'll probably need to go to the dentist after today.

Dad opens the door for me, and I let go of his arm and walk inside, smiling at the steel eyes that are thin with a big ass grin.

"Hey, Kira-Kira," Paxton rasps, wiping down his table.

I head his direction, tossing my mane up into a messy bun. "Thank you for doing this on short notice. I still can't believe you drew all that up within a few hours."

He stretches an arm out, wrapping me into a side hug. "It's no problem. Jax's art has been inspiring me to practice trad Japanese work. So, I'm stoked to do this."

I look at him, pouting my bottom lip. "Awh, Paxton, is Jax your muse?" I ask playfully.

Mom sets her basket of nail polish down on the table across from his, a sweet laugh humming out of her grin. "Can you blame him, honey? Jax is a beautiful man."

A twinge of annoyance simmers my blood. She has no idea what Jax said about her on Thanksgiving. But I'm still really aggravated about it and don't really care to hear about their sexual attraction to each other.

I thin my lips, tuning out her and Paxton and watching my dad roll his stainless-steel tray littered with blood drawing equipment over to the exam table.

My surprise might've taken a tad longer than I expected. Ten minutes into me being at the sanctuary, Jax called my dad in a full-blown panic asking if I was there.

Dad lied to him.

So, I have no clue what Jax has been doing for ten hours. Possibly ripping his hair out or burning shit down.

I guess I'll see in about thirty seconds.

I shift in my seat, peeling my shirt away from the heat trapped in my back and shoulders, and tunnel in on the large shadow rushing up to the glass front door.

My heart starts beating heavier, drying my tongue out and causing my palms to sweat.

He's already sprinting outside, scowl drawn taut with vexation. I frown, uncomfortably pulling up in front of the shop and side-eyeing the behemoth storming up to my driver door.

I barely have it in park before he's ripping at the handle—glaring at me for not unlocking it.

I turn the engine off, slowly looking over at pissed off Satan through the dark tint on my window. I smile. Awkwardly.

"Out. Of. The car. Now," he warns, deep voice seeping through the metal and glass between us.

Well, now I'm even more fucking nervous.

I take a deep breath and open the door. He instantly maneuvers around to stand in front of me, and I try to get out without making it obvious what I was up to.

"What the fuck, Tala?" he barks, eyes barbed with vexation.

He's never yelled at me like that before.

My fast heart rate drops to my stomach and the whites of my eyes begin to sting. I suck it up, flip the asshole off, and shove past him. "I'm not telling you shit if you can't speak to me at a normal volume," I snip. His hand wraps around my wrist, twisting me around and jerking me into him. "Ow, asshole!"

"You can't just fucking leave like that!" he snaps, and I draw back, gaping at the ticking jaw of a goddamn bomb. "I've been…" He shakes his head, loosening his iron vice-grip from my wrist and caging me in his arms. "It doesn't matter. You're here."

My lips curl to my teeth, harboring a cry of agony as he roughly hugs me. He smells really good though… "I just wanted to surprise you, Jax," I mumble, then shimmy from his possessive hug. Holding my nails out, I smile at the way his brows knit over them. "I thought they'd be pretty wrapped around your cock."

He slowly blinks, directing his thin pools of Hell at my face. He grabs my hand, looking back down at the glossy crimson paint on my sharp nails. "Such a fuckin' manipulator," he huffs.

Hooking my free fingers into his belt, I walk backwards, urging him to follow. "Come upstairs with me and I'll show you the rest," I say smokily, and tear away from him, dashing for the front door.

I laugh, knowing he's hot on my heels as I run inside and weave around the dogs. Nadia and Leon are watching from the kitchen and Maverick's shaking his head from the stairs.

"What?" I ask irritably, thundering past him.

"At least take your damn phone with you, killer."

"It wouldn't be a surprise then!" I holler back and run down the hallway.

My fast strides skitter to a halt, almost missing the bedroom and having to hook a hand around the doorframe to bolt inside. Large hands grab my hips, whisking my body around. I yelp in response, lazily backing away from Jax kicking the door closed.

He follows my steps, gliding a hand up my stomach and over my chest. "I like your hair like that," he grumbles, pinching the zipper in between my boobs and teasing it down the metal teeth. "You better have a really fuckin' good explanation for having it pulled up and out of the way."

The tight fabric of my jacket loosens, revealing my bare tits and ugly scars and stitches. I stop walking and grab his hand, maintaining heated eye contact while running his rough palm up to the dog tag resting in my cleavage.

"How do you want it?" I ask. He hikes a brow, tilting his head. "Do you want to see what it would look like in action? Or do you want me to stand here like a canvas on an easel?"

Smoothing his hand up to my throat, he easily joins his fingers around the back of my neck, hungry eyes boring into my soul. "You've been a bad girl, baby. You have about two seconds to show me before I shove you to your knees and make you wrap your pouty lips around my cock. Your pretty ass nails too."

Pressure falls in between my thighs, liking the idea more than I should. I strip my jacket off, letting him look at the Japanese peonies on my shoulders, then spin around and bend over the new memory foam bed.

His old bed was like a slab of concrete. I never complained though. I basically sleep on top of him when Sirohi isn't wedged in between us.

He brought my grandma's ornate mirror from my house and propped it up in the corner across from the bed. I watch him in it, biting my lip at the way his brows pinch with a gruff groan.

He presses his hard cock into my ass, hooking his fingertips into the waistband of my leggings to ease them farther down. "You and Paxton weren't at *Wyvern's*. So, where the fuck were you?" His eyes meet mine in the mirror, and he scans over the fresh ink on my back.

A large dragon coils around the dagger scale and covers the majority of my back, Japanese peonies filling the empty spaces. I eventually want to get my sleeves done. So, Paxton did the peonies on my shoulders to have a flawless transition into them.

And of course—I got his last name fixed.

"You can't be mad at him. But I told Dad to lie to you so I could attempt to surprise you. Mom did my nails while Paxton drilled into my back… That's not all though."

He firmly rubs over my ass, swerving his hands around my hips. His mouth opens to say something, but his face tightens, and he begins messing with the lump in my leggings.

It tickles, drawing out a laugh that makes my face smash into the fur blanket. "S-stop messing with it and just pull it out," I titter.

His fingers fish the warm metal out, and I push off the bed, swiveling around to sit in front of him.

His face softens, obsidian investigating the thick crimson filling a dagger charm.

"I didn't know if you'd want a separate chain for it, or if you'd want to stack it with your dog tag. So, I got one just in case."

He dangles the necklace from the back of his hand, adoration warming his twinkling eyes. "You spilled it for me."

Skimming my hands up his thighs, I stop on his belt and begin to unbuckle it. "It's a token of my devotion. A reminder that I'm always with you."

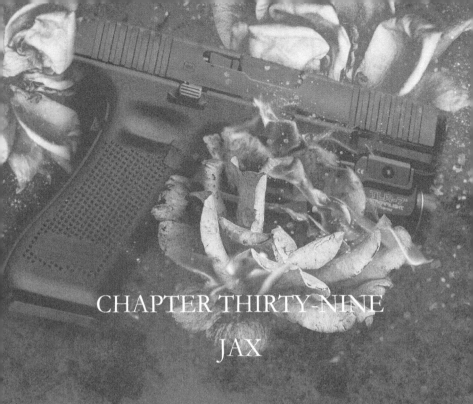

CHAPTER THIRTY-NINE

JAX

Every step towards the door removes a weight off my shoulders and chest. The shackles that have had me bound to him are finally. Fucking finally. Coming off.

I hope my father's proud, beaming his ridiculous smile that's capable of clearing cloudy skies.

Lifting Tala's blood out from under my hoodie, I grab the charm and press my lips to it, letting it slide back against my skin and shoving the metal door open.

Well, isn't this a mighty fine sight.

I can't help but smile at the pissed off, smug face that has my initials scarred into it. It's the first time I've come in here since we got our hands on him a few days ago. Since he wanted to starve the dogs and women, I've been letting him, and Ashton starve.

Ashton's light is slowly fading out naturally. He's gray, sweaty, and trembling from not having his insulin.

Grabbing the metal chair next to the embalming table, I scoot it across the floor, intentionally creating a god-awful scraping sound until I park it in front of Brutus' chained up body.

I straddle it backwards, resting my arms over the back with a cocky grin. "I take it you don't remember my face."

His heavy, hazel-brown eyes lock on me, and I smack the back of the chair, causing his eyes to twitch.

"I'll save you the trouble, you old fuck. Chihiro Otake, two-thousand-nine, got a bullet of yours lodged in between his eyes while he was enjoying breakfast with his kid son... Can you take a guess as to who that might be?"

Ashton's head slumps forward, spine bent like a shrimp and chest no longer rising.

I lazily point at him. "Oh, shit. I think we just lost your buddy," I jeer impassively.

"What makes you think I give a shit, boy?" he snarls.

"Watch your mouth when you're talking to me," I warn. "I know a pretty, little thing that likes teeth." I stop for a fake laugh. "I'm fuckin' with you. I'm taking them anyway." I stand my ass up, shoving the chair to the side.

"Oh, man," he smiles in revelation. "Your mama's Susannah?"

"Mm-hmm." I grab the curved jaw pliers off the stainless-steel table next to him, then snatch his jaw with my free hand, brutally digging my fingers into his sweaty cheeks.

He bucks around, grunting in agony, and I press harder, glowering at him as his jaws stretch open for me. Ignoring his despair and useless thrashes, I shove the pliers into his mouth and grip around a decaying molar. And I crank that shit to the right—and rip it out.

Holding it up for him to see, my lips curl in disgust. But something interesting is tingling my skin, and my face relaxes with infatuation, looking over to the man-eater standing in the threshold.

It's like seeing her for the first time all over again.

Except, her hair's thrown up in a bun, wavy tendrils falling out of it and framing her heart-shaped face. She's wearing Liam's wisdom teeth, adding to the celestial silver decorating her ears. And dear God, the black bodysuit she has on with her big ass furry boots is enough to make me forget my own name.

She sways over, not tearing her eyes from me. "Dinner's almost done. Is there anything in particular you want to drink?"

I catch Brutus staring at her, whimpers of pain emitting from his bleeding mouth. Tossing the pliers and his tooth over onto the table, my lip twitches and I whisk my balisong from my pocket, rolling the blade into an ice pick and stabbing his eye. Just enough to fuck it up.

"Whatever you spit into my mouth is fine, baby," I say over his shrieks, and shoot her fine ass a wink.

Paying no mind to the fucker that just lost an eye, she tilts her head, cheeks flushing with a foxy grin. "We have Stella Rosa," she says smoothly, husky voice drowning out the annoying cretin.

I unlatch my hand from his face, giving him a firm slap across the cheek before turning to the vixen and grabbing her waist. My eyes fall heavily, pinpointing the gloss on her pouty lips. "Are you trying to wine and dine me, little wolf?"

Brutus laughs menacingly, grunts and rough breaths following behind. "Now, I wouldn't get too cozy," he sneers.

Tala rolls her eyes, and I huff irritably, looking at the one eye that's beginning to turn red from broken blood vessels. "And why is that?"

The crimson seeping from his eye drips over his lip, spreading through the cracks of his smile. "Victor and Susannah are a peachy pair now. They're probably already here."

I'm not giving him the satisfaction of getting under my skin. Even though it feels like rats are chewing through my chest.

I honestly didn't think they'd still be alive.

Grabbing the metal handles of my knife, I rip the blade out of his eye, deadpanning at the ear-splitting scream this guy's capable of.

"Susannah… Is that your mom?" Tala asks.

"Yes, ma'am," I nod, pinching in between my brows.

He has the same *IR* tattoo on his middle finger.

Most likely has a fucking tracker too.

Tacking my blade to the leathery flesh above his knuckle, a bead of crimson bubbles out, swelling into the webs of his finger.

"What?" he chortles. "You didn't think I'd have people lookin' for me? I'm their fuckin' God, boy! Their savior!"

I look him dead in the one eye he has now, slowly letting a smile stretch. His smug amusement drops to a snarl, and I hammer my knife down into his finger, instantly confiscating the severed digit and holding it up in front of his straining face.

"Good thing I've been looking for them too… You just made this so easy for me." I wipe my knife off on his sleeve, roll it closed, and shove it into my pocket. "Keep that one eye on the fuckin' rats."

Tala's little fingers graze mine, taking his finger from my possession and dropping it down into a dirty bandana. She tips her head towards the door, turning around and rolling her hips away from me.

I follow her, closing and locking the metal door behind me. I watch the waves in her ass the entire walk through the shop, still in disbelief that she's real—and mine.

I've been planning something for her. Something that will tie the final knot in our joined souls. And I know she's going to love it.

She stops and watches me lock the side door of the shop, then reaches up to me. I smile and bend down, cupping under her ass and hauling her curvy, little body up. Her arms and legs encage me, and she rubs the tip of her nose against mine as I carry my little snow bunny through the ten fucking inches of cold fluff on the ground.

"You can talk to me about how you're feeling," she says softly, amber eyes trailing my face. "You know that, right?"

I'm not sure how I got so lucky.

I never needed anything outside of the essentials for survival. Aside from my father's guitar collection, I never found comfort in materialistic items that would fill space. And I think it's because deep down I've always known—I just need her.

I shift one hand underneath her, opening the door to the boys that are pissed their Mama left without them. "I know, little wolf. I'm doin' just fine. I promise."

Stepping inside, I close the door and set the alarm—getting lost in the sparkling Venus before me.

"Tala, I need help! I'm scared!" Nadia shouts gravely from the kitchen.

Tala throws her head back on a smoky laugh, shedding light on the pink scar low on her throat. "Th-they're just noodles," she giggles out.

Leave it to Nadia to burn a house down from boiling water.

"Goddamn it, angel," Maverick huffs irritably, storming from the living room and into the kitchen. "I left you alone for one minute."

Stalking towards the chaos, I squeeze Tala's ass, just enough to brand my hand into her.

She rolls closer into me, snaking a hand up the back of my head and igniting pinpricks on my scalp. Liquid desire warms my veins, and I set her down on the island, moving my face impossibly close to hers.

The coconut on her lips is too enticing.

My lips part, closing the centimeter separating us, and I capture her glossy pout, ever so slightly teasing my tongue over her bottom lip.

I have to tear away from her, otherwise her sexy bodysuit will be ripped in half, and I'll end up fucking her on the island in front of everyone.

She whines, not letting me pull away.

It makes me laugh a little. And another shot of novocaine numbs my head as her lips lock onto mine, her sweet fucking tongue slipping inside my mouth.

"Ah, man, you know what? I'm not even mad. I've never heard you laugh until you met her."

"Shut up, Leon, you're going to ruin it," Nadia hisses.

Tala's lips stretch against mine, and another smoky laugh comes out of her.

I pull away, fixing my sights on Leon. "Guess who's still breathing?"

His lips thin, eyes volleying around in thought. It dawns on him, and his eyes round. "No shit... Your mom?"

CHAPTER FORTY

TALA

Nadia's been rubbing her feet against mine on the couch for five minutes now. It's just one of those things I've grown to accept that she does. Must give her a boost of serotonin with how giddy she gets.

I don't know how she's smiling without vomiting. I ate way too much spaghetti and now my stomach feels like a damn bowling ball. I could fall off the couch and roll away forever.

I groan in discomfort and lay my open book flat on my chest, closing my eyes and yanking the hair tie out of my hair. I shake my waves out, almost moaning from the relief tingling my scalp.

"Will you carry me upstairs and undress me?" I ask coyly.

She locks her phone, sitting up with a bland expression.

"Tala, I love you and would do anything for you. But I am not capable of lifting your planet-sized ass up."

My jaw drops, and she shrugs irreverently

"You got cake, girl. I think Jax is the only baker that can handle all that." She bobs her head to the lewd tune of her words.

A disconnected laugh filters out of my agape mouth, and I snap my teeth together. She's not wrong.

That man picks me up like I'm a blade of grass.

I close my book and sit up, folding my legs in with a dorky grin. The little wine I was able to swallow is making my tongue loose. Excitement flashes through her hazel eyes, and she shuffles closer with a big ass smile, awaiting the slutty secrets to spill out of me.

"He can hold my weight up. In the shower. With soap making everything slippery. And still fuck me like a sex god," I utter secretively.

She screams. Squeals. I'm not sure. But it scares me, and all three dogs jump to their paws, barking at her aroused theatrics.

"Nadia," I hiss, cupping my hand over her mouth and silencing both her and the dogs. "You're going to make them think something's wrong!"

Too fucking late.

Loud steps are thundering down the stairs in a hurry.

I remove my hand from her, slowly blinking at the amused smile that's revealed. The embers are already tingling the right side of my body, warning me of Satan storming up to us. Silently.

"What happened? Are you okay?" Jax asks tensely, fighter body towering over me.

I gape up at the behemoth, craning my damn neck just to gaze into his hellish eyes. "We, uh… I…" Suddenly, I've forgotten English. Nadia laughing at me doesn't help the abrupt storm of nervousness.

But Jesus, he's devilishly handsome.

His brow raises, and he lightly wraps his hand around my throat—feeling my pulse. He cocks his head, a wolfish smirk showing off his sharp canines, tendrils of black hair falling over his eye. "Why so nervous, little rabbit?" He drops to a dangerous octave, making my heart race faster.

"Angel, you can't cry wolf when we still have people running around," Maverick sighs.

Out of my peripheral vision, I see him pick her up off the couch. But I'm still at war with the Devil and can't seem to win.

"I wasn't crying wolf, Maverick," she says cattily, getting carried away.

Jax's fingertips skim down my neck, the feathery touch sending a shudder down my spine as his fingers travel farther down my chest. He bends over me, using his free hand to unfold my legs, and a heavy throb begins pounding in my core. "Do you like what you're wearing, baby?" he asks darkly, teasing his middle finger down my nipple.

Heat floods my cheeks, and a breath hitches in my throat as his hand rubs the fabric concealing my needy clit. I glance around, making sure Viper's freaky ass isn't perched somewhere and watching. My gaze lands on Jax's close face, sweeping down to the scar on his lip.

"Yes," I answer timidly.

"Hmm. Then I suggest you change before I destroy it." His lips brush up mine, carnivorous eyes thinned to slits.

Desperately, I inch closer, barely getting his bottom lip sealed in between mine before he draws back.

My face scrunches at the fucking Punisher, and I yank his hand out from in between my thighs.

"And what is it that you want me to put on, sir?" I bite out.

His bottom lip curls within his teeth, and he quickly grabs under my arms. Picking me up like a damn feather. I mold around him, letting out a heavy breath from his lips skimming my ear.

"Something you don't mind me ripping to shreds," he whispers, hooking his hands under my ass and carrying me off.

"Why don't I just stay naked?" I question.

He kisses my jaw, hiking up the stairs. "Because I don't want anyone seeing my girl running through the woods naked."

I slowly blink. "Jax, there are at least ten inches of snow outside and it's freezing."

"I'll keep you warm, baby," he drawls, igniting a hunger that spills in between my thighs.

"It's the full moon," I point out, gazing up into sultry obsidian. "Are you trying to write up a soul contract, Mr. Scythe?"

"Little wolf… I already have your soul."

I gape at Satan, heart pulsing in my wind whipped cheeks. He's shoving along zombified Brutus through the glacial night air and snow. The horror of him somehow getting away again is constricting my tongue. I'm following mechanically, still unsure as to why Jax made me change and come out here to watch him torture a zombie in the woods.

"Here's the deal, Brutus. We'll give you a ten second head start since your old ass is about to meet the Grim Reaper. If you manage to escape, then you get to make it out of here alive. That's if sepsis doesn't take you the fuck out before you find your way through the trees," he grumbles, pushing Brutus into a small clearing blanketed in white.

"Jax," I growl, slowly blinking and hoping that I'm just losing my fucking marbles.

"Baby, look at him." He barely shoves him and Brutus staggers forward, falling to his knees with unintelligible noises straining out of his agape mouth.

"I'm aware that he's a mummy," I hum, grabbing his hand and shivering. "Stop playing with your food and just kill him. It won't matter in the end."

The moon's splashing over his scowl, shedding light on the carnal hunger in his hunter eyes. "Yes, ma'am."

Without looking, he whips his gun out from his waistband and fires a shot in Brutus' direction. My soul leaps out of my body, the resounding ring amplifying the steady incline of my heart rate. I'm not shocked to see the cavity on the back of Brutus' head, but I will never get used to Jax's inhumane range of sight.

The deep breath puffing out of me is a sigh of relief. Sure, it would've been sweeter to see Brutus cry and die painfully. But the weight unloading off my chest feels way better than vengeful torture.

Though, I'm not sure that was my call to make.

And I now realize that...

"How do you feel?" I ask Jax—who's tilting his head like a predator and sizing me up.

His arm extends out, and he wraps his large hand around the back of my neck, pulling me into him. "Starving," he growls quietly, raising the cold barrel to my temple.

A rupture of thrill pulses through my body. My pussy clenches, and I feel my pupils dilate, tunneling in on the wolfish grin that's slowly stretching wider.

"Would you take it for me?" he questions.

"Yes," I answer without hesitation. "I would do anything for you."

The metal skims down my cheekbone, and his hand retracts from my neck, moving in between us to undo his belt. I tremble, not from the cold air eating through my sweatpants and long sleeve shirt, from the barrel sliding over my lips and the domineering sharpness in his eyes.

"Take your clothes off," he demands.

My eyes narrow. "Didn't you make me change so you-" I yelp, snapping my teeth closed as he presses the end of the barrel to my forehead.

"Now, Tala." His belt cracks at his side, representing the little patience he has right now.

I grab the bottom of my shirt, pulling it off inside out and over my head as his gun moves from my damn cranium. I don't know what his deal is. But I'd be a liar if I said it's not making me weep down my thighs.

He's a little fucking crazy. And I love it.

Tossing my shirt to the side, the icy air nips at my skin. The image of him clawing at the back of his hoodie, ripping it off in a fluid motion, brings my blood to a rolling boil and floods my body with fire and ice.

His necklaces tink and swing as he throws it to the snow, fervently running his hand up my spine and into my hair while the other grazes his gun down the valley of my breasts. He tacks it to the thump in my sternum, and I swallow roughly, slipping my pants off as much as I can with him rendering my movement impossible.

"You could help," I mutter, kicking my shoes off and awkwardly shimmying out of my pants.

He smiles sharply, firmly dragging his gun along my scar and down my mound. Terror sizzles the utter excitement blasting through my veins, feeling the smooth metal course downward and slowly. So fucking slowly. Glide within my slit. "Keep going, little wolf," he orders, teasing his gun back and forth over my bud.

The blooming pleasure crafts a whimper, and I continue stepping out of my pants, getting more pressure applied to the slick motion with each inch I manage to get down.

I stand on top of the fabric, opening my legs wider and moaning as the build up begins. My hand flies to his chest, my nails clawing into his designed muscles, and I hike my leg up with my free hand, shamelessly belting out the smoky moans that I cannot contain.

"You like playing with my gun, baby?" he asks brusquely, tilting my head back and kissing along the collar I wear for him.

"Yes," I pant, frantic breaths burning my lungs. The danger, the thrill of playing with fire, is making me shake with the overwhelming hysteria that's heightening the orgasm exploding inside me like a box of grenades. "Oh, my fu-" My eyes disappear from my fucking skull, and my whine breaks out into a loud, husky cry of euphoria.

His lips stretch against my vibrating throat, and his sharp teeth sink down into my skin. The concoction of pain and pleasure is a paradisiac, altering my synapses and tipping me back and forth until my receptors smoke up into a haze of blissful anguish.

He laps over the stinging bite marks, blowing cool air that kisses his saliva and brands the sensation into me. "Attagirl," he whispers in my ear, removing his gun from my twitching clit. "Now lay your ethereal ass down for me."

Panting to catch my breath, I look at him like he's crazy.

Well, he is. But that's beside the point.

"In the fucking snow? Naked? Are you trying to kill me, Jax?"

His brow raises in warning, and I lightly growl in annoyance—then rip his hand from my hair and lay my ass down.

I whine, tightening my eyes as the fluffy ice melts into my backside, my hair only offering a small amount of warmth to my back. The snow crunching next to me makes my eyes pop open—and horror seizes the muscles in my face.

Jax has Brutus by the hair on the back of his head, dragging him right over to me and holding his dripping head above my stomach. I'm not given the chance to question him, or protest.

His blade glistens in the moonlight, moving in front of Brutus' throat and slashing it open.

The abrupt geyser of crimson makes me flinch, the warm liquid waterfalling over my body making my face tighten in a horrified cringe. I'm not saying shit though. Jax is scaring the fuck out of me right now and I'd like to be able to say a proper goodbye to my loved ones before his blade finds me next.

He rips Brutus away, hungrily tearing his pants off and coming down on top of me, pushing his slutty hips within my open legs. "I told you I'd keep you warm," he says wickedly, flashing me a dangerous smile.

I pop my lips, easily getting over whatever the fuck that was, and cup around his ears, guiding his mouth to mine. "You better be careful," I warn through a whisper. "I'll kill you if his blood gets inside me."

He groans in agreement, sealing our lips together, and his palm skates in between us, directing the stench of iron up to my throat.

It's really warm though.

And I'm aware that it's fucked up to say that. But I don't care.

Jax is rubbing his criminal body against mine, smearing the crimson around while making out with me like a horny teenager.

We only stop once our bodies begin dry humping in desperation. Our flesh is barely visible under the glistening crimson, Jax's appearing more intense because of his dark ink.

He jumps to his feet, eyeing me like I'm a queen on a bed of roses as he tears his briefs down.

My eyes grow heavy, watching his monster cock bob out, the anticipation on his rosy tip begging for me to lap it up. "You are darkly divine," he rumbles vehemently, getting down on his knees in between my legs.

I faintly laugh, smiling at the beast sliding up my sticky body. *"Divine and all mine,"* I quote him, mocking his subtle accent.

"Hmm," he growls amusedly, placing one hand by my head, the other gliding through the stickiness down to my thigh. "You mockin' me, baby girl?" He hooks his hand under my knee, stretching my leg, opening me up even more for him.

His hips rock back until the head of his cock is centered to my entrance, and a gush of anticipation shocks me, trapping me in the obsidian above me. "You know I love your voice. That includes the accent you try concealing," I say, running my wet hands up the back of his head.

He rocks his hips forward, easing me into the stretch that always makes my eyes roll, and he drops down to his elbow, cupping the back of my head and thrusting inside me until his shaven hilt rubs my clit.

"You're not supposed to know that," he rumbles playfully. My hands curl into his hair, the overfilled sensation producing a moan that bows my head back. "Tsk, tsk. Eyes on me. I want to be able to see how pretty they are under the moon."

I meet his sultry gaze, barely able to hold myself together as he rolls back, just to thrust in deeper than humanly possible. "If you don't fuck them out of my head," I groan, burrowing my heels into the snow.

My blood's running like furious sparks, clashing with the ice burning into my back and manifesting a tremble that his dick isn't helping.

I feel him in my fucking bones. They're shattering and mending back together with the fire he consistently feeds.

His pace quickens, each stroke rolling to his tip and bottoming out. He's gazing into my heavy eyes with affection, lips parted for the breaths that are bleeding into mine. "I want all of you," he whispers.

"I think you've got it all," I pant, brushing his hair away from his eye.

He shakes his head with a slight grin, and I expect him to drive into me for my attitude, but he thrusts in once more, slowly pulling out until I'm left empty.

I whine, clawing at the bloody behemoth sitting up in between my legs. "I'm sorry, come back," I plead, grinding my pussy in the air from how fucking desperate I am for him.

He leans over for his belt, and I immediately spring up with anxiety clawing into my chest. The moisture gets stripped from my tongue, negating any mumbling nonsense the flies would produce.

"Palms together, little wolf," he demands, feeding the leather through his lax grip.

My cheeks flame, feeling stupid for thinking he'd beat me with it. I swallow thickly and bring my hands together how he likes. "It's really cold," I point out, meeting his gaze.

"I can help you with that." Without breaking eye contact, he grabs a handful of snow and rubs it all over his mouth and cheeks. He repeats it, clearing away the majority of the crimson on his face.

I've said it before, and I'll say it again.

I might start howling.

Belt in hand, he scoots out from my legs and lays down in the snow. "Sit on my fucking face, Tala," he orders, monster cock fully erect in the air.

I bite my lip staring at it, almost considering straddling his hips to sink down onto him. But he'd probably rip me off by my hair and force me onto his face anyway.

Getting on my fours, my eyes turn hungry as I languidly crawl in between his legs, stitching my eyes to his and hunting him like prey.

I brace the snow on either side of his slutty hips, flattening my tongue over my bottom lip and lowering my mouth to his cock. His lips part for a warning, his contradicting eyes flashing with excitement. I don't stop. I lap up his velvety flesh, drawing his tip into my mouth.

"Fuck, baby," he groans, bringing his hand to the back of my head. "Crawl your sexy ass up to me and saddle my face before I put you there."

My own musk is blooming on my tongue, amplifying the craving of being overfilled until I'm one with the stars. I slowly work his tip out of my mouth, kissing it goodbye before crawling up to him. "I'm so serious, Jax," I say sternly, parking my knees on either side of his pretty face. "If a drop of his blood enters my pussy, I will kill you and wear your skin."

"Mmm," he groans with a wicked smile. "Sit the fuck down." He grabs my hips, roughly jerking my pussy down to his awaiting tongue.

His cold face and warm tongue send a shock of pleasure up my core. I buckle over, chest shaking with a ragged, breathy moan, and watch this man suck on me like a piece of fucking candy.

MADISON JO

He pins my hands together, flattening my palms into a prayer, and works the icy belt into a knotted loop around my wrists, tightening it until I'm unable to move my hands.

The glacial temperature no longer matters. My blood is burning hot, percolating my skin with a mist as his tongue sucks, flicks, and swirls my nerves into a flaming tension.

The heat expands through my hips and up my throat, and I swear flames are obstructing my vision.

My hips begin rolling on their own accord, encouraging the riptide of fiery pleasure to destroy my body. "Oh… oh, my God, Jax," I moan, getting a firm pat on my ass in encouragement.

Pain smarts on my ass cheek, sizzling from the icy air. He rubs it, massaging it into warm bliss, and the extra sensation pushes my body into overdrive.

There's too much coursing through my body and crafting a big aura of euphoria. It sparks and radiates from my head to my toes, and my head tosses back on an obnoxious moan that sends birds flapping their wings overhead. Fleeing the scene of my pussy getting murdered.

340

CHAPTER FORTY-ONE

JAX

I'm powering through the waterfall that's pouring into my mouth and down my face. It's like drinking straight juice, making me groan and crave more as I strip her of the last drop she's able to spill for me.

The sight is something else.

The moon's glow is raining hauntingly on the crimson of our common enemy, highlighting the macabre passion of her hips twitching, the way her tight waist is convulsing as she prays. To me.

"Fuck yes," she groans, snapping her gold eyes down to me.

I let her velvety bud go, and she nimbly lifts up, hovering her freshly fucked and eaten pussy above my face. God, I want to dive back in. But she starts working her way down my body before I can force her back onto my tongue without the chance of his blood getting on her.

"You wear my favorite color so well, baby," I drawl, smearing the sticky liquid up her wild ass hips.

She bites her lip, grinning and slowly rolling her hips backwards. "You know, my favorite color has always been black. It's just easy and forgiving. But I'm really starting to favor a certain shade of red… now that I've seen it on you," she tells me, eyeing me up and down like she's ready to go for a ride.

Dear God. My dick's pulsing with need.

I sit up, possessing her bound arms and slipping them over my head. "How's your back?" I ask hungrily, coasting my hands down to her hips.

"Now you're asking me?" she titters, centering her tight cunt to the head of my cock. My brow raises, and she tosses her head back on a smoky laugh, whipping her spine straight and crashing her lips to mine. She lets me dip inside her mouth once before she's tearing away, staying so close, I can only see her gold irises clashing with the moon and the crimson. "Fuck me like you hate me, Jax. Don't worry about hurting me."

She… has never said anything like that before. Jesus.

We've fucked several times over the past few days, and I've been taking extra precaution, so I don't hurt, or scare her.

The consent to get wild as hell is exploding my veins like a bomb and conjuring up a tsunami of wicked fire.

Scooping under her thighs and grabbing her ass, I launch to my feet, pounding through the snow towards the closest tree. I get her there, roughly backing her into the cold bark and using my elbows to push her knees out—stretching her wide the fuck open for me.

She moans, bucking her hips to swipe her weeping pussy on my cock. I note the trail of blood running down to her glistening clit, and I shift my arm out from under her, quickly wiping it away while widening my stance. "You gettin' hungry, baby girl? You want me to fill you up until you can't fuckin' take it anymore?" I move my arm back in place under her thigh, molding my hands to the creases of her juicy fucking hips and ass.

"Yes! God fucking damn it, Jax, just fuck me!"

I give the goddamn queen what she wants and drive into her. Black washes my vision out for a moment, the utter fucking Hell of her pussy blasting my nerve endings with unholy pleasure. I force them back open, moaning shamelessly into the husky cry smoking out of her pouty lips, and roll my hips back, just to thrust in deeper, and deeper, and deeper, until I set a steady pace that has both of us panting like animals.

I have to shake my head like a damn dog to get my hair out of my eyes. She's unbelievable, swallowing my cock and clenching impossibly tight around it. "Attagirl, baby. Come apart for me. Let me see you break so I can put those pieces back together, just to break you all over again." My hands sail underneath her thighs, hooking under her knees and pushing them back into the tree.

Her eyes roll back and her hellish grip turns supersonic—and here comes the whine that weakens my knees. "Oh, my God, I think my brain is bleeding," she whines raspily, her stomach hollowing and twitching.

If her pussy wasn't geysering on my cock and making the blood run thin down my legs, I'd be concerned that I was hurting her. But my girl's dramatic as fuck. Clearly.

I fight off the tingles that are tightening my balls and move a hand over her landing strip, making sure my thumb is somewhat clean before pressing it to her swollen bud and teasing it in circles. "Give me one more, baby girl."

Her brows draw taut over her heavy eyes. She nods, stammering unintelligible words, and it drives me fucking crazy. I growl, panting and praising her, and giving her all that I've got. I'm sweating against the icy air, rolling my hips how she likes and thrusting into her at a speed that I haven't gone at since before Thanksgiving.

Her pussy is just so fucking warm and wet… and fuck.

The tingles burn too fiercely to suppress. Everything within me is on fire, and the moment the loud, husky moan stretches her throat open and her cunt clamps around my dick, I let the fire spread and give in to the flames that could burn the world down. "Fuckin' hell, little wolf," I groan, releasing deep inside her.

I don't let my hips give out. I won't.

I keep thrusting through her grip and working my thumb in circles on her clit until a scream I've never heard before comes rasping out of her hoarse throat. "Jax!" She tightens her eyes, and I rush to her lips to taste the sweet whines of her catastrophic pleasure.

My heart swells, sending up a shock wave of courage that blasts over my chest, and I slow down, and press my misted forehead to hers—locking in on the most incredible Venus eyes that have taught me how to love. Possibly too much.

"Will you marry me?"

Surrealism softens her face, the euphoric glow beaming through the crimson and lighting her up like my dark fucking siren, my ethereal goddamn goddess.

She smiles, and the gold in her eyes turns to glass. "Yes," she whispers. A solo tear drips through her long lashes, veining through the blood on her cheek.

There wasn't a doubt in my mind that she wouldn't say yes. But actually hearing it, getting confirmation that she wants to take my last name, wear my blood on her finger, and be bound to me for the rest of our days in these vessels… I'm speechless.

All I can do is smile and lock our lips.

It's different though. Her touch has always torched my soul and radiated a hypnotic wildfire throughout my body.

Right now?

It's a rapture that's palpitating my heart, syncing it to the beat of hers and unifying our cardiac muscles. I wouldn't be surprised if bright ass lights were banding and glowing around us. Our joined souls are ascending. Together.

All of the "nexts" are with her.

My fiancé.

We pry away from each other, both smiling like absolute hell as I undo the belt and help her get dressed before covering my naked ass.

Pulling my jeans up, I fetch out the small loop of steel from my pocket and bring my hand to hers. Getting on one knee before her, her pretty nails dart up to her mouth, muffling the cutest fucking squeal that makes my cheeks hurt with the sharpest smile I can manage.

"This is just your engagement ring. I've already worked out the plans for both of our wedding rings. So, for now-" I slip my looped guitar string on her fourth finger "-this will hold its place... Mrs. Scythe."

I never see her excited. So, the little hops and giggles she's doing while looking at the ring honestly gives me fucking butterflies.

She's cute as hell when she's thrilled.

She waits for me to get my hoodie back on, then lunges up at me, encaging me with her limbs and biting her smiling pout. "I don't suppose your mom is invited to our wedding."

I palm her ass with both hands, walking through the snow and towards the house. "Abso-fuckin-lutely not, baby girl. She's been living it up in Florida. Apparently, Victor's been incarcerated there for three years for beating her to a pulp. And she's still making sappy ass posts on social media about *her man* getting out in a few months. She also has a nine-year-old son. So, that makes this all-" I halt, observing the cheerfulness depleting to sorrow in her face. "Baby, I'm okay. If anything, I'm worried about him."

She leans in, kissing me tenderly and gliding her nails in comforting circles on my back. The sorrow doesn't leave her face as she pulls away, gazing at me with eyes that see all. "So, what's the plan with them? I thought they were coming to Brutus' rescue. So he said."

"He's full of shit. He just wanted to get a rise out of me," I shake my head. "And as for the plan, I'm ready to let that sleeping dog lie. She hasn't been a thought in my mind in over eight years. I'll make sure their kid is okay and they're not pitting dogs anymore. But that's as far as I'm going to take it unless action is needed."

Walking through the front door, Sirohi, Killer, and Gemini begin skittering around us, whimpering and whining because evidently, they thought they'd never see Tala again.

She grins, her magical eyes roaming my face. "Whatever you choose, I support. I'll always be by your side. I'm your partner forever."

I stop, falling deep into her eyes. "Forever isn't long enough."

CHAPTER FORTY-TWO

TALA

Honey brown hair is bouncing around through the air. And for once—I'm joining the Tasmanian devil. So is Mom.

All three of us are jumping on my childhood bed. Which, we should definitely stop. The old floor is moaning and groaning like a train is being run on it.

But I'm getting fucking married! To Satan!

It's been a few days since he proposed to me in the passionate, macabre way that I was not expecting, and I still have stupid butterflies and a big grin on my face.

I collapse onto the mattress, falling heavily onto my side and propping my head in my hand.

Mom and Nadia follow the much-needed break, both creaking the bed as they plop down onto their butts.

"Okay-okay," Mom cheers, crisscrossing her legs. "What are you thinking for the color scheme? And flowers? Oh! I saw a catalog with a beautiful lace-"

"Mom," I interject lightheartedly, placing a hand on her knee. "It's been like three days. We're both just soaking it in right now."

Nadia snickers, "I'm sure Jax is really soaking it in."

"Nadia," I hiss, awkwardly looking back at my mom.

Mom laughs and Nadia shrugs irreverently. "You guys are really loud sometimes. It's a constant reminder that my vagina probably has spiders in it from being vacant for so long."

I deadpan at her, my cheeks flaming with embarrassment.

"Honey," Mom coos, sweeping the hair from my frozen face. "You guys weren't necessarily quiet on Thanksgiving."

"Oh, my God," I whine. The embarrassment is coiling around the butterflies, making me shy away from both of them. I grab a pillow from behind me and smash it into my face. "Nads, you know Maverick would sweep those cobwebs away in a heartbeat," I mumble into the pillow.

The silence is thick for a beat, then Mom gasps, and I rip the pillow away, following her line of sight to the increase of peach on Nadia's cheeks.

My jaw drops. I lurch myself forward and onto my ass, smacking my hair out my face to gape at her in amusement. "Nadia Arabella Adair," I croon in shock. Her bottom lip twitches, telling me that she's refraining from saying something, and I gasp. "When?"

"I don't know what you're talking about," she says impassively, a sheepish grin beginning to stretch her lips. "I wouldn't touch him with a ten-foot pole."

"But did you let him touch you with his?" Mom titters.

I fall in with Mom's laughter, having to roll onto my back and cover the burn firing up on my cheeks.

"Okay, you know what! Fine! I had a moment of weakness and let his face in between my legs. Are you happy?"

I lunge to my knees across from her, dramatically throwing my head back on a howl. And I mean a literal howl. Not a fucking laugh. She and Maverick are endgame, they're kismet just like Jax and I.

I have been decaying, just waiting for the moment that they'd finally give in. And for some goddamn reason it's exciting me and morphing me into an animal.

Mom chimes in, howling and stirring up the pack a mile away from the house.

"It was really good too!" Nadia shouts sourly over our noise, twisting her face for a theatrical cry.

Mom and I stop pestering her, and I giggle, sitting sideways with a look of content. "Well, yeah, Nads. I'm sure it was nice doing more with your mouths than bitch at each other. I mean, come on, we're going on ten years of your guys' bullshit. But my question for you is, did it mean something? And don't lie. I can read right into your soul."

She cringes, her body toppling backwards onto fur that's still matted from Jax and I disrespecting my parents' house.

Mom rubs her leg, smiling sweetly. "Nads, you girls are growing up. And as much as it pains Dad and I to accept that you guys aren't still playing fairies in the woods, we'd really like to see both of you settle down and just be happy. Especially with Mav, our special boy."

The faint creak in my doorway catches my attention. I lock eyes with Maverick and gape at him, gesturing for him to go away. He holds a finger up, pretending like his tall ass can hide behind the doorframe as he listens for Nadia's response.

I will disintegrate from vicarious embarrassment if she gets snippy and pretends like it didn't mean anything.

It clearly did to him. He wouldn't be on the edge of his seat, intently listening to her sigh.

"You guys can't say anything to him. Promise me," she says gravely, staring up at the ceiling.

"Promise," Mom and I hum together.

I can't avoid looking in his direction again.

He must've sensed that she's not ready to tell him herself, because he's no longer plastered up against the wall.

She trills her lips, bringing her arms over her stomach for comfort. "It meant more to me than I'll ever admit to myself. It felt right. I didn't feel like a toy or like I was using him to get what I wanted just to send him on his way. And all he did was shove his pretty face in between my legs... And yet... it felt like..." She rotates her hand, searching for the word.

"Dynamite," I fill her silence.

She's rarely ever serious. And as much as I love Nadia's bubbliness and carefree attitude, I love it when she's raw, and real, and unapologetically in tune with how she's truly feeling.

It's making my eyes sting.

Her hazel eyes land on me, contrition weaseling through the softness she's finally letting out. "Dynamite," she echoes.

A tear streams through my lower lashes, and I gently scoot in next to her, casting an arm and leg around her body. "Dynamite blows up. But it's so beautiful when it does," I whisper, eyeing the droplet rolling down her temple. I wipe it, cuddling her extra hard as Mom comes in on her other side.

Chewing, I fall into the hunter's gaze across the table from me, the lit candles in between us dancing in his obsidian irises.

Nadia's sitting next to me, scoffing at Maverick who's across from her as if she didn't just open her heart up about him an hour ago.

Mom and Dad are on either end, talking in circles about the future wedding and whether snow or flowers would be prettier.

And all I can think about is crawling up onto the table and parting my legs where Jax's empty plate is.

He's probably still hungry.

I stretch my leg out, running the toe of my boot up his leg. His jaw sets and he leans back, folding an arm up on the back of his chair—holding the heated tension.

My foot can only stretch so far. I manage to get his denim rolled up halfway before bringing my leg back to my side and grabbing my wine. I watch him over the brim of the glass, taking a slow drink that dribbles down my chin.

His eyes dart to the spill, and knowing he wants to lunge over and lap it up brings a foxy smile to my face. Isolating my ring finger, I flash him his guitar string, languidly wiping the red liquid away and cleaning it off my finger.

"Oh, honey, wouldn't that be so pretty?" Mom asks gleefully.

I don't know what the fuck was said.

I breeze over Maverick's smirk to get to my mom's dreamy expression, briskly sharpening my eyes at him. "I'm going to be completely honest. I got lost and started tuning everything out," I say tonelessly.

Mom frowns. "Where'd I lose you?"

Nadia's arm flings across my face, her French tip nail pointing at Jax. I gasp, furrowing my brows at Nadia. "What the hell? Why are you ratting me out?" I whisper-shout, ushering her arm back down beside her salad.

Her lips curl to her teeth, and her chest begins shaking with the suppressed laugh that's filtering disconnectedly through her nose.

"In some ways, they'll never grow up," Dad quips, his hands joined together in front of his smile.

"Speaking of growing up," Mom croons, rolling her head dramatically towards Nadia.

Enjoy the wolves, Nads. You've been thrown to them and I'm not saving you, you beautiful fucking angel.

"I have to pee!" she announces, scooting her chair back, the legs making a horrible screech. She springs up and runs around the back of my chair, fleeing from the kitchen.

I catch the flush in Maverick's cheeks, and I'm dying to say something. I don't, though. I have killer eyes eating through my face and burning my skull.

Maverick rips his phone from his pocket, instantly standing up and holding it to his ear. "I'm sorry, I need to take this. I'll be back in to help clean up." He starts to walk off, but quickly backpedals and places a light kiss on Mom's head. "Thank you for dinner."

I deadpan at him, watching as he pretends to rush towards the living room, only to hook back around and silently jog down the hall in route to the bathroom.

My head shakes with a slow blink, and I can do nothing to contain my lips curling in disgust, only imagining what they're doing, or what they could have already done in there.

"The front door never opened," Mom points out quietly.

I take a giant drink, focusing on Jax's lean body standing up and stacking empty plates. I'm no better than Nads and Mav. If the opportunity was presented, I'd maul Jax's clothes off and let him bend me over whatever was closest.

"This house is seeing more action now than what it did when they were in high school," Dad sighs, then pats Jax's arm with a smile as he takes his plate. "Thank you, son."

Jax's jaw tics, taking my dad's words too literally. He forces a grin on, stalking around the table—and stopping behind me. "Thank you, guys, for dinner. I understand why Tala's meals always taste exceptional." His arm comes over my shoulder, wafting his addicting scent of dark spices as he grabs my plate.

He's not talking about the preparation of food. And that pollutes my mind with images that scorch my cheeks.

I squeeze the heavy pressure in between my thighs, grazing his arm as it draws back over my shoulder. "Thank you, da-" I gulp, snapping my eyes to my actual father. "Thank you, Dad." I turn to my mom. "Thank you, Mom."

They're none the wiser to me almost fucking up and calling my fiancé "daddy" in front of people.

I'm not proud of it. Nor do I know how it happened. But he loves that shit, and for some reason it's been a bad habit the past few days.

"You two can come over whenever," Mom hums, grabbing his arm and flashing doe eyes up at him.

Is she flirting with him? ... Surely not. Right?

Jax smiles sharply, stacking her plate with the rest.

Flirt with her in front of me and I'll rip your larynx out with my teeth.

I stalk him like prey, standing up from my chair.

Waiting for him to piss me off.

He meets my eyes, a sliver of war flashing in his haunted obsidian. "Thank you, Ev. I'm sure Tala would love to spend more time over here." He tears away from my glare, smiling to himself as he strides off to the sink.

Really nice of him to punish me over my dad's poor choice of words. And that man is clueless as hell. He's smiling as all get out, sipping on his beer as he strolls out of the kitchen.

"I'll help Jax clean up, Mom," I insist, hastily snatching the wine glasses from the table. "I'm thinking red peonies and black silk, if you want to start-"

"Yes!" She flies around the table, bringing her arms around the back of me and resting her chin in the crook of my neck. "I can already see it, honey. My beautiful girl is going to be the most beautiful bride."

"Mmm," Jax groans, shaking his head in delight while rinsing the plates. "I already want the image burned into my retinas."

Mom giggles, releasing me and treading out of the kitchen. I ignore Jax's eyes tracking me like prey and grab the last glass. Striding up to his side, I set them down in the sink, side-eyeing the movement of him slipping away.

His presence doesn't disappear.

My jaded eyes sweep up to his reflection towering over me in the window, and my stupid heart palpitates, rushing a wave of excitement through my stomach.

He grabs my hips, pressing into me zealously. "Hmm," he growls, coasting a hand past the hem of my dress. "What was my girl doing in high school?" he asks in a quiet rumble, dripping with ire.

I part my legs, biting my lip to hold back a moan as he gently glides his fingers over the sheer material in between my thighs. "What we're doing right now. Sneaking around," I pant.

His eyes darken. He roughly grabs my tights, swiftly tugging until a loud rip opens me up for him. A breath hitches in my throat, and I clutch the sink, withering as he teases his fingers underneath my thong. "Yeah? Did you ever get caught?" he whispers, easing his long fingers inside me.

My head falls back to his sternum, throat filling with the moan that's on the verge of rupturing out.

All I can do is shake my head and let my eyes roll back without risking the chance of screaming "daddy" or some shit.

He plunges them deeper, and my back arches in tandem with my jaw falling. The desperate moan isn't able to escape before his free hand comes over my mouth. He starts scissoring his fingers into my inner walls, using his palm to stimulate my thumping bud.

Satan's been reading my smut. I'm sure it was porn that taught him everything prior to meeting me, but he's been surprising me with stuff written by my favorite authors.

Shout-out to those beautiful specimens.

I'm going to have a lazy eye by the time we get married.

He grinds his hard cock into my ass, tightening his hand over the whimper that coasts through my flaring nostrils. "Shh. I know, I know. You're almost there," he murmurs, gazing right into my fucking eyes.

My hips begin shaking, the pressure within them compressing and spiking in temperature.

And I shatter into pleasurable pieces.

My inner walls quake violently, and he doesn't stop. He keeps working his fingers and palm, indenting my cheeks from the rough force he's having to implement to muffle the slutty moan vibrating my throat.

"Attagirl," he breathes elatedly, then slowly withdraws his fingers.

His hand moves from my panting mouth, fitting snugly around my throat and against my jaw. With no warning, or dominant order, his full lips purse, and a bead of saliva falls from between them.

The moment the sweet liquid splashes on my tongue, he raises his wet fingers to my mouth and slides them over his DNA.

"Suck," he whispers sharply, a faint snarl making my stomach flip.

I nod, whining as my lips curl around his fingers, and I clean my mess, languidly working my tongue with hollowed cheeks.

The footsteps getting closer instill panic to tighten my chest.

My eyes widen, and the asshole smiles sharper than fucking ever.

He pulls his hand from my mouth and down to my waist, stealthily smoothing his other one towards my shoulder.

As if he's holding me in a loving embrace.

Even though I just came on his fingers. In my childhood kitchen. In front of the window my mom used to watch me play fairies from.

All I can taste is my own musk and it's freaking me out, thinking the smell of my arousal is permeating the air as my fucking mother waltzes up to our side with a magazine.

"Oh, honey, look how beautiful these candelabras are," Mom coos, stopping a foot away and twisting the open magazine around.

CHAPTER FORTY-THREE

JAX

"Goddamn, baby," I groan, watching her leather-clad leg swing over the glossy black paint of her Ninja. Twisting my throttle to rev the engine, I shake my head in my helmet, in awe that I get to marry her in one week.

Her smoky laughs filters through my earpiece. "If we weren't meeting Dad, I'd throw my leg over you and take you for a ride instead," she purrs.

I hike a brow, unable to say the lewd words on my tongue before she takes off down the driveway.

I don't know how she's riding her bike in her fuck-me boots.

I twist my throttle, the rumbles bleeding into hers, and quickly catch up to my succubus. Her infectious laugh fills my head like nitrous oxide, and then we cruise in the comfortable silence of each other, enjoying the greens that are coming back after the utter fucking hell of the snow season.

I haven't been able to take my hands off her for five months. Honestly, this is the longest we've gone without fucking or getting each other off.

She crawled under the table this morning while Nadia and Evelyn were sitting around me going over the seating chart and getting the catering scheduled, and my girl unzipped my pants and gave me the best fucking head that made me slam a fist into the table.

I had to pretend like Uncle Ben sitting next to Aunt Marie was exciting enough to warrant a broken tabletop. There's no chance they didn't catch on to what was happening. I was sweating and heaving for air by the time she swallowed my load.

After cruising around for twenty minutes, we roll up next to Damascus' Harley in the *Moonlight Bloom* parking lot.

Calliope was beyond thrilled to work on Tala's precise floral requests. We had to put the order in way back in January because Tala wants everything dead and peonies have to be shipped here during the winter.

Over three thousand flowers will be delivered to the venue once Tala gives the okay on everything. Which, she will. Even if she isn't pleased with the arrangements, she wouldn't have it in her to speak up and say something.

But I want her to have the wedding of her darkest desires.

I want her to have everything she's ever wanted and dreamed of.

Even if that means I have to be the bad guy to Calliope.

"Well, don't you two look as smooth as ever ridin' up together like that!" Damascus hollers over the rumbles getting cut off.

It makes me smile as I get my ass up. The long, raven braids getting shaken out to my right stop my heart and fill my muscles with cement, making me incapable of speech.

She sets her helmet down on her gas tank, approaching Damascus' embrace with a gleeful smile. "You ready to see the flowers?" she asks softly, pulling him into a tight hug.

His eyes mist over, and I look away from the intimate moment to yank my helmet off and set it down.

"Yes, and no," he chokes out. "You're my little baby girl. My sweetheart."

I'm terribly sorry, sir. You're not the only man she calls Daddy.

Listen, I didn't force her to start calling me that. She did it all on her own. And fuck if it doesn't make me want to test out her fallopian tube.

Damascus gives me a firm pat on the back, grinning with glassy eyes as we head towards the entrance.

None the wiser to the filthy thoughts circulating in my mind.

The floral arrangements were exactly how Tala envisioned them. And I paid close attention to make sure she wasn't just waving it off because she didn't want to hurt Calliope's feelings.

With Damascus getting elected as mayor, the old castle has fallen into his palms. That's where Tala and I have decided to get married. So, we rode out there, gave the place another look around while Tala pointed her sharp, crimson nail, explaining what will go where, and we made the call to Calliope to go ahead and schedule the delivery.

God, she's so fucking excited. And that alone excites me.

Ever since she barged into that room, all I've wanted is to have her melted into me. So deep, there'd be no distinction between our bodies.

I look over at her on her bike, green trees whizzing by in the background, and the groan that rumbles up my throat cannot be contained.

I still get worried that I'll look for her and she'll be gone. It happened so fast back in November. So, anytime I get the validation that her curvy, little body is within reach, the reassurance fills my lungs and zaps my veins with need.

"Pull over," I demand unwarrantedly, squeezing the brake.

She doesn't protest. She matches my speed, running off the road and following me into the tree line. As we come to a stop in a little clearing, she kills her engine and yanks her helmet off, dismounting the sexy metal.

"Are you wanting that ride I mentioned?" she asks salaciously, tossing her helmet down to the grass.

Killing the engine, I rip mine off, launching it out of my way and hungrily tracking her as she stops next to me. "Saddle up," I growl, and deftly undo my belt.

Thrill blazes in her golden eyes, and she hastily undoes her leather pants, yanking them and her thong off her wild legs and boots.

Anticipation fuels my body with heat while I unzip my jeans, reaching a hand in my briefs and wrapping around my stiff cock. I pull it out, groaning from the relief and the sexual vanilla wafting from her.

Bringing a hand to my shoulder, she throws her leg over my lap, squeezing her thighs around mine to stay mounted. I kick my kickstand out, heart lurching up my throat—passionately staring at her incredible heart-shaped face.

I let out a heavy breath, bringing a hand to her hip to center her to my cock. "You already wet for me, baby?"

With her eyes set on me, her pretty fingers coast down her mound, two of them running through her slit. My dick pulses at the erotic sight. I lazily stroke it, wetting my lips as her slick fingers slide out.

"I'm always soaked for you, Jax," she rasps, bringing her arousal towards my mouth.

The sweet smell has my lips parting, inviting her fingers over my tongue, and I suck her mess off.

Her addictive taste only spurs me on.

I guide her down, biting her nails as they retract from my teeth.

Her tight warmth surrounds my cock, and my eyes roll back, instant pleasure coiling down my spine. "Goddamn, Tala. The power your pussy holds," I groan with gritted teeth.

Her hand curls in the neckline of my shirt, the other tangling up in my hair, and her dark brows pinch with a whine of pleasure as she slowly slides down me.

"Will you promise to never get bored of me?" she asks breathlessly, tone soft with worry.

My brows snap together, and I collect her braids in one hand, wrapping them tightly around my loose fist, the hand on her hip keeping her steady. "Without you, my heart fails to beat properly. As long as I'm breathing, I will constantly be chasing after you. And when I die, I will always watch you. So, yeah, I promise, baby girl. Now sink all the way fucking down and ride my cock until you can't take it anymore," I finish barbarously.

She mewls, nodding and biting her bottom lip.

I know I fucking told her to, but her slamming down and bottoming out sends shock waves through my nerve endings.

Black threatens my sight and my hips twitch, not being offered a single moment before she's cowgirling up and riding it like she fucking stole it.

Her husky moans carry with the breeze, resounding through the woods and serenading my spinning head like a fervent prayer.

My fist curls tightly around her braids, tilting her head back and rushing towards her throat. I kiss in between the Japanese peonies elegantly designed to the shape of her neck, groaning once the adrenaline spreads tingles up my abdomen. "God, I'm so pissed off I didn't meet you sooner," I snarl, then lick up the sweat misting on her throat, sucking on the sensitive skin above her collar.

Steadily bouncing up and down my straining shaft, her ass rhythmically claps off the denim on my thighs, harmonizing with her wet pussy and the staccato moans breaking through her intense breaths.

The skin on her throat pops out of my mouth, and I let her lift her head up, becoming awestruck by her salacious smile and heavy eyelids. "I wonder how many times I was grinding on strangers while you were right under my feet," she pants cunningly.

My lip twitches, and vexation would be sharpening my eyes to swords if her cunt wasn't clenching around me and making them heavier than hell.

It's not a new discovery that she gets off on pissing me off. But—it's kind of hot that she likes the twitch in my lip.

Her stomach contracts, siphoning the flesh right off my fucking dick, and her long lashes flutter over her thin honey pools. I'm breathing heavily, groaning and watching her glossy lips fall apart, and my balls tighten vigorously as a slutty, pornstar moan smokes out of her lungs.

Cracking my palm across her ass, I firmly squeeze the mass of muscle and fat, shaking my head at the waves that never fail to amaze me.

She moans my favorite thing, her hips twitching and slowing down, and I almost forget I'm supporting both our weight. The electric shock of pleasure surges through my veins, wrapping around my spine like a flaming lasso, negating my sight and conjuring a growl of euphoria. "Fuck, baby, fuck." I gnash my teeth, steadying the bike wobbling underneath us.

Once upon a time, Liam promised me that her pussy isn't worth torturing someone over. And I beg to fucking differ.

Her pussy houses the arcane wisdom of the goddamn oracle, the mighty power of the gods that strike humans down.

"Good boy," she draws out breathlessly, working her trembling hips to milk me.

I smile, panting for the air she's stripping me of. "I'm not done with you," I say wickedly, voice rumbling with appetite.

She sinks down, resting her twitching muscles and staring beyond my soul with half-lidded gold. It's not possible to go soft when my cock is being swallowed by the siren's tight grip.

It pumps me harder, and I swiftly grab the bottom of her shirt, ripping it up and off her arms. Tossing it to the ground, I yank my own off, then bring her weight into me and throw a leg over my bike, easily getting off it. Her hand in my hair tightens, igniting pinpricks along my scalp, and she starts working her hips again, fucking me before I can fully set my damn foot down.

She rushes in, sloppily sucking my bottom lip into her mouth and whimpering.

"Goddamn, my little wolf's hungry," I groan, words muffling through my teeth.

She snaps her teeth into the sensitive skin, riding me harder, faster—and her pussy clamps with vigor, our mixed liquids sloshing out of her and smattering my soaked jeans.

Right as I believe my lip is going to get shredded off, her head rips back, possibly taking some of my flesh with her, and she smashes her forehead into mine, moaning her husky cries directly onto my mouth.

Heaving through the second round of sparks growing with impressive speed, I wet my dry lips, tasting the iron seeping through her mark of claim. We've been increasing how rough we get.

This is the first time she's made me bleed.

And fuck if it doesn't incite me to lift her shaking body off my cock, flipping her around and bending her over my bike.

She moans, widening her trembling legs for me, and I whip my belt off, deftly cracking the leather against her ass in passing.

"Oh, God," she whines, throwing her head forward, her long braids falling around her hourglass curves.

I palm the red mark on her ass, massaging the pain into pleasure. "I'm right here, little wolf. And fuck, I'm ready to get on my knees and sip from your waterfall of enigmatic power."

Doubling over my belt, I lasso it around her neck, getting on my knees behind her. She arches her back, whimpering as my breath skates over her freshly fucked pussy.

Still rubbing her ass, I swipe my flat tongue up the ocean spilling from her, groaning the second her sweet musk overrules the iron lingering on my taste buds.

"Jax," she whines, bringing her hand to the one I have on her ass and squeezing. "I'm not going to be able to walk at Brynn's funeral tomorrow."

I drink my source of life from her, lips popping as I draw back a bit. "I'll push you around if it comes to that," I say haughtily, smirking at the fond memory. Then, dive right back into her weeping cunt.

I work my tongue in the motions that make her tense up, and lightly twist the belt, tightening it with each chant of my name until her voice gives out.

Her skull crushers crush my skull, nails clawing into my hand, her hips quaking and sending the vibration through her legs, and a raspy cry of euphoria follows the waterfall that geysers down my face.

I release the belt, drinking her like juice and rubbing up her back in encouragement as she draws in a deep breath.

My cock is pulsing, in dire need of plunging back inside her.

Smoothing my hand down her ass, I trail my tongue up her other cheek, biting down on the mark I left on her last night. Her sharp inhale burns into a smoky moan, arching into me and grabbing my hair. I swirl my tongue over the burgundy teeth marks in between the leaves flowing with her curves, gripping her hip and standing my ass up.

If it weren't for her boots, I'd have to squat down in order to fuck her in this position.

I eagerly curl my hand around my shaft, centering my tip to her hungry cunt, eyes rolling back as I slam inside her.

Her ass folds over her back, one of her heels coming up and kicking my ass. "Jesus fucking fuck, Jax! Oh, my God!" she whines loudly.

I shudder, my cock twitching inside her, and I pull her head back by the belt, looking into her eyes while thrusting in and out of carnal Hell.

"You're such a good fuckin' girl. God, I want to go deeper. I want to feel how fast your heart is beating for me right now."

Using my feet, I open her legs wider, grinning at her irises vanishing, her mouth falling open on a silent moan.

What a mighty fine sight.

My girl's decked her curvy, little body out with black ink. The only scar left visible is the faint line in between the Japanese peonies around her neck.

She didn't want to cover it completely; said it's a scar of being brave, but also a reminder of her "fuck up."

I crowd over her, running my palm up her rib and cupping her breast. Her fluttering eyes lazily focus on me, and I drop the belt, replacing the leather with my hand while sliding my tongue over hers.

Her moans warm my chin, languidly tasting the leftover wine on her taste buds, feeling her heart racing on the tip of my dick as I reach in between her and the seat, rubbing her swollen clit in circles. My fingers curl into her cheeks, pressing into her teeth, and I suck on her pouty fucking lip, gently grazing it with my teeth while letting it free.

My addiction demands more.

She starts shaking underneath me, panting for the air I steal, sealing my lips to hers and driving in and out of her iron-vice grip. I keep a steady pace on her clit, knowing that the slightest change in speed can fuck up the orgasm shattering her, breaking her in the way I promised.

Her broken pieces have always fascinated me. But they look so much better when I'm the one fracturing them.

I tear away, taking in the sight of her jaw stretching open for a husky moan that triggers the flames burning my nerve endings. "Atta-fuckin-girl," I groan, working her release, my entire body lighting up in a soul-altering high.

I never want to come down from the paradisiac that she floods me with. I never want to be without her.

Stopping the circles on her clit, I coast my hand down her cunt, spreading my fingers around our joined bodies. Still kissing her, tasting the whimpers and whines that dance on her tongue.

Releasing inside of her is nothing short of celestial. Feeling my cock twitch against my fingers from the the blinding pleasure amplifies the spiritual rapture that's veiling my body.

I draw back from her lips, slowing my thrusts—and dive into her amber eyes.

Her cheeks are the rosiest I've ever seen, enhancing the gold that designs the windows to her hypnotic soul.

She breathes heavily, tugging her swollen bottom in between her teeth, and I take my time pulling out, my soaked shaft sliding along the sides of my fingers. "Not that I'd let you…" I swallow roughly, watching her warm eyes cruise around my face while I grow the damn balls to say what's on my tongue. "Please don't ever leave."

Relaxing my hand on her throat, I gently caress down the charm she wears for me, allowing her to read what I tuck away in a closet full of cobwebs and dust.

And that is my one fear. Losing her.

Her heart, that is.

The love she's given me. The comforting sense of home.

She backs into me, and I stand up, heart running a goddamn marathon. She turns around on her boots, instantly clenching her maddening thighs together. Knowing my cum is spilling out of her, a laugh breezes through my nose as I quickly tuck myself back.

I get on my knees before her and fetch my shirt from the ground, parting her legs open to dry her off.

She cups under my jaw, pulling my eyes directly to hers. "Our souls have been in love far longer than these bodies have known each other. I've always belonged to you, Jax. And I always will."

CHAPTER FORTY-FOUR

TALA

"Hey, Siri…"

"Uh-huh."

"Can a heart fall out of an ass?" I wait a moment, gaping at my screen.

"I can't help you with that."

I groan, jamming my thumb into the lock button and tossing my phone onto the vanity. I might be the first case of someone's heart falling straight out of their ass.

Knowing Jax, he'd pick it up and force it back in place just so he can marry me. Then, he'd let it fall back out and rip his own out to follow me in death.

That makes me laugh quietly to myself.

I needed a few minutes to breathe without tears surrounding me, so I kicked Nadia and Mom out of the room we have set up for me to get ready in and have been listening to the loud tempo of my heart drumming in my temples.

Everyone's been fighting tooth and nail to get everything set up to my liking around the castle. I never wanted to be a bridezilla. It's not in my character. But there's something so fucking aggravating about a man not being able to tell when there are too many shades of red in one spot.

I ended up doing it myself, so I didn't snap on my dad.

I think my testiness is a result of not seeing Jax in over twenty-four hours. Mom made Nadia and I stay the night with her last night while Dad kept Jax, Leon, and Maverick company at our house.

I miss him.

Swatting the swoop away from my eyes, I stand up from my chair and head over to my grandma's mirror in the corner of the room. A knot works its way up my throat, threatening my eyes with the tears that would ruin my makeup.

I wish they could be here. Grandma would fawn over the embroidery on my dress.

No one's seen it besides Mom and Nadia.

I know. Shocker. Jax actually let me pick it out myself and has no idea what I'll be walking down the aisle in. All he knows is that it's black, which is not surprising. Our entire wedding is black with pops of red, dark green, and some shades of cream and pink.

I do a final turn around in the mirror, smoothing my hands down the custom-made dress that's tight to my hourglass shape.

I almost went with silk, but Mom and I came up with a strapless tulle design with a pattern that Grandma would always embroider. It flows right down to my simple black heels, the high split on my hip giving it enough movement to move gracefully with my steps. The bodice and embroidery are covered in black sequins that reflect minimal light, just as a little something so it's not too dull for a wedding.

The matching gloves were Mom's idea. They run up to the Japanese peonies on my biceps, appearing to be connected to the dress. She even had the woman measure my nails to make sure they'd fit seamlessly within the tulle.

Of course I did Jax's favorite body waves. I wanted to make him happy all while keeping it simple under my long, black veil. I finished it all off with the smokey eyes and cherry glazed lips that had him too stunned to speak before the gala.

The lipstick he now wears on his neck.

I catch myself blushing and quickly fan my face. One thought always leads to another with him, and I cannot afford having to redo my makeup from sweating like a whore in church.

The old, wooden door behind me creaks open. I spin around, gasping over how handsome Dad looks in a suit. He closes the door behind him, walking my way with glassy eyes and taking in everything he possibly can.

"Mr. Mayor, you might steal the spotlight! Wow!" I marvel, taking a few steps to close the space between us.

He sniffles, bringing a hand to his mouth as the droplets roll down his cheeks. "My little girl," he chokes out.

I look up and rapidly blink, shunning the waterworks welling in my eyes. "I need everyone to stop crying or this wedding will never happen. I can only re-paint my face so many times before the guests start leaving," I say lightheartedly.

Roughly rubbing his face, he drops his arms and gestures for me to spin around.

I tilt my head, grinning with jaded eyes. I do it though. I pop a dramatic arm up and give him a slow twirl.

"Sweetheart," he cries out, and rushes me into a warm hug. "The moment Jax told me he knew you I just had a feeling that it would evolve into somethin' as beautiful as you two have made it. Your love was destined, kiddo. Cherish that and never let go."

"I wouldn't be able to even if I tried," I laugh.

He pulls away, placing his hands on my arms and sweeping down me one last time with a grin. "He'd hunt you down... Speakin' of the man, we should probably get you down to the courtyard before he punches someone. I don't think he ever went to bed last night. He was pacin' around when I woke my ass up, and when I asked him if he got any sleep, all he said was, *'No rest for the wicked.'* He does his best impression of Jax's subtle accent, drawing out a laugh from me.

The nerves settle in my stomach like stones and my hands begin trembling. "Were you and Mom nervous when you got married?" I question, curling an arm around his as he leads the way out.

"Shoot, I remember Mom being an anxious mess for an entire month. She almost called it off because she was making herself so sick. Grandma ended up talking her down and got her to relax." He opens the door, offering me a somber grin. "You know she'd be right by your side, giving you the same encouragement, sweetheart."

I nod, then take a polite vow of silence, focusing on box breathing until we make it to the grand staircase.

Everyone must be in their seats outside. Not a soul is left wandering around the vast space that's elegantly decorated with red peonies, black dahlias, light pink roses, and black and cream pampas grass to add texture alongside the dark green leaves.

It's everything I've ever dreamed of. Everything I never thought I'd get. It's macabre and dark, but romantic and… well—us. It's a reflection of our connection, a visual representation of the passion Jax has filled my life with.

Though, I very well could vomit at any moment.

Walking through a floral archway, the stones in my stomach evolve into fluttering butterflies. I clutch onto Dad a little tighter, slowing my steps with his as we approach Mom getting the boys ready for their moment.

Jax, the dog whisperer, has been training them to walk in a V formation. Sirohi being in front with the rings and Gemini and Killer on either side with black rose petals.

I never told Jax, but I used the petals from the first bouquet he ever got me. Gemini and Killer don't actually toss them around, so I figured it'd be a nice homage to how far we've come since he stalked me into loving him.

I wave to my babies holding their little baskets of silk and petals, growing way too misty-eyed for having to walk down the aisle in approximately two minutes.

Knowing Jax is on the other side of the door, patiently watching Nadia and Maverick, and Loxley and Leon walk down the aisle in their silk gowns and black suits—makes my heart race.

You've got this, bitch. Don't fall, don't throw up, and definitely don't drop your heart out of your ass. Just breathe.

I take my own advice, box breathing and rubbing my glossed lips together, looking for an escape from the crippling anxiety clawing at my chest.

Mom refuses to look at me as she sticks my bouquet out to take from her grasp. "I'm sorry, honey. If I look, I'll cry. I'll preserve the tears for when he finally sees you."

"It's okay, Mom," I titter, bringing the dark bouquet of dead peonies to my chest. "I really appreciate your efforts to save my face from melting off."

She laughs sweetly, grabbing the door handle. "Okay, boys. Your turn," she croons.

Dad and I step away from any possible eyes, and she opens the door, letting in the sounds of the violin.

I can taste the anticipation radiating off everyone waiting. It collects with the bees and swarms my head, making me dizzy while watching the boys stride out the door with their sharp ears up and heads held high.

Even with the door closing I can hear the cooing and noises of contentment coming from the guests.

It's cute as hell. I'm just trying to not piss down my legs right now, otherwise I'd steal a quick look while everyone is distracted. The photographer is capturing everything, so I'll be able to look back on this day and relive it without anxiety controlling me.

"Okay, honey," Mom hums, finally gracing me with her glassy eyes. "That large man out there is probably about to start running down the aisle if we don't get you out there."

"Away from me, or to me?" I titter nervously.

She stares at me for a moment, her laugh breaking through her nose first, then she covers her mouth to hide the amusement bubbling from her throat. "Okay-okay," she collects herself, fanning her face and taking her position by the door.

This is the moment. The legal binding of our vessels.

The unification of twin flames that will never die.

"Breathe in... Breathe out," Dad says softly, gazing at me in adoration. "You are the most beautiful bride, sweetie."

I breathe in—and out, heart swelling the longer I take in the uncontrollable tears falling from the softest eyes that have always looked out for me.

There was never a moment where Dad didn't have my back. He was the first man to show me real love, and for some reason I settled for less… before Jax. And now, I truly don't know what to do with the immense affection and utter enchantment I'm consumed with. All I can do is feel it—and pray that it never fades.

"Honey…"

I tear away from Dad's spilled love, heart lodging in my throat as my gaze settles on Mom's smile.

"It's time," she tells me.

Swallowing thickly, I follow Dad's steps to our place in front of the door, giving my hair one last toss away from my eye before nodding at Mom, letting her know I'm ready.

Dad gives me a comforting pat, then holds his head high, the light from outside beaming over his wet cheeks and the violin serenading the emotions swelling in my chest.

"Slow and steady, wolf princess," Dad whispers, keeping his attention aimed out the door.

While stepping out onto the peony littered silk, my eyes find home.

I lock onto the hunter eyes that are stitched to me from underneath the massive floral arch, the embers of his intense gaze burning through my dress and lighting my skin up in a frenzy.

The loud rhythm of my heart drowns the violin, taking in the all-black suit snug to his lean build. "Holy shit," I murmur to myself.

Sweeping up his tall body, I land on his devastatingly beautiful face, noting his perfectly messy hair and how it's framing the mist in his eyes.

And the pending tears finally break free.

He brings a hand up to his mouth, and he blinks, releasing a droplet that's loaded with so much passion I can see it from halfway down the aisle.

Through the waves washing over my vision, I breeze over Loxley and Nadia's sniffles, and then pay some attention to Maverick and Leon who are crying harder than Dad was.

But I go back home.

Each step past the candelabras amplifies the intense drum inside my chest, following the rope tugging me towards the emotional man waiting for me.

I smile lightheartedly at him, wanting to run and catch the tears he's no longer holding back.

The empty chair on Jax's side spreads heat up my throat, and my smile falls, and my lip quivers, and I fucking lose it, releasing the floodgates that have been knocking on the dam I built myself.

He saved a seat for his dad. And the chair wouldn't be empty if it weren't for Brutus fucking Tuffin taking an innocent life.

The streams rolling down my cheeks are nothing short of the raw and deep emotional connection I have with Jax Scythe. The other half of my soul. My best friend. And the flaming love of my life.

It's taking everything within him to not run to me and scoop me up. When his hands aren't wiping his face, they're flexing at his sides as if he's fighting the urge to get me out of here.

My heart explodes like a bomb, coming to a stop close enough to smell his dark spices and see the tears clinging to his lashes.

I flick my blurry eyes over to Dad, getting a sweet kiss on my forehead from him. He lets my arm go, only to wrap both arms around me and pull me into a protective hug. I know he's telling me that he'll always be my knight in shining armor, but that it's time to let the Dark Stallion wield the sword and be my lovesick protector.

Both of us sniffle as he steps back and pulls out his handkerchief. Although he has his own tears to catch, he gently blots my face with the red fabric and gives me a final heartfelt once over—before giving me away.

I bring my trembling hands around my bouquet as I step up onto the platform, taking my place directly in front of my darkest desires, the man that has held my heart in the palms of his hands ever since he turned to look at me.

He wets his full lips, raking down me with his glassy pools of coffee. It flames my cheeks, and I look away, only to look right back to his sharp smile. "You've truly outdone yourself, Mrs. Scythe," he says heartily, rich voice carrying over the violin.

I smile, bringing a hand to his awaiting palm. "I'm having very inappropriate thoughts about you right now, Mr. Scythe. Ones that I'll have to share when we don't have an audience."

Maverick chokes and Leon gasps. I don't have to turn to see Nadia's cheeks blown up to contain her throaty laugh. I think she starts fixing my veil to distract herself from letting it out.

My eyes are on the little indent in Jax's bottom lip, as if he's thinking about what could be circulating in my mind.

"Stained. Glass," I mouth to him, watching his eyes fly over my lips to decipher what I said.

He tries his best to hold it together, but the groan comes out right as the music fades and Mom steps up as our officiant.

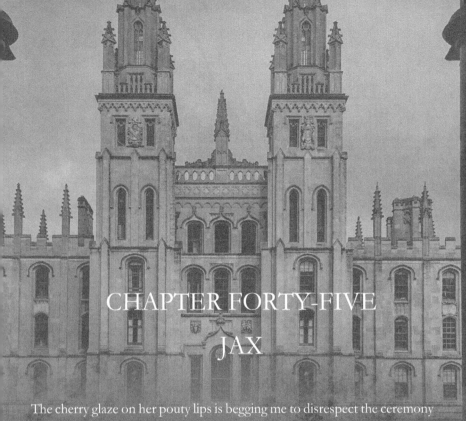

CHAPTER FORTY-FIVE

JAX

The cherry glaze on her pouty lips is begging me to disrespect the ceremony and taste the champagne I know she was sipping on while doing her hair.

I drove myself crazy while writing vows that would accurately depict the all-consuming, stellar love I have for Tala. The love that will never die. Therefore, I was able to recite them flawlessly given the siren standing before me and fucking with my head.

God, she is divine.

I didn't plan on showing my weakness to the mass amount of domes watching us.

But when your weakness is the love of your life, a specimen made up of Heaven and Hell and is walking down an aisle of silk, wearing a custom-made dress that molds to her curvy shape, her hair elegantly bending alongside her harmonious features—it's inevitable.

I flick down to my blood on her gloved finger, then right back up to her eyes of Venus, my heart thundering wildly as her lips part for the last two words needed to complete our unification.

"I do," she says, devotion making her words sweeter than honey.

Come on, Ev, give me the fucking go ahead before I scar everyone here.

Evelyn sniffles, her smile radiating in the periphery of my flickering vision. "I pronounce you husband and wife... Show us what you've got."

"Don't mind if I do," I say vehemently, bending down and throwing my arms around her tight waist.

The moment our lips seal together—galaxies are born.

My skin sets on fire, burning through my muscles and right down to the bones that have been charred with her love for who knows how many lifetimes. But given the fiery connection, the heavy weight that always pulls us back to each other, I'd say it's too many to count. A number that isn't comprehendible to human life.

I lift her up, one of her arms coming around the back of my neck, the other resting against my arm and hiding our kiss with her dead bouquet. I don't hold back. I can't. I haven't felt her lips in over twenty-four hours and the hunger, the tingles, the fucking fireworks take a hold of me, and I hungrily slip my tongue inside her sweet mouth.

The violin swells through the clapping and whistling, and I want to keep feeding the flames burning in my eyes. But I let her tongue coast so fucking smoothly one last time before setting her back down on her pretty heels.

I draw back, gazing at her with undeniable captivation, and my girl presses right back into me. My hands brace her hips, holding her steady as another wave of unholy passion rolls through us.

She whimpers, just enough for my ears and tongue to obtain. And the jolt that runs down my abdomen shoots right into my cock. Showing everyone here how fucking obsessed I am with the vixen before me.

Making rounds through the ballroom to pay our thanks, I stop by a contact of mine that went to college with Leon and I but ended up moving off to Florida for some job with a cellular provider.

I didn't think he'd actually come when Leon mentioned extending an invite to him. We don't speak unless he has questions regarding hunting someone down.

"Zeke Hemings, I know you didn't make the trip all the way up north just to meet my goddess of a wife," I say cordially, deftly running my thumb along her hip.

His vibrant smile flashes out, and his brown eyes sweep right to Tala.

He stretches his arm out, offering her a polite handshake. "Never thought I'd see the day when Jax Scythe was getting married. It's a pleasure to meet you, Tala," he says placidly.

She takes his hand, her hypnotic smile lighting his face up that much more. My eyes want to barb. I have to remind myself that he's a friendly guy who knows all too well that I'm capable of ripping his jaw off right here.

"Likewise. Thank you for making the trip and being with us on such a big day," she says kindly.

I'm well aware of the effect her otherworldly beauty and husky voice has on people. So, it's no surprise that he hangs on to her every word while intently roaming her face.

While their hands separate his attention settles on me. "Of course, I wanted to meet the woman that caught your attention-"

"But," I interject.

He laughs, swirling the champagne in his flute and darting his eyes around coyly. "I have a business proposal that I'd like to speak to you face to face about. I don't want to discuss business on your big day, but this was the only way I'd get off the hook with work and you are the only man I know to go to for an idea like this."

Before I can tell him to fuck off, Tala gazes up at me with warm eyes that are telling me to hear him out.

"I can step away and check on the boys."

"No, ma'am. My business is yours," I insist. Even though I'd rather get her alone and hear her sweet moans echo off the stained glass.

But sure. Let's fucking hear this guy out.

"I'll make it quick," Zeke insists with a tilt in his head. "I want to start a Secret Service operation. It'd be underground, of course, so it'd be highly illegal in Florida. I'll wire four million to your account today as a startup fee and tack on an additional mill each month it takes to get it up and running. I have no idea what I'm doing, dude. But it's calling to me like the sea. I already have a few guys that I'm certain will take jobs."

He's made a few comments recently about wanting to protect the victims failed by the government, so his idea isn't coming out of left field or taking me by surprise.

It would be a tricky business to run where the laws are enforced. He'd have to be sly as hell and hire stealthy people.

I scratch my scruff, thinking it over and falling into the twinkling honey gazing up at me. Her little hand brushes over my belt—and fiery tingles spread up my chest like a wildfire.

Snapping my eyes back to Zeke who is tracking her hand with a smirk, my hand on her hip smooths around to her insane ass, squeezing just enough to brand the shape of my fingers into her.

"We have a deal," I say definitively. He pumps his fist, gesturing his silent excitement, and I pull Tala in closer. "We'll stay in touch. My siren of a wife will be receiving my undivided attention for the rest of the evening. Thank you again for coming, Zeke. I look forward to seeing the impact your operation has."

Leaving him with his big ass smile, I guide Tala through the gowns and suits in the ballroom and make a left towards the sunroom.

"How did you meet Zeke?" she asks softly, then offers a smile to some random fuck passing by and scans the art lining the walls of the gallery.

I just watch her. My masterpiece. "He went to college with Leon and I. He was actually going to help us bust dogfights, but he got a nice job offer and ended up dropping his classes to move to Florida."

Stepping into the sunroom, I quickly look around for any domes.

I haven't eaten since yesterday.

I'm fucking starving.

Not seeing any lurking eyes, I twirl her into me and back her ass up against the back of an old couch.

Her magical eyes fall heavy, and she grins cunningly. "The Big Bad Wolf will have to catch me if he wants to eat me." And with that, she slips out from under me and runs off, her little heels clacking furiously against the wooden floor.

Knowing where she's running off to has thrill coiling down my spine— and I chase after my little wolf.

My wife.

My best fucking friend.

MADISON JO

Until death do us part. And I find her again.

CHAPTER FORTY-SIX

TALA

I cannot hear anything over my own giggles and the powerful clicks of my heels, hooking right and sprinting down the long hallway.

His embers are weaving into the hysteria, tingling my skin in the highest vibration I have yet to feel.

I'm not convinced this feeling will ever go away.

Not that I would ever want it to. It's just intense, searing down into my branded bones and making a *welcomed* home within them.

My strides come to a stagger around the bend, and his large hands slip around my waist. I squeal, breaking free of them and dashing towards the hidden door, my head tipping back on the laugh that's knotting my stomach.

I drift to a stop, reaching for the doorknob, and his hands return to my waist. My tense stomach swirls with the movement of him spinning me into him, the butterflies making me giggle even more.

He rushes down, colliding our lips with brute hunger and pinning me against the door. My head knocks into the wood, the sound reverberating throughout the abandoned space.

His rich laugh smokes out onto me, one of his hands coming up and cupping the back of my head.

Looking into his haunted obsidian, I smile, snapping my teeth around his bottom lip and tugging it.

He groans, releasing my head and roughly gripping my hips. My hands dart to his belt, and I suck his lip into my mouth, swirling my tongue around the pulse while he hikes my tight dress up.

The metal of his belt clatters loose, and I pop his lip out my mouth, taking in a deep breath that spins my head. "I missed you last night," I rasp out, quickly kissing him again as my dress comes up my waist. "My fingers just aren't the same."

Though it's dark with only a dim light diffusing over him, I can still see his thick brows knit together, his hands putting in overtime to yank my dress off my head. I stick my arms up and black briefly abates my sight of him. As the tulle slips off my gloved hands, I look back at the growling beast. The God.

"Yeah? How many times did you come on your pretty, little fingers to the thought of me?" he asks quietly, tossing my dress to the floor.

A chill rolls over my bare skin, pebbling my nipples and intensifying the heavy pressure in between my thighs. I don't answer him. I can't admit how many times I had an orgasm in my childhood bed.

I twist around and jerk the door open, having to step back into his monster cock to fly through the door and up the stairs.

My tits are out and bouncing the fuck around.

"That's fine, baby. You can run. And you can hide... But you know what happens when I get my hands on you." His deep voice echoes through the staircase, sending a chill up my spine.

My pussy pulses, a stream running down my thighs and getting smeared around as I propel myself towards the center of the room.

I'm not bothering with the light this time. The sun is setting and sending in its sherbet glow through the stained glass, the dull blocks of rainbow casting over the entire space.

It's mesmerizing.

My heart thumps violently as I come to a stop near the swing, marveling at the colors. But it's short lived.

Satan is extra hungry now that he knows I played with my pussy without him.

He presses into me, grabbing my hips and roughly grinding his hard-on into my ass, the open zipper grating against my skin. "Bend over and grab your ankles."

My eyes widen, the thrill of something new flushing my face. "Yes, sir," I purr, and bend over, wrapping my hands around the thin straps on my ankles.

One of his hands sails over my ass, and the closer it gets to my entrance, the more the thrum burns.

"How many times, Tala?" he questions, hooking a finger into my soaked thong and easing it down my thighs.

Looking at his dress shoes in anticipation, I swallow thickly, wishing I never told the Punisher. "S-six," I stammer.

He crouches down, looking at me from between my legs while tugging my thong down to my hands. "And all six were to the thought of me. Correct?"

No, the ghost in my old bedroom really had me going.

"Yes."

"Attagirl, baby." His rough palms slide around the dark scales and florals on my thighs, and he leans in, languidly skating his warm tongue over my clit.

Every muscle in my face goes slack, eyes fluttering lazily, skin percolating with need, and a moan puffs out soundlessly. His glistening tongue rolls, disappearing and slipping inside me, just to unroll and collect my juices.

"Oh, my God," I pant, hazily watching his tongue skate the sticky wetness over my clit.

All so he can suck it off, groaning as if it's dessert.

My hips twitch, a jolt of electric pleasure shooting up my spine. The sucking and swirling feed into the blood rush in my head, putting me somewhere else other than Earth and weighing my pelvis heavy with the destructive embers of my desire for him.

I mewl, my cheeks pulsing in tandem with the quake in my stomach. Pulling a hand out from his makeshift bondage, I reach back, cupping under his working jaw—and the fire surges inside me.

My nails tack to his inked skin, a loud moan splitting through the drumming in my ears. I whine, calling him his favorite thing and caressing over his bobbing throat.

My legs are about to give the fuck out.

They're shaking like vibrators, my heels tapping with the velocity and crafting a hum on the floor.

He squeezes my thighs, releasing my clit and standing up to crowd me. One of his hands comes around my throat, the other bracing my stomach, and he guides my way up, holding my shaking body tightly against him.

"I'm never letting you go, Tala Akira Scythe. Even if you grow to hate me. I will never let you break free of me," he rumbles, the devotion in his tone reverberating on my back.

Even if I wanted to reassure him that it would never be possible to hate him, I wouldn't be allowed to.

His hand travels up to my jaw, forcing my head back. I get a glimpse of him soaking up the rainbow aura before he's leaning over me and stealing my lips.

Our tongues meet halfway, swirling around each other in a synced dance. The moment our lips part, I hungrily spin around and start tearing his clothes off, fumbling with buttons and tossing black fabric to the side—until his tattoos are out, absorbing the heavenly halo that kisses the scarred Devil with forgiveness.

I gasp, stepping back to ogle the ruthless savage before me. "Do you want to have babies with me?"

His tongue swipes over his wolfish smile, large hand wrapping around his cock and slowly stroking up. The relieving touch has his pecs flexing, and he steps closer.

"You already call me Daddy. So, we're halfway there, mama."

My stomach flips, eyes rounding. I've never heard him call me "mama" before. The richness in his drawl is making me reconsider my decision of forswearing crotch goblins.

Later, though.

I'll decide later.

EPILOGUE

JAX

Waves roll and crash, the seagulls overheard squawking and looking for domes to peck. A curvy, heavily tattooed, divine vessel in a little, black bikini is knee deep in the blue water, rough housing with the three boys that I have to share her heart with.

What a fucking sight.

I often find myself wanting to burn the image of her into my retinas. But I want this moment burned onto a disc. I want to be able to replay the memory of a darkly ethereal woman in the ocean with her Hellhounds whenever I damn well please.

Her crimson nails wave elegantly through the air, her pretty hand beckoning me to step closer to the siren's enchanting trap.

I'm under her spell. The several times I thought I'd never get my heart back has only amplified the compulsion I've fallen under.

I don't realize I'm walking through the water until I'm close enough to hook a finger under her chin and lock my lips with the pout that should be illegal. "Hmm," I growl in delight against her lips. "You want to show me where you drag men to eat them, little wolf?"

She smiles, gliding her smooth hand up my bare abdomen, showing off the ring that matches her nails. "If you want me to eat you, all you have to do is ask. I promise I'll make it feel like Heaven," she purrs.

I'm buzzing. Not only is she captivating, gazing up with amber eyes that are inhumanely golden in the sun, her husky voice always spills lewd words that spike my heart rate.

I grab her hand, a sharp smile forming on my face as I bend her fingers down, marveling at my blood encased with silver. "Are you trying to dirty talk, Mrs. Scythe?" I intentionally drop an octave, inspecting the goosebumps that pebble her diamond hugged nipples.

She grabs my hand, biting her lip while analyzing the blood she spilled for me. "I always want to play with you."

"Yeah? Let's play." Swiftly, I cage my arms around her tight waist, rotating around and lifting her through the air.

Her yelp of excitement is music to my ears before I fall backwards, crashing us through the salt water. I unlatch from her, burning my eyes just to take in the magnificent sight of a siren swirling around on top of me, eating me up with insatiable eyes.

If it weren't for the black legs bombing through the water, panicking while searching for her, I'd think she has plans of saddling up and riding me right here.

She hooks her arms around my neck, and I push off the sand, exploring the hips I'll never wrap my mind around as I stand us up.

The water crashes around, her long hair slicked back and waterfalling down my hands. Steady beads roll over her heart-shaped face, trailing down the creamy skin that's now completely covered in black ink.

"You never did tell me why," she says serenely.

I hike a brow. "Why what?"

Her nails tingle my scalp, sending embers coiling down my spine. "Why didn't you swim?"

Walking out of the water, I whistle for the dogs to follow, then return my attention to her sultry eyes. "Because I thought slipping into the darkness would take me home... take me to you."

She frowns, playing with my hair and getting carried to the daybed like the goddess she is. "That's why you asked me that," she states softly. "You really didn't know if you actually died or not."

Setting her ungodly body down on her cheetah print towel on the daybed, I say, "I didn't. All I knew was my heart started beating again the second I saw you."

She lays back, propping her glistening body up on her elbows, her eyes roaming my body a little too hungrily for having the whole beach to ourselves. "Well, Mr. Scythe... I say we open our book back up, read until our skin tingles with need, and see how fast our hearts can beat."

I tilt my chin up, filtering a groan towards the blue sky. "You're gonna be the death of me, baby," I huff, and look back down to her widening her inked legs, salaciously running her fingers in between two black pages containing porn.

My phone lights up next to her with an unknown Florida number. I bend over and grab it, meeting the concern scrunching her face as I answer it.

"Jax Scythe," an unfamiliar masculine voice says from the other side. "A mutual contact told me you were the man to go to for a canine problem. I'm requesting you and your wife's services in St. Augustine, Florida."

"How big of a problem are we talkin'?"

"Several warehouses stretched out over the state. Arrangements will be made and paid and sent from a black number."

The dead call has me pulling my phone from my ear, reading over the immediate text message popping up.

I was worried *The Inner Realm* leaked out of Alaska. Guess Brutus was right that day. We shouldn't have gotten comfortable.

"What is it now?"

I lock my phone, taking in the majestic view of my wife sitting in a siren pose with Sirohi, Killer, and Gemini surrounding her. "Those grenades might come in handy, baby girl… We're facing big dogs now. And we're facing them where the laws are enforced."

ACKNOWLEDGMENT

I'll keep it simple and sweet. Thank you, my reader. I know I mentioned it last time but thank you for taking a chance and opening this book up. I'm always open for discussion, so please reach out to me, even if you just want to chat. I'm very interested in knowing who your favorite character is and what scenes will live rent-free in your head.

Jax and Tala truly became my best friends. They started as an idea that presented itself to me in vivid images—and over time they became real. In a sense, of course. The comfort, the attachment, the stellar love—it was *and* is real for me. Putting the finishing touches on their duet was bittersweet. I felt like I was saying a final goodbye and closing the door on two people that loved me unconditionally, that stayed by my side through trials and tribulations.

Although, *"It's never goodbye, little wolf. It's until I see you again."*

ABOUT THE AUTHOR

Madison Jo began typing away, not realizing it would open the door to a vaulted passion. Although she is pervaded with anxiety and will cry if you yell at her, she is a horror fanatic and loves all things dark and twisted. If she's not ripping her hair out while writing, she's usually talking to the hidden cameras she's convinced are in her home or the ghosts that live in the walls.

If you enjoy her atrocities, you can find her on Instagram @madison.jo.author to find out what's coming next.

Made in United States
Cleveland, OH
11 March 2025

15087475R00223